The Stories of

Edith Wharton

The Stories of
Edith Wharton

Volume 2

Selected and introduced by
Anita Brookner

Stoddart

Published in Great Britain by
Simon and Schuster
West Garden Place
Kendal Street
London, England W2 2AQ

First published in Canada in 1990 by
Stoddart Publishing Co. Limited
34 Lesmill Road
Toronto, Canada M3B 2T6

Canadian Cataloguing in Publication Data

Wharton, Edith, 1862-1937
The stories of Edith Wharton
Includes bibliographical references.

ISBN 0-7737-5362-1 (v. 2)

I. Brookner, Anita. II. Title.
PS3545.H16A15 1989   813'.52   C88-095162-1

Printed and bound in Great Britain by
Richard Clay Ltd, Bungay, Suffolk

Contents

Introduction

IT WAS as a short story writer that Edith Wharton made her literary debut in the 1890s. She continued to write short stories throughout her life: her last collection – *The World Over* – came out one year before her death in 1937. There is a remarkable consistency in her work, with puzzlingly few hints as to how or why she started to write these consummately professional pieces, or how she departed from this restrained format to write her finest novel, the brilliant and worldly-wise *House of Mirth*. If one charts a graph of her progress one sees a reassuring regularity in her biannual, sometimes annual, production, starting in 1895 and ending in 1936, with the years of greatest maturity between 1905 and 1920, the years that saw the publication of her major novels, *The House of Mirth* (1905), *Ethan Frome* (1911), *The Reef* (1912), *The Custom of the Country* (1913), and *The Age of Innocence* (1920). Few short stories were written in these years, which also saw Edith Wharton established in Paris, and in love, for the first time in her life, with the evasive Morton Fullerton. No great lady ever stooped more whole-heartedly to folly, yet whatever her grief on a human level the experience mysteriously benefited her powers of invention. The novels written in this period have a depth and a brilliance that are, on the whole, denied to the short stories, which remain harnessed to a possibly restrictive formula: situation, said the author, is what makes a short story, whereas the study of character is the preserve of the novel.

The situations which she appropriates – and which are all firmly set before the reader in her first paragraph – have to do with matters that might have been discussed among New York hostesses or New York clubmen: the laughable attempts of the New Rich to get on in society, the stratagems that ladies and gentlemen, reduced to the status of companions or secretaries, must employ in order to satisfy their desire for luxury, the gullibility of the fashionable many and the shrewdness of the unfashionable few, the power of art and the dubious impulses of the collector, and the abiding fascination for the comfortably established of haunted houses and revenants, wives or husbands betrayed, or dead too soon. '*Do New York*!', Henry James instructed her, thinking thus to distance her from himself, and reserving for himself the great theme of innocence abroad, native Americans coming to grips with the lures and deceptions and ironies of old Europe. But Edith Wharton lived in Europe (far more comfortably, it must be said, than Henry James ever did) and what she retains of New York is a sense of amusement at its pretention. She is, in fact, more of a New Yorker than James, who found in Europe a complexity that answered to the complexity of his own mind. Where James is profuse Edith Wharton is sharp, sunny, alert; where James is frequently terror-stricken Edith Wharton remains very much on the safe side of the line dividing sanity from madness.

Yet in her own life there were episodes that drove her off her balance. Between 1894 and 1895 she suffered a protracted nervous breakdown, characterized by exhaustion, nausea, and profound melancholia. This may have been – probably was – occasioned by the disappointments of her marriage to the unstable Teddy Wharton. She managed to find the cure for herself: she simply wrote her way out of her disarray and enjoyed outstandingly good health for the rest of her life. Thus one is justified in making the claim that for Edith Wharton writing and good health were synonymous.

Her other stratagem was to remove herself from the restrictions of her well-bred background and suitable marriage to live as a free woman and a grand hostess in Paris, at 53 rue de Grenelle. In this beautiful house she entertained lavishly and received scores of visitors and guests, departing regularly for a 'motor-tour' of Italy, France, Germany, Austria, Spain, Morocco – trips that would take the cautious modern writer a year to prepare and unimaginable wealth to pursue. Edith Wharton was, of course, a rich woman, but she also had a sense of magnificence: *nothing* was allowed to hold her back, and the sense of liberty which she gained in exile empowered her, so that she was able to combine a life of fêtes, travels, and visits with the simple routine of a working day, with the morning reserved for writing and the afternoon for company. Her enormously wide range of reading was reserved for the small hours, when her guests had gone to bed.

The other strange episode in her life was her love for Morton Fullerton, a handsome and probably bisexual journalist with whom she conducted an affair between 1907 and 1909. The recent publication of 400 of her estimated 4000 letters provided an unexpected sidelight onto Edith Wharton the queenly novelist (photographs show her firm-jawed, with bird's nest hair and pearl choker) and her abrupt descent into Edith Wharton the powerless mistress. To her enormous credit she emerged from the experience, perhaps the most bitter she was ever to know, to urge friendship on the unworthy and possibly embarrassed recipient of her passion. Yet however noble her overtures the wretched Fullerton seems to have been unable to respond in kind. It may be that her friendship was a little overwhelming. Henry James is known to have groaned before succumbing to her invitations. Yet her conception of friendship was an elevated one, which managed to forgive or overlook an inadequate return. The friendship of Henry James she described as 'the pride and honour of my life'. An equally strong sentiment bound her to the lawyer Walter Berry, with whom she enjoyed an *amitié amoureuse* that was terminated only by Berry's death.

James could not quite overlook the fact that Edith Wharton sold tremendously and made a great deal of money from her writing. It has been calculated that between 1920 and 1924 she earned the modern equivalent of three million dollars before tax. She needed this money to sustain a particularly lavish and by all accounts beautiful way of life, yet she never ceased to consider herself a professional writer, and one whose position she had established at the very outset of her career. Her literary taste was simple and straightforward: she disliked anything effortful, obscure, tricky or subjective, and it is true that her work is distinguished by a directness and a certain bright clarity. She had tremendous reservations about James's late style (although there is more than a hint of his influence in the story called *The Moving Finger*) and one is not surprised to learn that her favourite among the Master's novels was *The Portrait of a Lady*. James Joyce, Eliot, and Scott Fitzgerald were condemned without the slightest hesitation, although the latter made her feel her age. She was in fact found to be old-fashioned when a reviewer in a London paper scrutinized Virginia Woolf's *Mrs. Dalloway* together with Edith Wharton's *The Mother's Recompense* in the same article, to the detriment of the latter. 'My heroine belongs to the day when scruples existed,' retorted Mrs. Wharton.

Indeed, scruples exist in everything she writes, and are particularly in evidence in the short stories. In making this second selection I have concentrated on less familiar work, and have included examples from every stage of Edith Wharton's career. The connecting link is the writer's own firmness of purpose and her refusal to sacrifice abundant good sense to tricks of the trade. If 'good sense' sounds rather too reductive a term of praise the reader should reflect how much he is being spared in the way of mystification. Good sense in this instance goes hand in hand with great style: there is not a clumsy sentence in the whole of her 86 short stories. Indeed, the reader might, for his own benefit and delight, measure the length of one of Mrs. Wharton's sentences and see how lightly it falls into place.

She was not unaware that her reputation was a little too popular to be taken seriously. She wrote to a cousin, 'As my work reaches its close I feel so sure that it is either nothing, or far more than they know. And I wonder, a little desolately, which?' As her fame increases – and there are signs that it continues to do so – her question is answered by an ever larger and more discriminating public. She is, in every sense, 'far more than they know'.

ANITA BROOKNER

The Lamp of Psyche

DELIA CORBETT was too happy; her happiness frightened her. Not on theological grounds, however; she was sure that people had a right to be happy; but she was equally sure that it was a right seldom recognized by destiny. And her happiness almost touched the confines of pain – it bordered on that sharp ecstasy which she had known, through one sleepless night after another, when what had now become a reality had haunted her as an unattainable longing.

Delia Corbett was not in the habit of using what the French call *gros mots* in the rendering of her own emotions; she took herself, as a rule, rather flippantly, with a dash of contemptuous pity. But she felt that she had now entered upon a phase of existence wherein it became her to pay herself an almost reverential regard. Love had set his golden crown upon her forehead, and the awe of the office allotted her subdued her doubting heart. To her had been given the one portion denied to all other women on earth, the immense, the unapproachable privilege of becoming Laurence Corbett's wife.

Here she burst out laughing at the sound of her own thoughts, and rising from her seat walked across the drawing room and looked at herself in the mirror above the mantelpiece. She was past thirty and had never been very pretty; but she knew herself to be capable of loving her husband better and pleasing him longer than any other woman in the world. She was not afraid of rivals; he and she had seen each other's souls.

She turned away, smiling carelessly at her insignificant reflection, and went back to her armchair near the balcony. The room in which she sat was very beautiful; it pleased Corbett to make all his surroundings beautiful. It was the drawing room of his hotel in

Paris, and the balcony near which his wife sat overlooked a small bosky garden framed in ivied walls, with a mouldering terra-cotta statue in the center of its cup-shaped lawn. They had now been married some two months and, after traveling for several weeks, had both desired to return to Paris; Corbett because he was really happier there than elsewhere, Delia because she passionately longed to enter as a wife the house where she had so often come and gone as a guest. How she used to find herself dreaming in the midst of one of Corbett's delightful dinners (to which she and her husband were continually being summoned) of a day when she might sit at the same table, but facing its master, a day when no carriage should wait to whirl her away from the brightly lit porte-cochère, and when, after the guests had gone, he and she should be left alone in his library and she might sit down beside him and put her hand in his! The high-minded reader may infer from this that I am presenting him, in the person of Delia Corbett, with a heroine whom he would not like his wife to meet; but how many of us could face each other in the calm consciousness of moral rectitude if our inmost desire were not hidden under a convenient garb of lawful observance?

Delia Corbett, as Delia Benson, had been a very good wife to her first husband; some people (Corbett among them) had even thought her laxly tolerant of 'poor Benson's' weaknesses. But then she knew her own; and it is admitted that nothing goes so far toward making us blink the foibles of others as the wish to have them extend a like mercy to ourselves. Not that Delia's foibles were of a tangible nature; they belonged to the order which escapes analysis by the coarse process of our social standards. Perhaps their very immateriality, the consciousness that she could never be brought to book for them before any human tribunal, made her the more restive under their weight; for she was of a nature to prefer buying her happiness to stealing it. But her rising scruples were perpetually being allayed by some fresh indiscretion of Benson's, to which she submitted with an undeviating amiability which flung her into the opposite extreme of wondering if she didn't really influence him to do wrong – if she mightn't help him to do better. All these psychological subtleties exerted, however, no influence over her conduct which, since the day of her marriage, had been a model of delicate circumspection. It was only necessary to look at Benson to see that the most eager reformer could have done little to improve him. In the first place he must have encountered the initial difficulty, most disheartening to reformers, of making his neophyte distinguish between right and wrong. Undoubtedly it was within the measure even of Benson's primitive perceptions to recognize that some actions were permissible and others were not; but his sole means of classifying them was to try both, and then deny having committed those of which his wife disapproved. Delia had once owned a poodle who greatly desired to sleep on a white fur rug which she destined to other uses. She and the poodle disagreed on the subject, and the latter, though submitting to her authority (when reinforced by a whip), could never be made to see the justice of her demand, and consequently (as the rug frequently revealed) never missed an opportunity of evading it when her back was turned. Her husband often reminded her of the poodle, and, not having a whip or its moral equivalent to control him with, she had long since resigned herself to seeing him smudge the whiteness of her early illusions. The worst of it was that her resignation was such a cheap virtue. She had to be perpetually rousing herself to a sense of Benson's enormities; through the ever-lengthening perspective of her indifference they looked as small as the details of a landscape seen through the wrong end of a telescope. Now and then she tried to remind herself that she had married him for love; but she was well aware that the sentiment she had once entertained for him had nothing in common with the state of mind which the words now represent to her; and this naturally diminished the force of the argument. She had married him at nineteen, because he had beautiful blue eyes and always wore a gardenia in his coat; really, as far as she could remember, these considerations had been the determining factors in her choice. Delia as a child (her parents were since dead) had been a much-indulged daughter, with a liberal allowance of pocket-money, and permission to spend it unquestioned and unadvised. Subsequently, she used sometimes to look, in a critical humor, at the various articles which she had purchased in her teens; futile chains and lockets, valueless china knickknacks, and poor engravings of sentimental pictures. These, as a chastisement to her taste, she religiously preserved; and they often made her think of Benson. No one, she could not but reflect, would have blamed her if, with the acquirement of a fuller discrimination, she had thrown them all out of the window and replaced them by some object of permanent merit; but she was expected not only to keep Benson for life, but to conceal the fact that her taste had long since discarded him.

It could hardly be expected that a woman who reasoned so dispassionately about her mistakes should attempt to deceive herself about her preferences. Corbett personified all those finer amenities of mind and manners which may convert the mere act of being into a beneficient career; to Delia he seemed the most admirable man she had ever met, and she would have thought it disloyal to her best aspirations not to admire him. But she did not attempt to palliate her warmer feeling under the mask of a plausible esteem; she knew that she loved him, and scorned to disavow that also. So well, however, did she keep her secret that Corbett himself never suspected it, until her husband's death freed her from the obligation of concealment. Then, indeed, she glorified in its confession; and after two years of widowhood, and more than two months of marriage, she was still under the spell of that moment of exquisite avowal.

She was reliving it now, as she often did in the rare hours which separated her from her husband; when presently she heard his step on the stairs, and started up with the blush of eighteen. As she walked across the room to meet him she asked herself perversely (she was given to such obliqueness of self-scrutiny) if to a dispassionate eye he would appear as complete, as supremely well-equipped as she beheld him, or if she walked in a cloud of delusion, dense as the god-concealing mist of Homer. But whenever she put this question to herself, Corbett's appearance instantly relegated it to the limbo of solved enigmas; he was so obviously admirable that she wondered that people didn't stop her in the street to attest her good fortune.

As he came forward now, his renewal of satisfaction was so strong in her that she felt an impulse to seize him and assure herself of his reality; he was so perilously like the phantasms of joy which had mocked her dissatisfied past. But his coat sleeve was convincingly tangible; and, pinching it, she felt the muscles beneath.

'What – all alone?' he said, smiling back her welcome.

'No, I wasn't – I was with you!' she exclaimed; then fearing to appear fatuous, added, with a slight shrug, 'Don't be alarmed – it won't last.'

'That's what frightens me,' he answered, gravely.

'Precisely,' she laughed; 'and I shall take good care not to reassure you!'

They stood face to face for a moment, reading in each other's eyes the completeness of their communion; then he broke the silence by saying, 'By the way, I'd forgotten; here's a letter for you.'

She took it unregardingly, her eyes still deep in his; but as her glance turned to the envelope she uttered a note of pleasure.

'Oh, now nice – it's from your only rival!'

'Your Aunt Mary?'

She nodded. 'I haven't heard from her in a month – and I'm afraid I haven't written to her either. You don't know how many beneficent intentions of mine you divert from their proper channels.'

'But your Aunt Mary has had you all your life – I've only had you two months,' he objected.

Delia was still contemplating the letter with a smile. 'Dear thing!' she murmured. 'I wonder when I shall see her?'

'Write and ask her to come and spend the winter with us.'

'What – and leave Boston, and her kindergartens, and associated charities, and symphony concerts, and debating clubs? You don't know Aunt Mary!'

'No, I don't. It seems so incongruous that you should adore such a bundle of pedantries.'

'I forgive that, because you've never seen her. How I wish you could!'

He stood looking down at her with the all-promising smile of the happy lover. 'Well, if she won't come to us we'll go to her.'

'Laurence – and leave this!'

'It will keep – we'll come back to it. My dear girl, don't beam so; you make me feel as if you hadn't been happy until now.'

'No – but it's your thinking of it!'

'I'll do more than think; I'll act; I'll take you to Boston to see your Aunt Mary.'

'Oh, Laurence, you'd hate doing it.'

'Not doing it together.'

She laid her hand for a moment on his. 'What a difference that does make in things!' she said, as she broke the seal of the letter.

'Well, I'll leave you to commune with Aunt Mary. When you've done, come and find me in the library.'

Delia sat down joyfully to the perusal of her letter, but as her eye traveled over the closely-written pages her gratified expression turned to one of growing concern; and presently, thrusting it back into the envelope, she followed her husband to the library. It was a charming room and singularly indicative, to her fancy, of its occupant's character; the expanse of harmonious bindings, the fruity bloom of Renaissance bronzes, and the imprisoned sunlight of two or three old pictures fitly epitomizing the delicate ramifications of her husband's taste. But now her glance lingered less appreciatively than usual on the warm tones and fine lines which formed so expressive a background for Corbett's fastidious figure.

'Aunt Mary has been ill – I'm afraid she's been seriously ill,' she announced as he rose to receive her. 'She fell in coming downstairs from one of her tenement house inspections, and it brought on water on the knee. She's been laid up ever since – some three or four weeks now. I'm afraid it's rather bad at her age; and I don't know how she will resign herself to keeping quiet.'

'I'm very sorry,' said Corbett, sympathetically; 'but water on knee isn't dangerous, you know.'

'No – but the doctor says she mustn't go out for weeks and weeks; and that will drive her mad. She'll think the universe has come to a standstill.'

'She'll find it hasn't,' suggested Corbett, with a smile which took the edge from his comment.

'Ah, but such discoveries hurt – especially if one makes them late in life!'

Corbett stood looking affectionately at his wife.

'How long is it,' he asked, 'since you have seen your Aunt Mary?'

'I think it must be two years. Yes, just two years; you know I went home on business after – ' She stopped; they never alluded to her first marriage.

Corbett took her hand. 'Well,' he declared, glancing rather wistfully at the Paris Bordone above the mantelpiece, 'we'll sail next month and pay her a little visit.'

• II •

CORBETT was really making an immense concession in going to America at that season; he disliked the prospect at all times, but just as his hotel in Paris had reopened its luxurious arms to him for the winter, the thought of departure was peculiarly distasteful. Delia knew it, and winced under the enormity of the sacrifice which he had imposed upon himself; but he bore the burden so lightly, and so smilingly derided her impulse to magnify the heroism of his conduct, that she gradually yielded to the undisturbed enjoyment of her anticipations. She was really very glad to be returning to Boston as Corbett's wife; her occasional appearances there as Mrs. Benson had been so eminently unsatisfactory to herself and her relatives that she naturally desired to efface them by so triumphal a re-entry. She had passed so great a part of her own life in Europe that she viewed with a secret leniency Corbett's indifference to his native land; but though she did not mind his not caring for his country she was intensely anxious that his country should care for him. He was a New Yorker, and entirely unknown, save by name, to her little circle of friends and relatives in Boston; but she reflected, with tranquil satisfaction, that, if he were cosmopolitan enough for Fifth Avenue, he was also cultured enough for Beacon Street. She was not so confident of his being altruistic enough for Aunt Mary; but Aunt Mary's appreciations covered so wide a range that there seemed small doubt of his coming under the head of one of her manifold enthusiasms.

Altogether Delia's anticipations grew steadily rosier with the approach to Sandy Hook; and to her confident eye the Statue of Liberty, as they passed under it in the red brilliance of a winter sunrise, seemed to look down upon Corbett with her Aunt Mary's most approving smile.

Delia's Aunt Mary – known from the Back Bay to the South End as Mrs. Mason Hayne – had been the chief formative influence of her niece's youth. Delia, after the death of her parents, had even spent two years under Mrs. Hayne's roof, in direct contrast with all her apostolic ardors, her inflammatory zeal for righteousness in everything from baking powder to municipal government; and though the girl never felt any inclination to interpret her aunt's influence in action, it was potent in modifying her judgment of herself and others. Her parents had been incurably frivolous, Mrs.

Hayne was incurably serious, and Delia, by some unconscious powers of selection, tended to frivolity of conduct, corrected by seriousness of thought. She would have shrunk from the life of unadorned activity, the unsmiling pursuit of Purposes with a capital letter, to which Mrs. Hayne's energies were dedicated; but it lent relief to her enjoyment of the purposeless to measure her own conduct by her aunt's utilitarian standards. This curious sympathy with aims so at variance with her own ideals would hardly have been possible to Delia had Mrs. Hayne been a narrow enthusiast without visual range beyond the blinders of her own vocation; it was the consciousness that her aunt's perceptions included even such obvious inutility as hers which made her so tolerant of her aunt's usefulness. All this she had tried, on the way across the Atlantic, to put vividly before Corbett; but she was conscious of a vague inability on his part to adjust his conception of Mrs. Hayne to his wife's view of her; and Delia could only count on her aunt's abounding personality to correct the one-sidedness of his impression.

Mrs. Hayne lived in a wide brick house on Mount Vernon Street, which had belonged to her parents and grandparents, and from which she had never thought of moving. Thither, on the evening of their arrival in Boston, the Corbett's were driven from the Providence Station. Mrs. Hayne had written to her niece that Cyrus would meet them with a 'hack'; Cyrus was a sable factotum designated in Mrs. Hayne's vocabulary as a 'chore man.' When the train entered the station he was, in fact, conspicuous on the platform, his smile shining like an open piano, while he proclaimed with abundant gesture the proximity of 'de hack,' and Delia, descending from the train into his dusky embrace, found herself guiltily wishing that he could have been omitted from the function of their arrival. She could not help wondering what her husband's valet would think of him. The valet was to be lodged at a hotel: Corbett himself had suggested that his presence might disturb the routine of Mrs. Hayne's household, a view in which Delia had eagerly acquiesced. There was, however, no possibility of dissembling Cyrus, and under the valet's depreciatory eye the Corbetts suffered him to precede them to the livery stable landau, with blue shades and a confidentially disposed driver, which awaited them outside the station.

During the drive to Mount Vernon Street Delia was silent; but as they approached her aunt's swell-fronted domicile she said, hurriedly, 'You won't like the house.'

Corbett laughed. 'It's the inmate I've come to see,' he commented.

'Oh, I'm not afraid of her,' Delia almost too confidently rejoined.

The parlormaid who admitted them to the hall (a discouraging hall, with a large-patterned oilcloth and buff walls stenciled with a Greek border) informed them that Mrs. Hayne was above; and ascending to the next floor they found her genial figure, supported on crutches, awaiting them at the drawing room door. Mrs. Hayne was a tall, stoutish woman, whose bland expanse of feature was accentuated by a pair of gray eyes of such surpassing penetration that Delia often accused her of answering people's thoughts before they had finished thinking them. These eyes, through the close fold of Delia's embrace, pierced instantly to Corbett, and never had that accomplished gentleman been more conscious of being called upon to present his credentials. But there was no reservation in the uncritical warmth of Mrs. Hayne's welcome, and it was obvious that she was unaffectedly happy in their coming.

She led them into the drawing room, still clinging to Delia, and Corbett, as he followed, understood why his wife had said that he would not like the house. One saw at a glance that Mrs. Hayne had never had time to think of her house or her dress. Both were scrupulously neat, but her gown might have been an unaltered one of her mother's, and her drawing room wore the same appearance of contented archaism. There was a sufficient number of armchairs, and the tables (mostly marble-topped) were redeemed from monotony by their freight of books; but it had not occurred to Mrs. Hayne to substitute logs for hard coal in her fireplace, nor to replace by more personal works of art the smoky expanses of canvas 'after' Raphael and Murillo which lurched heavily forward from the walls. She had even preserved the knotty antimacassars on her high-backed armchairs, and Corbett, who was growing bald, resignedly reflected that during his stay in Mount Vernon Street he should not be able to indulge in any lounging.

• III •

DELIA held back for three days the question which burned her lip; then, following her husband upstairs after an evening during which Mrs. Hayne had proved herself especially comprehensive (even questioning Corbett upon the tendencies of modern French art), she let escape the imminent 'Well?'

'She's charming,' Corbett returned, with the fine smile which always seemed like a delicate criticism.

'Really?'

'Really, Delia. Do you think me so narrow that I can't value such a character as your aunt's simply because it's cast in different lines from mine? I once told you that she must be a bundle of pedantries, and you prophesied that my first sight of her would correct that impression. You were right; she's a bundle of extraordinary vitalities. I never saw a woman more thoroughly alive; and that's the great secret of living – to be thoroughly alive.'

'I knew it; I knew it!' his wife exclaimed. 'Two such people couldn't help liking each other.'

'Oh, I should think she might very well help liking me.'

'She doesn't; she admires you immensely; but why?'

'Well, I don't precisely fit into any of her ideals, and the worst part of having ideals is that the people who don't fit into them have to be discarded.'

'Aunt Mary doesn't discard anybody,' Delia interpolated.

'Her heart may not, but I fancy her judgment does.'

'But she doesn't exactly fit into any of your ideals, and yet you like her,' his wife persisted.

'I haven't any ideals,' Corbett lightly responded. '*Je prends mon bien où je le trouve*; and I find a great deal in your Aunt Mary.'

Delia did not ask Mrs. Hayne what she thought of her husband; she was sure that, in due time, her aunt would deliver her verdict; it was impossible for her to leave anyone unclassified. Perhaps, too, there was a latent cowardice in Delia's reticence; an unacknowledged dread lest Mrs. Hayne should range Corbett among the intermediate types.

After a day or two of mutual inspection and adjustment the three lives under Mrs. Hayne's roof lapsed into their separate routines. Mrs. Hayne once more set in motion the complicated machinery of her own existence (rendered more intricate by the accident of her lameness), and Corbett and his wife began to dine out and return the visits of their friends. There were, however, some hours which Corbett devoted to the club or to the frequentation of the public libraries, and these Delia gave to her aunt, driving with Mrs. Hayne from one committee meeting to another, writing business letters at her dictation, or reading aloud to her the reports of the various philanthropic, educational, or political institutions in which she was interested. She had been conscious on her arrival of a certain aloofness from her aunt's militant activities; but within a week she was swept back into the strong current of Mrs. Hayne's existence. It was like stepping from a gondola to an ocean steamer; at first she was dazed by the throb of the screw and the rush of parting waters, but gradually she felt herself infected by the exhilaration of getting to a fixed place in the shortest possible time. She could make sufficient allowance for the versatility of her moods to know that, a few weeks after her return to Paris, all that seemed most strenuous in Mrs. Hayne's occupations would fade to unreality; but that did not defend her from the strong spell of the moment. In its light her own life seemed vacuous, her husband's aims trivial as the subtleties of Chinese ivory carving; and she wondered if he walked in the same revealing flash.

Some three weeks after the arrival of the Corbetts in Mount Vernon Street, it became manifest that Mrs. Hayne had overtaxed her strength and must return for an undetermined period to her lounge. The life of restricted activity to which this necessity condemned her left her an occasional hour of leisure when there seemed no more letters to be dictated, no more reports to be read; and Corbett, always sure to do the right thing, was at hand to speed such unoccupied moments with the ready charm of his talk.

One day when, after sitting with her for some time, he departed to the club, Mrs. Hayne, turning to Delia, who came in to replace him, said, emphatically, 'My dear, he's delightful.'

'Oh, Aunt Mary, so are you!' burst gratefully from Mrs. Corbett.

Mrs. Hayne smiled. 'Have you suspended your judgment of me until now?' she asked.

'No; but your liking each other seems to complete you both.'

'Really, Delia, your husband couldn't have put that more gracefully. But sit down and tell me about him.'

'Tell you about him?' repeated Delia, thinking of the voluminous letters in which she had enumerated to Mrs. Hayne the sum of her husband's merits.

'Yes,' Mrs. Hayne continued, cutting, as she talked, the pages of a report on state lunatic asylums; 'for instance, you've never told me why so charming an American has condemned America to the hard fate of being obliged to get on without him.'

'You and he will never agree on that point, Aunt Mary,' said Mrs. Corbett, coloring.

'Never mind; I rather like listening to reasons that I know beforehand I'm bound to disagree with; it saves so much mental effort. And besides, how can you tell? I'm very uncertain.'

'You are very broad-minded, but you'll never understand his just having drifted into it. Any definite reason would seem to you better than that.'

'Ah – he drifted into it?'

'Well, yes. You know his sister, who married the Comte de Vitrey and went to live in Paris, was very unhappy after her marriage; and when Laurence's mother died there was no one left to look after her; and so Laurence went abroad in order to be near her. After a few years Monsieur de Vitrey died too; but by that time Laurence didn't care to come back.'

'Well,' said Mrs. Hayne. 'I see nothing so shocking in that. Your husband can gratify his tastes much more easily in Europe than in America; and, after all, that is what we're all secretly striving to do. I'm sure if there were more lunatic asylums and poorhouses and hospitals in Europe that there are here I should be very much inclined to go and live there myself.'

Delia laughed. 'I knew you would like Laurence,' she said, with a wisdom bred of the event.

'Of course I like him; he's a liberal education. It's very interesting to study the determining motives in such a man's career. How old is your husband, Delia?'

'Laurence is fifty-two.'

'And when did he go abroad to look after his sister?'

'Let me see – when he was about twenty-eight; it was in 1867, I think.'

'And before that he had lived in America?'

'Yes, the greater part of the time.'

'Then of course he was in the war?' Mrs. Hayne continued, laying down her pamphlet. 'You've never told me about that. Did he see any active service?'

As she spoke Delia grew pale; for a moment she sat looking blankly at her aunt.

'I don't think he was in the war at all,' she said at length in a low tone.

Mrs. Hayne stared at her. 'Oh, you must be mistaken,' she said, decidedly. 'Why shouldn't he have been in the war? What else could he have been doing?'

Mrs. Corbett was silent. All the men of her family, all the men of her friends' families, had fought in the war; Mrs. Hayne's husband had been killed at Bull Run, and one of Delia's cousins at Gettysburg. Ever since she could remember it had been regarded as a matter of course by those about her that every man of her husband's generation who was neither lame, halt, nor blind should have fought in the war. Husbands had left their wives, fathers their children, young men their sweethearts, in answer to that summons; and those who had been deaf to it she had never heard designated by any name but one.

But all that had happened long ago; for years it had ceased to be a part of her consciousness. She had forgotten about the war; about her uncle who fell at Bull Run, and her cousin who was killed at Gettysburg. Now, of a sudden, it all came back to her, and she asked herself the question which her aunt had just put to her – why had her husband not been in the war? What else could he have been doing?

But the very word, as she repeated it, struck her as incongruous; Corbett was a man who never did anything. His elaborate intellectual processes bore no flower of result; he simply *was* – but had she not hitherto found that sufficient? She rose from her seat, turning away from Mrs. Hayne.

'I really don't know,' she said, coldly. 'I never asked him.'

• IV •

Two weeks later the Corbetts returned to Europe. Corbett had really been charmed with his visit, and had in fact shown a marked inclination to outstay the date originally fixed for their departure. But Delia was firm; she did not wish to remain in Boston. She acknowledged that she was sorry to leave her Aunt Mary; but she wanted to get home.

'You turncoat!' Corbett said, laughing. 'Two months ago you reserved that sacred designation for Boston.'

'One can't tell where it is until one tries,' she answered, vaguely.

'You mean that you don't want to come back and live in Boston?'

'Oh, no – no!'

'Very well. But pray take note of the fact that I'm very sorry to leave. Under your Aunt Mary's tutelage I'm becoming a passionate patriot.'

Delia turned away in silence. She was counting the moments which led to their departure. She longed with an unreasoning intensity to get away from it all; from the dreary house in Mount Vernon Street, with its stenciled hall and hideous drawing room, its monotonous food served in unappetizing profusion; from the rarefied atmosphere of philanthropy and reform which she had once found so invigorating; and most of all from the reproval of her aunt's altruistic activities. The recollection of her husband's delightful house in Paris, so framed for a noble leisure, seemed to mock the aesthetic barrenness of Mrs. Hayne's environment. Delia thought tenderly of the mellow bindings, the deep-piled rugs, the pictures, bronzes, and tapestries; of the 'first nights' at the Français, the eagerly discussed *conférences* on art or literature, the dreaming hours in galleries and museums, and all the delicate enjoyments of the life to which she was returning. It would be like passing from a hospital ward to a flower-filled drawing room; how could her husband linger on the threshold?

Corbett, who observed her attentively, noticed that a change had come over her during the last two weeks of their stay in Mount Vernon Street. He wondered uneasily if she were capricious; a man who has formed his own habits upon principles of the finest selection does not care to think that he has married a capricious woman. Then he reflected that the love of Paris is an insidious disease, breaking out when its victim least looks for it, and concluded that Delia was suffering from some such unexpected attack.

Delia certainly was suffering. Ever since Mrs. Hayne had asked her that innocent question – 'Why shouldn't your husband have been in the war?' – she had been repeating it to herself day and night with the monotonous iteration of a monomaniac. Whenever Corbett came into the room, with that air of giving the simplest act its due value which made episodes of his entrances, she was tempted to cry out to him – 'Why weren't you in the war?' When she heard him, at a dinner, point one of his polished epigrams, or smilingly demolish the syllogism of an antagonist, her pride in his achievement was chilled by the question – 'Why wasn't he in the war?' When she saw him in the street, give a coin to a crossing sweeper, or lift his hat ceremoniously to one of Mrs. Hayne's maidservants (he was always considerate of poor people and servants) her approval winced under the reminder – 'Why wasn't he in the war?' And when they were alone together, all through the spell of his talk and the exquisite pervasion of his presence ran the embittering undercurrent, 'Why wasn't he in the war?'

At times she hated herself for the thought; it seemed a disloyalty to life's best gift. After all, what did it matter now? The war was over and forgotten; it was what the newspapers call 'a dead issue.' And why should any act of her husband's youth affect their present happiness together? Whatever he might once have been, he was perfect now; admirable in every relation of life; kind, generous, upright; a loyal friend, an accomplished gentleman, and, above all, the man she loved. Yes – but why had he not been in the war? And so began again the reiterant torment of the question. It rose up and lay down with her; it watched with her through sleepless nights, and followed her into the street; it mocked her from the eyes of strangers, and she dreaded lest her husband should read it in her own. In her saner moments she told herself that she was under the influence of a passing mood, which would vanish at the contact of her wonted life in Paris. She had become overstrung in the high air of Mrs. Hayne's moral enthusiasms; all she needed was to descend again to regions of more temperate virtue. This thought increased her impatience to be gone; and the days seemed interminable which divided her from departure.

The return to Paris, however, did not yield the hoped-for alleviation. The question was still with her, clamoring for a reply, and reinforced, with separation, by the increasing fear of her aunt's unspoken verdict. That shrewd woman had never again alluded to the subject of her brief colloquy with Delia; up to the moment of his farewell she had been unreservedly cordial to Corbett; but she was not the woman to palter with her convictions.

Delia knew what she must think; she knew what name, in the old days, Corbett would have gone by in her aunt's uncompromising circle.

Then came a flash of resistance – the heart's instinct of self-preservation. After all, what did she herself know of her husband's reasons for not being in the war? What right had she to set down to cowardice a course which might have been enforced by necessity, or dictated by unimpeachable motives? Why should she not put to him the question which she was perpetually asking herself? And not having done so, how dared she condemn him unheard?

A month or more passed in that torturing indecision. Corbett had returned with fresh zest to his accustomed way of life, weaned, by his first glimpse of the Champs Élysées, from his factitious enthusiasm for Boston. He and his wife entertained their friends delightfully, and frequented all the 'first nights' and 'private views' of the season, and Corbett continued to bring back knowing 'bits' from the Hotel Drouot, and rare books from the quays; never had he appeared more cultivated, more decorative and enviable; people agreed that Delia Benson had been uncommonly clever to catch him.

One afternoon he returned later than usual from the club, and finding his wife alone in the drawing room, begged her for a cup of tea. Delia reflected, in complying, that she had never seen him look better; his fifty-two years sat upon him like a finish which made youth appear crude, and his voice, as he recounted his afternoon's doings, had the intimate inflections reserved for her ear.

'By the way,' he said presently, as he set down his teacup, 'I had almost forgotten that I've brought you a present – something I picked up in a little shop in the Rue Bonaparte. Oh, don't look too expectant; it's not a *chef-d'oeuvre*; on the contrary, it's about as bad as it can be. But you'll see presently why I bought it.'

As he spoke he drew a small, flat parcel from the breast pocket of his impeccable frock coat and handed it to his wife.

Delia, loosening the paper which wrapped it, discovered within an oval frame studded with pearls and containing the crudely executed miniature of an unknown young man in the uniform of a United States cavalry officer. She glanced inquiringly at Corbett.

'Turn it over,' he said.

She did so, and on the back, beneath two unfamiliar initials, read the brief inscription:

'Fell at Chancellorsville, May 3, 1863.'

The blood rushed to her face as she stood gazing at the words.

'You see now why I bought it?' Corbett continued. 'All the pieties of one's youth seemed to protest against leaving it in the clutches of a Jew pawnbroker in the Rue Bonaparte. It's awfully bad, isn't it? – but some poor soul might be glad to think that it had passed again into the possession of fellow countrymen.' He took it back from her, bending to examine it critically. 'What a daub!' he murmured. 'I wonder who he was? Do you suppose that by taking a little trouble one might find out and restore it to his people?'

'I don't know – I dare say,' she murmured, absently.

He looked up at the sound of her voice. 'What's the matter, Delia? Don't you feel well?' he asked.

'Oh, yes. I was only thinking' – she took the miniature from his hand. 'It was kind of you, Laurence, to buy this – it was like you.'

'Thanks for the latter clause,' he returned, smiling.

Delia stood staring at the vivid flesh tints of the young man who had fallen at Chancellorsville.

'You weren't very strong at his age, were you, Laurence? Weren't you often ill?' she asked.

Corbett gave her a surprised glance. 'Not that I'm aware of,' he said; 'I had the measles at twelve, but since then I've been unromantically robust.'

'And you – you were in America until you came abroad to be with your sister?'

'Yes – barring a trip of a few weeks in Europe.'

Delia looked again at the miniature; then she fixed her eyes upon her husband's.

'Then why weren't you in the war?' she said.

Corbett answered her gaze for a moment; then his lids dropped, and he shifted his position slightly.

'Really,' he said, with a smile, 'I don't think I know.'

They were the very words which she had used in answering her aunt.

'You don't know?' she repeated, the question leaping out like an electric shock. 'What do you mean when you say that you don't know?'

'Well – it all happened some time ago,' he answered, still smiling, 'and the truth is that I've completely forgotten the excellent reasons that I doubtless had at the time for remaining at home.'

'Reasons for remaining at home? But there were none; every man of your age went to the war; no one stayed at home who wasn't lame, or blind, or deaf, or ill, or – ' Her face blazed, her voice broke passionately.

Corbett looked at her with rising amazement.

'Or – ?' he said.

'Or a coward,' she flashed out. The miniature dropped from her hands, falling loudly on the polished floor.

The two confronted each other in silence; Corbett was very pale.

'I've told you,' he said, at length, 'That I was neither lame, deaf, blind, nor ill. Your classification is so simple that it will be easy for you to draw your own conclusion.'

And very quietly, with that admirable air which always put him in the right, he walked out of the room. Delia, left alone, bent down and picked up the miniature; its protecting crystal had been broken by the fall. She pressed it close to her and burst into tears.

An hour later, of course, she went to ask her husband's forgiveness. As a woman of sense she could do no less; and her conduct had been so absurd that it was the more obviously pardonable. Corbett, as he kissed her hand, assured her that he had known it was only nervousness; and after dinner, during which he made himself exceptionally agreeable, he proposed their ending the evening at the Palais Royal, where a new play was being given.

Delia had undoubtedly behaved like a fool, and was prepared to do meet penance for her folly by submitting to the gentle sarcasm of her husband's pardon; but when the episode was over, and she realized that she had asked her question and received her answer, she knew that she had passed a milestone in her existence. Corbett was perfectly charming; it was inevitable that he should go on being charming to the end of the chapter. It was equally inevitable that she should go on being in love with him; but her love had undergone a modification which the years were not to efface.

Formerly he had been to her like an unexplored country, full of bewitching surprises and recurrent revelations of wonder and beauty; now she had measured and mapped him, and knew beforehand the direction of every path she trod. His answer to her question had given her the clue to the labyrinth; knowing what he had once done, it seemed quite simple to forecast his future conduct. For that long-past action was still a part of his actual being; he had not outlived or disowned it; he had not even seen that it needed defending.

Her ideal of him was shivered like the crystal above the miniature of the warrior of Chancellorsville. She had the crystal replaced by a piece of clear glass which (as the jeweler pointed out to her) cost much less and looked equally well; and for the passionate worship which she had paid her husband she substituted a tolerant affection which possessed precisely the same advantages.

A Journey

As she lay in her berth, staring at the shadows overhead, the rush of the wheels was in her brain, driving her deeper and deeper into circles of wakeful lucidity. The sleeping car had sunk into its night silence. Through the wet windowpane she watched the sudden lights, the long stretches of hurrying blackness. Now and then she turned her head and looked through the opening in the hangings at her husband's curtains across the aisle. . . .

She wondered restlessly if he wanted anything and if she could hear him if he called. His voice had grown very weak within the last months and it irritated him when she did not hear. This irritability, this increasing childish petulance seemed to give expression to their imperceptible estrangement. Like two faces looking at one another through a sheet of glass they were close together, almost touching, but they could not hear or feel each other: the conductivity between them was broken. She, at least, had this sense of separation, and she fancied sometimes that she saw it reflected in the look with which he supplemented his failing words. Doubtless the fault was hers. She was too impenetrably healthy to be touched by the irrelevancies of disease. Her self-reproachful tenderness was tinged with the sense of his irrationality: she had a vague feeling that there was a purpose in his helpless tyrannies. The suddenness of the change had found her so unprepared. A year ago their pulses had beat to one robust measure; both had the same prodigal confidence in an exhaustless future. Now their energies no longer kept step: hers still bounded ahead of life, pre-empting unclaimed regions of hope and activity, while his lagged behind, vainly struggling to overtake her.

When they married, she had such arrears of living to make up: her days had been as bare as the whitewashed schoolroom where she forced innutritious facts upon reluctant children. His coming had broken in on the slumber of circumstance, widening the present till it became the encloser of remotest chances. But imperceptibly the horizon narrowed. Life had a grudge against her: she was never to be allowed to spread her wings.

At first the doctors had said that six weeks of mild air would set him right; but when he came back this assurance was explained as having of course included a winter in a dry climate. They gave up their pretty house, storing the wedding presents and new furniture, and went to Colorado. She had hated it there from the first. Nobody knew her or cared about her; there was no one to wonder at the good match she had made, or to envy her the new dresses and the visiting cards which were still a surprise to her. And he kept growing worse. She felt herself beset with difficulties too evasive to be fought by so direct a temperament. She still loved him, of course; but he was gradually, undefinably ceasing to be himself. The man she had married had been strong, active, gently masterful: the male whose pleasure it is to clear a way through the material obstructions of life; but now it was she who was the protector, he who must be shielded from importunities and given his drops or his beef juice though the skies were falling. The routine of the sickroom bewildered her; this punctual administering of medicine seemed as idle as some uncomprehended religious mummery.

There were moments, indeed, when warm gushes of pity swept away her instinctive resentment of his condition, when she still found his old self in his eyes as they groped for each other through the dense medium of his weakness. But these moments had grown rare. Sometimes he frightened her: his sunken expressionless face seemed that of a stranger; his voice was weak and hoarse; his thin-lipped smile a mere muscular contraction. Her hand avoided his damp soft skin, which had lost the familiar roughness of health: she caught herself furtively watching him as she might have watched a strange animal. It frightened her to feel that this was the man she loved; there were hours when to tell him what she suffered seemed the one escape from her fears. But in general she judged herself more leniently, reflecting that she had perhaps been too long alone with him, and that she would feel differently when they were at home again, surrounded by her robust and buoyant family. How she had rejoiced when the doctors at last gave their consent to his going home! She knew, of course, what the decision meant; they both knew. It meant that he was to die; but they dressed the truth in hopeful euphemisms, and at times, in the joy of preparation, she really forgot the purpose of their journey, and slipped into an eager allusion to next year's plans.

At last the day of leaving came. She had a dreadful fear that they would never get away; that somehow at the last moment he would fail her; that the doctors held one of their accustomed treacheries in reserve; but nothing happened. They drove to the station, he was installed in a seat with a rug over his knees and a cushion at his back, and she hung out of the window waving unregretful farewells to the acquaintances she had really never liked till then.

The first twenty-four hours had passed off well. He revived a little and it amused him to look out of the window and to observe the humors of the car. The second day he began to grow weary and to chafe under the dispassionate stare of the freckled child with the lump of chewing gum. She had to explain to the child's mother that her husband was too ill to be disturbed: a statement received by that lady with a resentment visibly supported by the maternal sentiment of the whole car. . . .

That night he slept badly and the next morning his temperature frightened her: she was sure he was growing worse. The day passed slowly, punctuated by the small irritations of travel. Watching his tired face, she traced in its contractions every rattle and jolt of the train, till her own body vibrated with sympathetic fatigue. She felt the others observing him too, and hovered restlessly between him and the line of interrogative eyes. The freckled child hung about him like a fly; offers of candy and picture books failed to dislodge her: she twisted one leg around the other and watched him imperturbably. The porter, as he passed, lingered with vague proffers of help, probably inspired by philanthropic passengers swelling with the sense that 'something ought to be done'; and one nervous man in a skull cap was audibly concerned as to the possible effect on his wife's health.

The hours dragged on in a dreary inoccupation. Towards dusk she sat down beside him and he laid his hand on hers.

The touch startled her. He seemed to be calling her from far off. She looked at him helplessly and his smile went through her like a physical pang.

'Are you very tired?' she asked.

'No, not very.'

'We'll be there soon now.'

'Yes, very soon.'

'This time tomorrow – '

He nodded and they sat silent. When she had put him to bed and crawled into her own berth she tried to cheer herself with the thought that in less than twenty-four hours they would be in New York. Her people would all be at the station to meet her – she pictured their round unanxious faces pressing through the crowd. She only hoped they would not tell him too loudly that he was looking splendidly and would be all right in no time: the subtler sympathies developed by long contact with suffering were making her aware of a certain coarseness of texture in the family sensibilities.

Suddenly she thought she heard him call. She parted the curtains and listened. No, it was only a man snoring at the other end of the car. His snores had a greasy sound, as though they passed through tallow. She lay down and tried to sleep. . . . Had she not heard him move? She started up trembling. . . . The silence frightened her more than any sound. He might not be able to make her hear – he might be calling her now. . . . What made her think of such things? It was merely the familiar tendency of an overtired mind to fasten itself on the most intolerable chance within the range of its forebodings. . . . Putting her head out, she listened: but she could not distinguish his breathing from that of the other pairs of lungs about her. She longed to get up and look at him, but she knew the impulse was a mere vent for her restlessness, and the fear of disturbing him restrained her. . . . The regular movement of his curtain reassured her, she knew not why; she remembered that he had wished her a cheerful good night; and the sheer inability to endure her fears a moment longer made her put them from her with an effort of her whole sound-tired body. She turned on her side and slept.

She sat up stiffly, staring out at the dawn. The train was rushing through a region of bare hillocks huddled against a lifeless sky. It looked like the first day of creation. The air of the car was close, and she pushed up her window to let in the keen wind. Then she looked at her watch: it was seven o'clock, and soon the people about her would be stirring. She slipped into her clothes, smoothed her disheveled hair and crept to the dressing room. When she had washed her face and adjusted her dress she felt more hopeful. It was always a struggle for her not to be cheerful in the morning. Her cheeks burned deliciously under the coarse towel and the wet hair about her temples broke into strong upward tendrils. Every inch of her was full of life and elasticity. And in ten hours they would be at home!

She stepped to her husband's berth: it was time for him to take his early glass of milk. The window shade was down, and in the dusk of the curtained enclosure she could just see that he lay sideways, with his face away from her. She leaned over him and drew up the shade. As she did so she touched one of his hands. It felt cold. . . .

She bent closer, laying her hand on his arm and calling him by name. He did not move. She spoke again more loudly; she grasped his shoulder and gently shook it. He lay motionless. She caught hold of his hand again: it slipped from her limply, like a dead thing. A dead thing?

Her breath caught. She must see his face. She leaned forward, and hurriedly, shrinkingly, with a sickening reluctance of the flesh, laid her hands on his shoulders and turned him over. His head fell back; his face looked small and smooth; he gazed at her with steady eyes.

She remained motionless for a long time, holding him thus; and they looked at each other. Suddenly she shrank back: the longing to scream, to call out, to fly from him, had almost overpowered her. But a strong hand arrested her. Good God! If it were known that he was dead they would be put off the train at the next station –

In a terrifying flash of remembrance there arose before her a scene she had once witnessed in traveling, when a husband and wife, whose child had died in the train, had been thrust out at some chance station. She saw them standing on the platform with the child's body between them; she had never forgotten the dazed look with which they followed the receding train. And this was what would happen to her. Within the next hour she might find herself on the platform of some strange station, alone with her husband's body. . . . Anything but that! It was too horrible – She quivered like a creature at bay.

As she cowered there, she felt the train moving more slowly. It was coming then – they were approaching a station! She saw again the husband and wife standing on the lonely platform; and with a violent gesture she drew down the shade to hide her husband's face.

Feeling dizzy, she sank down on the edge of the berth, keeping away from his outstretched body, and pulling the curtains close, so that he and she were shut into a kind of sepulchral twilight. She tried to think. At all costs she must conceal the fact that he was dead. But how? Her mind refused to act: she could not plan, combine. She could think of no way but to sit there, clutching the curtains, all day long. . . .

She heard the porter making up her bed; people were beginning to move about the car; the dressing-room door was being opened and shut. She tried to rouse herself. At length with a supreme effort she rose to her feet, stepping into the aisle of the car and drawing the curtains tight behind her. She noticed that they still parted slightly with the motion of the car, and finding a pin in her dress she fastened them together. Now she was safe. She looked round and saw the porter. She fancied he was watching her.

'Ain't he awake yet?' he inquired.

'No,' she faltered.

'I got his milk all ready when he wants it. You know you told me to have it for him by seven.'

She nodded silently and crept into her seat.

At half-past eight the train reached Buffalo. By this time the other passengers were dressed and the berths had been folded back for the day. The porter, moving to and fro under his burden of sheets and pillows, glanced at her as he passed. At length he said: 'Ain't he going to get up? You know we're ordered to make up the berths as early as we can.'

She turned cold with fear. They were just entering the station.

'Oh, not yet,' she stammered. 'Not till he's had his milk. Won't you get it, please?'

'All right. Soon as we start again.'

When the train moved on he reappeared with the milk. She took it from him and sat vaguely looking at it: her brain moved slowly from one idea to another, as though they were steppingstones set far apart across a whirling flood. At length she became aware that the porter still hovered expectantly.

'Will I give it to him?' he suggested.

'Oh, no,' she cried, rising. 'He – he's asleep yet, I think – '

She waited till the porter had passed on; then she unpinned the curtains and slipped behind them. In the semiobscurity her husband's face stared up at her like a marble mask with agate eyes. The eyes were dreadful. She put out her hand and drew down the lids. Then she remembered the glass of milk in her other hand: what was she to do with it? She thought of raising the window and throwing it out; but to do so she would have to lean across his body and bring her face close to his. She decided to drink the milk.

She returned to her seat with the empty glass and after a while the porter came back to get it.

'When'll I fold up his bed?' he asked.

'Oh, not now – not yet; he's ill – he's very ill. Can't you let him stay as he is? The doctor wants him to lie down as much as possible.'

He scratched his head. 'Well, if he's *really* sick – '

He took the empty glass and walked away, explaining to the passengers that the party behind the curtains was too sick to get up just yet.

She found herself the center of sympathetic eyes. A motherly woman with an intimate smile sat down beside her.

'I'm real sorry to hear your husband's sick. I've had a remarkable amount of sickness in my family and maybe I could assist you. Can I take a look at him?'

'Oh, no – no please! He mustn't be disturbed.'

The lady accepted the rebuff indulgently.

'Well, it's just as you say, of course, but you don't look to me as if you'd had much experience in sickness and I'd have been glad to assist you. What do you generally do when your husband's taken this way?'

'I – I let him sleep.'

'Too much sleep ain't any too healthful either. Don't you give him any medicine?'

'Y – yes.'

'Don't you wake him to take it?'

'Yes.'

'When does he take the next dose?'

'Not for – two hours – '

The lady looked disappointed. 'Well, if I was you I'd try giving it oftener. That's what I do with my folks.'

After that many faces seemed to press upon her. The passengers were on their way to the dining car, and she was conscious that as they passed down the aisle they glanced curiously at the closed curtains. One lantern-jawed man with prominent eyes stood still and tried to shoot his projecting glance through the division between the folds. The freckled child, returning from breakfast, waylaid the passers with a buttery clutch, saying in a loud whisper, 'He's sick'; and once the conductor came by, asking for tickets. She shrank into her corner and looked out of the window at the flying trees and houses, meaningless hieroglyphs of an endlessly unrolled papyrus.

Now and then the train stopped,and the newcomers on entering the car stared in turn at the closed curtains. More and more people seemed to pass – their faces began to blend fantastically with the images surging in her brain. . . .

Later in the day a fat man detached himself from the mist of faces. He had a creased stomach and soft pale lips. As he pressed himself into the seat facing her she noticed that he was dressed in black broadcloth, with a soiled white tie.

'Husband's pretty bad this morning, is he?'

'Yes.'

'Dear, dear! Now that's terribly distressing, ain't it?' An apostolic smile revealed his gold-filled teeth. 'Of course you know there's no sech thing as sickness. Ain't that a lovely thought? Death itself is but a deloosion of our grosser senses. On'y lay yourself open to the influx of the sperrit, submit yourself passively to the action of the divine force, and disease and dissolution will cease to exist for you. If you could indooce your husband to read this little pamphlet – '

The faces about her again grew indistinct. She had a vague recollection of hearing the motherly lady and the parent of the freckled child ardently disputing the relative advantages of trying several medicines at once, or of taking each in turn; the motherly lady maintaining that the competitive system saved time; the other objecting that you couldn't tell which remedy had effected the cure; their voices went on and on, like bell buoys droning through a fog. . . . The porter came up now and then with questions that she did not understand, but somehow she must have answered since he went away again without repeating them; every two hours the motherly lady reminded her that her husband ought to have his drops; people left the car and others replaced them. . . .

Her head was spinning and she tried to steady herself by clutching at her thoughts as they swept by, but they slipped away from her like bushes on the side of a sheer precipice down which she seemed to be falling. Suddenly her mind grew clear again and she found herself vividly picturing what would happen when the train reached New York. She shuddered as it occurred to her that he would be quite cold and that someone might perceive he had been dead since morning.

She thought hurriedly: 'If they see I am not surprised they will suspect something. They will ask questions, and if I tell them the truth they won't believe me – no one would believe me! It will be terrible' – and she kept repeating to herself – 'I must pretend I don't know. I must pretend I don't know. When they open the curtains I must go up to him quite naturally – and then I must scream! She had an idea that the scream would be very hard to do.

Gradually new thoughts crowded upon her, vivid and urgent: she tried to separate and restrain them, but they beset her clamorously, like her school children at the end of a hot day, when she was too tired to silence them. Her head grew confused, and she felt a sick fear of forgetting her part, of betraying herself by some unguarded word or look.

'I must pretend I don't know,' she went on murmuring. The words had lost their significance, but she repeated them mechanically, as though they had been a magic formula, until suddenly she heard herself saying: 'I can't remember, I can't remember!'

Her voice sounded very loud, and she looked about her in terror; but no one seemed to notice that she had spoken.

As she glanced down the car her eye caught the curtains of her husband's berth, and she began to examine the monotonous arabesques woven through their heavy folds. The pattern was intricate and difficult to trace; she gazed fixedly at the curtains and as she did so the thick stuff grew transparent and through it she saw her husband's face – his dead face. She struggled to avert her look, but her eyes refused to move and her head seemed to be held in vice. At last, with an effort that left her weak and shaking, she turned away; but it was of no use; close in front of her, small and smooth, was her husband's face. It seemed to be suspended in the air between her and the false braids of the woman who sat in front of her. With an uncontrollable gesture she stretched out her hand to push the face away, and suddenly she felt the touch of his smooth skin. She repressed a cry and half started from her seat. The woman with the false braids looked around, and feeling that she must justify her movement in some way she rose and lifted her traveling bag from the opposite seat. She unlocked the bag and looked into it; but the first object her hand met was a small flask of her husband's, thrust there at the last moment, in the haste of departure. She locked the bag and closed her eyes . . . his face was there again, hanging between her eyeballs and lids like a waxen mask against a red curtain. . . .

She roused herself with a shiver. Had she fainted or slept? Hours seemed to have elapsed; but it was still broad day, and the people about her were sitting in the same attitudes as before.

A sudden sense of hunger made her aware that she had eaten nothing since morning. The thought of food filled her with disgust, but she dreaded a return of faintness, and remembering that she had some biscuits in her bag she took one out and ate it. The dry crumbs choked her, and she hastily swallowed a little brandy from her husband's flask. The burning sensation in her throat acted as a counterirritant, momentarily relieving the dull ache of her nerves. Then she felt a gently-stealing warmth, as though a soft air fanned her, and the swarming fears relaxed their clutch, receding through the stillness that enclosed her, a stillness soothing as the spacious quietude of a summer day. She slept.

Through her sleep she felt the impetuous rush of the train. It seemed to be life itself that was sweeping her on with headlong inexorable force – sweeping her into darkness and terror, and the awe of unknown days. – Now all at once everything was still – not a sound, not a pulsation. . . . She was dead in her turn, and lay beside him with smooth upstaring face. How quiet it was! – and yet she heard feet coming, the feet of the men who were to carry them away. . . . She could feel too – she felt a sudden prolonged vibration, a series of hard shocks, and then another plunge into darkness: the darkness of death this time – a black whirlwind on which they were both spinning like leaves, in wild uncoiling spirals, with millions and millions of the dead. . . .

She sprang up in terror. Her sleep must have lasted a long time, for the winter day had paled and the lights had been lit. The car was in confusion, and as she regained her self-possession she saw that the passengers were gathering up their wraps and bags. The woman with the false braids had brought from the dressing room a sickly ivy plant in a bottle, and the Christian Scientist was reversing his cuffs. The porter passed down the aisle with his impartial brush. An impersonal figure with a gold-banded cap asked for her husband's ticket. A voice shouted 'Baig-gage *ex*press!' and she heard the clicking of metal as the passengers handed over their checks.

Presently her window was blocked by an expanse of sooty wall, and the train passed into the Harlem tunnel. The journey was over; in a few minutes she would see her family pushing their joyous way through the throng at the station. Her heart dilated. The worst terror was past. . . .

'We'd better get him up now, hadn't we?' asked the porter, touching her arm.

He had her husband's hat in his hand and was meditatively revolving it under his brush.

She looked at the hat and tried to speak; but suddenly the car grew dark. She flung up her arms, struggling to catch at something, and fell face downward, striking her head against the dead man's berth.

The Line of Least Resistance

MILLICENT WAS LATE – as usual. Mr. Mindon, returning unexpectedly from an interrupted yacht race, reached home with the legitimate hope of finding her at luncheon; but she was still out. 'Was she lunching out then?' he asked the butler, who replied, with the air of making an uncalled-for concession to his master's curiosity, that Mrs. Mindon had given no orders about the luncheon.

Mr. Mindon, on this negative information (it was the kind from which his knowledge of his wife's movements was mainly drawn), sat down to the grilled cutlet and glass of Vichy that represented his share in the fabulous daily total of the chef's book. Mr. Mindon's annual food consumption probably amounted to about half of one per cent on his cook's perquisites, and of the other luxuries of his complicated establishment he enjoyed considerably less than this fraction. Of course, it was nobody's fault but his own. As Millicent pointed out, she couldn't feed her friends on mutton chops and Vichy because of his digestive difficulty, nor could she return their hospitality by asking them to play croquet with the children because that happened to be Mr. Mindon's chosen pastime. If that was the kind of life he wanted to lead he should have married a dyspeptic governess, not a young confiding girl, who little dreamed what marriage meant when she passed from her father's roof into the clutches of a tyrant with imperfect gastric secretions.

It was his fault, of course, but then Millicent had faults too, as she had been known to concede when she perceived that the contemplation of her merits was beginning to pall; and it did seem unjust to Mr. Mindon that their life should be one long adaptation to Millicent's faults at the expense of his own, Millicent was unpunctual – but that gave a sense of her importance to the people she kept waiting; she had nervous attacks – but they served to excuse her from dull dinners and family visits; she was bad-tempered – but that merely made the servants insolent to Mr. Mindon; she was extravagant – but that simply necessitated Mr. Mindon's curtailing his summer holiday and giving a closer attention to business. If ever a woman had the qualities of her faults, the woman was Millicent. Like the legendary goose, they laid golden eggs for her, and she nurtured them tenderly in return. If Millicent had been a perfect wife and mother, she and Mr. Mindon would probably have spent their summer in the depressing promiscuity of hotel piazzas. Mr. Mindon was shrewd enough to see that he reaped the advantages of his wife's imperfect domesticity, and that if her faults were the making of her, she was the making of him. It was therefore unreasonable to be angry with Millicent, even if she were late for luncheon, and Mr. Mindon, who prided himself on being a reasonable man, usually found some other outlet for his wrath.

On this occasion it was the unpunctuality of the little girls. They came in with their governess some minutes after he was seated: two small Millicents, with all her arts in miniature. They arranged their frocks carefully before seating themselves and turned up their little Greek noses at the food. Already they showed signs of finding fault with as much ease and discrimination as Millicent; and Mr. Mindon knew that this was an accomplishment not to be undervalued. He himself, for example, though Millicent charged him with being a discontented man, had never acquired her proficiency in deprecation; indeed, he sometimes betrayed a mortifying indifference to trifles that afforded opportunity for the display of his wife's fastidiousness. Mr. Mindon, though no biologist, was vaguely impressed by the way in which that accomplished woman had managed to transmit an acquired characteristic to her children: it struck him with wonder that traits of which he had marked the incipience in Millicent should have become intuitions in her offspring. To rebuke such costly replicas of their mother seemed dangerously like scolding Millicent – and Mr. Mindon's hovering resentment prudently settled on the governess.

He pointed out to her that the children were late for luncheon.

The governess was sorry, but Gladys was always unpunctual. Perhaps her papa would speak to her.

Mr. Mindon changed the subject. 'What's that at my feet? There's a dog in the room!'

He looked round furiously at the butler, who gazed impartially over his head. Mr. Mindon knew that it was proper for him to ignore his servants, but was not sure to what extent they ought to reciprocate his treatment.

The governess explained that it was Gwendolen's puppy.

'Gwendolen's puppy? Who gave Gwendolen a puppy?'

Fwank Antwin,' said Gwendolen through a mouthful of mushroom soufflé.

'Mr. Antrim,' the governess suggested, in a tone that confessed the futility of the correction.

'*We* don't call him Mr. Antrim; we call him Frank; he likes us to,' said Gladys icily.

'You'll do no such thing!' her father snapped.

A soft body came in contact with his toe. He kicked out viciously, and the room was full of yelping.

'Take the animal out instantly!' he stormed; dogs were animals to Mr. Mindon. The butler continued to gaze over his head, and the two footmen took their cue from the butler.

'I won't – I won't – I won't let my puppy go!' Gwendolen violently lamented.

But she should have another, her father assured her – a much handsomer and more expensive one; his darling should have a prize dog; he would telegraph to New York on the instant.

'I don't want a pwize dog; I want Fwank's puppy!'

Mr. Mindon laid down his fork and walked out of the room, while the governess, cutting up Gwendolen's nectarine, said, as though pointing out an error in syntax, 'You've vexed your papa again.'

'I don't mind vexing papa – nothing happens,' said Gwendolen, hugging her puppy; while Gladys, disdaining the subject of dispute, contemptuously nibbled caramels. Gladys was two years older than Gwendolen and had outlived the first freshness of her enthusiasm for Frank Antrim, who, with the notorious indiscrimination of the grownup, always gave the nicest presents to Gwendolen.

Mr. Mindon, crossing his marble hall between goddesses whose dishabille was still slightly disconcerting to his traditions, stepped out on the terrace above the cliffs. The lawn looked as expensive as a velvet carpet woven in one piece; the flower borders contained only exotics; and the stretch of blue-satin Atlantic had the air of being furrowed only by the keels of pleasure boats. The scene, to Mr. Mindon's imagination, never lost the keen edge of its costliness; he had yet to learn Millicent's trick of regarding a Newport villa as a mere *pied-à-terre*; but he could not help reflecting that, after all, it was to him she owed her fine sense of relativity. There are certain things one must possess in order not to be awed by them, and it was he who had enabled Millicent to take a Newport villa for granted. And still she was not satisfied! She had reached the point where taking the exceptional as a matter of course becomes in itself a matter of course; and Millicent could not live without novelty. That was the worst of it: she discarded her successes as rapidly as her gowns; Mr. Mindon felt a certain breathlessness in retracing her successive manifestations. And yet he had always made allowances: literally and figuratively, he had gone on making larger and larger allowances, till his whole income, as well as his whole point of view, was practically at Millicent's disposal. But after all, there was a principle of give and take – if only Millicent could have been brought to see it! One of Millicent's chief sources of strength lay in her magnificent obtuseness: there were certain obligations that simply didn't exist for her, because she couldn't be brought to see them, and the principle of give and take (a favorite principle of Mr. Mindon's) was one of them.

There was Frank Antrim, for instance. Mr. Mindon, who had a high sense of propriety, had schooled himself, not without difficulty, into thinking Antrim a charming fellow. No one was more alive than Mr. Mindon to the expediency of calling the Furies the Eumenides. He knew that as long as he chose to think Frank Antrim a charming fellow, everything was as it should be and his home a temple of the virtues. But why on earth did Millicent let the fellow give presents to the children? Mr. Mindon was dimly conscious that Millicent had been guilty of the kind of failure she would least have liked him to detect – a failure in taste – and a certain exultation tempered his resentment. To anyone who had suffered as Mr. Mindon had from Millicent's keenness in noting such lapses in others, it was not unpleasant to find she could be 'bad form.' A sense of unwonted astuteness fortified Mr. Mindon's wrath. He felt that he had every reason to be angry with Millicent, and decided to go and scold the governess; then he remembered that it was bad for him to lose his temper after eating, and, drawing a small phial from his pocket, he took a pepsin tablet instead.

Having vented his wrath in action, he felt calmer, but scarcely more happy. A marble nymph smiled at him from the terrace; but he knew how much nymphs cost, and was not sure that they were worth the price. Beyond the shrubberies he caught a glimpse of domed glass. His greenhouses were the finest in Newport; but since he neither ate fruit nor wore orchids, the yielded at best an indirect satisfaction. At length he decided to go and play with the little girls; but on entering the nursery he found them dressing for a party, with the rapt gaze and fevered cheeks with which Millicent would presently perform the same rite. They took no notice of him, and he crept downstairs again.

His study table was heaped with bills, and as it was bad for his digestion to look over them after luncheon, he wandered on into the other rooms. He did not stay long in the drawing room; it evoked too vividly the evening hours when he delved for platitudes under the inattentive gaze of listeners who obviously resented his not being somebody else. Much of Mr. Mindon's intercourse with ladies was clouded by the sense of this resentment, and he sometimes avenged himself by wondering if they supposed he would talk to them if he could help it. The sight of the dining-room increased his depression by recalling the long dinners where, with the pantry draft on his neck, he languished between the dullest women of the evening. He turned away; but the ballroom beyond roused even more disturbing association: an orchestra playing all night (Mr. Mindon crept to bed at eleven), carriages shouted for under his windows, and a morrow like the day after an earthquake.

In the library he felt less irritated but not more cheerful. Mr. Mindon had never quite known what the library was for; it was like one of those mysterious ruins over which archaeology endlessly disputes. It could not have been intended for reading, since no one in the house ever read, except an under-housemaid charged with having set fire to her bed in her surreptitious zeal for fiction; and smoking was forbidden there, because the hangings held the odor of tobacco. Mr. Mindon felt a natural pride in being rich enough to permit himself a perfectly useless room; but not liking to take the bloom from its inutility by sitting in it, he passed on to Millicent's boudoir.

Here at least was a room of manifold purposes, the center of Millicent's complex social system. Mr. Mindon entered with the awe of the modest investor treading the inner precincts of finance. He was proud of Millicent's social activities and liked to read over her daily list of engagements and the record of the invitations she received in a season. The number was perpetually swelling like a rising stock. Mr. Mindon had a vague sense that she would soon be declaring an extra dividend. After all, one must be lenient to a woman as hard-working as Millicent. All about him were the evidences of her toil: her writing table disappeared under an avalanche of notes and cards; the wastepaper basket overflowed with torn correspondence; and, glancing down, Mr. Mindon saw a crumpled letter at his feet. Being a man of neat habits, he was often tried by Millicent's genial disorder; and his customary rebuke was the act of restoring the strayed object to its place.

He stopped to gather the bit of paper from the floor. As he picked it up his eyes caught the words; he smoothed the page and read on. . . .

• II •

He seemed to be cowering on the edge of a boiling flood, watching his small thinking faculty spin round out of reach on the tumult of his sensations. Then a fresh wave of emotion swept the tiny object – the quivering imperceptible ego – back to shore, and it began to reach out drowned tentacles in a faint effort after thought.

He sat up and glanced about him. The room looked back at him, coldly, unfamiliarly, as he had seen Millicent look when he asked her to be reasonable. And who are you? the walls seemed to say. Who am I? Mr. Mindon heard himself retorting. I'll tell you, by God! I'm the man that paid for you – paid for every scrap of you: silk hangings, china rubbish, glasses, chandeliers – every Frenchified rag of you. Why, if it weren't for me and my money you'd be nothing but a brick-and-plaster shell, naked as the day you were built – no better than a garret or a coal hole. Why, you wouldn't *be* at all if I chose to tear you down. I could tear the whole house down, if I chose.

He paused, suddenly aware that his eyes were on a photograph of Millicent, and that it was his wife he was apostrophizing. Her lips seemed to shape a 'hush'; when he said things she didn't like she always told him not to talk so loud. Had he been talking loud? Well, who was to prevent him? Wasn't the house his and everything in it? Who was Millicent, to bid him hush?

Mr. Mindon felt a sudden increase of stature. He strutted across the room. Why, of course, the room belonged to him, the house belonged to him, and he belonged to himself! That was the best of it! For years he had been the man that Millicent thought him, the mere projection of her disdain; and now he was himself.

It was odd how the expression of her photograph changed, melting, as her face did, from contempt to cajolery, in one of those transitions that hung him breathless on the skirts of her mood. She was looking at him gently now, sadly almost, with the little grieved smile that seemed always to anticipate and pardon his obtuseness. Ah, Millicent! The clock struck and Mr. Mindon stood still. Perhaps she was smiling so now – or the other way. He could have told the other fool where each of her smiles led. There was a fierce enjoyment in his sense of lucidity. He saw it all now. Millicent had kept him for years in bewildered subjection to exigencies as inscrutable as the decrees of Providence; but now his comprehension of her seemed a mere incident in his omniscience.

His sudden translation to the absolute gave him a curious sense of spectatorship; he seemed to be looking on at his own thoughts. His brain was like a brightly-lit factory, full of flying wheels and shuttles. All the machinery worked with the greatest rapidity and precision. He was planning, reasoning, arguing, with unimagined facility; words flew out like sparks from each revolving thought. But suddenly he felt himself caught in the wheels of his terrific logic, and swept round, red and shrieking, till he was flung off into space.

The acuter thrill of one sobbing nerve detached itself against his consciousness. What was it that hurt so? Someone was speaking; a voice probed to the central pain –

'Any orders for the stable, sir?'

And Mr. Mindon found himself the mere mouthpiece of a roving impulse that replied –

'No; but you may telephone for a cab for me – at once.'

• III •

HE drove to one of the hotels. He was breathing more easily now, restored to the safe level of conventional sensation. His late ascent to the rarefied heights of the unexpected had left him weak and exhausted; but he gained reassurance from the way in which his thoughts were slipping back of themselves into the old grooves. He was feeling, he was sure, just as a gentleman ought to feel; all the consecrated phrases – 'outraged honor,' 'a father's heart,' 'the sanctity of home' – were flocking glibly at his call. He had the self-confidence that comes of knowing one has on the right clothes. He had certainly done the proper thing in leaving the house at once; but, too weak and tired to consider the next step, he yielded himself to one of those soothing intervals of abeyance when life seems to wait submissively at the door.

As his cab breasted the current of the afternoon drive he caught the greeting of the lady with whom he and Millicent were to have dined. He was troubled by the vision of that disrupted dinner. He had not yet reached the point of detachment at which offending Mrs. Targe might become immaterial, and again he felt himself jerked out of his grooves. What ought he to do? Millicent, now, could have told him – if only he might have consulted Millicent! He pulled himself together and tried to think of his wrongs.

At the hotel, the astonished clerk led him upstairs, unlocking the door of a room that smelt of cheap soap. The window had been so long shut that it opened with a jerk, sending a shower of dead flies to the carpet. Out along the sea front, at that hour, the south wind was hurrying the waters, but the hotel stood in one of the sheltered streets, where in midsummer there is little life in the air. Mr. Mindon sat down in the provisional attitude of a visitor who is kept waiting. Over the fireplace hung a print of the 'Landing of Columbus'; a fly-blown portrait of General Grant faced it from the opposite wall. The smell of soap was insufferable, and hot noises came up irritatingly from the street. He looked at his watch; it was just four o'clock.

He wondered if Millicent had come in yet, and if she had read his letter. The occupation of picturing how she would feel when she read it proved less exhilarating than he had expected, and he got up and wandered about the room. He opened a drawer in the dressing table, and seeing in it some burnt matches and a fuzz of hair, shut it with disgust; but just as he was ringing to rebuke the housemaid he remembered that he was not in his own house. He sat down again, wondering if the afternoon post were in, and what letters it had brought. It was annoying not to get his letters. What would be done about them? Would they be sent after him? Sent where? It suddenly occurred to him that he didn't in the least know where he was going. He must be going somewhere, of course; he hadn't left home to settle down in that stifling room. He supposed he should go to town, but with the heat at ninety the prospect was not alluring. He might decide on Lenox or Saratoga; but a doubt as to the propriety of such a course set him once more adrift on a chartless sea of perplexities. His head ached horribly and he threw himself on the bed.

When he sat up, worn out with his thoughts, the room was growing dark. Eight o'clock! Millicent must be dressing – but no; tonight at least, he grimly reflected, she was condemned to the hateful necessity of dining alone; unless, indeed, her audacity sent her to Mrs. Targe's in the always acceptable role of the pretty woman whose husband has been 'called away.' Perhaps Antrim would be asked to fill his place!

The thought flung him on his feet, but its impetus carried him no farther. He was borne down by the physical apathy of a traveler who has a week's journey in his bones. He sat down and thought of the little girls, who were just going to bed. They would have welcomed him at that hour: he was aware that they cherished him chiefly as a pretext, a sanctuary from bedtime and lessons. He had never in his life been more than an alternative to anyone.

A vague sense of physical apprehension resolved itself into hunger stripped of appetite, and he decided that he ought to urge himself to eat. He opened his door on a rising aroma of stale coffee and fry.

In the dining room, where a waiter offered him undefinable food in thick-lipped saucers, Mr. Mindon decided to go to New York. Retreating from the heavy assault of a wedge of pie, he pushed back his chair and went upstairs. He felt hot and grimy in the yachting clothes he had worn since morning, and the Fall River boat would at least be cool. Then he remembered the playful throngs that held the deck, the midnight hilarity of the waltz tunes, the horror of the morning coffee. His stomach was still tremulous from its late adventure into the unknown, and he shrank from further risks. He had never before realized how much he loved his home.

He grew soft at the vision of his vacant chair. What were they doing and saying without him? His little ones were fatherless – and Millicent? Hitherto he had evaded the thought of Millicent, but now he took a doleful pleasure in picturing her in ruins at his feet. Involuntarily he found himself stooping to her despair; but he straightened himself and said aloud, 'I'll take the night train, then.' The sound of his voice surprised him, and he started up. Was that a footstep outside? – a message, a note? Had they found out where he was, and was his wretched wife mad enough to sue for mercy? His ironical smile gave the measure of her madness; but the step passed on, and he sat down rather blankly. The impressiveness of his attitude was being gradually sapped by the sense that no one knew where he was. He had reached the point where he could not be sure of remaining inflexible unless someone asked him to relent.

• IV •

At the sound of a knock he clutched his hat and bag.

'Mindon, I say!' a genial voice adjured him; and before he could take counsel with his newly-acquired dignity, which did not immediately respond to a first summons, the door opened on the reassuring presence of Laurence Meysy.

Mr. Mindon felt the relief of a sufferer at the approach of the eminent specialist. Laurence Meysy was the past tense of a dangerous man: though timeworn, still a favorite; a circulating library romance, dog-eared by many a lovely hand, and still perused with pleasure, though, alas! no longer on the sly. He was said to have wrought much havoc in his youth; and it being now his innocent pleasure to repair the damage done by others, he had become the consulting physician of injured husbands and imprudent wives.

Two gentlemen followed him: Mr. Mindon's uncle and senior partner, the eminent Ezra Brownrigg, and the Reverend Doctor Bonifant, rector of the New York church in which Mr. Mindon owned a pew that was almost as expensive as his opera box.

Mr. Brownrigg entered silently; to get at anything to say he had to sink an artesian well of meditation; but he always left people impressed by what he would have said if he had spoken. He greeted his nephew with the air of a distinquished mourner at a funeral – the mourner who consciously overshadows the corpse; and Doctor Bonifant did justice to the emotional side of the situation by fervently exclaiming, 'Thank heaven, we are not too late!'

Mr. Mindon looked about him with pardonable pride. This scene suggested something between a vestry meeting and a conference of railway directors; and the knowledge that he himself was its central figure, that even his uncle was an accessory, an incident, a mere bit of still life brushed in by the artist Circumstance to throw Mr. Mindon into fuller prominence, gave that gentleman his first sense of equality with his wife. Equality? In another moment he towered above her, picturing her in an attitude of vaguely imagined penance at Doctor Bonifant's feet. Mr. Mindon had always felt about the clergy much as he did about his library: he had never quite known what they were for; but, with the pleased surprise of the pious naturalist, he now saw that they had their uses, like every other object in the economy of nature.

'My dear fellow,' Meysy persuasively went on, 'we've come to have a little chat with you.'

Mr. Brownrigg and the Rector seated themselves. Mr. Mindon mechanically followed their example, and Meysy, asking the others if they minded his cigarette, cheerfully accommodated himself to the edge of the bed.

From the lifelong habit of taking the chair, Mr. Brownrigg coughed and looked at Doctor Bonifant. The Rector leaned forward, stroking his cheek with a hand on which a massive intaglio seemed to be rehearsing the part of the episcopal ring;

then his deprecating glance transferred the burden of action to Laurence Meysy. Meysy seemed to be surveying the case through the mitigating medium of cigarette smoke. His view was that of the professional setting to rights the blunders of two amateurs. It was his theory that the art of carrying on a love affair was very nearly extinct; and he had a far greater contempt for Antrim than for Mr. Mindon.

'My dear fellow,' he began, 'I've seen Mrs. Mindon – she sent for me.'

Mr. Brownrigg, peering between guarded lids, here interposed a 'Very proper.'

Of course Millicent had done the proper thing! Mr. Mindon could not repress a thrill of pride at her efficiency.

'Mrs. Mindon,' Meysy continued, 'showed me your letter.' He paused. 'She was perfectly frank – she throws herself on your mercy.'

'That should be remembered in her favor,' Doctor Bonifant murmured in a voice of absolution.

'It's a wretched business, Mindon – the poor woman's crushed – crushed. Your uncle here has seen her.'

Mr. Brownrigg glanced suspiciously at Meysy, as though not certain whether he cared to corroborate an unauthorized assertion; then he said, 'Mrs. Brownrigg has *not*.'

Doctor Bonifant sighed; Mrs. Brownrigg was one of his most cherished parishioners.

'And the long and short of it is,' Meysy summed up, 'that we're here as your friends – and as your wife's friends – to ask you what you mean to do.'

There was a pause. Mr. Mindon was disturbed by finding the initiative shifted to his shoulders. He had been talking to himself so volubly for the last six hours that he seemed to have nothing left to say.

'To do – to do?' he stammered. 'Why, I mean to go away – leave her – '

'Divorce her?'

'Why – y - yes – yes – '

Doctor Bonifant sighed again, and Mr. Brownrigg's lips stirred like a door being cautiously unbarred.

Meysy knocked the ashes off his cigarette. 'You've quite made up your mind, eh?'

Mr. Mindon faltered another assent. Then, annoyed at the uncertain sound of his voice, he repeated loudly, 'I mean to divorce her.'

The repetition fortified his resolve; and his declaration seemed to be sealed by the silence of his three listeners. He had no need to stiffen himself against entreaty; their mere presence was a pedestal for his wrongs. The words flocked of themselves, building up his conviction like a throng of masons buttressing a weak wall.

Mr. Brownrigg spoke upon his first pause. 'There's the publicity – it's the kind of thing that's prejudicial to a man's business interests.'

An hour earlier the words would have turned Mr. Mindon cold; now he brushed them aside. His business interests, forsooth! What good had his money ever done him? What chance had he ever had of enjoying it? All his toil hadn't made him a rich man – it had merely made Millicent a rich woman.

Doctor Bonifant murmured, 'The children must be considered.'

'They've never considered me!' Mr. Mindon retorted – and turned afresh upon his uncle. Mr. Brownrigg listened impassively. He was a very silent man, but his silence was not a receptacle for the speech of others – it was a hard convex surface on which argument found no footing. Mr. Mindon reverted to the Rector. Doctor Bonifant's attitude towards life was full of a benignant receptivity; as though, logically, a man who had accepted the Thirty-nine Articles was justified in accepting anything else that he chose. His attention had therefore an absorbent quality peculiarly encouraging to those who addressed him. He listened affirmatively, as it were.

Mr. Mindon's spirits rose. It was the first time that he had ever had an audience. He dragged his hearers over every stage of his wrongs, losing sight of the vital injury in the enumeration of incidental grievances. He had the excited sense that at last Millicent would know what he had always thought of her.

Mr. Brownrigg looked at his watch, and Doctor Bonifant bent his head as though under the weight of a pulpit peroration. Meysy, from the bed, watched the three men with the air of an expert who holds the solution of the problem.

He slipped to his feet as Mr. Mindon's speech flagged.

'I suppose you've considered, Mindon, that it rests with you to proclaim the fact that you're no longer – well, the chief object of your wife's affection?'

Mr. Mindon raised his head irritably; interrogation impeded the flow of his diatribe.

'That you – er – in short, created the situation by making it known?' Meysy glanced at the Rector. 'Am I right, Bonifant?'

The Rector took meditative counsel of his finger tips; then slowly, as though formulating a dogma, 'Under certain conditions,' he conceded, 'what is unknown may be said to be nonexistent.'

Mr. Mindon looked from one to the other.

'Damn it, man – before it's too late,' Meysy followed up, 'can't you see that *you're* the only person who can make you ridiculous?'

Mr. Brownrigg rose, and Mr. Mindon had the desperate sense that the situation was slipping out of his grasp.

'It rests with you,' Doctor Bonifant murmured, 'to save your children from even the shadow of obloquy.'

'You can't stay here, at any rate,' said Mr. Brownrigg heavily.

Mr. Mindon, who had risen, dropped weakly into his chair. His three counsellors were now all on their feet, taking up their hats with the air of men who have touched the limit of duty. In another moment they would be gone, and with them Mr. Mindon's audience, his support, his confidence in the immutability of his resolve. He felt himself no more than an evocation of their presence; and, in dread of losing the identity they had created, he groped for a dedaining word. 'I shan't leave for New York till tomorrow.'

'Tomorrow everything will be known,' said Mr. Brownrigg, with his hand on the door.

Meysy glanced at his watch with a faint smile. 'It's tomorrow now,' he added.

He fell back, letting the older men pass out; but, turning as though to follow, he felt a drowning clutch upon his arm.

'It's for the children,' Mr. Mindon stammered.

The Moving Finger

THE NEWS of Mrs. Grancy's death came to me with the shock of an immense blunder – one of fate's most irretrievable acts of vandalism. It was as though all sorts of renovating forces had been checked by the clogging of that one wheel. Not that Mrs. Grancy contributed any perceptible momentum to the social machine: her unique distinction was that of filling to perfection her special place in the world. So many people are like badly-composed statues, overlapping their niches at one point and leaving them vacant at another. Mrs. Grancy's niche was her husband's life; and if it be argued that the space was not large enough for its vacancy to leave a very big gap, I can only say that, at the last resort, such dimensions must be determined by finer instruments than any ready-made standard of utility. Ralph Grancy's was in short a kind of disembodied usefulness: one of those constructive influences that, instead of crystallizing into definite forms, remain as it were a medium for the development of clear thinking and fine feeling. He faithfully irrigated his own dusty patch of life, and the fruitful moisture stole far beyond his boundaries. If, to carry on the metaphor, Grancy's life was a sedulously-cultivated enclosure, his wife was the flower he had planted in its midst – the embowering tree, rather, which gave him rest and shade at its foot and the wind of dreams in its upper branches.

We had all – his small but devoted band of followers – known a moment when it seemed likely that Grancy would fail us. We had watched him pitted against one stupid obstacle after another – ill-health, poverty, misunderstanding and, worst of all for a man of his texture, his first wife's soft insidious egotism. We had seen him sinking under the leaden embrace of her affection like a swimmer in a drowning clutch; but just as we despaired he had always come to the surface again, blinded, panting, but striking out fiercely for the shore. When at last her death released him it became a question as to how much of the man she had carried with her. Left alone, he revealed numb withered patches, like a tree from which a parasite has been stripped. But gradually he began to put out new leaves; and when he met the lady who was to become his second wife – his one *real* wife, as his friends reckoned – the whole man burst into flower.

The second Mrs. Grancy was past thirty when he married her, and it was clear that she had harvested that crop of middle joy which is rooted in young despair. But if she had lost the surface of eighteen she had kept its inner light; if her cheek lacked the gloss of immaturity her eyes were young with the stored youth of half a lifetime. Grancy had first known her somewhere in the East – I believe she was the sister of one of our consuls out there – and when he brought her home to New York she came among us as a stranger. The idea of Grancy's remarriage had been a shock to us all. After one such calcining most men would have kept out of the fire; but we agreed that he was predestined to sentimental blunders, and we awaited with resignation the embodiment of his latest mistake. Then Mrs. Grancy came – and we understood. She was the most beautiful and the most complete of explanations. We shuffled our defeated omniscience out of sight and gave it hasty burial under a prodigality of welcome. For the first time in years we had Grancy off our minds. 'He'll do something great now!' the least sanguine of us prophesied; and our sentimentalist amended: 'He *has* done it – in marrying her!'

It was Claydon, the portrait painter, who risked this hyperbole; and who soon afterward, at the happy husband's request, prepared to defend it in a portrait of Mrs. Grancy. We were all – even Claydon – ready to concede that Mrs. Grancy's unwontedness was in some degree a matter of environment. Her graces were complementary and it needed the mate's call to reveal the flash of color beneath her neutral-tinted wings. But if she needed Grancy to interpret her, how much greater was the service she rendered him! Claydon professionally described her as the right frame for him; but if she defined she also enlarged, if she threw the whole into perspective she also cleared new ground, opened fresh vistas, reclaimed whole areas of activity that had run to waste under the harsh husbandry of privation. This interaction of sympathies was not without its visible expression. Claydon was not alone in maintaining that Grancy's presence – or indeed the mere mention of his name – had a perceptible effect on his wife's appearance. It was as though a light were shifted, a curtain drawn back, as though, to borrow another of Claydon's metaphors, Love the indefatigable artist were perpetually seeking a happier 'pose' for his model. In this interpretative light Mrs. Grancy acquired the charm which makes some women's faces like a book of which the last page is never turned. There was always something new to read in her eyes. What Claydon read there – or at least such scattered hints of the ritual as reached him through the sanctuary doors – his portrait in due course declared to us. When the picture was exhibited it was at once acclaimed as his masterpiece; but the people who knew Mrs. Grancy smiled and said it was flattered. Claydon, however, had not set out to paint *their* Mrs. Grancy – or ours even – but Ralph's; and Ralph knew his own at a glance. At the first confrontation he saw that Claydon had understood. As for Mrs. Grancy, when the finished picture was shown to her she turned to the painter and said simply: 'Ah, you've done me facing the east!'

The picture, then, for all its value, seemed a mere incident in the unfolding of their double destiny, a footnote to the illuminated text of their lives. It was not till afterward that it acquired the significance of last words spoken on a threshold never to be recrossed. Grancy, a year after his marriage, had given up his town house and carried his bliss an hour's journey away, to a little place among the hills. His various duties and interest brought him frequently to New York but we necessarily saw him less often than when his house had served as the rallying point of kindred enthusiasms. It seemed a pity that such an influence should be withdrawn, but we all felt that his long arrears of happiness should be paid in whatever coin he chose. The distance from which the fortunate couple radiated warmth on us was not too great for friendship to traverse; and our conception of glorified leisure took the form of Sundays spent in the Grancys' library, with its sedative rural outlook, and the portrait of Mrs. Grancy illuminating its studious walls. The picture was at its best in that setting; and we used to accuse Claydon of visiting Mrs. Grancy in order to see her portrait. He met this by declaring that the portrait *was* Mrs. Grancy; and there were moments when the statement seemed unanswerable. One of us, indeed – I think it must have been the novelist – said that Claydon had been saved from falling in love with Mrs. Grancy only by falling in love with his picture of her; and it was noticeable that he, to whom his finished work was no more than the shed husk of future effort, showed a perennial tenderness for this one achievement. We smiled afterward to think how often, when Mrs. Grancy was in the room, her presence reflecting itself in our talk like a gleam of sky in a hurrying current, Claydon, averted from the real woman, would sit as it were listening to the picture. His attitude, at the time, seemed only a part of the unusualness of those picturesque afternoons, when the most familiar combinations of life underwent a magical change. Some human happiness is a landlocked lake; but the Grancys' was an open sea, stretching a buoyant and illimitable surface to the voyaging interests of life. There was room and to spare on those waters for all our separate ventures; and always, beyond the sunset, a mirage of the fortunate isles toward which our prows were bent.

• II •

It was in Rome that, three years later, I heard of her death. The notice said 'suddenly'; I was glad of that. I was glad too – basely perhaps – to be away from Grancy at a time when silence must have seemed obtuse and speech derisive.

I was still in Rome when, a few months afterward, he suddenly arrived there. He had been appointed secretary of legation at Constantinople and was on the way to his post. He had taken the place, he said frankly, 'to get away.' Our relations with the Porte held out a prospect of hard work, and that, he explained, was what he needed. He could never be satisfied to sit down among the ruins. I saw that, like most of us in moments of extreme moral tension, he was playing a part, behaving as he thought it became a man to behave in the eye of disaster. The instinctive posture of grief is a shuffling compromise between defiance and prostration; and pride feels the need of striking a worthier attitude in face of such a foe. Grancy, by nature musing and retrospective, had chosen the role of the man of action, who answers blow for blow and opposes a mailed front to the thrusts of destiny; and the completeness of the equipment testified to his inner weakness. We talked only of what we were not thinking of, and parted, after a few days, with a sense of relief that proved the inadequacy of friendship to perform, in such cases, the office assigned to it by tradition.

Soon afterward my own work called me home, but Grancy remained several years in Europe. International diplomacy kept its promise of giving him work to do, and during the year in which he acted as *chargé d'affaires* he acquitted himself, under trying conditions, with conspicuous zeal and discretion. A political redistribution of matter removed him from office just as he had proved his usefulness to the government; and the following summer I heard that he had come home and was down at his place in the country.

On my return to town I wrote him and his reply came by the next post. He answered as it were in his natural voice, urging me to spend the following Sunday with him, and suggesting that I should bring down any of the old set who could be persuaded to join me. I thought this a good sign, and yet – shall I own it? – I was vaguely disappointed. Perhaps we are apt to feel that our friends' sorrows should be kept like those historic monuments from which the encroaching ivy is periodically removed.

That very evening at the club I ran across Claydon. I told him of Grancy's invitation and proposed that we should go down together; but he pleaded an engagement. I was sorry, for I had always felt that he and I stood nearer Ralph than the others, and if the old Sundays were to be renewed I should have preferred that we two should spend the first alone with him. I said as much to Claydon and offered to fit my time to his; but he met this by a general refusal.

'I don't want to go to Grancy's,' he said bluntly. I waited a moment, but he appended no qualifying clause.

'You've seen him since he came back?' I finally ventured.

Claydon nodded.

'And is he so awfully bad?'

'Bad? No, he's all right.'

'All right? How can he be, unless he's changed beyond all recognition?'

'Oh, you'll recognize *him*,' said Claydon, with a puzzling deflection of emphasis.

His ambiguity was beginning to exasperate me, and I felt myself shut out from some knowledge to which I had as good a right as he.

'You've been down there already, I suppose?'

'Yes; I've been down there.'

'And you've done with each other – the partnership is dissolved?'

'Done with each other? I wish to God we had!' He rose nervously and tossed aside the review from which my approach had diverted him. 'Look here,' he said, standing before me, 'Ralph's the best fellow going and there's nothing under heaven I wouldn't do for him – short of going down there again.' And with that he walked out of the room.

Claydon was incalculable enough for me to read a dozen different meanings into his words; but none of my interpretations satisfied me. I determined, at any rate, to seek no farther for a companion; and the next Sunday I traveled down to Grancy's alone. He met me at the station and I saw at once that he had changed since our last meeting. Then he had been in fighting array, but now if he and grief still housed together it was no longer as enemies. Physically the transformation was as marked but less reassuring. If the spirit triumphed the body showed its scars. At five-and-forty he was gray and stooping, with the tired gate of an old man. His serenity, however, was not the resignation of age. I saw that he did not mean to drop out of the game. Almost immediately he began to speak of our old interests; not with an effort, as at our former meeting, but simply and naturally, in the tone of a man whose life has flowed back into its normal channels. I remembered, with a touch of self-reproach, how I had distrusted his reconstructive powers; but my admiration for his reserved force was now tinged by the sense that, after all, such happiness as his ought to have been paid with his last coin. The feeling grew as we neared the house and I found how inextricably his wife was interwoven with my remembrance of the place: how the whole scene was but an extension of that vivid presence.

Within doors nothing was changed, and my hand would have dropped without surprise into her welcoming clasp. It was luncheon time, and Grancy led me at once to the dining room, where the walls, the furniture, the very plate and porcelain, seemed a mirror in which a moment since her face had been reflected. I wondered whether Grancy, under the recovered tranquillity of his smile, concealed the same sense of her nearness, saw perpetually between himself and the actual her bright unappeasable ghost. He spoke of her once or twice, in an easy incidental way, and her name seemed to hang in the air after he had uttered it, like a chord that continues to vibrate. If he felt her presence it was evidently as an enveloping medium, the moral atmosphere in which he breathed. I had never before known how completely the dead may survive.

After luncheon we went for a long walk through the autumnal fields and woods, and dusk was falling when we re-entered the house. Grancy led the way to the library, where, at this hour, his wife had always welcomed us back to a bright fire and a cup of tea. The room faced the west, and held a clear light of its own after the rest of the house had grown dark. I remembered how young she had looked in this pale gold light, which irradiated her eyes and hair, or silhouetted her girlish outline as she passed before the windows. Of all the rooms the library was most peculiarly hers; and here I felt that her nearness might take visible shape. Then, all in a moment, as Grancy opened the door, the feeling vanished and a kind of resistance met me on the threshold. I looked about me. Was the room changed? Had some desecrating hand effaced the traces of her presence? No; here too the setting was undisturbed. My feet sank into the same deep-piled Daghestan; the bookshelves took the firelight on the same rows of rich subdued bindings; her armchair stood in its old place near the tea table; and from the opposite wall her face confronted me.

Her face – but *was* it hers? I moved nearer and stood looking up at the portrait. Grancy's glance had followed mine and I heard him move to my side.

'You see a change in it?' he said.

'What does it mean?' I asked.

'It means – that five years have passed.'

'Over *her*?'

'Why not? – Look at me!' He pointed to his gray hair and furrowed temples. 'What do you think kept *her* so young? It was happiness! But now – ' he looked up at her with infinite tenderness. 'I like her better so,' he said. 'It's what she would have wished.'

'Have wished?'

'That we should grow old together. Do you think she would have wanted to be left behind?'

I stood speechless, my gaze traveling from his worn grief-beaten features to the painted face above. It was not furrowed like his; but a veil of years seemed to have descended on it. The bright hair had lost its elasticity, the cheek its clearness, the brow its light: the whole woman had waned.

Grancy laid his hand on my arm. 'You don't like it?' he said sadly.

'Like it? I – I've lost her!' I burst out.

'And I've found her,' he answered.

'In *that*?' I cried with a reproachful gesture.

'Yes, in that.' He swung round on me almost defiantly. 'The other had become a sham, a lie! This is the way she would have looked – does look, I mean. Claydon ought to know, oughtn't he?'

I turned suddenly. 'Did Claydon do this for you?'

Grancy nodded.

'Since your return?'

'Yes. I sent for him after I'd been back a week – ' He turned away and gave a thrust to the smoldering fire. I followed, glad to leave the picture behind me. Grancy threw himself into a chair near the hearth, so that the light fell on his sensitive variable face. He leaned his head back, shading his eyes with his hand, and began to speak.

• III •

'You fellows knew enough of my early history to guess what my second marriage meant to me. I say guess, because no one could understand – really. I've always had a feminine streak in me, I suppose: the need of a pair of eyes that should see with me, of a pulse that should keep time with mine. Life is a big thing, of course: a magnificent spectacle; but I got so tired of looking at it alone! Still, it's always good to live, and I had plenty of happiness – of the evolved kind. What I'd never had a taste of was the simple inconscient sort that one breathes in like the air.

'Well – I met her. It was like finding the climate in which I was meant to live. You know what she was – how indefinitely she multiplied one's point of contact with life, how she lit up the caverns and bridged the abysses! Well, I swear to you (though I suppose the sense of all that was latent in me) that what I used to think of on my way home at the end of the day, was simply that when I opened this door she'd be sitting over there, with the lamplight falling in a particular way on one little curl in her neck. When Claydon painted her he caught just the look she used to lift to mine when I came in – I've wondered, sometimes, at his knowing how she looked when she and I were alone. How I rejoiced in that picture! I used to say to her, 'You're my prisoner now – I shall never lose you. If you grew tired of me and left me you'd leave your real self there on the wall!' It was always one of our jokes that she was going to grow tired of me.

'Three years of it – and then she died. It was so sudden that there was no change, no diminution. It was as if she had suddenly become fixed, immovable, like her own portrait: as if Time had ceased at its happiest hour, just as Claydon had thrown down his brush one day and said, 'I can't do better than that.'

'I went away, as you know, and stayed over there five years. I worked as hard as I knew how, and after the first black months a little light stole in on me. From thinking that she would have been interested in what I was doing I came to feel that she *was* interested – that she was there and that she knew. I'm not talking any psychical jargon – I'm simply trying to express the sense I had that an influence so full, so abounding as hers couldn't pass like a spring shower. We had so lived into each other's hearts and minds that the consciousness of what she would have thought and felt illuminated all I did. At first she used to come back shyly; tentatively, as though not sure of finding me; then she stayed longer and longer, till at last she became again the very air I breathed. There was bad moments, of course, when her nearness mocked me with the loss of the real woman; but gradually the distinction between the two was effaced and the mere thought of her grew warm as flesh and blood.

'Then I came home. I landed in the morning and came straight down here. The thought of seeing her portrait possessed me and my heart beat like a lover's as I opened the library door. It was in the afternoon and the room was full of light. It fell on her picture – the picture of a young and radiant woman. She smiled at me coldly across the distance that divided us. I had the feeling that she didn't even recognize me. And then I caught sight of myself in the mirror over there – a gray-haired broken man whom she had never known!

'For a week we two lived together – the strange woman and the strange man. I used to sit night after night and question her smiling face; but no answer ever came. What did she know of me, after all? We were irrevocably separated by the five years of life that lay between us. At times, as I sat here, I almost grew to hate her; for her presence had driven away my gentle ghost, the real wife who had wept, aged, struggled with me during those awful years. It was the worst loneliness I've ever known. Then, gradually, I began to notice a look of sadness in the picture's eyes; a look that seemed to say: 'Don't you see that *I* am lonely too?' And all at once it came over me how she would have hated to be left behind! I remembered her comparing life to a heavy book that could not be read with ease unless two people held it together; and I thought how impatiently her hand would have turned the pages that divided us! So the idea came to me: 'It's the picture that stands between us; the picture that is dead, and not my wife. To sit in this room is to keep watch beside a corpse.' As this feeling grew on me the portrait became like a beautiful mausoleum in which she had been buried alive: I could hear her beating against the painted walls and crying to me faintly for help.

'One day I found I couldn't stand it any longer and I sent for Claydon. He came down and I told him what I'd been through and what I wanted him to do. At first he refused point-blank to touch the picture. The next morning I went off for a long tramp, and when I came home I found him sitting here alone. He looked at me sharply for a moment and then he said: "I've changed my mind; I'll do it." I arranged one of the north rooms as a studio and he shut himself up there for a day; then he sent for me. The picture stood there as you see it now – it was as though she'd met me on the threshold and taken me in her arms! I tried to thank him, to tell him what it meant to me, but he cut me short.

"There's an up train at five, isn't there?" he asked. "I'm booked for a dinner tonight. I shall just have time to make a bolt for the station and you can send my traps after me." I haven't seen him since.

'I can guess what it cost him to lay hands on his masterpiece; but, after all, to him it was only a picture lost, to me it was my wife regained!'

• IV •

After that, for ten years or more, I watched the strange spectacle of a life of hopeful and productive effort based on the structure of a dream. There could be no doubt to those who saw Grancy during this period that he drew his strength and courage from the sense of his wife's mystic participation in his task. When I went back to see him a few months later I found the portrait had been removed from the library and placed in a small study upstairs, to which he had transferred his desk and a few books. He told me he always sat there when he was alone, keeping the library for his Sunday visitors. Those who missed the portrait of course made no comment on its absence, and the few who were in his secret respected it. Gradually all his old friends had gathered about him and our Sunday afternoons regained something of their former character; but Claydon never reappeared among us.

As I look back now I see that Grancy must have been failing from the time of his return home. His invincible spirit belied and disguised the signs of weakness that afterward asserted themselves in my remembrance of him. He seemed to have an inexhaustible fund of life to draw on, and more than one of us was a pensioner on his superfluity.

Nevertheless, when I came back one summer from my European holiday and heard that he had been at the point of death, I understood at once that we had believed him well only because he wished us to.

I hastened down to the country and found him midway in a slow convalescence. I felt then that he was lost to us and he read my thought at a glance.

'Ah,' he said, 'I'm an old man now and no mistake. I suppose we shall have to go half-speed after this; but we shan't need towing just yet!'

The plural pronoun struck me, and involuntarily I looked up at Mrs. Grancy's portrait. Line by line I saw my fear reflected in it. It was the face of a woman *who knows that her husband is dying*. My heart stood still at the thought of what Claydon had done.

Grancy had followed my glance. 'Yes, it's changed her,' he said quietly. 'For months, you know, it was touch and go with me – we had a long fight of it, and it was worse for her than for me.' After a pause he added: 'Claydon has been very kind; he's so busy nowadays that I seldom see him, but when I sent for him the other day he came down at once.'

I was silent and we spoke no more of Grancy's illness; but when I took leave it seemed like shutting him in alone with his death warrant.

The next time I went down to see him he looked much better. It was a Sunday and he received me in the library, so that I did not see the portrait again. He continued to improve and toward spring we began to feel that, as he had said, he might yet travel a long way without being towed.

One evening, on returning to town after a visit which had confirmed my sense of reassurance, I found Claydon dining alone at the club. He asked me to join him and over the coffee our talk turned to his work.

'If you're not too busy,' I said at length, 'you ought to make time to go down to Grancy's again.'

He looked up quickly. 'Why?' he asked.

'Because he's quite well again,' I returned with a touch of cruelty. 'His wife's prognostications were mistaken.'

Claydon stared at me a moment. 'Oh, *she* knows,' he affirmed with a smile that chilled me.

'You mean to leave the portrait as it is then?' I persisted.

He shrugged his shoulders. 'He hasn't sent for me yet!'

A waiter came up with the cigars and Claydon rose and joined another group.

It was just a fortnight later that Grancy's housekeeper telegraphed for me. She met me at the station with the news that he had been 'taken bad' and that the doctors were with him. I had to wait for some time in the deserted library before the medical men appeared. They had the baffled manner of empirics who have been superseded by the Great Healer; and I lingered only long enough to hear that Grancy was not suffering and that my presence could do him no harm.

I found him seated in his armchair in the little study. He held out his hand with a smile.

'You see she was right after all,' he said.

'She?' I repeated, perplexed for the moment.

'My wife.' He indicated the picture. 'Of course I knew she had no hope from the first. I saw that' – he lowered his voice – 'after Claydon had been here. But I wouldn't believe it at first!'

I caught his hands in mine. 'For God's sake don't believe it now!' I adjured him.

He shook his head gently. 'It's too late,' he said. 'I might have known that she knew.'

'But, Grancy, listen to me,' I began; and then I stopped. What could I say that would convince him? There was no common ground of argument on which we could meet; and after all it would be easier for him to die feeling that she *had* known. Strangely enough, I saw that Claydon had missed his mark.

• V •

GRANCY'S will named me as one of his executors; and my associate, having other duties on his hands, begged me to assume the task of carrying out our friend's wishes. This placed me under the necessity of informing Claydon that the portrait of Mrs. Grancy had been bequeathed to him; and he replied by the next post that he would send for the picture at once. I was staying in the deserted house when the portrait was taken away; and as the door closed on it I felt that Grancy's presence had vanished too. Was it his turn to follow her now, and could one ghost haunt another?

After that, for a year or two, I heard nothing more of the picture, and though I met Claydon from time to time we had little to say to each other. I had no definable grievance against the man and I tried to remember that he had done a fine thing in sacrificing his best picture to a friend; but my resentment had all the tenacity of unreason.

One day, however, a lady whose portrait he had just finished begged me to go with her to see it. To refuse was impossible, and I went with the less reluctance that I knew I was not the only friend she had invited. The others were all grouped around the easel when I entered, and after contributing my share to the chorus of approval I turned away and began to stroll about the studio. Claydon was something of a collector and his things were generally worth looking at. The studio was a long tapestried room with a curtained archway at one end. The curtains were looped back, showing a smaller apartment, with books and flowers and a few fine bits of bronze and porcelain. The tea table standing in this inner room proclaimed that it was open to inspection, and I wandered in. A *bleu poudré* vase first attracted me; then I turned to examine a slender bronze Ganymede, and in so doing found myself face to face with Mrs. Grancy's portrait. I stared up at her blankly and she smiled back at me in all the recovered radiance of youth. The artist had effaced every trace of his later touches and the original picture had reappeared. It throned alone on the paneled wall, asserting a brilliant supremacy over its carefully chosen surroundings. I felt in an instant that the whole room was tributary to it: that Claydon had heaped his treasures at the feet of the woman he loved. Yes – it was the woman he had loved and not the picture; and my instinctive resentment was explained.

Suddenly I felt a hand on my shoulder.

'Ah, how could you?' I cried, turning on him.

'How could I?' he retorted. 'How could I *not*? Doesn't she belong to me now?'

I moved away impatiently.

'Wait a moment,' he said with a detaining gesture. 'The others have gone and I want to say a word to you. Oh, I know what you've thought of me – I can guess! You think I killed Grancy, I suppose?'

I was startled by his sudden vehemence. 'I think you tried to do a cruel thing,' I said.

'Ah – what a little way you others see into life!' he murmured. 'Sit down a moment – here, where we can look at her – and I'll tell you.'

He threw himself on the ottoman beside me and sat gazing up at the picture, with his hands clasped about his knee.

'Pygmalion,' he began slowly, 'turned his statue into a real woman; *I* turned my real woman into a picture. Small compensation, you think – but you don't know how much of a woman belongs to you after you've painted her! Well, I made the best of it, at any rate – I gave her the best I had in me; and she gave me in return what such a woman gives by merely being. And after all she rewarded me enough by making me paint as I shall never paint again! There was one side of her, though, that was mine alone, and that was her beauty; for no one else understood it. To Grancy even it was the mere expression of herself – what language is to thought. Even when he saw the picture he didn't guess my secret – he was so sure she was all his! As though a man should think he owned the moon because it was reflected in the pool at his door.

'Well – when he came home and sent for me to change the picture it was like asking me to commit murder. He wanted me to make an old woman of her – of her who had been so divinely, unchangeably young! As if any man who really loved a woman would ask her to sacrifice her youth and beauty for his sake! At first I told him I couldn't do it – but afterward, when he left me alone with the picture, something queer happened. I suppose it was because I was always so confoundedly fond of Grancy that it went against me to refuse what he asked. Anyhow, as I sat looking up at her, she seemed to say, 'I'm not yours but his, and I want you to make me what he wishes.' And so I did it. I could have cut my hand off when the work was done – I dare say he told you I never would go back and look at it. He thought I was too busy – he never understood.

'Well – and then last year he sent for me again – you remember. It was after his illness, and he told me he'd grown twenty years older and that he wanted her to grow older too – he didn't want her to be left behind. The doctors all thought he was going to get well at that time, and he thought so too; and so did I when I first looked at him. But when I turned to the picture – ah, now I don't ask you to believe me; but I swear it was *her* face that told me he was dying, and that she wanted him to know it! She had a message for him and she made me deliver it.'

He rose abruptly and walked toward the portrait; then he sat down beside me again.

'Cruel! Yes, it seemed so to me at first; and this time, if I resisted, it was for *his* sake and not for mine. But all the while I felt her eyes drawing me, and gradually she made me understand. If she'd been there in the flesh (she seemed to say) wouldn't she have seen before any of us that he was dying? Wouldn't he have read the news first in her face? And wouldn't it be horrible if now he should discover it instead in strange eyes? – Well – that was what she wanted of me and I did it – I kept them together to the last!' He looked up at the picture again. 'But now she belongs to me,' he repeated. . . .

Expiation

'I CAN NEVER,' said Mrs. Fetherel, 'hear the bell ring without a shudder.'

Her unruffled aspect – she was the kind of woman whose emotions never communicate themselves to her clothes – and the conventional background of the New York drawing room, with its pervading implication of an imminent tea tray and of an atmosphere in which the social functions have become purely reflex, lent to her declaration a relief not lost on her cousin Mrs. Clinch, who, from the other side of the fireplace, agreed, with a glance at the clock, that it *was* the hour for bores.

'Bores!' cried Mrs. Fetherel impatiently, 'If I shuddered at *them*, I should have a chronic ague!'

She leaned forward and laid a sparkling finger on her cousin's shabby black knee. 'I mean the newspaper clippings,' she whispered.

Mrs. Clinch returned a glance of intelligence. 'They've begun already?'

'Not yet; but they're sure to now, at any minute, my publisher tells me.'

Mrs. Fetherel's look of apprehension sat oddly on her small features, which had an air of neat symmetry somehow suggestive of being set in order every morning by the housemaid. Someone (there were rumours that it was her cousin) had once said that Paula Fetherel would have been very pretty if she hadn't looked so like a moral axiom in a copybook hand.

Mrs. Clinch received her confidence with a smile. 'Well,' she said, 'I suppose you were prepared for the consequences of authorship?'

Mrs. Fetherel blushed brightly. 'It isn't their coming,' she owned – 'it's their coming *now*.'

'Now?'

'The Bishop's in town.'

Mrs. Clinch leaned back and shaped her lips to a whistle which deflected in a laugh. 'Well!' she said.

'You see!' Mrs. Fetherel triumphed.

'Well – weren't you prepared for the Bishop?'

'Not now – at least, I hadn't thought of his seeing the clippings.'

'And why should he see them?'

'Bella – *won't* you understand? It's John.'

'John?'

'Who has taken the most unexpected tone – one might almost say out of perversity.'

'Oh, perversity – ' Mrs. Clinch murmured, observing her cousin between lids wrinkled by amusement. 'What tone has John taken?'

Mrs. Fetherel threw out her answer with the desperate gesture of a woman who lays bare the traces of a marital fist. 'The tone of being proud of my book.'

The measure of Mrs. Clinch's enjoyment overflowed in laughter.

'Oh, you may laugh,' Mrs. Fetherel insisted, 'but it's no joke to me. In the first place, John's liking the book is so – so – such a false note – it puts me in such a ridiculous position; and then it has set him watching for the reviews – who would ever have suspected John of knowing that books were *reviewed*? Why, he's actually found out about the clipping bureau, and whenever the postman rings I hear John rush out of the library to see if there are any yellow envelopes. Of course, when they *do* come he'll bring them into the drawing room and read them aloud to everybody who happens to be here – and the Bishop is sure to happen to be here!'

Mrs. Clinch repressed her amusement. 'The picture you draw is a lurid one,' she conceded, 'but your modesty strikes me as abnormal, especially in an author. The chances are that some of the clippings will be rather pleasant reading. The critics are not all union men.'

Mrs. Fetherel stared. 'Union men?'

'Well, I mean they don't all belong to the well-known Society-for-the-Persecution-of-Rising-Authors. Some of them have even been known to defy its regulations and say a good word for a new writer.'

'Oh, I dare say,' said Mrs. Fetherel, with the laugh her cousin's epigram exacted. 'But you don't quite see my point. I'm not at all nervous about the success of my book – my publisher tells me I have no need to be – but I *am* afraid of its being a *succès de scandale*.'

'Mercy!' said Mrs. Clinch, sitting up.

The butler and footman at this moment appeared with the tea tray and when they had withdrawn, Mrs. Fetherel, bending her brightly rippled head above the kettle, continued in a murmur of avowal, 'The title, even, is a kind of challenge.'

'*Fast and Loose*,' Mrs. Clinch mused. 'Yes, it ought to take.'

'I didn't choose it for that reason!' the author protested. 'I should have preferred something quieter – less pronounced; but I was determined not to shirk the responsibility of what I had written. I want people to know beforehand exactly what kind of book they are buying.'

'Well,' said Mrs. Clinch, 'that's a degree of conscientiousness that I've never met with before. So few books fulfill the promise of their titles that experienced readers never expect the fare to come up to the menu.'

'*Fast and Loose* will be no disappointment on that score,' her cousin significantly returned. 'I've handled the subject without gloves. I've called a spade a spade.'

'You simply make my mouth water! And to think I haven't been able to read it yet because every spare minute of my time has been given to correcting the proofs of "How the Birds Keep Christmas"! There's an instance of the hardships of an author's life!'

Mrs. Fetherel's eye clouded. 'Don't joke, Bella, please. I suppose to experienced authors there's always something absurd in the nervousness of a new writer, but in my case so much is at stake; I've put so much of myself into this book and I'm so afraid of being misunderstood . . . of being, as it were, in advance of my time . . . like poor Flaubert. . . . I *know* you'll think me ridiculous . . . and if only my own reputation were at stake, I should never give it a thought . . . but the idea of dragging John's name through the mire. . . .'

Mrs. Clinch, who had risen and gathered her cloak about her, stood surveying from her genial height her cousin's agitated countenance.

'Why did you use John's name, then?'

'That's another of my difficulties! I *had* to. There would have been no merit in publishing such a book under an assumed name; it would have been an act of moral cowardice. *Fast and Loose* is not an ordinary novel. A writer who dares to show up the hollowness of social conventions must have the courage of her convictions and be willing to accept the consequences of defying society. Can you imagine Ibsen or Tolstoi writing under a false name?' Mrs. Fetherel lifted a tragic eye to her cousin. 'You don't know, Bella, how often I've envied you since I began to write. I used to wonder sometimes – you won't mind my saying so? – why, with all your cleverness, you hadn't taken up some more exciting subject than natural history; but I see now how wise you were. Whatever happens, you will never be denounced by the press!'

'Is that what you're afraid of?' asked Mrs. Clinch, as she grasped the bulging umbrella which rested against her chair. 'My dear, if I had ever had the good luck to be denounced by the press, my brougham would be waiting at the door for me at this very moment, and I shouldn't have had to ruin this umbrella by using it in the rain. Why, you innocent, if I'd ever felt the slightest aptitude for showing up social conventions, do you suppose I should waste my time writing "Nests Ajar" and "How to Smell the Flowers"? There's a fairly steady demand for pseudo-science and colloquial ornithology, but it's nothing, simply nothing, to the ravenous call for attacks on social institutions – especially by those inside the institutions!'

There was often, to her cousin, a lack of taste in Mrs. Clinch's pleasantries, and on this occasion they seemed more than usually irrelevant.

'*Fast and Loose* was not written with the idea of a large sale.'

Mrs. Clinch was unperturbed. 'Perhaps that's just as well,' she returned, with a philosophic shrug. 'The surprise will be all the pleasanter, I mean. For of course it's going to sell tremendously; especially if you can get the press to denounce it.'

'Bella, how *can* you? I sometimes think you say such things expressly to tease me; and yet I should think you of all women would understand my purpose in writing such a book. It has always seemed to me that the message I had to deliver was not for myself alone, but for all the other women in the world who have felt the hollowness of our social shams, the ignominy of bowing down the idols of the market, but have lacked either the courage or the power to proclaim their independence; and I have fancied, Bella dear, that, however severely society might punish me for revealing its weaknesses, I could count on the sympathy of those who like you' – Mrs. Fetherel voice sank – 'have passed through the deep waters.'

Mrs. Clinch gave herself a kind of canine shake, as though to free her ample shoulders from any drop of the element she was supposed to have traversed.

'Oh, call them muddy rather than deep,' she returned; 'and you'll find, my dear, that women who've had any wading to do are rather shy of stirring up mud. It sticks – especially on white clothes.'

Mrs. Fetherel lifted an undaunted brow. 'I'm not afraid,' she proclaimed; and at the same instant she dropped her teaspoon with a clatter and shrank back into her seat. 'There's the bell,' she exclaimed, 'and I know it's the Bishop!'

It was in fact the Bishop of Ossining, who impressively announced by Mrs. Fetherel's butler, now made an entry that may best be described as not inadequate to the expectations the announcement raised. The Bishop always entered a room well; but, when unannounced, or preceded by a low church butler who gave him his surname, his appearance lacked the impressiveness conferred on it by the due specification of his diocesan dignity. The Bishop was very fond of his niece, Mrs. Fetherel, and one of the traits he most valued in her was the possession of a butler who knew how to announce a bishop.

Mrs. Clinch was also his niece; but, aside from the fact that she possessed no butler at all, she had laid herself open to her uncle's criticism by writing insignificant little books which had a way of going into five or ten editions, while the fruits of his own episcopal leisure – 'The Wail of Jonah' (twenty cantos in blank verse), and 'Through a Glass Brightly'; or, 'How to Raise Funds for a Memorial Window' – inexplicably languished on the back shelves of a publisher noted for his dexterity in pushing 'devotional goods.' Even this indiscretion the Bishop might, however, have condoned, had his niece thought fit to turn to him for support and advice at the painful juncture of her history when, in her own words, it became necessary for her to invite Mr. Clinch to look out for another situation. Mr. Clinch's misconduct was of the kind especially designed by Providence to test the fortitude of a Christian wife and mother, and the Bishop was absolutely distended with seasonable advice and edification; so that when Bella met his tentative exhortations with the curt remark that she preferred to do her own house cleaning unassisted, her uncle's grief at her ingratitude was not untempered with sympathy for Mr. Clinch.

It is not surprising, therefore, that the Bishop's warmest greetings were always reserved for Mrs. Fetherel; and on this occasion Mrs. Clinch thought she detected, in the salutation which fell to her share, a pronounced suggestion that her own presence was superfluous – a hint which she took with her usual imperturbable good humor.

• II •

LEFT alone with the Bishop, Mrs. Fetherel sought the nearest refuge from conversation by offering him a cup of tea. The Bishop accepted with the preoccupied air of a man to whom, for the moment, tea is but a subordinate incident. Mrs. Fetherel's nervousness increased; and knowing that the surest way of distracting attention from one's own affairs is to affect an interest in those of one's companion, she hastily asked if her uncle had come to town on business.

'On business – yes – ' said the Bishop in an impressive tone. 'I had to see my publisher, who has been behaving rather unsatisfactorily in regard to my last book.'

'Ah – your last book?' faltered Mrs. Fetherel, with a sickening sense of her inability to recall the name or nature of the work in question, and a mental vow never again to be caught in such ignorance of a colleague's productions.

' "Through a Glass Brightly," ' the Bishop explained, with an emphasis which revealed his detection of her predicament. 'You may remember that I sent you a copy last Christmas?'

'Of course I do!' Mrs. Fetherel brightened. 'It was that delightful story of the poor consumptive girl who had no money, and two little brothers to support – '

'Sisters – idiot sisters – ' the Bishop gloomily corrected.

'I mean sisters; and who managed to collect money enough to put up a beautiful memorial window to her – her grandfather, whom she had never seen – '

'But whose sermons had been her chief consolation and support during her long struggle with poverty and disease.' The Bishop gave the satisfied sigh of the workman who reviews his completed task. 'A touching subject, surely; and I believe I did it justice; at least so my friends assured me.'

'Why, yes – I remember there was a splendid review of it in the *Reredos*!' cried Mrs. Fetherel, moved by the incipient instinct of reciprocity.

'Yes – by my dear friend Mrs. Gollinger, whose husband, the late Dean Gollinger, was under very particular obligations to me. Mrs. Gollinger is a woman of rare literary acumen, and her praise of my book was unqualified; but the public wants more highly seasoned fare, and the approval of a thoughtful churchwoman carries less weight than the sensational comments of an illiterate journalist.' The Bishop bent a meditative eye on his spotless gaiters. 'At the risk of horrifying you, my dear,' he added, with a slight laugh, 'I will confide to you that my best chance of a popular success would be to have my book denounced by the press.'

'Denounced?' gasped Mrs. Fetherel. 'On what ground?'

'On the ground of immorality.' The Bishop evaded her startled gaze, 'Such a thing is inconceivable to you, of course; but I am only repeating what my publisher tells me. If, for instance, a critic could be induced – I mean, if a critic were to be found, who called in question the morality of my heroine in sacrificing her own health and that of her idiot sisters in order to put up a memorial window to her grandfather, it would probably raise a general controversy in the newspapers, and I might count on a sale of ten or fifteen thousand within the next year. If he described her as morbid or decadent, it might even run to twenty thousand; but that is more than I permit myself to hope. In fact I should be satisfied with any general charge of immorality.' The Bishop sighed again. 'I need hardly tell you that I am actuated by no mere literary ambition. Those whose opinion I most value have assured me that the book is not without merit; but, though it does not become me to dispute their verdict, I can truly say that my vanity as an author is not at stake. I have, however, a special reason for wishing to increase the circulation of "Through a Glass Brightly"; it was written for a purpose – a purpose I have greatly at heart – '

'I know,' cried his niece sympathetically. 'The chantry window – ?'

'Is still empty, alas! and I had great hopes that, under Providence my little book might be the means of filling it. All our wealthy parishioners have given lavishly to the cathedral, and it was for this reason that in writing "Through a Glass," I addressed my appeal more especially to the less well-endowed, hoping by the example of my heroine to stimulate the collection of small sums throughout the entire diocese, and perhaps beyond it. I am sure,' the Bishop feelingly concluded, 'the book would have a widespread influence if people could only be induced to read it!'

His conclusion touched a fresh threat of association in Mrs. Fetherel's vibrating nerve centers. 'I never thought of that!' she cried.

The Bishop looked at her inquiringly.

'That one's books may not be read at all! How dreadful!' she exclaimed.

He smiled faintly. 'I had not forgotten that I was addressing an authoress,' he said. 'Indeed, I should not have dared to inflict my troubles on anyone not of the craft.'

Mrs. Fetherel was quivering with the consciousness of her involuntary self-betrayal. 'Oh, Uncle!' she murmured.

'In fact,' the Bishop continued, with a gesture which seemed to brush away her scruples, 'I came here partly to speak to you about your novel. "Fast and Loose," I think you call it?'

Mrs. Fetherel blushed assentingly.

'And is it out yet?' the Bishop continued.

'It came out about a week ago. But you haven't touched your tea and it must be quite cold. Let me give you another cup.'

'My reason for asking,' the Bishop went on, with the bland inexorableness with which, in his younger days, he had been known to continue a sermon after the senior warden had looked four times at his watch, '– my reason for asking it, that I hoped I might not be too late to induce you to change the title.'

Mrs. Fetherel set down the cup she had filled. 'The title?' she faltered.

The Bishop raised a reassuring hand. 'Don't misunderstand me, dear child; don't for a moment imagine that I take it to be in any way indicative of the contents of the book. I know you too well for that. My first idea was that it had probably been forced on you by an unscrupulous publisher. I know too well to what ignoble compromises one may be driven in such cases!' He paused, as though to give her the opportunity of confirming this conjecture, but she preserved an apprehensive silence, and he went on, as though taking up the second point in his sermon: 'Or, again, the name may have taken your fancy without your realizing all that implies to minds more alive than yours to offensive innuendoes. It is – ahem – excessively suggestive, and I hope I am not too late to warn you of the false impression it is likely to produce on the very readers whose approbation you would most value. My friend Mrs. Gollinger, for instance – '

Mrs. Fetherel, as the publication of her novel testified, was in theory a woman of independent views; and if in practice she sometimes failed to live up to her standard, it was rather from an irresistible tendency to adapt herself to her environment than from any conscious lack of moral courage. The Bishop's exordium had excited in her that sense of opposition which such admonitions are apt to provoke; but as he went on she felt herself gradually enclosed in an atmosphere in which her theories vainly gasped for breath. The Bishop had the immense dialectical advantage of invalidating any conclusions at variance with his own by always assuming that his premises were among the necessary laws of thought. This method, combined with the habit of ignoring any classifications but his own, created an element in which the first condition of existence was the immediate adoption of his standpoint; so that his niece, as she listened, seemed to feel Mrs. Gollinger's Mechlin cap spreading its conventual shadow over her rebellious brow and the *Revue de Paris* at her elbow turning into a copy of the *Reredos*. She had meant to assure her uncle that she was quite aware of the significance of the title she had chosen, that it had been deliberately selected as indicating the subject of her novel, and that the book itself had been written in direct defiance of the class of readers for whose susceptibilities he was alarmed. The words were almost on her lips when the irresistible suggestion conveyed by the Bishop's tone and language deflected them into the apologetic murmur, 'Oh, Uncle, you mustn't think – I never meant – ' How much farther this current of reaction might have carried her the historian is unable to compute, for at this point the door opened and her husband entered the room.

'The first review of your book!' he cried, flourishing a yellow envelope. 'My dear Bishop, how lucky you're here!'

Though the trials of married life have been classified and catalogued with exhaustive accuracy, there is one form of conjugal misery which had perhaps received inadequate attention; and that is the suffering of the versatile woman whose husband is not equally adapted to all her moods. Every woman feels for the sister who is compelled to wear a bonnet which does not 'go' with her gown; but how much sympathy is given to her whose husband refuses to harmonize with the pose of the moment? Scant justice has, for instance, been done to the misunderstood wife whose husband persists in understanding her; to the submissive helpmate whose taskmaster shuns every opportunity of browbeating her, and to the generous and impulsive being whose bills are paid with philosophic calm. Mrs. Fetherel, as wives go, had been fairly exempt from trials of this nature, for her husband, if undistinguished by pronounced brutality or indifference, had at least the negative merit of being her intellectual inferior. Landscape gardeners, who are aware of the usefulness of a valley in emphasizing the height of a hill, can form an idea of the account to which an accomplished woman may turn such deficiencies; and it need scarcely be said that Mrs. Fetherel had made the most of her opportunities. It was agreeably obvious to everyone, Fetherel included, that he was not the man to appreciate such a woman; but there are no limits to man's perversity, and he did his best to invalidate this advantage by admiring her without pretending to understand her. What she most suffered from was this fatuous approval: the maddening sense that, however she conducted herself, he would always admire her. Had he belonged to the class whose conversational supplies are drawn from the domestic circle, his wife's name would never have been off his lips; and to Mrs. Fetherel's sensitive perceptions his frequent silences were indicative of the fact that she was his one topic.

It was, in part, the attempt to escape this persistent approbation that had driven Mrs. Fetherel to authorship. She had fancied that even the most infatuated husband might be counted on to resent, at least negatively, an attack on the sanctity of the hearth; and her anticipations were heightened by a sense of the unpardonableness of her act. Mrs. Fetherel's relations with her husband were in fact complicated by an irrepressible tendency to be fond of him; and there was a certain pleasure in the prospect of a situation that justified the most explicit expiation.

These hopes Fetherel's attitude had already defeated. He read the book with enthusiasm, he pressed it on his friends, he sent a copy to his mother; and his very soul now hung on the verdict of the reviewers. It was perhaps this proof of his general inaptitude that made his wife doubly alive to his special defects; so that his inopportune entrance was aggravated by the very sound of his voice and the hopeless aberration of his smile. Nothing, to the observant, is more indicative of a man's character and circumstances than his way of entering a room. The Bishop of Ossining, for instance, brought with him not only an atmosphere of episcopal authority, but an implied opinion on the verbal inspiration of the Scriptures and on the attitude of the Church toward divorce; while the appearance of Mrs. Fetherel's husband produced an immediate impression of domestic felicity. His mere aspect implied that there was a well-filled nursery upstairs; that his wife, if she did not sew on his buttons, at least superintended the performance of that task; that they both went to church regularly, and that they dined with his mother every Sunday evening punctually at seven o'clock.

All this and more was expressed in the affectionate gesture with which he now raised the yellow envelope above Mrs. Fetherel's clutch; and knowing the uselessness of begging him not to be silly, she said, with a dry despair, 'You're boring the Bishop horribly.'

Fetherel turned a radiant eye on that dignitary. 'She bores us all horribly, doesn't she, sir?' he exulted.

'Have you read it?' said his wife uncontrollably.

'Read it? Of course not – it's just this minute come. I say, Bishop, you're not going – ?'

'Not till I've heard this,' said the Bishop, settling himself in his chair with an indulgent smile.

His niece glanced at him despairingly 'Don't let John's nonsense detain you,' she entreated.

'Detain him? That's good,' guffawed Fetherel. 'It isn't as long as one of his sermons – won't take me five minutes to read. Here, listen to this, ladies and gentlemen: "In this age of festering pessimism and decadent depravity, it is no surprise to the nauseated reviewer to open one more volume saturated with the fetid emanations of the sewer – " '

Fetherel, who was not in the habit of reading aloud, paused with a gasp, and the Bishop glanced sharply at his niece, who kept her gaze fixed on the teacup she had not yet succeeded in transferring to his hand.

' "Of the sewer," ' her husband resumed; ' "but his wonder is proportionately great when he lights on a novel as sweetly inoffensive as Paula Fetherel's *Fast and Loose.* Mrs. Fetherel is, we believe, a new hand at fiction, and her work reveals frequent traces of inexperience; but these are more than atoned for by her pure fresh view of life and her altogether unfashionable regard for the reader's moral susceptibilities. Let no one be induced by its distinctly misleading title to forego the enjoyment of this pleasant picture of domestic life, which, in spite of a total lack of force in character drawing and of consecutiveness in incident, may be described as a distinctly pretty story." '

• III •

It was several weeks later that Mrs. Clinch once more brought the plebeian aroma of heated tramcars and muddy street crossings into the violet-scented atmosphere of her cousin's drawing room.

'Well,' she said, tossing a damp bundle of proofs into the corner of a silk-cushioned bergère, 'I've read it at last and I'm not so awfully shocked!'

Mrs. Fetherel, who sat near the fire with her head propped on a languid hand, looked up without speaking.

'Mercy, Paula,' said her visitor, 'you're ill.'

Mrs. Fetherel shook her head. 'I was never better,' she said, mournfully.

'Then may I help myself to tea? Thanks.'

Mrs. Clinch carefully removed her mended glove before taking a buttered tea cake; then she glanced again at her cousin.

'It's not what I said just now – ?' she ventured.

'Just now?'

'About *Fast and Loose*? I came to talk it over.'

Mrs. Fetherel sprang to her feet. 'I never,' she cried dramatically, 'want to hear it mentioned again!'

'Paula!' exclaimed Mrs. Clinch, setting down her cup.

Mrs. Fetherel slowly turned on her an eye brimming with the incommunicable; then, dropping into her seat again, she added, with a tragic laugh: 'There's nothing left to say.'

'Nothing – ?' faltered Mrs. Clinch, longing for another tea cake, but feeling the inappropriateness of the impulse in an atmosphere so charged with the portentous. 'Do you mean that everything *has* been said?' She looked tentatively at her cousin. 'Haven't they been nice?'

'They've been odious – odious – ' Mrs. Fetherel burst out, with an ineffectual clutch at her handkerchief. 'It's been perfectly intolerable!'

Mrs. Clinch, philosophically resigning herself to the propriety of taking no more tea, crossed over to her cousin and laid a sympathizing hand on that lady's agitated shoulder.

'It *is* a bore at first,' she conceded; 'but you'll be surprised to see how soon one gets used to it.'

'I shall – never – get – used to it – ' Mrs. Fetherel brokenly declared.

'Have they been so very nasty – all of them?'

'Every one of them!' the novelist sobbed.

'I'm so sorry, dear; it *does* hurt, I know – but hadn't you rather expected it?'

'Expected it?' cried Mrs. Fetherel, sitting up.

Mrs. Clinch felt her way warily. 'I only mean, dear, that I fancied from what you said before the book came out that you rather expected – that you'd rather discounted – '

'Their recommending it to everybody as a perfectly harmless story?'

'Good gracious! Is *that* what they've done?'

Mrs. Fetherel speechlessly nodded.

'Every one of them?'

'Every one.'

'Phew!' said Mrs. Clinch, with an incipient whistle.

'Why, you've just said it yourself!' her cousin suddenly reproached her.

'Said what?'

'That you weren't so *awfully* shocked – '

'I? Oh, well – you see, you'd keyed me up to such a pitch that it wasn't quite as bad as I expected – '

Mrs. Fetherel lifted a smile steeled for the worst. 'Why not say at once,' she suggested, 'that it's a distinctly pretty story?'

'They haven't said *that*?'

'They've all said it.'

'My poor Paula!'

'Even the Bishop – '

'The Bishop called it a pretty story?'

'He wrote me – I've his letter somewhere. The title rather scared him – he wanted me to change it; but when he'd read the book he wrote that it was all right and that he'd sent several copies to his friends.'

'The old hypocrite!' cried Mrs. Clinch. 'That was nothing but professional jealousy.'

'Do you think so?' cried her cousin, brightening.

'Sure of it, my dear. His own books don't sell, and he knew the quickest way to kill yours was to distribute it through the diocese with his blessing.'

'Then you don't really think it's a pretty story?'

'Dear me, no! Not nearly as bad as that – '

'You're so good, Bella – but the reviewers?'

'Oh, the reviewers,' Mrs. Clinch jeered. She gazed meditatively at the cold remains of her tea cake. 'Let me see,' she said suddenly; 'do you happen to remember if the first review came out in an important paper?'

'Yes – the *Radiator*.'

'That's it! I thought so. Then the others simply followed suit: they often do if a big paper sets the pace. Saves a lot of trouble. Now if you could only have got the *Radiator* to denounce you – '

'That's what the Bishop said!' cried Mrs. Fetherel.

'He did?'

'He said his only chance of selling "Through a Glass Brightly" was to have it denounced on the ground of immorality.'

'H'm,' said Mrs. Clinch, 'I thought he knew a trick or two.' She turned an illuminated eye on her cousin.'You ought to get *him* to denounce *Fast and Loose*!' she cried.

Mrs. Fetherel looked at her suspiciously. 'I suppose every book must stand or fall on its own merits,' she said in an unconvinced tone.

'Bosh! That view is as extinct as the post chaise and the packet ship – it belongs to the time when people read books. Nobody does that now; the reviewer was the first to set the example, and the public was only too thankful to follow it. At first people read the reviews; now they read only the publishers' extracts from them. Even these are rapidly being replaced by paragraphs borrowed from the vocabulary of commerce. I often have to look twice before I am sure if I am reading a department store advertisement or the announcement of a new batch of literature. The publishers will soon be having their "fall and spring openings" and their "special importations for Horse Show Week." But the Bishop is right, of course – nothing helps a book like a rousing attack on its morals; and as the publishers can't exactly proclaim the impropriety of their own wares, the task has to be left to the press or the pulpit.'

'The pulpit?' Mrs. Fetherel mused.

'Why, yes. Look at those two novels in England last year.'

Mrs. Fetherel shook her head hopelessly. 'There is so much more interest in literature in England than here.'

'Well, we've got to make the supply create the demand. The Bishop could run your novel up into the hundred thousands in no time.'

'But if he can't make his own sell – '

'My dear, a man can't very well preach against his own writings!'

Mrs. Clinch rose and picked up her proofs.

'I'm awfully sorry for you, Paula dear,' she concluded, 'but I can't help being thankful that there's no demand for pessimism in the field of natural history. Fancy having to write "The Fall of a Sparrow," or "How the Plants Misbehave"!'

• IV •

MRS. FETHEREL, driving up to the Grand Central Station one morning about five months later, caught sight of the distinguished novelist, Archer Hynes, hurrying into the waiting room ahead of her. Hynes, on his side, recognising her brougham, turned back to greet her as the footman opened the carriage door.

'My dear colleague! Is it possible that we are traveling together?'

Mrs. Fetherel blushed with pleasure. Hynes had given her two columns of praise in the *Sunday Meteor*, and she had not yet learned to disguise her gratitude.

'I am going to Ossining,' she said smilingly.

'So am I. Why, this is almost as good as an elopement.'

'And it will end where elopements ought to – in church.'

'In church? You're not going to Ossining to go to church?'

'Why not? There's a special ceremony in the cathedral – the chantry window is to be unveiled.'

'The chantry window? How picturesque! What *is* a chantry? And why do you want to see it unveiled? Are you after copy – doing something in the Huysmans manner? "La Cathédrale," eh?'

'Oh, no,' Mrs. Fetherel hesitated. 'I'm going simply to please my uncle,' she said at last.

'Your uncle?'

'The Bishop, you know.' She smiled.

'The Bishop – the Bishop of Ossining? Why, wasn't he the chap who made the ridiculous attack on your book? Is that prehistoric ass your uncle? Upon my soul, I think you're mighty forgiving to travel all the way to Ossining for one of his stained-glass sociables!'

Mrs. Fetherel's smiles flowed into a gentle laugh. 'Oh, I've never allowed that to interfere with our friendship. My uncle felt dreadfully about having to speak publicly against my book – it was a great deal harder for him than for me – but he thought it his duty to do so. He has the very highest sense of duty.'

'Well,' said Hynes, with a shrug, 'I don't know that he didn't do you a good turn. Look at that!'

They were standing near the bookstall and he pointed to a placard surmounting the counter and emblazoned with the conspicuous announcement: '*Fast and Loose*. New Edition with Author's Portrait. Hundred and Fiftieth Thousand.'

Mrs. Fetherel frowned impatiently. 'How absurd! They've no right to use my picture as a poster!'

'There's our train,' said Hynes; and they began to push their way through the crowd surging toward one of the inner doors.

As they stood wedged between circumferent shoulders, Mrs. Fetherel became conscious of the fixed stare of a pretty girl who whispered eagerly to her companion: 'Look, Myrtle! That's Paula Fetherel right behind us – I knew her in a minute!'

'Gracious – where?' cried the other girl, giving her head a twist which swept her Gainsborough plumes across Mrs. Fetherel's face.

The first speaker's words had carried beyond her companion's ear, and a lemon-colored woman in spectacles, who clutched a copy of the 'Journal of Psychology' in one drab cotton-gloved hand, stretched her disengaged hand across the intervening barrier of humanity.

'Have I the privilege of addressing the distinguished author of *Fast and Loose*? If so, let me thank you in the name of the Woman's Psychological League of Peoria for your magnificent courage in raising the standard of revolt against – '

'You can tell us the rest in the car,' said a fat man, pressing his good-humored bulk against the speaker's arm.

Mrs. Fetherel, blushing, embarrassed and happy, slipped into the space produced by this displacement, and a few moments later had taken her seat in the train.

She was a little late, and the other chairs were already filled by a company of elderly ladies and clergymen who seemed to belong to the same party, and were still busy exchanging greetings and settling themselves in their places.

One of the ladies, at Mrs. Fetherel's approach, uttered an exclamation of pleasure and advanced with outstretched hand. 'My dear Mrs. Fetherel! I am so delighted to see you here. May I hope you are going to the unveiling of the chantry window? The dear Bishop so hoped that you would do so! But perhaps I ought to introduce myself. I am Mrs. Gollinger' – she lowered her voice expressively – 'one of your uncle's oldest friends, one who has stood close to him through all this sad business, and who knows what he suffered when he felt obliged to sacrifice family affection to the call of duty.'

Mrs. Fetherel, who had smiled and colored slightly at the beginning of this speech, received its close with a depreciating gesture.

'Oh, pray don't mention it,' she murmured. 'I quite understood how my uncle was placed – I bore him no ill will for feeling obliged to preach against my book.'

'He understood that, and was so touched by it! He has often told me that it was the hardest task he was ever called upon to perform – and, do you know, he quite feels that this unexpected gift of the chantry window is in some way a return for his courage in preaching that sermon.'

Mrs. Fetherel smiled faintly. 'Does he feel that?'

'Yes; he really does. When the funds for the window were so mysteriously placed at his disposal, just as he had begun to despair of raising them, he assured me that he could not help connecting the fact with his denunciation of your book.'

'Dear Uncle!' sighed Mrs. Fetherel. 'Did he say that?'

'And now,' continued Mrs. Gollinger, with cumulative rapture – 'now that you are about to show, by appearing at the ceremony today, that there had been no break in your friendly relations, the dear Bishop's happiness will be complete. He was so longing to have you come to the unveiling!'

'He might have counted on me,' said Mrs. Fetherel, still smiling.

'Ah, that is so beautifully forgiving of you!' cried Mrs. Gollinger enthusiastically. 'But then, the Bishop has always assured me that your real nature was very different from that which – if you will pardon my saying so – seems to be revealed by your brilliant but – er – rather subversive book. "If you only knew my niece, dear Mrs. Gollinger," he always said, "you would see that her novel was written in all innocence of heart"; and to tell you the truth, when I first read the book I didn't think it so very, *very*, shocking. It wasn't till the dear Bishop had explained to me – but, dear me, I mustn't take up your time in this way when so many others are anxious to have a word with you.'

Mrs. Fetherel glanced at her in surprise, and Mrs. Gollinger continued with a playful smile: 'You forget that your face is familiar to thousands whom you have never seen. We all recognized you the moment you entered the train, and my friends here are so eager to make your acquaintance – even those' – her smile deepened – 'who thought the dear Bishop not *quite unjustified* in his attack on your remarkable novel.'

• V •

A RELIGIOUS light filled the chantry of Ossining Cathedral, filtering through the linen curtain which veiled the central window and mingling with the blaze of tapers on the richly adorned altar.

In this devout atmosphere, agreeably laden with the incense-like aroma of Easter lilies and forced lilacs, Mrs. Fetherel knelt with a sense of luxurious satisfaction. Beside her sat Archer Hynes, who had remembered that there was to be a church scene in his next novel and that his impressions of the devotional environment needed refreshing. Mrs. Fetherel was very happy. She was conscious that her entrance had sent a thrill through the female devotees who packed the chantry, and she had humor enough to enjoy the thought that, but for the good Bishop's denunciation of her book, the heads of his flock would not have been turned so eagerly in her direction. Moreover, as she entered she had caught sight of a society reporter, and she knew that her presence, and the fact that she was accompanied by Hynes, would be conspicuously proclaimed in the morning papers. All these evidences of the success of her handiwork might have turned a calmer head than Mrs. Fetherel's; and though she had now learned to dissemble her gratification, it still filled her inwardly with a delightful glow.

The Bishop was somewhat late in appearing, and she employed the interval in meditating on the plot of her next novel, which was already partly sketched out, but for which she had been unable to find a satisfactory dénouement. By a not uncommon process of ratiocination, Mrs. Fetherel's success had convinced her of her vocation. She was sure now that it was her duty to lay bare the secret plague spots of society, and she was resolved that there should be no doubt as to the purpose of her new book. Experience had shown her that where she had fancied she was calling a spade a spade she had in fact been alluding in guarded terms to the drawing-room shovel. She was determined not to repeat the same mistake, and she flattered herself that her coming novel would not need an episcopal denunciation to insure its sale, however likely it was to receive this crowning evidence of success.

She had reached this point in her meditations when the choir burst into song and the ceremony of the unveiling began. The Bishop, almost always felicitous in his addresses to the fair sex, was never more so than when he was celebrating the triumph of one of his cherished purposes. There was a peculiar mixture of Christian humility and episcopal exultation in the manner with which he called attention to the Creator's promptness in responding to his demand for funds, and he had never been more happily inspired than in eulogizing the mysterious gift of the chantry window.

Though no hint of the donor's identity had been allowed to escape him, it was generally understood that the Bishop knew who had given the window, and the congregation awaited in a flutter of suspense the possible announcement of a name. None came, however, though the Bishop deliciously titillated the curiosity of his flock by circling ever closer about the interesting secret. He would not disguise from them, he said, that the heart which had divined his inmost wish had been a woman's – is it not to woman's institutions that more than half the happiness of earth is owing? What man is obliged to learn by the laborious process of experience, woman's wondrous instinct tells her at a glance; and so it had been with this cherished scheme, this unhoped-for completion of their beautiful chantry. So much, at least, he was allowed to reveal; and indeed, had he not done so, the window itself would have spoken for him, since the first glance at its touching subject and exquisite design would show it to have originated in a woman's heart. This tribute to the sex was received with an audible sigh of contentment, and the Bishop, always stimulated by such evidence of his sway over his hearers, took up his theme with gathering eloquence.

Yes – a woman's heart had planned the gift, a woman's hand had executed it, and, might he add, without too far withdrawing the veil in which Christian beneficence ever loved to drape its acts – might he add that, under Providence, a book, a simple book, a mere tale, in fact, had had its share in the good work for which they were assembled to give thanks?

At this unexpected announcement, a ripple of excitement ran through the assemblage, and more than one head was abruptly turned in the direction of Mrs. Fetherel, who sat listening in an agony of wonder and confusion. It did not escape the observant novelist at her side that she drew down her veil to conceal an uncontrollable blush, and this evidence of dismay caused him to fix an attentive gaze on her, while from her seat across the aisle Mrs. Gollinger sent a smile of unctuous approval.

'A book – a simple book – ' the Bishop's voice went on above this flutter of mingled emotions. 'What is a book? Only a few pages and a little ink – and yet one of the mightiest instruments which Providence has devised for shaping the destinies of man . . . one of the most powerful influences for good or evil which the Creator has placed in the hands of his creatures. . . .'

The air seemed intolerably close to Mrs. Fetherel, and she drew out her scent bottle, and then thrust it hurriedly away, conscious that she was still the center of an unenviable attention. And all the while the Bishop's voice droned on. . . .

'And of all forms of literature, fiction is doubtless that which has exercised the greatest sway, for good or ill, over the passions and imagination of the masses. Yes, my friends, I am the first to acknowledge it – no sermon, however eloquent, no theological treatise, however learned and convincing, has ever inflamed the heart and imagination like a novel – a simple novel. Incalculable is the power exercised over humanity by the great magicians of the pen – a power ever enlarging its boundaries and increasing its responsibilities as popular education multiplies the number of readers. . . . Yes, it is the novelist's hand which can pour balm on countless human sufferings, or inoculate mankind with the festering poison of a corrupt imagination. . . .'

Mrs. Fetherel had turned white, and her eyes were fixed with a blind stare of anger on the large-sleeved figure in the center of the chancel.

'And too often alas, it is the poison and not the balm which the unscrupulous hand of genius proffers to its unsuspecting readers. But, my friends, why should I continue? None know better than an assemblage of Christian women, such as I am now addressing, the beneficent or baleful influences of modern fiction; and so, when I say that this beautiful chantry window of ours owes its existence in part to the romancer's pen' – the

Bishop paused, and bending forward, seemed to seek a certain face among the countenances eagerly addressed to his – 'when I say that this pen, which for personal reasons it does not become me to celebrate unduly – '

Mrs. Fetherel at this point half rose, pushing back her chair, which scraped loudly over the marble floor; but Hynes involuntarily laid a warning hand on her arm, and she sank down with a confused murmur about the heat.

'When I confess that this pen, which for once at least has proved itself so much mightier than the sword, is that which was inspired to trace the simple narrative of "Through a Glass Brightly" ' – Mrs. Fetherel looked up with a gasp of mingled relief and anger – 'when I tell you, my dear friends, that it was your Bishop's own work which first roused the mind of one of his flock to the crying need of a chantry window, I think you will admit that I am justified in celebrating the triumphs of the pen, even though it be the modest instrument which your own Bishop wields.'

The Bishop paused impressively, and a faint gasp of surprise and disappointment was audible throughout the chantry. Something very different from this conclusion had been expected, and even Mrs. Gollinger's lips curled with a slightly ironic smile. But Archer Hynes's attention was chiefly reserved for Mrs. Fetherel, whose face had changed with astonishing rapidity from surprise to annoyance, from annoyance to relief, and then back again to something very like indignation.

The address concluded, the actual ceremony of the unveiling was about to take place, and the attention of the congregation soon reverted to the chancel, where the choir had grouped themselves beneath the veiled window, prepared to burst into a chant of praise as the Bishop drew back the hanging. The moment was an impressive one, and every eye was fixed on the curtain. Even Hynes's gaze strayed to it for a moment, but soon returned to his neighbor's face; and then he perceived that Mrs. Fetherel, alone of all the persons present, was not looking at the window. Her eyes were fixed in an indignant stare on the Bishop; a flush of anger burned becomingly under her veil, and her hands nervously crumpled the beautifully printed program of the ceremony.

Hynes broke into a smile of comprehension. He glanced at the Bishop, and back at the Bishop's niece; then, as the episcopal hand was solemnly raised to draw back the curtain, he bent and whispered in Mrs. Fetherel's ear:

'Why, you gave it yourself! You wonderful woman, of course you gave it yourself!'

Mrs. Fetherel raised her eyes to his with a start. Her blush deepened and her lips shaped a hasty 'No'; but the denial was deflected into the indignant murmur – 'It wasn't *his* silly book that did it, anyhow!'

Les Metteurs en scène

It was tea time at the Hotel Nouveau-Luxe.

For several moments now Jean Le Fanois had been standing in the doorway of one of the small Louis XV drawing rooms that opened onto the spacious lounge. Of medium height, lean and well-built in his impeccably tailored frock coat, he had the knowing and slightly impertinent air of the aristocratic Parisian too long caught up in the exotic, noisy world of first-class hotels and fashionable cabarets. From time to time, however, his pale, finely chiseled face was clouded by an anxious expression, which the carefree smile he bestowed on passing acquaintances did little to hide.

Several times he glanced impatiently at his watch; then his expression cleared, and he advanced rapidly to meet a young woman who had just appeared on the threshold of the lounge. Exquisite and slender in a street dress of understated elegance, she balanced on a long, slim neck the head of an ephebe. Her exceedingly pale pink lips and large limpid eyes complemented an intelligent forehead crowned with a soft haze of indecisively blond hair. Glancing about for the young man, she made her way across the room alone, with the confident air, the serenely audacious carriage, of the young American used to making her own way in life. A closer scrutiny, however, revealed that the slightly naïve air of independence characteristic of her compatriots was tempered in her by a nuance of Parisian refinement – as if a florid complexion had been softened by a film of tulle. Contact with another civilization had affected her in a totally different way than it had Le Fanois; she had gained, in this cosmopolitan exchange, as much as he seemed to have lost.

The young man approached her with a brotherly gesture of familiarity. 'You're alone! Did your friends leave you in the lurch?' he asked her, shaking her hand.

Miss Lambart smiled reassuringly as she scanned the room. 'No, I don't think so. I was supposed to find Mrs. Smithers and her daughter in one of the drawing rooms over there.' She pointed with her tortoise-shell lorgnette toward the series of rooms just off the lounge. 'If we look for them . . .,' she continued, but Le Fanois held her back.

'No, wait a moment,' he said, lowering his voice and propelling the young woman to one of the large glassed-in bays overlooking the hotel garden. 'Tell me what you told them about me and just what role I'm supposed to play.' He hesitated; then, with a vaguely ironic smile, 'In brief, what stage of social ambition have your friends reached?'

Miss Lambart smiled too. 'They still seem quite naïve to me,' she said; 'but one always has to be on one's guard. The most naïve are sometimes the most distrustful.' She threw him a teasing glance. 'Do you remember that pretty widow in Trouville – you know, from last year? If you'd been willing to present her to the Duchess of Sestre, what a marvelous trick you would have played!'

The young man shrugged slightly. 'She was simply asking too much,' he returned. 'And then – and then was she really a widow as we understand it here, or had she simply mislaid her last husband? Your country is so vast that such accidents must be common. Decidedly, her past was much too nebulous!'

The girl broke into a chuckle that revealed her even pearl-white teeth beneath pale pink lips that were a bit too thin. 'Well, as far as "nebulous pasts" go, I can't answer for Mrs. Smithers' because I've never raised the veil that surrounds it. But I *will* vouch for the fact that her daughter is charming and that you're terribly finicky if you don't agree.'

The young man shot her an indefinable glance which seemed to color his customary mockery with a nuance of affection.

'As charming as you are?' he asked banteringly.

Miss Lambart frowned and her eyes suddenly turned a cold metallic gray. 'Now then, my dear fellow, you're not speaking in character. Besides,' she went on, self-possessed and smiling once again, 'it's my job to point such things out to you. As

I was saying, I believe that for the moment Mrs. Smithers' ambitions are rather amorphous. Like many Americans who find themselves rich overnight, she wasn't able to establish the proper social connections in New York. So half out of spite and half out of sheer desire to spend her money, she jumped aboard the first available steamer with her daughter, no doubt hoping to acquire immediate social standing in a world where people are received in society without embarrassing inquiries into their past, provided they are wealthy and come from far enough away! As you know, it's only recently that I met Mrs. Smithers – on the liner that brought me back here – and she admitted to me with positively *noble* frankness that she wanted to establish ties with the French aristocracy, since her own aristocratic tastes made life in a plebeian society unbearable. Look, there she is,' she added with a subtly malicious smile.

Le Fanois turned around and saw a large woman with pale, puffy features and a complicated coiffure, on which was poised a hat laden with the remains of an entire aviary of exotic birds. She advanced toward them, her shoulders weighed down by a magnificent silver fox coat, her movements impeded by the folds of a lavishly embroidered dress, trailing in her wake a tall, rosy girl. Dressed with the same exaggerated elegance as her mother, the girl held in her hands a sable muff, a gold purse set with precious stones and a diamond-studded lorgnette, and her incredibly blond hair was crowned with a floral abundance as varied as the ornithological trimmings of the maternal bonnet. 'Here are Mrs. Smithers and her daughter Catherine,' Blanche Lambart repeated, and Le Fanois, following her toward the new arrivals, could not suppress a sigh; 'Oh, those poor people . . . those poor people!'

• II •

FOR almost ten years, Jean Le Fanois had led the tiresome and ambiguous life of a promoter of *nouveaux riches* in Parisian society. He had let himself be drawn into it little by little, as a result of accidental dealings with an extremely wealthy American at a time when he himself was down on his luck. How could this luxury-craving boy, accustomed from early youth to the easy-going and costly life of the Parisian club-man, have resisted the unhoped-for windfall such a relationship represented? His new friend, goodhearted and simple-minded, asked only to enjoy his millions in the company of a few choice friends. A dabbler in art collecting, like many of his compatriots, he was able to appreciate the artistic tastes of Le Fanois and commissioned him to furnish and decorate the elegant town house he had just bought from a bankrupt adventurer. Jean was delighted with the opportunity to distinguish himself in the role of enlightened amateur and, in acquiring handsome works of art for his friend, he experienced a little of the pleasure he would have had in buying them for himself. Then he learned that the stakes in this game included more durable rewards than mere altruistic pleasure. He received large sums of money from secondhand dealers highly pleased with the client he brought them; and although this arrangement embarrassed him slightly the first time it was proposed, he quickly grew accustomed to it, especially in view of the fact that sizeable gambling losses had seriously depreciated his modest fortune.

He enjoyed in more disinterested fashion the idle, luxurious life in which he found himself involved. The compatriots surrounding his friend led a completely empty existence, devoid of fixed occupations and stable relationships – but how artfully they hid its yawning emptiness under the appearances of frantic activity! Cruises on yachts, automobile trips, sumptuous dinners in fashionable restaurants, afternoons of elegant strolling at Bagatelle or Saint-James, trips to the race track and to art exhibits, evenings at those small theaters designed for tourists in the know: all of these expensive and monotonous diversions followed in succession time and time again without exhausting a need to be busy inherited from enterprising and tenacious ancestors, who had directed the same furious activity toward amassing fortunes that their descendants devoted to squandering them. Needless to say, Le Fanois was often bored in this childish and shifting milieu. Yet he found such sweet compensations in it! Not only did his transactions with antique dealers enable him to purchase at a fraction of their worth some of the exquisite objects with which he liked to surround himself, but his parasitic existence saved him a considerable sum of money, which finally allowed him to organize a life of his own.

One fine day his Maecenas died, leaving his entire fortune to American relatives – to the great disappointment of Le Fanois.

Happily, a successor soon appeared on the scene, and little by little the young man became accustomed to the role of 'metteur en scène' – his own definition – serving as advisor extraordinary to foreign pilgrims quickened by the pious desire to spend their millions for the benefit of idle Parisians.

His family ties and charming personality had enabled him to remain in contact with the exclusive social circles that keep their distance from the madding crowd; Le Fanois acted as intermediary between the renegades from this milieu, each of them tormented by a craving for luxury and movement, and the explorers from the New World who longed to penetrate their closed society.

His task had not assumed significant proportions, however – he had not really turned professional – until he met Miss Blanche Lambart at a gathering of the foreign colony. Her fine intelligence and open-mindedness had struck him immediately; he had frequented her compatriots too long not to realize promptly that she came from more refined stock than most Americans who try to storm Parisian society. Everything about her betrayed a careful education, an abundance of social graces, the habit of moving in elegant circles. He had soon guessed, however, that like himself, she lived at the expense of people she despised.

At the time of their meeting, Miss Lambart was the traveling companion of a wealthy widow from Chicago who had visions of an advantageous marriage. In no time at all, Le Fanois and Miss Lambart had joined forces to present her to society and look for a husband who met her specifications. But it seems that the widow was as ungrateful as Le Fanois' patron; for the moment she was married she dismissed Miss Lambart who was forced to search for another benefactress. Having found one without delay, she once again asked Le Fanois' assistance in introducing her protégée to society.

Their unspoken agreement was three or four years old now. Le Fanois still did not know what pressing circumstances had prompted her to choose such a life. Was it the taste for luxury or the need for perpetual motion that so often motivated her fellow-countrymen? Did she come from one of those small towns whose sad, monotonous atmosphere he had heard described, where the women die of boredom in idle solitude while their husbands pile up a fortune that neither of them can enjoy? Le Fanois thought he detected in her, rather, a casualty of New

York society, too poor to resist the luxury that surrounded her, yet too proud and particular to tie herself down to a second-rate marriage. But whatever her past, Le Fanois found her attractive in a unique and undefinable way. He had never spoken to her of love. In spite of her free manner and ultra-modern vocabulary, he sensed in her an almost aggressive uprightness, that shielded her from his advances even more effectively than her deliberately ironic way of speaking.

So they simply remained the best of friends, enjoying their meetings and at the same time protecting themselves from the humiliation of their secret complicity by openly and cynically making fun of it.

Blanche Lambart had guessed right; Mrs. Smithers and her daughter were naïve souls.

Catherine in particular asked no more than to enjoy herself, aspired to no more stable happiness. She wanted to go to the races and the theater, to display her lovely outfits at the American colony's dances and to meet the greatest possible number of waltzers. Mrs. Smithers, however, already envisioned for her daughter the inevitable 'marriage to a French count.' But she realized only too well that she could not set her plan in motion by herself. Won over immediately by Miss Lambart's charm, she entrusted to her the creation of an existence consonant with her social aspirations. The young woman secured the services of Le Fanois, and before long the two of them had installed Mrs. Smithers in the town house formerly owned by Le Fanois' first patron and decorated by Le Fanois himself. Next they arranged a splendid succession of dinners and balls, to which Le Fanois' friends flocked with a pleasure they sometimes forgot to express to the hostess. But they did take notice of Catherine. In spite of her awkwardness, her twangy voice, her ear-splitting laugh, she projected such freshness and youthful radiance that her lack of *savoir-faire* was soon forgotten. She was a 'nice girl' and her naïveté and joviality were much appreciated.

'After all the designing women you've sent us over here, that child is a real relief,' Le Fanois remarked jestingly to Blanche. 'I think her very faults will help us to marry her off.'

They were sitting at the tea table in Miss Lambart's tiny sitting room. Two years ago she had been able to move into an unpretentious fifth-floor apartment, where she received callers with the independence of a married woman.

('What else could I do?' she would say. 'I have no source of income, no husband and no companion, so I have to be all three to myself.')

She smiled at the young man's mild impertinence.

'I admit that the Americans we send you are not always models of democratic pride,' she said. 'But are they any worse than the husbands you unearth for them so effortlessly?'

He did not reply and she went on: 'I don't know if we'll find it quite as easy to settle Catherine. I share your opinion of her and I wouldn't want to see her unhappily married for anything in the world.'

Le Fanois mused for a moment. Then he said:

'What would you say to Jean de Sestre?'

She started. 'You mean the young prince? He's the eldest son, isn't he? That means he'll be the Duke of Sestre!'

'Exactly.'

'And you think . . .'

'I think he's sincerely smitten with our charming Catherine and I don't foresee any difficulty in obtaining his parents' consent.'

She blinked at him as dumbfounded as ever.

'Now that's what's called a splendid match!' she said. 'And he's a fine person, isn't he?'

'He's no genius, but I think he'll be an exemplary husband. You'll be able to entrust your protégée to him without fear.'

Miss Lambart seemed lost in thought. Then she got up with a sigh and took several steps across the tiny room.

'What's the matter?' the young man inquired, tilting his head against the back of his chair to follow her graceful movements more easily.

She came toward him and leaned against the mantelpiece.

'Well, I . . . it's just that I keep thinking about the awful power of money. Quite an original thought, isn't it? But I can't help it when I look at that sweet young thing, who is certainly goodhearted enough, but who, when you come right down to it, is neither beautiful, witty, imaginative nor charming. And yet all she has to do is reach out her hand – oh! that pudgy red paw – and pluck herself a name from the social register, security for life and the heart of a respectable young man!'

Le Fanois was still gazing at her, with that indefinable gleam that sometimes came to his eyes when she was present.

'While you, poor dear, who have all that . . .'

'Oh, be quiet!' she interrupted.

A brick-red flush crept to her temples, and she returned abruptly to her place at the tea table.

Le Fanois shrugged.

'I thought we could be frank with one another.'

Her smile was full of bitterness.

'Very well, then. I'm worn out, I've had enough. But I've lived too long among the rich and the happy – the need for luxury is in my blood. And when I think that I'll have to start over again – put up another good fight . . .! Once Catherine is married, Mrs. Smithers will probably go back to America to conquer New York. If not, Catherine's position will make my services quite expendable.' An ironic laugh burst from her throat. 'Believe me, I've had enough!'

Le Fanois looked at her for a moment with a faintly sad expression; then he reassumed his bantering tone:

'Well, perhaps this time they'll give you a dowry, and I'll make a fine match for you.'

Their eyes met again; then she said smilingly:

'Oh! the dowry . . . the dowry I've dreamed of! How much do you think I would need to find a suitable husband?'

He seemed to reflect on it.

'A suitable husband? Why, for an income of sixty thousand francs, I solemnly promise to find you a man who adores you.'

She blushed a little, laughing incredulously.

'A man who adores me? Does such a person exist?'

'Trust me,' he said as he rose from his chair. 'And in the meantime, we're agreed, aren't we, that you'll feel out Mrs. Smithers while I take care of the de Sestres. I think our little affair is all but settled.

• III •

TEN days later, the two friends found themselves together again, this time in one of the gilded drawing rooms of the Smithers town house. Mrs. Smithers and her daughter had decided to go for a long drive, and Blanche had telephoned the young man to let him know she would wait for him alone at their house.

'My dear colleague,' he said, shaking her hand, 'it seems that your half of our venture has dragged on a bit! I had no difficulty at all with mine – I've just been waiting for a sign from you.'

Miss Lambart motioned him to an armchair opposite her own.

'And I couldn't give you a sign till this morning. It's been a fight to the finish.'

'A fight? What do you mean? They don't want my suitor?'

'Mrs. Smithers wants nothing more, as you might suspect.' She smiled wanly. 'But Catherine has other ideas.'

'What! That brainless girl?' Le Fanois frowned. 'What happened?'

Blanche hesitated, playing distractedly with the silk tassels that fringed the lapels of her dress. Finally she said, 'Well, in spite of myself, I sided with Catherine – I protected her from her mother.'

Le Fanois looked at her aghast.

'But what in the world does the child want? I'm completely lost.'

'On the contrary. You've *arrived,* my friend, because it's *you* she wants.'

The words, borne on her mocking laugh, struck him like a challenger's glove. He bolted from his chair, his face suddenly ashen, and began stroking his moustache nervously as if to hide his contorted lips.

'What? What do you mean by that?' he stammered.

'Just what I said. Catherine intends to marry the man she loves, and that man is you.'

He stood before her, bearing down with both hands on the bronze-laden table that separated them.

'Me? She loves *me*?' he repeated.

Blanche's laugh was tinged with a distinct note of mockery.

'Oh, come now! You can't be *that* surprised.'

'Surprised? I'm flabbergasted!' He glanced at her suddenly. 'Wait a minute. You don't think . . .'

'Oh, of course not! I'm well aware that you laid your cards on the table. Only, it's not the first time, is it, that someone has fallen in love with you without your assistance?'

He shrugged disdainfully; then he turned on his heel, paced the room once or twice, and came back to where Blanche was sitting.

'But the mother – the mother would never give her consent, would she?' he asked abruptly.

A sudden rush of color inflamed Blanche Lambart's cheeks. She stood up.

'Then it's all right with you?' she said, looking straight into his eyes.

He reddened too, and began to twist his gloves between his agitated fingers. 'All right with me? I have no idea. I was only asking . . .'

'In that case, the matter is settled. I have obtained Mrs. Smithers' permission.'

He looked at her, dumbfounded.

'You've obtained her permission? But how? It's unbelievable!'

'Not at all. She's a good woman at heart, and she adores Catherine. She wouldn't make her unhappy for anything in the world. The two of us broke down her resistance in no time. Catherine will marry for love – and Mrs. Smithers herself will make the brilliant match.'

Le Fanois gasped at this final surprise.

'Good Lord, you mean that *she* wants to marry Sestre?'

'Oh no! I don't think she intends to replace her daughter. But we should certainly be able to find someone her own age. You'll take care of it, won't you? She's really not too bad since she lost weight and began to wear dark colors.'

Blanche suddenly broke off. 'I hear the doorbell. They've come back.'

And, as Le Fanois looked around, searching for a way to escape without being seen, Blanche smiled and went on:

'No, don't go. You know we don't stand on ceremony in this household. Besides, I promised Catherine I would keep you here.'

She added softly as she left him. 'She's desperately in love with you. You'll be good to her, won't you?'

• IV •

SIX weeks later, Jean Le Fanois was again pacing Mrs. Smithers' gilded salon.

This time, he was alone; but, when he had crisscrossed the room several times and paced back and forth before the handsome bronze clock on the mantelpiece, he heard the soft rustle of a skirt behind him and turned to greet Miss Lambart.

It was the first time they had seen each other since the engagement.

The very day after her last conversation with him, she had left for London to visit some friends. In spite of Mrs. Smithers' supplications, she prolonged her stay far beyond the date set for her return. She wrote that she had caught a bad case of influenza, then alleged a slow convalescence which made her fear the strain of the trip home.

Her decision was finally triggered by a telegram stating that Catherine Smithers had become critically ill, and she had only been back for a few hours when Le Fanois arrived.

The moment she appeared, he was struck by the extreme pallor of her thin features, as drawn from anxiety over Catherine as from the traces of her own indisposition.

'It's really serious, then?' the young man asked after shaking hands with her.

'I'm afraid so. The poor child has double pneumonia, and her fever is raging.'

They continued to speak in hushed tones of Catherine's illness. Pneumonia had set in only the day before, complicating what had been a neglected cold. Mrs. Smithers, half out of her mind, never left her daughter's bedside. Four doctors and three nurses gave her the finest of care, and the mother, in despair, spoke of calling in a specialist from New York. For the time being, the symptoms were quite serious. However, the doctors would not be able to make their prognosis for twenty-four hours.

'The poor girl often asks for you, but they're afraid your visit might upset her. So Mrs. Smithers asked me to take her a message for you.'

Le Fanois had tears in his eyes.

'The poor child! Tell her, tell her that I . . .' He hesitated and suddenly seemed uncomfortable under Miss Lambart's serene gaze.

The hint of a sardonic smile crossed her pale lips.

'I'll know what to tell her,' she replied with a slightly bitter intonation.

Le Fanois looked at her; then he took her hand and kissed it.

'Would you?' he said. And she left him.

Two days later Catherine died. Her mother, having imagined till the very last minute that she could save her by sheer force of money, was profoundly shaken by the disaster, which seemed to show her for the time the impotence of her millions. She questioned Blanche and Le Fanois over and over again: 'What more could I have spent?' and blamed herself for not having sent for the specialist from New York, forgetting that Catherine had died before he could have arrived. Nevertheless, she was consoled a bit when she learned that Parisian high society, touched by the girl's tragic death, was bent on attending the funeral and she sent for a hundred copies of the *Paris Herald* to send to her friends in America.

Le Fanois and Miss Lambart did not see each other after the funeral. Greatly saddened by Catherine's death, Blanche had been forced to stay in bed by a recurrence of influenza; and the very next day Mrs. Smithers had asked Le Fanois to accompany her to Cannes, where she spoke of hiding her sorrow, in spite of the fact that the social season was at its height. The young man could hardly refuse the woman who was to have been his mother-in-law, so Miss Lambart remained alone in the luxurious hotel where she had stayed since her return from London.

Weeks slipped by. Mrs. Smithers did not write a word, so that Blanche, knowing that her patroness found spelling an insurmountable obstacle, finally wrote to Le Fanois to ask how she was. His answer was a week in arriving. Then he wrote from Barcelona, where he and Mrs. Smithers had gone by car in the hope that she would be diverted by a brief excursion in Spain.

Several days later, Blanche received from San Sebastian a card hastily scribbled by Mrs. Smithers, telling her that she would be home shortly and instructing her to order a selection of 'suitable' outfits from the couturiers of the rue de la Paix. In a postscript, she asked her to pick up at the jewelers her long strand of black pearls, 'the only ornament she would dream of wearing.' Miss Lambart carried out her orders and moved back into the town house on the eve of Mrs. Smithers return.

The next day at tea time Blanche was expecting a visit from Le Fanois, whom she had asked to stop by. When he appeared, paler and thinner than usual in his mourning clothes, she went to meet him with a sad smile somehow touched with tenderness. Le Fanois was struck by the soft luminosity of her wide gray eyes.

For the first time in her life, she seemed unafraid to take off the mask of irony that usually blurred her lovely features.

She put her hand in his and looked at him lingeringly.

'I've been so anxious to talk with you! I have so many things to tell you,' she said in a soft, affectionate tone of voice, motioning him to the armchair next to hers.

He sat down without saying a word and for a moment both were silent. Then, in a voice quavering with emotion, she began to speak of Catherine.

Le Fanois' face clouded and he made an almost irritated gesture.

'What's the matter?' asked Blanche astonished.

He stumbled over his words. 'It's . . . that that innocent child's love weighs me down. I . . . I'm ashamed I couldn't love her in return – the way I wanted to . . . the way she deserved. Please, let's not talk about it any more.'

Miss Lambart replied, smiling:

'She never suspected a thing. She thought you were sincerely in love.'

He reddened.

'Can't you see I'm ashamed of that too?'

She continued to gaze at him with a tender smile.

'Let's talk about Mrs. Smithers, then. I only saw her for a minute this morning. She was so busy with her dressmakers that I beat a hasty retreat.'

Le Fanois lowered his eyes.

'She seems better now. She's looking for activities to occupy her time,' he said casually.

'Yes, and I think she'll succeed. She spoke of an intimate luncheon she hopes to give next week for a grand duke passing through Paris. . . . Don't you think I'm right?' she went on, as Le Fanois remained silent. 'Don't you think Mrs. Smithers will find a good catch?'

'Really, this is hardly the moment to think about such things.'

'You don't think so? Well, I disagree. It seems to me that the poor woman needs to be diverted. She sincerely loved her daughter, but she doesn't know how to live with her sorrow. Besides, mourning suits her quite well. Her black dresses make her appear thinner, and she looks ten years younger since she stopped dyeing her hair. Was that your bright idea?'

Le Fanois frowned and uttered a short irritated burst of laughter.

'My dear girl, do you think I have nothing better to do than to supervise Mrs. Smithers' hairdresser?'

Miss Lambart smiled.

'If it bothers you to talk about Mrs. Smithers, why don't we talk about me for a while?'

Immediately he seemed more at ease.

'About you? That's a subject I never tire of.'

She was seated before him, slender and delicate in a dark dress which brought out the transparent pallor of her skin, making her lips seem even redder than they were. Golden highlights shimmered on her blond hair. Le Fanois decided she had never looked prettier, more captivating. When he felt her eyes softly meet his, however, he glanced away.

'Yes,' she continued, 'I want to talk to you about myself. I have some news – big news – to tell you.'

His head jerked up.

'You're getting married?'

'Perhaps. It's possible. I really don't know!'

She still enveloped him in her calm, sweet gaze, which seemed infused with an inner light.

'You asked me just a moment ago not to bring up the love of the poor child we're grieving over. However, I have to tell you that she was so ecstatic over your love for her that she wanted a little of her happiness to spill over onto others. The poor dear . . . She knew I was the one who had pleaded your cause with her mother – that I had fought for it loyally – and the very day she got sick she called me to her room to let me know how grateful she was.'

Le Fanois had pushed back his chair. He rose halfway, almost involuntarily, then changed his mind and sat down again.

'Go on,' he said in a low voice.

'She was so choked with emotion that she could hardly speak; but I knew instinctively what she wanted to tell me, and I hugged her and told her to be still for a moment and calm down. Then she answered that she couldn't enjoy her own happiness without doing her best to ensure my own. She knew I had almost no means of support and couldn't bear the idea of my continuing to live at others' expense. She had learned that a girl can't get married without a dowry in France, and she begged me to accept a gift that her feverish hand slipped into mine. I was already worried by the way she looked, so I accepted her present and kissed her without even glancing at the paper. The next day pneumonia set in, and three days later she was dead. I had put the paper away in my writing case, and I only looked at it the day after the burial.'

She stopped for a moment; then she slipped her hand under the lace of her bodice and withdrew a folded piece of paper that she gave to Le Fanois.

'Look,' she said, her voice trembling.

He unfolded the piece of paper automatically, and was astounded by what he saw.

'A million dollars, a million dollars . . .,' he stammered.

'Yes indeed! It's hard to believe how wealthy these people are. They give you a gift of a million dollars as if they were paying their butcher's bill.'

She said nothing, and their eyes met.

'It's like a fairy tale, isn't it?' she said with a short, high-pitched laugh.

Le Fanois had risen and given back the paper with a faintly trembling hand.

Again they fell silent. He had gone to lean against the mantelpiece, while Blanche, still seated, kept her hands crossed on her lap and her head slightly bowed. Le Fanois spoke first.

'I'm so happy for you! You don't doubt it, do you?' he said with obvious emotion, but without moving toward Blanche.

She raised her head slowly and looked at him, blushing.

'Have you forgotten your promise?' she asked with a smile.

'My promise?'

Le Fanois' cheeks flushed crimson.

She continued to gaze at him with her tender, fathomless eyes, as if to decipher what was going on inside him. But, as he still said nothing and stood propped against the fireplace with no apparent intention of coming toward her, she turned pale all of a sudden and stood up.

'I see that you *have* forgotten it – just my luck!' she said, struggling to maintain a lively tone of voice as her eyes filled with tears.

At the sound of her voice, Le Fanois wheeled around and came toward her, seizing her wrists with a violent movement.

'No, no! I haven't forgotten it, I haven't forgotten,' he cried, pulling her toward him.

She uttered a cry of joy and fright; then, just as she was about to yield to his embrace, she looked at him again and jerked backward, pushing him away with all the force of her stiffened arms.

'What is it? What's the matter?' she cried in a terror-stricken voice.

Le Fanois still clutched her wrists in a vise-like grip, and they stood stock-still for an instant, their eyes riveted on each other.

'Jean, what's the matter? Say something, I implore you!' she gasped.

Suddenly he let go of her hands and turned away from her with a hopeless gesture.

'The matter is . . . that I have engaged to marry the mother,' he said, with a bitter laugh.

Full Circle

GEOFFREY BETTON woke rather late – so late that the winter sunlight sliding across his bedroom carpet struck his eyes as he turned on the pillow.

Strett, the valet, had been in, drawn the bath in the adjoining dressing room, placed the crystal and silver box at his side, put a match to the fire, and thrown open the windows to the bright morning air. It brought in, on the glitter of sun, all the crisp morning noises – those piercing notes of the American thoroughfare that seem to take a sharper vibration from the clearness of the medium through which they pass.

Betton raised himself languidly. That was the voice of Fifth Avenue below his windows. He remembered that, when he moved into his rooms eighteen months before, the sound had been like music to him: the complex orchestration to which the tune of his new life was set. Now it filled him with disgust and weariness, since it had become the symbol of the hurry and noise of that new life. He had been far less hurried in the old days when he had to be up at seven, and down at the office sharp at nine. Now that he got up when he chose, and his life had no fixed framework of duties, the hours hunted him like a pack of bloodhounds.

He dropped back on his pillow with a groan. Yes – not a year ago there had been a positively sensuous joy in getting out of bed, feeling under his barefeet the softness of the warm red carpet, and entering the shining sanctuary where his great porcelain bath proffered its renovating flood. But then a year ago he could still call up the horror of the communal plunge at his earlier lodging: the listening for other bathers, the dodging of shrouded ladies in crimping pins, the cold wait on the landing, the descent into a blotchy tin bath, and the effort to identify one's soap and nailbrush among the promiscuous implements of ablution. That memory had faded now, and Betton saw only the dark hours to which his tiled temple of refreshment formed a kind of glittering ante-chamber. For after his bath came his breakfast, and on the breakfast tray his letters. His letters!

He remembered – and *that* memory had not not faded! – the thrill with which, in the early days of his celebrity, he had opened the first missive in a strange feminine hand: the letter beginning: 'I wonder if you'll mind an unknown reader's telling you all that your book has been to her?'

Mind? Ye gods, he minded now! For more than a year after the publication of *Diadems and Faggots* the letters, the inane indiscriminate letters of commendation, of criticism, of interrogation, had poured in on him by every post. Hundreds of unknown readers had told him with unsparing detail all that his book had been to them. And the wonder of it was, when all was said and done, that it had really been so little – that when their thick broth of praise was strained through the author's searching vanity there remained to him so small a sediment of definite specific understanding! No – it was always the same thing, over and over and over again – the same vague gush of adjectives, the same incorrigible tendency to estimate his effort according to each writer's personal references, instead of regarding it as a work of art, a thing to be measured by fixed standards!

He smiled to think how little, at first, he had felt the vanity of it all. He had found a savour even in the grosser evidences of popularity: the advertisements of his book, the daily shower of 'clippings,' the sense that, when he entered a restaurant or a theater, people nudged each other and said 'That's Betton.' Yes, the publicity had been sweet to him – at first. He had been touched by the sympathy of his fellow men: had thought indulgently of the world, as a better place than the failures and the dyspeptics would acknowledge. And then his success began to submerge him: he gasped under the thickening shower of letters. His admirers were really unappeasable. And they wanted him to do such ridiculous things – to give lectures, to head movements, to be tendered receptions, to speak at banquets, to address mothers, to plead for orphans, to go up in balloons, to lead the struggle for sterilized milk. They wanted his photograph for literary supplements, his autograph for charity bazaars, his name on committees, literary, educational, and social; above all, they wanted his opinion on everything: on Christianity, Buddhism, tight lacing, the drug habit, democratic government, female suffrage and love. Perhaps the chief benefit of this demand was his incidentally learning from it how few opinions he really had: the only one that remained with him was a rooted horror of all forms of correspondence. He had been unspeakably thankful when the letters began to fall off.

Diadems and Faggots was now two years old, and the moment was at hand when its author might have counted on regaining the blessed shelter of oblivion – if only he had not written another book! For it was the worst part of his plight that the result of his first folly had goaded him to the perpetration of the next – that one of the incentives (hideous thought!) to his new work had been the desire to extend and perpetuate his popularity. And this very week the book was to come out, and the letters, the cursed letters, would begin again!

Wistfully, almost plaintively, he looked at the breakfast tray with which Strett presently appeared. It bore only two notes and the morning journals, but he knew that within the week it would groan under his epistolary burden. The very newspaper flung the fact at him as he opened them.

READY ON MONDAY.
GEOFFREY BETTON'S NEW NOVEL
ABUNDANCE.
BY THE AUTHOR OF 'DIADEMS AND FAGGOTS.'
FIRST EDITION OF ONE HUNDRED AND FIFTY THOUSAND
ALREADY SOLD OUT.
ORDER NOW.

A hundred and fifty thousand volumes! And an average of three readers to each! Half a million of people would be reading him within a week, and every one of them would write to him, and their friends and relations would write too. He laid down the paper with a shudder.

The two notes looked harmless enough, and the caligraphy of one was vaguely familiar. He opened the envelope and looked at the signature: *Duncan Vyse*. He had not seen the name in years – what on earth could Duncan Vyse have to say? He ran over the page and dropped it with a wondering exclamation, which the watchful, Strett, re-entering, met by a tentative 'Yes, sir?'

'Nothing. Yes – that is – ' Betton picked up the note. 'There's a gentleman, Mr. Vyse, coming at ten.'

Strett glanced at the clock. 'Yes, sir. You'll remember that ten was the hour you appointed for the secretaries to call, sir.'

Betton nodded. 'I'll see Mr. Vyse first. My clothes, please.'

As he got into them, in the state of nervous hurry that had become almost chronic with him, he continued to think about Duncan Vyse. They had seen a great deal of each other for the few years after both had left Harvard: the hard happy years when Betton had been grinding at his business and Vyse – poor devil! – trying to write. The novelist recalled his friend's attempts with a smile; then the memory of the one small volume came back to him. It was a novel: 'The Lifted Lamp.' There was stuff in that, certainly. He remembered Vyse's tossing it down on his table with a gesture of despair when it came back from the last publisher. Betton, taking it up indifferently, had sat riveted till daylight. When he ended, the impression was so strong that he said to himself: 'I'll tell Apthorn about it – I'll go and see him tomorrow.' His own secret literary yearnings increased his desire to champion Vyse, to see him triumph over the dullness and timidity of the publishers. Apthorn was the youngest of the guild, still capable of opinions and the courage of them, a personal friend of Betton's, and, as it happened, the man afterward to become known as the privilege publisher of *Diadems and Faggots*. Unluckily the next day something unexpected turned up, and Betton forgot about Vyse and his manuscript. He continued to forget for a month, and then came a note from Vyse, who was ill, and wrote to ask what his friend had done. Betton did not like to say 'I've done nothing,' so he left the note unanswered, and vowed again: 'I'll see Apthorn.'

The following day he was called to the West on business, and was away a month. When he came back, there was a third note from Vyse, who was still ill, and desperately hard up. 'I'll take anything for the book, if they'll advance me two hundred dollars.' Betton, full of compunction, would gladly have advanced the sum himself; but he was hard up too, and could only swear inwardly: 'I'll write to Apthorn.' Then glanced again at the manuscript, and reflected: 'No – there are things in it that need explaining. I'd better see him.'

Once he went so far as to telephone Apthorn, but the publisher was out. Then he finally and completely forgot.

One Sunday he went out of town, and on his return, rummaging among the papers on his desk, he missed 'The Lifted Lamp,' which had been gathering dust there for half a year. What the deuce could have become of it? Betton spent a feverish hour in vainly increasing the disorder of his documents, and then bethought himself of calling the maid-servant, who first indignantly denied having touched anything ('I can see that's true from the dust,' Betton scathingly remarked), and then mentioned with hauteur that a young lady had called in his absence and asked to be allowed to get a book.

'A lady? Did you let her come up?'

She said somebody'd sent her.'

Vyse, of course – Vyse had sent her for his manuscript! He was always mixed up with some woman, and it was just like him to send the girl of the moment to Betton's lodgings, with instructions to force the door in his absence. Vyse had never been remarkable for delicacy. Betton, furious, glanced over the table to see if any of his own effects were missing – one couldn't tell, with the company Vyse kept! – and then dismissed the matter from his mind, with a vague sense of magnanimity in doing so. He felt himself exonerated by Vyse's conduct.

The sense of magnanimity was still uppermost when the valet opened the door to announce 'Mr. Vyse,' and Betton, a moment later, crossed the threshold of his pleasant library.

His first thought was that the man facing him from the hearthrug was the very Duncan Vyse of old: small, starved, bleached-looking, with the same sidelong movements, the same air of anemic truculence. Only he had grown shabbier, and bald.

Betton held out a hospitable hand.

'This is a good surprise! Glad you looked me up, my dear fellow.'

Vyse's palm was damp and bony: he had always had a disagreeable hand.

'You got my note? You know what I've come for?'

'About the secretaryship? (Sit down). Is that really serious?'

Betton lowered himself luxuriously into one of his vast maple armchairs. He had grown stouter in the last year, and the cushion behind him fitted comfortably into the crease of his nape. As he leaned back he caught sight of his image in the mirror between the windows, and reflected uneasily that Vyse would not find *him* unchanged.

'Serious?' Vyse rejoined. 'Why not? Aren't *you*?'

'Oh, perfectly.' Betton laughed apologetically. 'Only – well, the fact is, you may not understand what rubbish a secretary of mine would have to deal with. In advertising for one I never imagined – I didn't aspire to anyone above the ordinary hack.'

'I'm the ordinary hack,' said Vyse drily.

Betton's affable gesture protested. 'My dear fellow – . You see it's not business – what I'm in now,' he continued with a laugh.

Vyse's thin lips seemed to form a noiseless '*Isn't* it?' which they instantly transposed into the audible reply: 'I judged from your advertisement that you want someone to relieve you in your literary work. Dictation, shorthand – that kind of thing?'

'Well, no: not that either. I type my own things. What I'm looking for is somebody who won't be above tackling my correspondence.'

Vyse looked slightly surprised. 'I should be glad of the job,' he then said.

Betton began to feel a vague embarrassment. He had supposed that such a proposal would be instantly rejected. 'It would be only for an hour or two a day – if you're doing any writing of your own?' he threw out interrogatively.

'No. I've given all that up. I'm in an office now – business. But it doesn't take all my time, or pay enough to keep me alive.'

'In that case, my dear fellow – if you could come every morning; but it's mostly awful bosh, you know,' Betton again broke off, with growing awkwardness.

Vyse glanced at him humorously. 'What you want me to write?'

'Well, that depends – ' Betton sketched the obligatory smile. 'But I was thinking of the letters you'll have to answer. Letters about my books, you know – I've another one appearing next week. And I want to be beforehand now – dam the flood before it swamps me. Have you any idea of the deluge of stuff that people write to a successful novelist?'

As Betton spoke, he saw a tinge of red on Vyse's thin cheek, and his own reflected it in a richer glow of shame. 'I mean – I mean – ' he stammered helplessly.

'No, I haven't,' said Vyse, 'but it will be awfully jolly finding out.'

There was a pause, groping and desperate on Betton's part, sardonically calm on his visitor's.

'You – you've given up writing altogether?' Betton continued.

'Yes; we've changed places, as it were.' Vyse paused. 'But about these letters – you dictate the answers?'

'Lord, no! That's the reason why I said I wanted somebody – er – well used to writing. I don't want to have anything to do with them – not a thing! You'll have to answer them as if they were written to *you* – ' Betton pulled himself up again, and rising in confusion jerked opened one of the drawers of his writing table.

'Here – this kind of rubbish,' he said, tossing a packet of letters onto Vyse's knee.

'Oh – you keep them, do you?' said Vyse simply.

'I – well – some of them; a few of the funniest only.'

Vyse slipped off the band and began to open the letters. While he was glancing over them Betton again caught his own reflection in the glass, and asked himself what impression he had made on his visitor. It occurred to him for the first time that his high-colored well-fed person presented the image of commercial rather than of intellectual achievement. He did not look like his own idea of the author of *Diadems and Faggots* – and he wondered why.

Vyse laid the letters aside. 'I think I can do it – if you'll give me a notion of the tone I'm to take.'

'The tone?'

'Yes – that is, if you expect me to sign your name.'

'Oh, of course you're to sign for me. As for the tone, say just what you'd – well, say all you can without encouraging them to answer.'

Vyse rose from his seat. 'I could submit a few specimens,' he suggested.

'Oh, as to that – you always wrote better than I do,' said Betton handsomely.

'I've never had this kind of thing to write. When do you wish me to begin?' Vyse inquired, ignoring the tribute.

'The book's out on Monday. The deluge will probably begin about three days after. Will you turn up on Thursday at this hour?' Betton held his hand out with real heartiness. 'It was great luck for me, your striking that advertisement. Don't be too harsh with my correspondents – I owe them something for having brought us together.'

• II •

THE deluge began punctually on the Thursday, and Vyse, arriving as punctually, had an impressive pile of letters to attack. Betton, on his way to the Park for a ride, came into the library, smoking the cigarette of indolence, to look over his secretary's shoulder.

'How many of 'em? Twenty? Good Lord! It's going to be worse than *Diadems*. I've just had my first quiet breakfast in two years – time to read the papers and loaf. How I used to dread the sight of my letter box! Now I shan't know that I have one.'

He leaned over Vyse's chair, and the secretary handed him a letter.

'Here's rather an exceptional one – lady, evidently. I thought you might want to answer it yourself – '

'Exceptional?' Betton ran over the mauve pages and tossed them down. 'Why, my dear man, I get hundreds like that. You'll have to be pretty short with her, or she'll send her photograph.'

He clapped Vyse on the shoulder and turned away, humming a tune. 'Stay to luncheon,' he called back gaily from the threshold.

After luncheon Vyse insisted on showing a few of his answers to the first batch of letters. 'If I've struck the note I won't bother you again,' he urged; and Betton groaningly consented.

'My dear fellow, they're beautiful – too beautiful. I'll be let in for a correspondence with every one of these people.'

Vyse, in reply, mused for a while above a blank sheet. 'All right – how's this?' he said, after another interval of rapid writing.

Betton glanced over the page. 'By George – by George! Won't she *see* it?' he exulted, between fear and rapture.

'It's wonderful how little people see,' said Vyse reassuringly.

The letters continued to pour in for several weeks after the appearance of *Abundance*. For five or six blissful days Betton did not even have his mail brought to him, trusting to Vyse to single out his personal correspondence, and to deal with the rest of the letters according to their agreement. During those days he luxuriated in a sense of wild and lawless freedom; then, gradually, he began to feel the need of fresh restraints to break, and learned that the zest of liberty lies in the escape from specific obligations. At first he was conscious only of a vague hunger, but in time the craving resolved itself into a shame-faced desire to see his letters.

'After all, I hated them only because I had to answer them'; and he told Vyse carelessly that he wished all his letters submitted to him before the secretary answered them.

The first morning he pushed aside those beginning: 'I have just laid down *Abundance* after a third reading,' or: 'Everyday for the last month I have been telephoning my bookseller to know when your novel would be out.' But little by little the freshness of his interest revived, and even this stereotyped homage began to arrest his eye. At last a day came when he read all the letters, from the first word to the last, as he had done when *Diadems and Faggots* appeared. It was really a pleasure to read them, now that he was relieved of the burden of replying: his new relation to his correspondents had the glow of a love affair unchilled by the contingency of marriage.

One day it struck him that the letters were coming in more slowly and in smaller numbers. Certainly there had been more of a rush when *Diadems and Faggots* came out. Betton began to wonder if Vyse were exercising an unauthorised discrimination, and keeping back the communications he deemed least important. This conjecture carried the novelist straight to his library, where he found Vyse bending over the writing table with his usual inscrutable pale smile. But once there, Betton hardly knew how to frame his question, and blundered into an inquiry for a missing invitation.

'There's a note – a personal note – I ought to have had this morning. Sure you haven't kept it back by mistake among the others?'

Vyse laid down his pen. 'The others? But I never keep back any.'

Betton had foreseen the answer. 'Not even the worst twaddle about my book?' he suggested lightly, pushing the papers about.

'Nothing. I understood you wanted to go over them all first.'

'Well, perhaps it's safer,' Betton conceded, as if the idea were new to him. With an embarrassed hand he continued to turn over the letters at Vyse's elbow.

'Those are yesterday's,' said the secretary; 'here are today's,' he added, pointing to a meager trio.

'H'm – only these?' Betton took them and looked them over lingeringly. 'I don't see what the deuce that chap means about the first part of *Abundance* "certainly justifying the title" – do you?'

Vyse was silent, and the novelist continued irritably: 'Damned cheek, his writing, if he doesn't like the book. Who cares what he thinks about it, anyhow?'

And his morning ride was embittered by the discovery that it was unexpectedly disagreeable to have Vyse read any letters which did not express unqualified praise of his books. He began to fancy that there was a latent rancor, a kind of baffled sneer, under Vyse's manner; and he decided to return to the practice of having his mail brought straight to his room. In that way he could edit the letters before his secretary saw them.

Vyse made no comment on the change, and Betton was reduced to wondering whether his imperturbable composure were the mask of complete indifference or of a watchful jealousy. The latter view being more agreeable to his employer's self-esteem, the next step was to conclude that Vyse had not forgotten the episode of 'The Lifted Lamp,' and would naturally take a vindictive joy in any unfavorable judgments passed on his rival's work. This did not simplify the situation, for there was no denying that unfavorable criticisms preponderated in Betton's correspondence. *Abundance* was neither meeting with the unrestricted welcome of *Diadems and Faggots*, nor enjoying the alternative of an animated controversy: it was simply found dull, and its readers said so in language not too tactfully tempered by comparisons with its predecessor. To withhold unfavourable comments from Vyse was, therefore, to make it appear that correspondence about the book had died out; and its author, mindful of his unguarded predictions, found this even more embarrassing. The simplest solution would be to get rid of Vyse; and to this end Betton began to address his energies.

One evening, finding himself unexpectedly disengaged, he asked Vyse to dine; it had occurred to him that, in the course of an after-dinner chat, he might hint his feeling that the work he had offered his friend was unworthy so accomplished a hand.

Vyse surprised him by a momentary hesitation. 'I may not have time to dress.'

Betton brushed the objection aside. 'What's the odds? We'll dine here – and as late as you like.'

Vyse thanked him, and appeared, punctually at eight, in all the shabbiness of his daily wear. He looked paler and more shyly truculent than usual, and Betton, from the height of his florid stature, said to himself, with the sudden professional instinct for 'type': 'He might be an agent of something – a chap who carries deadly secrets.'

Vyse, it was to appear, did carry a deadly secret; but one less perilous to society than to himself. He was simply poor-unpardonably, irremediably poor. Everything failed him, had always failed him: whatever he put his hand to went to bits.

This was the confession that, reluctantly, yet with a kind of white-lipped bravado, he flung at Betton in answer to the latter's tentative suggestion that, really the letter-answering job wasn't worth bothering him with – a thing that any typewriter could do.

'If you mean that you're paying me more than it's worth, I'll take less,' Vyse rushed out after a pause.

'Oh, my dear fellow – ' Betton protested, flushing.

'What *do* you mean, then? Don't I answer the letters as you want them answered?'

Betton anxiously stroked his silken ankle. 'You do it beautifully, too beautifully. I mean what I say: the work's not worthy of you. I'm ashamed to ask you – '

'Oh, hang shame,' Vyse interrupted. 'Do you know why I said I shouldn't have time to dress tonight? Because I haven't any evening clothes. As a matter of fact, I haven't much but the clothes I stand in. One thing after another's gone against me; all the infernal ingenuities of chance. It's been a slow Chinese torture, the kind where they keep you alive to have more fun killing you.' He straightened himself with a sudden blush. 'Oh, I'm all right now – getting on capitally. But I'm still walking rather a narrow plank; and if I do your work well enough – if I take your idea – '

Betton stared into the fire without answering. He knew next to nothing of Vyse's history, of the mischance or mismanagement that had brought him, with his brains and the training, to so unlikely a pass. But a pang of compunction shot through him as he remembered the manuscript of 'The Lifted Lamp' gathering dust on his table for half a year.

'Not that it would have made any earthly difference – since he's evidently never been able to get the thing published.' But this reflection did not wholly console Betton, and he found it impossible, at the moment, to tell Vyse that his services were not needed.

• III •

DURING the ensuing weeks the letters grew fewer and fewer, and Betton foresaw the approach of the fatal day when his secretary, in common decency, would have to say: 'I can't draw my pay for doing nothing.'

What a triumph for Vyse!

The thought was intolerable, and Betton cursed his weakness in not having dismissed the fellow before such a possibility arose.

'If I tell him I've no use for him now, he'll see straight through it, of course; and then, hang it, he looks so poor!'

This consideration came after the other, but Betton, in re-arranging them, put it first, because he thought it looked better there, and also because he immediately perceived its value in justifying a plan of action that was beginning to take shape in his mind.

'Poor devil, I'm damned if I don't do it for him!' said Betton, sitting down at his desk.

Three or four days later he sent word to Vyse that he didn't care to go over the letters any longer, and that they would once more be carried directly to the library.

The next time he lounged in, on his way to his morning ride, he found his secretary's pen in active motion.

'A lot today,' Vyse told him cheerfully.

His tone irritated Betton: it had the inane optimism of the physician reassuring a discouraged patient.

'Oh, Lord – I thought it was almost over,' groaned the novelist.

'No: they've just got their second wind. Here's one from a Chicago publisher – never heard the name – offering you thirty per cent on your next novel, with an advance royalty of twenty thousand. And here's a chap who wants to syndicate it for a bunch of Sunday papers: big offer, too. That's from Ann Arbor. And this – oh, *this* one's funny!'

He held up a small scented sheet to Betton, who made no movement to receive it.

'Funny? Why's it funny?' he growled.

'Well, it's from a girl – a lady – and she thinks she's the only person who understands *Abundance* – has the clue to it. Says she's never seen a book so misrepresented by the critics – '

'Ha, ha! That *is* good!' Betton agreed with too loud a laugh.

'This one's from a lady, too – married woman. Says she's misunderstood, and would like to correspond.'

'Oh, Lord,' said Betton. 'What are you looking at?' he added sharply, as Vyse continued to bend his blinking gaze on the letters.

'I was only thinking I'd never seen such short letters from women. Neither one fills the first page.'

'Well, what of that?' queried Betton.

Vyse reflected. 'I'd like to meet a woman like that,' he said wearily; and Betton laughed again.

The letters continued to pour in, and there could be no further question of dispensing with Vyse's services. But one morning, about three weeks later, the latter asked for a word with his employer, and Betton, on entering the library, found his secretary with half a dozen documents spread out before him.

'What's up?' queried Betton, with a touch of impatience.

Vyse was attentively scanning the outspread letters.

'I don't know: can't make out.' His voice had a faint note of embarrassment. 'Do you remember a note signed "Hester Macklin" that came three or four weeks ago? Married – misunderstood – Western army post – wanted to correspond?'

Betton seemed to grope among his memories; then he assented vaguely.

'A short note,' Vyse went on: 'The whole story in half a page. The shortness struck me so much – and the directness – that I wrote her: wrote in my own name, I mean.'

'In your own name?' Betton stood amazed; then he broke into a groan.

'Good Lord, Vyse – you're incorrigible!'

The secretary pulled his thin mustache with a nervous laugh. 'If you mean I'm an ass, you're right. Look here.' He held out an envelope stamped with the words: 'Dead Letter Office.' 'My effusion has come back to me marked "unknown." There's no such person at the address she gave you.'

Betton seemed for an instant to share his secretary's embarrassment; then he burst into an uproarious laugh.

'Hoax, was it? That's rough on you, old fellow!'

Vyse shrugged his shoulders. 'Yes; but the interesting question is – why on earth didn't *your* answer come back, too?'

'My answer?'

'The official one – the one I wrote in your name. If she's unknown, what's become of *that*?'

Betton's eyes were wrinkled by amusement. 'Perhaps she hadn't disappeared then.'

Vyse disregarded the conjecture. 'Look here – I believe *all* these letters are a hoax,' he broke out.

Betton stared at him with a face that turned slowly red and angry. 'What are you talking about? All what letters?'

'These I've got spread out here: I've been comparing them. And I believe they're all written by one man.'

Betton's redness turned to a purple that made his ruddy mustache seem pale. 'What the devil are you driving at?' he asked.

'Well, just look at it,' Vyse persisted, still bent above the letters. 'I've been studying them carefully – those that have come within the last two or three weeks – and there's a queer likeness in the writing of some of them. The *g's* are all like corkscrews. And the same phrases keep recurring – the Ann Arbor news agent uses the same expressions as the President of the Girl's College at Euphorbia, Maine.'

Betton laughed. 'Aren't the critics always groaning over the shrinkage of the national vocabulary? Of course we all use the same expressions.'

'Yes,' said Vyse obstinately. 'But how about using the same *g's*?'

Betton laughed again, but Vyse continued without heeding him: 'Look here, Betton – could Strett have written them?'

'Strett?' Betton roared. '*Strett*?' He threw himself into his armchair to shake out his mirth at greater ease.

'I'll tell you why. Strett always posts all my answers. He comes in for them everyday before I leave. He posted the letter to the misunderstood party – the letter from *you* that the Dead Letter Office didn't return. *I* posted my own letter to her; and that came back.'

A measurable silence followed the emission of this ingenious conjecture; then Betton observed with gentle irony: 'Extremely neat. And of course it's no business of yours to supply any valid motive for this remarkable attention of my valet's part.'

Vyse cast on him a slanting glance.

'If you've found that human conduct's generally based on valid motives – !'

'Well, outside of madhouses it's supposed to be not quite incalculable.'

Vyse had an odd smile under his thin mustache. 'Every house is a madhouse at some time or another.'

Betton rose with a careless shake of the shoulders. 'This one will be if I talk to you much longer,' he said, moving away with a laugh.

• IV •

BETTON did not for a moment believe that Vyse suspected the valet of having written the letters.

'Why the devil don't he say out what he thinks? He was always a tortuous chap,' he grumbled inwardly.

The sense of being held under the lens of Vyse's mute scrutiny became more and more exasperating. Betton, by this time, had squared his shoulders to the fact that *Abundance* was a failure with the public: a confessed and glaring failure. The press told him so openly, and his friends emphasized the fact by their circumlocutions and evasions. Betton minded it a good deal more than he had expected, but not nearly as much as he minded Vyse's knowing it. That remained the central twinge in his diffused discomfort. And the problem of getting rid of his secretary once more engaged him.

He had set aside all sentimental pretexts for retaining Vyse; but a practical argument replaced them. 'If I ship him now he'll think it's because I'm ashamed to have him see that I'm not getting any more letters.'

For the letters had ceased again, almost abruptly, since Vyse had hazarded the conjecture that they were the product of Strett's devoted pen. Betton had reverted only once to the subject – to ask ironically, a day or two later: 'Is Strett writing to me as much as ever?' – and, on Vyse's replying with a neutral headshake, had added, laughing: 'If you suspect *him* you'll be thinking next that I write the letters myself!'

'There are very few today,' said Vyse, with an irritating evasiveness; and Betton rejoined squarely: 'Oh, they'll stop soon. The book's a failure.'

A few mornings later he felt a rush of shame at his own tergiversations, and stalked into the library with Vyse's sentence on his tongue.

Vyse was sitting at the table making pencil sketches of a girl's profile. Apparently there was nothing else for him to do.

'Is that your idea of Hester Macklin?' asked Betton jovially, leaning over him.

Vyse started back with one of his anemic blushes. 'I was hoping you'd be in. I wanted to speak to you. There've been no letters the last day or two,' he explained.

Betton drew a quick breath of relief. The man had some sense of decency, then! He meant to dismiss himself.

'I told you so, my dear fellow; the book's a flat failure,' he said, almost gaily.

Vyse made a deprecating gesture. 'I don't know that I should regard the absence of letters as the final test. But I wanted to ask you if there isn't something else I can do on the days when there's no writing.' He turned his glance toward the book-lined walls. 'Don't you want your library catalogued?' he asked insidiously.

'Had it done last year, thanks.' Betton glanced away from Vyse's face. It was piteous how he needed the job!

'I see. . . . Of course this is just a temporary lull in the letters. They'll begin again – as they did before. The people who read carefully read slowly – you haven't heard yet what *they* think.'

Betton felt a rush of puerile joy at the suggestion. Actually, he hadn't thought of that!

'There *was* a big second crop after *Diadems and Faggots*,' he mused aloud.

'Of course. Wait and see,' said Vyse confidently.

The letters in fact began again – more gradually and in smaller numbers. But their quality was different, as Vyse had predicted. And in two cases Betton's correspondents, not content to compress into one rapid communication the thoughts inspired by his work, developed their views in a succession of really remarkable letters. One of the writers was a professor in Western college; the other was a girl in Florida. In their language, their point of view, their reasons for appreciating *Abundance*, they differed almost diametrically; but this only made the unanimity of their approval the more striking. The rush of correspondence evoked by Betton's earlier novel had produced nothing so personal, so exceptional as these communications. He had gulped the praise of *Diadems and Faggots* as undiscriminatingly as it was offered; now he knew for the first time the subtler pleasures of the palate. He tried to feign indifference, even to himself; and to Vyse he made no sign. But gradually he felt a desire to know what his secretary thought of the letters, and, above all, what he was saying in reply to them. And he resented acutely the possibility of Vyse's starting one of his clandestine correspondences with the girl in Florida. Vyse's notorious lack of delicacy had never been more vividly present to Betton's imagination; and he made up his mind to answer the letters himself.

He would keep Vyse on, of course: there were other communications that the secretary could attend to. And, if necessary, Betton would invent an occupation: he cursed his stupidity in having betrayed the fact that his books were already catalogued.

Vyse showed no surprise when Betton announced his intention of dealing personally with the two correspondents who showed so flattering a reluctance to take their leave. But Betton immediately read a criticism in his lack of comment, and put forth, on a note of challenge: 'After all, one must be decent!'

Vyse looked at him with an evanescent smile. 'You'll have to explain that you didn't write the first answers.'

Betton halted. 'Well – I – more or less dictated them, didn't I?'

'Oh, virtually, they're yours, of course.'

'You think I can put it that way?'

'Why not?' The secretary absently drew an arabesque on the blotting pad. 'Of course they'll keep it up longer if you write yourself,' he suggested.

Betton blushed, but faced the issue. 'Hang it all, I shan't be sorry. They interest me. They're remarkable letters.' And Vyse, without observation, returned to his writings.

The spring, that year, was delicious to Betton. His college professor continued to address him tersely but cogently at fixed intervals, and twice a week eight serried pages came from Florida. There were other letters, too; he had the solace of feeling that at last *Abundance* was making its way, was reaching the people who, as Vyse said, read slowly because they read intelligently. But welcome as were all these proofs of his restored authority they were but the background of his happiness. His life revolved for the moment about the personality of his two chief correspondents. The professor's letters satisfied his craving for intellectual recognition, and the satisfaction he felt in them proved how completely he had lost faith in himself. He blushed to think that his opinion of his work had been swayed by the shallow judgments of a public whose taste he despised. Was it possible that he had allowed himself to think less well of *Abundance* because it was not to the taste of the average novel reader? Such false humility was less excusable than the crudest appetite for praise: it was ridiculous to try to do conscientious work if one's self-esteem were at the mercy of popular judgments. All this the professor's letters delicately and indirectly conveyed to Betton, with the results that the authors of *Abundance* began to recognize in it the ripest flower of his genius.

But if the professor understood his book, the girl from Florida understood *him*; and Betton was fully alive to the superior qualities of discernment which this implied. For his lovely correspondent his novel was but the starting point, the pretext of her discourse: he himself was her real object, and he had the delicious sense, as their exchange of thoughts proceeded, that she was interested in *Abundance* because of its author, rather than in the author because of his book. Of course she laid stress on the fact that his ideas were the object of her contemplation; but Betton's agreeable person had permitted him some insight into the incorrigible subjectiveness of female judgments, and he was pleasantly aware, from the lady's tone, that she guessed him to be neither old nor ridiculous. And suddenly he wrote to ask if he might see her . . . .

The answer was long in coming. Betton fidgeted at the delay, watched, wondered, fumed; then he received the one word 'Impossible.'

He wrote back more urgently, and awaited the reply with increasing eagerness. A certain shyness had kept him from once more modifying the instructions regarding his mail, and Strett still carried the letters directly to Vyse. The hour when he knew they were passing under the latter's eyes was now becoming intolerable to Betton, and it was a relief when the secretary, suddenly advised of his father's illness, asked permission to absent himself for a fortnight.

Vyse departed just after Betton had dispatched to Florida his second missive of entreaty, and for ten days he tasted the joy of a first perusal of his letters. The answer from Florida was not among them; but Betton said to himself 'She's thinking it over,' and delay, in that light, seemed favorable. So charming, in fact, was this phase of sentimental suspense that he felt a start of resentment when a telegram apprised him one morning that Vyse would return to his post that day.

Betton had slept later than usual, and, springing out of bed with the telegram in his hand, he learned from the clock that his secretary was due in half an hour. He reflected that the morning's mail must long since be in; and, too impatient to wait for its appearance with his breakfast tray, he threw on a dressing gown and went to the library. There lay the letters, half a dozen of them: but his eyes flew to one envelope, and as he tore it open a warm wave rocked his heart.

The letter was dated a few days after its writer must have received his own; it had all the qualities of grace and insight to which his unknown friend had accustomed him, but it contained no allusion, however, indirect, to the special purport of his appeal. Even a vanity less ingenious than Betton's might have read in the lady's silence one of the most familiar motions of consent; but the smile provoked by this inference faded as he turned to his other letters. For the uppermost bore the superscription 'Dead Letter Office,' and the document that fell from it was his own last letter to Florida.

Betton studied the ironic 'Unknown' for an appreciable space of time; then he broke into a laugh. He had suddenly recalled Vyse's similar experience with Hester Macklin, and the light he was able to throw on that episode was searching enough to penetrate all the dark corners of his own adventure. He felt a rush of heat to the ears; catching sight of himself in the glass, he saw a ridiculous congested countenance, and dropped into a chair to hide it between his fists. He was roused by the opening of the door, and Vyse appeared.

'Oh, I beg pardon – you're ill?' said the secretary.

Betton's only answer was an inarticulate murmur of derision; then he pushed forward the letter with the imprint of the Dead Letter Office.

'Look at that,' he jeered.

Vyse peered at the envelope, and turned it over slowly in his hands. Betton's eyes, fixed on him, saw his face decompose like a substance touched by some powerful acid. He clung to the envelope as if to gain time.

'It's from the young lady you've been writing to at Swazee Springs?' he asked at length.

'It's from the young lady I've been writing to at Swazee Springs.'

'Well – I suppose she's gone away,' continued Vyse, rebuilding his countenance rapidly.

'Yes; and in a community numbering perhaps a hundred and fifty souls, including the dogs and chicken, the local post office is so ignorant of her movements that my letter has to be sent to the Dead Letter Office.'

Vyse meditated on this; then he laughed in turn. 'After all, the same thing happened to me – with Hester Macklin, I mean,' he suggested sheepishly.

'Just so,' said Betton, bringing down his clenched fist on the table. '*Just so*,' he repeated, in italics.

He caught his secretary's glance, and held it with his own for a moment. Then he dropped it as, in pity, one releases something scared and squirming.

'The very day my letter was returned from Swazee Springs she wrote me this from there,' he said, holding up the last Florida missive.

'Ha! That's funny,' said Vyse, with a damp forehead.

'Yes, it's funny,' said Betton. He leaned back, his hands in his pockets, staring up at the ceiling, and noticing a crack in the cornice. Vyse, at the corner of the writing table, waited.

'Shall I get to work?' he began, after a silence measurable by minutes. Betton's gaze descended from the cornice.

'I've got your seat, haven't I?' he said politely, rising and moving away from the table.

Vyse, with a quick gleam of relief, slipped into the vacant chair, and began to stir about among the papers.

'How's your father?' Betton asked from the hearth.

'Oh, better – better, thank you. He'll pull out of it.'

'But you had a sharp scare for a day or two?'

'Yes – it was touch and go when I got there.'

Another pause, while Vyse began to classify the letters.

'And I suppose,' Betton continued in a steady tone, 'your anxiety made you forget your usual precautions – whatever they were – about this Florida correspondence, and before you'd had time to prevent it the Swazee post office blundered?'

Vyse lifted his head with a quick movement. 'What do you mean?' he asked, pushing back his chair.

'I mean that you saw I couldn't live without flattery, and that you've been ladling it out to me to earn your keep.'

Vyse sat motionless and shrunken, digging the blotting pad with his pen. 'What on earth are you driving at?' he repeated.

'Though why the deuce,' Betton continued in the same steady tone, 'you should need to do this kind of work when you've got such faculties at your service – those letters were wonderful, my dear fellow! Why in the world don't you write novels, instead of writing to other people about them?'

Vyse straightened himself with an effort. 'What are you talking about, Betton? Why the devil do you think *I* wrote those letters?'

Betton held back his answer with a brooding face. 'Because I wrote Hester Macklin's – to myself!'

Vyse sat stock still, without the least outcry of wonder.

'Well – ?' he finally said, in a low tone.

'And because you found me out (you see, you can't even feign surprise!) – because you saw through it at a glance, knew at once that the letters were faked. And when you'd foolishly put me on my guard by pointing out to me that they were a clumsy forgery, and had then suddenly guessed that *I* was the forger, you drew the natural inference that I had to have popular approval, or at least had to make *you* think I had it. You saw that, to me, the worst thing about the failure of the book was having *you* know it was a failure. And so you applied your superior – your immeasurably superior – abilities to carrying on the humbug, and deceiving me as I'd tried to deceive you. And you did it so successfully that I don't see why the devil you haven't made your fortune writing novels!'

Vyse remained silent, his head slightly bent under the mounting tide of Betton's denunciation.

'The way you differentiated your people – characterized them – avoided my stupid mistake of making the women's letters too short and too logical, of letting my different correspondents use the same expressions: the amount of ingenuity and art you wasted on it! I swear, Vyse, I'm sorry that damned post office went back on you.' Betton went on, piling up the waves of his irony.

'But at this height they suddenly paused, drew back on themselves, and began to recede before the sight of Vyse's misery. Something warm and emotional in Betton's nature – a lurking kindliness, perhaps, for anyone who tried to soothe and smooth his writhing ego – softened his eye as it rested on the figure of his secretary.

'Look here, Vyse – I'm sorry – not altogether sorry this has happened!' He moved across the room, and laid his hand on Vyse's drooping shoulder. 'In a queer illogical way it evens up things, as it were. I did you a shabby turn once, years ago – oh, out of the sheer carelessness, of course – about the novel of yours I promised to give to Apthorn. If I *had* given it, it might not have made any difference – I'm not sure it wasn't too good for success – but anyhow, I dare say you thought my personal influence might have helped you, might at least have got you a quicker hearing. Perhaps you thought it was because the thing *was* so good that I kept it back, that I felt some nasty jealously of your superiority. I swear to you it wasn't that – I clean forgot it. And one day when I came home it was gone: you'd sent and taken it away. And I've always thought since that you might have owed me a grudge – and not unjustly; so this . . . this business of the letters . . . the sympathy you've shown . . . for I suppose it is sympathy . . . ?'

Vyse startled and checked him by a queer crackling laugh.

'It's *not* sympathy?' broke in Betton, the moisture drying out of his voice. He withdrew his hand from Vyse's shoulder. 'What is it, then? The joy of uncovering my nakedness? An eye for an eye? Is it *that*?'

Vyse rose from his seat, and with a mechanical gesture swept into a heap all the letters he had sorted.

I'm stone-broke, and wanted to keep my job – that's what it is,' he said wearily. . . .

The Daunt Diana

'WHAT'S BECOME OF of the Daunt Diana? You mean to say you never heard the sequel?'

Ringham Finney threw himself back into his chair with the smile of the collector who has a good thing to show. He knew he had a good listener, at any rate. I don't think much of Ringham's snuffboxes, but his anecdotes are usually worth-while. He's a psychologist astray among *bibelots*, and the best bits he brings back from his raids on Christie's and the Hotel Drouot are the fragments of human nature he picks up on those historic battlefields. If his *flair* in enamel had been half as good we should have heard of the Finney collection by this time.

He really has – queer fatuous investigator! – an unusually sensitive touch for the human texture, and the specimens he gathers into his museum of memories have almost always some mark of the rare and chosen. I felt, therefore, that I was really to be congratulated on the fact that I didn't know what had become of the Daunt Diana, and on having before me a long evening in which to learn. I had just led my friend back, after an excellent dinner at Foyot's, to the shabby pleasant sitting room of my *Rive Gauche* hotel; and I knew that, once I had settled him in a good armchair, and put a box of cigars at his elbow, I could trust him not to budge till I had the story.

• II •

YOU remember old Neave, of course? Little Humphrey Neave, I mean. We used to see him pottering about Rome years ago.

He lived in two rooms over a wine shop, on polenta and lentils, and prowled among the refuse of the Ripetta whenever he had a few coppers to spend. But you've been out of the collector's world for so long that you may not know what happened to him afterward. . . .

He was always a queer chap, Neave; years older than you and me, of course – and even when I first knew him, in my raw Roman days, he produced on me an unusual impression of age and experience. I don't think I've ever known anyone who was at once so intelligent and so simple. It's the precise combination that results in romance; and poor little Neave was romantic.

He told me once how he'd come to Rome. He was *originaire* of Mystic, Connecticut – and he wanted to get as far away from it as possible. Rome seemed as far as anything on the same planet could be; and after he'd worried his way through Harvard – with shifts and shavings that you and I can't imagine – he contrived to be sent to Switzerland as tutor to a chap who'd failed in his examinations. With only the Alps between, he wasn't likely to turn back; and he got another fellow to take his pupil home, and struck out on foot for the seven hills.

I'm telling you these early details merely to give you a notion of the man. There was a cool persistency and a headlong courage in his dash for Rome that one wouldn't have guessed in the pottering chap we used to know. Once on the spot, he got more tutoring, managed to make himself a name for coaxing balky youths to take their fences, and was finally able to take up the more congenial task of expounding 'the antiquities' to cultured travelers. I call it more congenial – but how it must have seared his soul! Fancy unveiling the sacred scars of Time to ladies who murmur: 'Was this *actually* the spot – ?' while they absently feel for their hatpins! He used to say that nothing kept him at it but the exquisite thought of accumulating the *lire* for his collection. For the Neave collection, my dear fellow, began early, began almost with his Roman life, began in a series of little nameless odds and ends, broken trinkets, torn embroideries, the amputated extremities of maimed marbles: things that even the rag-picker had pitched away when he sifted his haul. But they weren't nameless or meaningless to Neave; his strength lay in his instinct for identifying, putting together, seeing significant relations. He was a regular Cuvier of bric-a-brac. And during those early years, when he had time to brood over trifles and note imperceptible differences, he gradually sharpened his instinct, and made it into the delicate and redoubtable instrument it is. Before he had a thousand francs' worth of *anticaglie* to his name he began to be known as an expert, and the big dealers were glad to consult him. But we're getting no nearer the Daunt Diana. . . .

Well, some fifteen years ago, in London, I ran across Neave at Christie's. He was the same little man we'd known, effaced, bleached, indistinct, like a poor impression' – as unnoticeable as one of his own early finds, yet, like them, with *a quality*, if one had an eye for it. He told me he still lived in Rome, and had contrived, by persistent self-denial, to get a few bits together – 'piecemeal, little by little, with fasting and prayer; and I mean the fasting literally!' he said.

He had run over to London for his annual 'lookround' – I fancy one or another of the big collectors usually paid his journey – and when we met he was on his way to see the Daunt collection. You know old Daunt was a surly brute, and the things weren't easily seen; but he had heard Neave was in London, and had sent – yes, actually sent! – for him to come and give his opinion on a few bits, including the Diana. The little man bore himself discreetly, but you can imagine how proud he was! In his exultation he asked me to come with him – 'Oh, I've the *grandes et petites entrées*, my dear fellow: I've made my conditions – ' and so it happened that I saw the first meeting between Humphrey Neave and his fate.

For that collection *was* his fate: or, one may say, it was embodied in the Diana who was queen and goddess of the realm. Yes – I shall always be glad I was with Neave when he had his first look at the Diana. I see him now, blinking at her through his white lashes, and stroking his wisp of a mustache to hide a twitch of the muscles. It was all very quiet, but it was the *coup de foudre*. I could see that by the way his hands worked when he turned away and began to examine the other things. You remember Neave's hands – thin and dry, with long inquisitive fingers thrown out like antennae? Whatever they hold – bronze or lace, enamel or glass – they seem to acquire the very texture of the thing, and to draw out of it, by every fingertip, the essence it has secreted. Well, that day, as he moved about among Daunt's treasures, the Diana followed him everywhere. He didn't look back at her – he gave himself to the business he was there for – but whatever he touched, he felt her. And on the threshold he turned and gave her his first free look – the kind of look that says: '*You're mine.*'

It amused me at the time – the idea of little Neave making eyes at any of Daunt's belongings. He might as well have coquetted with the Kohinoor. And the same idea seemed to strike him; for as we turned away from the big house in Belgravia he glanced up at it and said, with a bitterness I'd never heard in him: 'Good Lord! To think of that lumpy fool having those things to handle! Did you notice his stupid stumps of fingers? I suppose he blunted them gouging nuggets out of gold fields. And in exchange for the nuggets he gets all that in a year – only has to hold out his callous palm to have that ripe sphere of beauty drop into it! That's my idea of heaven – to have a great collection drop into one's hand, as success, or love, or any of the big shining things, suddenly drop on some men. And I've had to worry along for nearly fifty years, saving and paring, and haggling and managing, to get here a bit and there a bit – and not one perfection in the lot! It's enough to poison a man's life.'

The outbreak was so unlike Neave that I remember every word of it; remember, too, saying in answer: 'But, look here, Neave, you wouldn't take Daunt's hands for yours, I imagine?'

He stared a moment and smiled. 'Have all that, and grope my way through it like a blind cave fish? What a question! But the sense that it's always the blind fish that live in that kind of aquarium is what makes anarchists, sir!' He looked back from the corner of the square, where we had paused while he delivered himself of this remarkable metaphor. 'God, I'd like to throw a bomb at that place, and be in at the looting!'

And with that, on the way home, he unpacked his grievance – pulled the bandage off the wound, and showed me the ugly mark it made on his little white soul.

It wasn't the struggling, screwing, stinting, self-denying that galled him – it was the smallness of the result. It was, in short, the old tragedy of the discrepancy between a man's wants and his power to gratify them. Neave's taste was too fine for his means – was like some strange, delicate, capricious animal, that he cherished and pampered and couldn't satisfy.

'Don't you know those little glittering lizards that die if they're not fed on some rare tropical fly? Well, my taste's like that, with one important difference – if it doesn't get its fly, it simply turns and feeds on *me*. Oh, it doesn't die, my taste – worse luck! It gets larger and stronger and more fastidious, and takes a bigger bite of me – that's all.'

That was all. Year by year, day by day, he had made himself into this delicate register of perceptions and sensations – as far above the ordinary human faculty of appreciation as some scientific registering instrument is beyond the rough human senses – only to find that the beauty which alone could satisfy him was unattainable, that he was never to know the last deep identification which only possession can give. He had trained himself, in short, to feel, in the rare great thing – such an utterance of beauty as the Daunt Diana, say – a hundred elements of perfection, a hundred *reasons why*, imperceptible, inexplicable even, to the average 'artistic' sense; he had reached this point by a long process of discrimination and rejection, the renewed great refusals of the intelligence which perpetually asks more, which will make no pact with its self of yesterday, and is never to be beguiled from its purpose by the wiles of the next best thing. Oh, it's a poignant case, but not a common one; for the next best thing usually wins. . . .

You see, the worst of Neave's state was the fact of his not being a mere collector, even the collector raised to his highest pitch. The whole thing was blended in him with poetry – his imagination had romanticized the acquisitive instinct, as the religious feeling of the Middle Ages turned passion into love. And yet his could never be the abstract enjoyment of the philosopher who says: 'This or that object is really mine because I'm capable of appreciating it.' Neave *wanted* what he appreciated – wanted it with his touch and his sight as well as with his brain.

It was hardly a year afterward that, coming back from a long tour in India, I picked up a London paper and read the amazing headline: 'Mr. Humphrey Neave buys the Daunt collection' I rubbed my eyes and read again. Yes, it could only be our old friend Humphrey. 'An American living in Rome . . . one of our most discerning collectors'; there was no mistaking the description. I bolted out to see the first dealer I could find, and there I had the incredible details. Neave had come into a fortune – two or three million dollars, amassed by an uncle who had a corset factory, and who had attained wealth as the creator of the Mystic Superstraight. (Corset factory sounds odd, by the way, doesn't it? One had fancied that the corset was a personal, a highly specialized garment, more or less shaped on the form it was to modify; but, after all, the Tanagras were all made from two or three molds – and so, I suppose, are the ladies who wear the Mystic Superstraight.)

The uncle had a son, and Neave had never dreamed of seeing a penny of the money; but the son died suddenly, and the father followed, leaving a codicil that gave everything to our friend. Humphrey had to go out to 'realize' on the corset factory; and his description of *that*! . . . Well, he came back with his money in his pocket, and the day he landed old Daunt went to smash. It all fitted in like a puzzle. I believe Neave drove straight from Euston to Daunt House: at any rate, within two months the collection was his, and at a price that made the trade sit up. Trust old Daunt for that!

I was in Rome the following spring, and you'd better believe I looked him up. A big porter glared at me from the door of the Palazzo Neave: I had almost to produce my passport to get in. But that wasn't Neave's fault – the poor fellow was so beset by people clamoring to see his collection that he had to barricade himself, literally. When I had mounted the state *Scalone*, and come on him, at the end of half a dozen echoing salons, in the farthest, smallest *réduit* of the suite, I received the same welcome that he used to give us in his den over the wine shop.

'Well – so you've got her?' I said. For I'd caught sight of the Diana in passing against the bluish blur of an old *verdure* – just the background for her hovering loveliness. Only I rather wondered why she wasn't in the room where he sat.

He smiled. 'Yes, I've got her,' he returned, more calmly than I had expected.

'And all the rest of the loot?'

'Yes. I had to buy the lump.'

'Had to? But you wanted to, didn't you? You used to say it was your idea of heaven – to stretch out your hand and have a great ripe sphere of beauty drop into it. I'm quoting your own words, by the way.'

Neave blinked and stroked his seedy mustache. 'Oh, yes. I remember the phrase. It's true – it *is* the last luxury.' He paused, as if seeking a pretext for his lack of warmth. 'The thing that bothered me was having to move. I couldn't cram all the stuff into my old quarters.'

'Well, I should say not! This is rather a better setting.'

He got up. 'Come and take a look round. I want to show you two or three things – new attributions I've made. I'm doing the catalogue over.'

The interest of showing me the things seemed to dispel the vague apathy I had felt in him. He grew keen again in detailing his redistribution of values, and above all in convicting old Daunt and his advisers of their repeated aberrations of judgment. 'The miracle is that he should have got such things, knowing as little as he did what he was getting. And the egregious asses who bought for him were not better, were worse in fact, since they had all sorts of humbugging wrong reasons for admiring what old Daunt simply coveted because it belonged to some other rich man.'

Never had Neave had so wondrous a field for the exercise of his perfected faculty; and I saw then how, in the real, the great collector's appreciations, the keenest scientific perception is suffused with imaginative sensibility, and how it is to the latter undefinable quality that, in the last resort, he trusts himself.

Nevertheless, I still felt the shadow of that hovering apathy, and he knew I felt it, and was always breaking off to give me reasons for it. For one thing, he wasn't used to his new quarters – hated their bigness and formality; then the requests to show his things drove him mad. 'The women – oh, the women!' he wailed, and interrupted himself to describe a heavy-footed German princess who had marched past his treasures as if she were viewing a cavalry regiment, applying an unmodulated *Mugneeficent* to everything from the engraved gems to the Hercules torso.

'Not that she was half as bad as the other kind,' he added, as if with a last effort at optimism. 'The kind who discriminate and say: "I'm not sure if it's Botticelli or Cellini I mean, but *one of that school*, at any rate." And the worst of all are the ones who know – up to a certain point: have the schools, and the dates and the jargon pat, and yet wouldn't recognize a Phidias if it stood where they hadn't expected it.'

He had all my sympathy, poor Neave; yet these were trials inseparable from the collector's lot, and not always without their secret compensations. Certainly they did not wholly explain my friend's state of mind; and for a moment I wondered if it were due to some strange disillusionment as to the quality of his treasures. But no! the Daunt collection was almost above criticism; and as we passed from one object to another I saw there was no mistaking the genuineness of Neave's pride in his possessions. The ripe sphere of beauty was his, and he had found no flaw in it as yet. . . .

A year later came the amazing announcement that the Daunt collection was for sale. At first we all supposed it was a case of weeding out (though how old Daunt would have raged at the thought of anybody's weeding *his* collection!). But no – the catalogue corrected that idea. Every stick and stone was to go under the hammer. The news ran like wildfire from Rome to Berlin, from Paris to London and New York. Was Neave ruined, then? Wrong again – the dealers nosed that out in no time. He was simply selling because he chose to sell; and in due time the things came up at Christie's.

But you may be sure the trade had found an answer to the riddle; and the answer was that, on close inspection, Neave had found the things less good than he had supposed. It was a preposterous answer – but then there was no other. Neave, by this time, was pretty generally acknowledged to have the sharpest *flair* of any collector in Europe, and if he didn't choose to keep the Daunt collection it could be only because he had reason to think he could do better.

In a flash this report had gone the rounds, and the buyers were on their guard. I had run over to London to see the thing through, and it was the queerest sale I ever was at. Some of the things held their own, but a lot – and a few of the best among them – went for half their value. You see, they'd been locked up in old Daunt's house for nearly twenty years and hardly shown to anyone, so that the whole younger generation of dealers and collectors knew of them only by hearsay. Then you know the effect of suggestion in such cases. The undefinable sense we were speaking of is a ticklish instrument, easily thrown out of gear by a sudden fall of temperature; and the sharpest experts grow shy and self-distrustful when the cold current of deprecation touches them. The sale was a slaughter – and when I saw the Daunt Diana fall at the wink of a little third-rate *brocanteur* from Vienna I turned sick at the folly of my kind.

For my part, I had never believed that Neave had sold the collection because he'd 'found it out'; and within a year my incredulity was justified. As soon as the things were put in circulation they were known for the marvels that they are. There was hardly a poor bit in the lot; and my wonder grew at Neave's madness. All over Europe, dealers began to fight for the spoils; and all kinds of stuff were palmed off on the unsuspecting as fragments of the Daunt collection!

Meantime, what was Neave doing? For a long time I didn't hear, and chance kept me from returning to Rome. But one day, in Paris, I ran across a dealer who had captured for a song one of the best Florentine bronzes in the Daunt collection – a marvelous *plaquette* of Donatello's. I asked him what had become of it, and he said with a grin: 'I sold it the other day,' naming a price that staggered me.

'Ye gods! Who paid you that for it?'

His grin broadened, and he answered: 'Neave.'

'*Neave*? Humphrey Neave?'

'Didn't you know he was buying back his things?'

'Nonsense!'

'He is, though. Not in his own name – but he's doing it.'

And he *was*, do you know – and at prices that would have made a sane man shudder! A few weeks later I ran across his tracks in London, where he was trying to get hold of a Penicaud enamel – another of his scattered treasures. Then I hunted him down at his hotel, and had it out with him.

'Look here, Neave, what are you up to?'

He wouldn't tell me at first: stared and laughed and denied. But I took him off to dine, and after dinner, while we smoked, I happened to mention casually that I had a pull over the man who had the Penicaud – and at that he broke down and confessed.

'Yes, I'm buying them back, Finney – it's true.' He laughed nervously, twitching his mustache. And then he let me have the story.

'You know how I'd hungered and thirsted for the *real thing* – you quoted my own phrase to me once, about the "ripe sphere of beauty." So when I got my money, and Daunt lost his, almost at the same moment, I saw the hand of Providence in it. I knew that, even if I'd been younger, and had had more time, I could never hope, nowadays, to form such a collection as *that*. There was the ripe sphere, within reach; and I took it. But when I got it, and began to live with it, I found out my mistake. The transaction was a *marriage de convenance* – there'd been no wooing, no winning. Each of my little old bits – the rubbish I chucked out to make room for Daunt's glories – had its own personal history, the drama of my relation to it, of the discovery, the struggle, the capture, the first divine moment of possession. There was a romantic secret between us. And then, I had absorbed its beauties one by one, they had become a part of my imagination, they held me by a hundred threads of far-reaching association. And suddenly I had expected to create this kind of personal tie between myself and a roomful of new cold alien presences – things staring at me vacantly from the depths of unknown pasts! Can you fancy a more preposterous hope? Why, my other things, my *own* things had wooed me as passionately as I wooed them: there was a certain little Italian bronze, a little Venus, who had drawn me, drawn me, drawn me, imploring me to rescue her from her unspeakable surroundings in a vulgar bric-a-brac shop at Biarritz, where she shrank out of sight among sham Sèvres and Dutch silver, as one has seen certain women – rare, shy, exquisite – made almost invisible by the vulgar splendors surrounding them. Well! that little Venus, who was just a specious seventeenth-century attempt at an "antique," but who had penetrated me with her pleading grace, touched me by the easily guessed story of her obscure anonymous origin, was more to me imaginatively – yes! more – than the cold bought beauty of the Daunt Diana. . . .'

'The Daunt Diana!' I broke in. 'Hold up, Neave – *the Daunt Diana*?'

He smiled contemptuously. 'A professional beauty, my dear fellow – expected every head to be turned when she came into a room.'

'Oh, Neave,' I groaned.

'Yes, I know. You're thinking of what we felt that day we first saw her in London. Many a poor devil has sold his soul as the result of such a first sight! Well, I sold *her* instead. Do you want the truth about her? *Elle était bête à pleurer*.'

He laughed and turned away with a shrug of disenchantment.

'And so you're impenitent?' I insisted. 'And yet you're buying some of the things back?'

Neave laughed again, ironically. 'I knew you'd find me out and call me to account. Well, yes: I'm buying back.' He stood before me, half sheepish, half defiant. 'I'm buying back because there's nothing else as good in the market. And because I've a queer feeling that, this time, they'll be *mine*. But I'm ruining myself at the game!' he confessed.

It was true. Neave was ruining himself. And he's gone on ruining himself ever since, till now the job's pretty nearly done. Bit by bit, year by year, he has gathered in his scattered treasures, at higher prices than the dealers ever dreamed of getting for them. There are fabulous details in the story of his quest. Now and then I ran across him, and was able to help him recover a fragment; and it was touching to see his delight in the moment of reunion. Finally, about two years ago, we met in Paris, and he told me he had got back all the important pieces except the Diana.

'The Diana? But you told me you didn't care for her.'

'Didn't care?' He leaned across the restaurant table that divided us. 'Well, no, in a sense I didn't. I wanted her to want me, you see; and she didn't then! Whereas now she's crying to me to come to her. You know where she is?' he broke off.

Yes, I knew: in the center of Mrs. Willy P. Goldmark's yellow and gold drawing room, under a thousand candle power chandelier, with reflectors aimed at her from every point of the compass. I had seen her, wincing and shivering there in her outraged nudity, at one of the Goldmark 'crushes.'

'But you can't get her, Neave,' I objected.

'No, I can't get her,' he said.

Well, last month I was in Rome, for the first time in six or seven years, and of course I looked about for Neave. The Palazzo Neave was let to some rich Russians, and the new porter didn't know where the proprietor lived. But I got on his trail easily enough, and it led me to a strange old place in the Trastevere, a crevassed black palace turned tenement house and fluttering with pauper linen. I found Neave under the leads, in two or three cold rooms that smelt of the *cuisine* of all his neighbors: a poor shrunken figure, smaller and shabbier than ever, yet more alive than when we had made the tour of his collection in the Palazzo Neave.

The collection was around him again, not displayed in tall cabinets and on marble tables, but huddled on shelves, perched on chairs, crammed in corners, putting the gleam of bronze, the luster of marble, the opalescence of old glass, into all the angles of his dim rooms. There they were, the presences that had stared at him down the vistas of Daunt House, and shone in cold transplanted beauty under his own cornices: there they were, gathered about him in humble promiscuity, like superb wild creatures tamed to become the familiars of some harmless wizard.

As we went from bit to bit, as he lifted one piece after another, and held it to the light, I saw in his hands the same tremor that I had noticed when he first handled the same objects at Daunt House. All his life was in his fingertips, and it seemed to communicate life to the things he touched. But you'll think me infected by his mysticism if I tell you they gained new beauty while he held them . . .

We went the rounds slowly and reverently; and then, when I supposed our inspection was over, and was turning to take my leave, he opened a door I had not noticed, and showed me into a room beyond. It was a mere monastic cell, scarcely large enough for his narrow bed and the chest which probably held his few clothes; but there, in a niche, at the foot of the bed – there stood the Daunt Diana.

I gasped at the sight and turned to him; and he looked back at me without speaking.

'In the name of magic, Neave, how did you do it?'

He smiled as if from the depths of some secret rapture. 'Call it magic, if you like; but I ruined myself doing it,' he said.

I stared at him in silence, breathless with the madness of it; and suddenly, red to the ears, he flung out his confession. 'I lied to you that day in London – the day I said I didn't care for her. I always cared – always worshiped – always wanted her. But she wasn't mine then, and I knew it, and she knew it . . . and now at last we understand each other.' He looked at me shyly, and then glanced about the bare room. 'The setting isn't worthy of her, I know; she was meant for glories I can't give her; but beautiful things, my dear Finney, like beautiful spirits, live in houses not made with hands. . . .'

His face shone with an extraordinary kind of light as he spoke; and I saw he'd got hold of the secret we're all after. No, the setting isn't worthy of her, if you like. The rooms are as shabby and mean as those we used to see him in years ago over the wine shop. I'm not sure they're not shabbier and meaner. But she rules there at last, she shines and hovers there above him, and there at night, I doubt not, comes down from her cloud to give him the Latmian kiss. . . .

Afterward

'Oh, there *is* one, of course, but you'll never know it.'

The assertion, laughingly flung out six months earlier in a bright June garden, came back to Mary Boyne with a new perception of its significance as she stood, in the December dusk, waiting for the lamps to be brought into the library.

The words had been spoken by their friend Alida Stair, as they sat at tea on her lawn at Pangbourne, in reference to the very house of which the library in question was the central, the pivotal 'feature.' Mary Boyne and her husband, in quest of a country place in one of the southern or southwestern counties, had, on their arrival in England, carried their problem straight to Alida Stair, who had successfully solved it in her own case; but it was not until they had rejected, almost capriciously, several practical and judicious suggestions that she threw out: 'Well, there's Lyng, in Dorsetshire. It belongs to Hugo's cousins, and you can get it for a song.'

The reason she gave for its being obtainable on these terms – its remoteness from a station, its lack of electric light, hot water pipes, and other vulgar necessities – were exactly those pleading in its favor with two romantic Americans perversely in search of the economic drawbacks which were associated, in their tradition, with unusual architectural felicities.

'I should never believe I was living in an old house unless I was thoroughly uncomfortable,' Ned Boyne, the more extravagant of the two, had jocosely insisted; 'the least hint of convenience would make me think it had been bought out of an exhibition, with the pieces numbered, and set up again.' And they had proceeded to enumerate, with humorous precision, their various doubts and demands, refusing to believe that the house their cousin recommended was *really* Tudor till they learned it had no heating system, or that the village church was literally in the grounds till she assured them of the deplorable uncertainty of the water supply.

'It's too uncomfortable to be true!' Edward Boyne had continued to exult as the avowal of each disadvantage was successively wrung from her; but he had cut short his rhapsody to ask, with a relapse to distrust: 'And the ghost? You've been concealing from us the fact that there is no ghost!'

Mary, at the moment, had laughed with him, yet almost with her laugh, being possessed of several sets of independent perceptions, had been struck by a note of flatness in Alida's answering hilarity.

'Oh, Dorsetshire's full of ghosts, you know.'

'Yes, yes; but that won't do. I don't want to have to drive ten miles to see somebody else's ghost. I want one of my own on the premises. *Is* there a ghost at Lyng?'

His rejoinder had made Alida laugh again, and it was then that she had flung back tantalizingly: 'Oh, there *is* one, of course, but you'll never know it.'

'Never know it?' Boyne pulled her up. 'But what in the world constitutes a ghost except the fact of its being known for one?'

'I can't say. But that's the story.'

'That there's a ghost, but that nobody knows it's a ghost?'

'Well – not till afterward, at any rate.'

'Till afterward?'

'Not till long long afterward.'

'But if it's once been identified as an unearthly visitant, why hasn't it *signalement* been handed down in the family? How has it managed to preserve its incognito?'

Alida could only shake her head. 'Don't ask me. But it has.'

'And then suddenly' – Mary spoke up as if from cavernous depths of divination – 'suddenly, long afterward, one says to one's self "*That was it*?" '

She was startled at the sepulchral sound with which her question fell on the banter of the other two, and she saw the shadow of the same surprise flit across Alida's pupils. 'I suppose so. One just has to wait.'

'Oh, hang waiting!' Ned broke in. 'Life's too short for a ghost who can only be enjoyed in retrospect. Can't we do better than that, Mary?'

But it turned out that in the event they were not destined to, for within three months of their conversation with Mrs. Stair they were settled at Lyng, and the life they had yearned for, to the point of planning it in advance in all its daily details, had actually begun for them.

It was to sit, in the thick December dusk, by just such a wide-hooded fireplace, under just such black oak rafters, with the sense that beyond the mullioned panes the downs were darkened to a deeper solitude: it was for the ultimate indulgence of such sensations that Mary Boyne, abruptly exiled from New York by her husband's business, had endured for nearly fourteen years the soul-deadening ugliness of a Middle Western town, and that Boyne had ground on doggedly at his engineering till, with a suddenness that still made her blink, the prodigious windfall of the Blue Star Mine had put them at a stroke in possession of life and the leisure to taste it. They had never for a moment meant their new state to be one of idleness; but they meant to give themselves only to harmonious activities. She had her vision of painting and gardening (against a background of grey walls), he dreamed of the production of his long-planned book on the 'Economic Basic of Culture'; and with such absorbing work ahead no existence could be too sequestered: they could not get far enough from the world, or plunge deep enough into the past.

Dorsetshire had attracted them from the first by an air of remoteness out of all proportion to its geographical position. But to the Boynes it was one of the ever-recurring wonders of the whole incredibly compressed island – a nest of counties, as they put it – that for the production of its effects so little of a given quality went so far: that so few miles made a distance, and so short a distance a difference.

'It's that,' Ned had once enthusiastically explained, 'that gives such depth to their effects, such relief to their contrasts. They've been able to lay the butter so thick on every delicious mouthful.'

The butter had certainly been laid on thick at Lyng: the old house hidden under a shoulder of the downs had almost all the finer marks of commerce with a protracted past. The mere fact that it was neither large nor exceptional made it, to the Boynes, abound the more completely in its special charm – the charm of having been for centuries a deep dim reservoir of life. The life had probably not been of the most vivid order: for long periods, no doubt, it had fallen as noiselessly into the past as the quiet drizzle of autumn fell, hour after hour, into the fish pond between the yews; but these backwaters of existence sometimes breed, in their sluggish depths, strange acuities of emotion, and Mary Boyne had felt from the first the mysterious stir of intenser memories.

The feeling had never been stronger than on this particular afternoon when, waiting in the library for the lamps to come, she rose from her seat and stood among the shadows of the hearth. Her husband had gone off, after luncheon, for one of his long tramps on the downs. She had noticed of late that he preferred to go alone; and, in the tried security of their personal relations, had been driven to conclude that his book was bothering him, and that he needed the afternoons to turn over in solitude the problems left from the morning's work. Certainly the book was not going as smoothly as she had thought it would, and there were lines of perplexity between his eyes such as had never been there in his engineering days. He had often, then, looked fagged to the verge of illness, but the native demon of worry had never branded his brow. Yet the few pages he had so far read to her – the introduction, and a summary of the opening chapter – showed a firm hold on his subject, and an increasing confidence in his powers.

The fact threw her into deeper perplexity, since, now that he had done with business and its disturbing contingencies, the one other possible source of anxiety was eliminated. Unless it were his health, then? But physically he had gained since they had come to Dorsetshire, grown robuster, ruddier and fresher eyed. It was only within the last week that she had felt in him the undefinable change which made her restless in his absence, and as tongue-tied in his presence as though it were *she* who had a secret to keep from him!

The thought that there *was* a secret somewhere between them struck her with a sudden rap of wonder, and she looked about her down the long room.

'Can it be the house?' she mused.

The room itself might have been full of secrets. They seemed to be piling themselves up, as evening fell, like the layers and layers of velvet shadow dropping from the low ceiling, the rows of books, the smoke-blurred sculpture of the hearth.

'Why, of course – the house is haunted!' she reflected.

The ghost – Alida's imperceptible ghost – after figuring largely in the banter of their first month or two at Lyng, had been gradually left aside as too ineffectual for imaginative use. Mary had, indeed, as became the tenant of a haunted house, made the customary inquiries among her rural neighbors, but, beyond a vague 'They dü say so, Ma'am,' the villages had nothing to impart. The elusive specter had apparently never had sufficient identity for a legend to crystallize about it, and after a time the Boynes had set the matter down to their profit-and-loss account, agreeing that Lyng was one of the few houses good enough in itself to dispense with supernatural enhancements.

'And I suppose, poor ineffectual demon, that's why it beats its beautiful wings in vain in the void,' Mary had laughingly concluded.

'Or, rather,' Ned answered in the same strain, 'why, amid so much that's ghostly, it can never affirm its separate existence as *the* ghost.' And thereupon their invisible housemate had finally dropped out of their references, which were numerous enough to make them soon unaware of the loss.

Now, as she stood on the hearth, the subject of their earlier curiosity revived in her with a new sense of its meaning – a sense gradually acquired through daily contact with the scene of the lurking mystery. It was the house itself, of course, that possessed the ghost-seeing faculty, that communed visually but secretly with its own past; if one could only get into close enough communion with the house, one might surprise its secret, and acquire the ghost sight on one's own account. Perhaps, in his long hours in this very room, where she never trespassed till the afternoon, her husband *had* acquired it already, and was silently carrying about the weight of whatever it had revealed to him. Mary was too well versed in the code of the spectral world not to know that one could not talk about the ghosts one saw: to do so was almost as great a breach of taste as to name a lady in a club. But this explanation did not really satisfy her. 'What, after all, except for the fun of the shudder,' she reflected, 'would he really care for any of their old ghosts?' And thence she was thrown back once more on the fundamental dilemma: the fact that one's greater or less susceptibility to spectral influences had no particular bearing on the case, since, when one *did* see a ghost at Lyng, one did not know it.

'Not till long afterward,' Alida Stair had said. Well, supposing Ned *had* seen one when they first came, and had known only within the last week what had happened to him? More and more under the spell of the hour, she threw back her thoughts to the early days of their tenancy, but at first only to recall a lively confusion of unpacking, settling, arranging of books, and calling to each other from remote corners of the house as, treasure after treasure, it revealed itself to them. It was in this particular connection that she presently recalled a certain soft afternoon of the previous October, when, passing from the first rapturous flurry of exploration to a detailed inspection of the old house, she had pressed (like a novel heroine) a panel that opened on a flight of corkscrew stairs leading to a flat ledge of the roof – the roof which, from below, seemed to slope away on all sides too abruptly for any but practiced feet to scale.

The view from this hidden coign was enchanting, and she had flown down to snatch Ned from his papers and give him the freedom of her discovery. She remembered still how, standing at her side, he had passed his arm about her while their gaze flew to the long tossed horizon line of the downs, and then dropped contentedly back to trace the arabesque of yew hedges about the fish pond, and the shadow of the cedar on the lawn.

'And now the other way,' he had said, turning her about within his arm; and closely pressed to him, she had absorbed, like some long satisfying draught, the picture of the grey-walled court, the squat lions on the gates, and the lime avenue reaching up to the highroad under the downs.

It was just then, while they gazed and held each other, that she had felt his arm relax, and heard a sharp 'Hullo!' that made her turn to glance at him.

Distinctly, yes, she now recalled that she had seen, as she glanced, a shadow of anxiety, of perplexity, rather, fall across his face; and, following his eyes, had beheld the figure of a man – a man in loose greyish clothes, as it appeared to her – who was sauntering down the lime avenue to the court with the doubtful gait of a stranger who seeks his way. Her shortsighted eyes had given her but a blurred impression of slightness and greyishness, with something foreign, or at least unlocal, in the cut of the figure or its dress; but her husband had apparently seen more – seen enough to make him push past her with a hasty 'Wait!' and dash down the stairs without pausing to give her a hand.

A slight tendency to dizziness obliged her, after a provisional clutch at the chimney against which they had been leaning, to follow him first more cautiously; and when she had reached the landing she paused again, for a less definite reason, leaning over the banister to strain her eyes through the silence of the brown sun-flecked depths. She lingered there till, somewhere in those depths, she heard the closing of a door; then, mechanically impelled, she went down the shallow flights of steps till she reached the lower hall.

The front door stood open on the sunlight of the court, and hall and court were empty. The library door was open, too, and after listening in vain for any sound of voices within, she crossed the threshold, and found her husband alone, vaguely fingering the papers on his desk.

He looked up, as if surprised at her entrance, but the shadow of anxiety had passed from his face, leaving it even, as she fancied, a little brighter and clearer than usual.

'What was it? Who was it?' she asked.

'Who?' he repeated, with the surprise still all on his side.

'The man we saw coming toward the house.'

He seemed to reflect. 'The man? Why, I thought I saw Peters; I dashed after him to say a word about the stable drains, but he had disappeared before I could get down.'

'Disappeared? But he seemed to be walking so slowly when we saw him.'

Boyne shrugged his shoulders. 'So I thought; but he must have got up steam in the interval. What do you say to our trying a scramble up Meldon Steep before sunset?'

That was all. At the time the occurrence had been less than nothing, had, indeed, been immediately obliterated by the magic of their first vision from Meldon Steep, a height which they had dreamed of climbing ever since they had first seen its bare spine rising above the roof of Lyng. Doubtless it was the mere fact of the other incident's having occurred on the very day of their ascent to Meldon that had kept it stored away in the fold of memory from which it now emerged; for in itself it had no mark of the portentous. At the moment there could have been nothing more natural than that Ned should dash himself from the roof in the pursuit of dilatory tradesmen. It was the period when they were always on the watch for one or the other of the specialists employed about the place; always lying in wait for them, and rushing out at them with questions, reproaches or reminders. And certainly in the distance the grey figure had looked like Peters.

Yet now, as she reviewed the scene, she felt her husband's explanation of it to have been invalidated by the look of anxiety on his face. Why had the familiar appearance of Peters made him anxious? Why, above all, if it was of such prime necessity to confer with him on the subject of the stable drains, had the failure to find him produced such a look of relief? Mary could not say that any one of these questions had occurred to her at the time, yet, from the promptness with which they now marshalled themselves at her summons, she had a sense that they must all along have been there, waiting their hour.

• II •

WEARY with her thoughts, she moved to the window. The library was now quite dark, and she was surprised to see how much faint light the outer world still held.

As she peered out into it across the court, a figure shaped itself far down the perspective of bare limes: it looked a mere blot of deeper grey in the greyness, and for an instant, as it moved toward her, her heart thumped to the thought 'It's the ghost!'

She had time, in that long instant, to feel suddenly that the man of whom, two months earlier, she had had a distant vision from the roof, was now, at his predestined hour, about to reveal himself as *not* having been Peters; and her spirit sank under the impending fear of the disclosure. But almost with the next tick of the clock the figure, gaining substance and character, showed itself even to her weak sight as her husband's; and she turned to meet him, as he entered, with the confession of her folly.

'It's really too absurd,' she laughed out, 'but I never *can* remember!'

'Remember what?' Boyne questioned as they drew together.

'That when one sees the Lyng ghost one never knows it.'

Her hand was on his sleeve, and he kept it there, but with no response in his gesture or in the lines of his preoccupied face.

'Did you think you'd seen it?' he asked, after an appreciable interval.

'Why, I actually took *you* for it, my dear, in my mad determination to spot it!'

'Me – just now?' His arm dropped away, and he turned from her with a faint echo of her laugh. 'Really, dearest, you'd better give it up, if that's the best you can do.'

'Oh, yes, I give it up. Have *you*?' she asked, turning round on him abruptly.

The parlormaid had entered with letters and a lamp, and the light struck up into Boyne's face as he bent above the tray she presented.

'Have *you*?' Mary perversely insisted, when the servant had disappeared on her errand of illumination.

'Have I what?' he rejoined absently, the light bringing out the sharp stamp of worry between his brows as he turned over the letters.

'Given up trying to see the ghost.' Her heart beat a little at the experiment she was making.

Her husband, laying his letters aside, moved away into the shadow of the hearth.

'I never tried,' he said, tearing open the wrapper of a newspaper.

'Well, of course,' Mary persisted, 'the exasperating thing is that there's no use trying, since one can't be sure till so long afterward.'

He was unfolding the paper as if he had hardly heard her; but after a pause, during which the sheets rustled spasmodically between his hands, he looked up to ask, 'Have you any idea *how long*?'

Mary had sunk into a low chair beside the fireplace. From her seat she glanced over, startled, at her husband's profile, which was projected against the circle of lamplight.

'No; none. Have *you*?' she retorted, repeating her former phrase with an added stress of intention.

Boyne crumpled the paper into a bunch, and then, inconsequently, turned back with it toward the lamp.

'Lord, no! I only meant,' he exclaimed, with a faint tinge of impatience, 'is there any legend, any tradition, as to that?'

'Not that I know of,' she answered; but the impulse to add 'What makes you ask?' was checked by the reappearance of the parlormaid, with tea and a second lamp.

With the dispersal of shadows, and the repetition of the daily domestic office, Mary Boyne felt herself less oppressed by that sense of something mutely imminent which had darkened her afternoon. For a few moments she gave herself to the details of her task, and when she looked up from it she was struck to the point of bewilderment by the change in her husband's face. He had seated himself near the farther lamp, and was absorbed in the perusal of his letters; but was it something he had found in them, or merely the shifting of her own point of view, that had restored his features to their normal aspect? The longer she looked the more definitely the change affirmed itself. The lines of tension had vanished, and such traces of fatigue as lingered were of the kind easily attributable to steady mental effort. He glanced up, as if drawn by her gaze, and met her eyes with a smile.

'I'm dying for my tea, you know; and here's a letter for you,' he said.

She took the letter he held out in exchange for the cup she proffered him, and, returning to her seat, broke the seal with the languid gesture of the reader whose interests are all enclosed in the circle of one cherished presence.

Her next conscious motion was that of starting to her feet, the letter falling to them as she rose, while she held out to her husband a newspaper clipping.

'Ned! What's this? What does it mean?'

He had risen at the same instant, almost as if hearing her cry before she uttered it; and for a perceptible space of time he and she studied each other, like adversaries watching for an advantage, across the space between her chair and his desk.

'What's what? You fairly made me jump!' Boyne said at length, moving toward her with a sudden half-exasperated laugh. The shadow of apprehension was on his face again, not now a look of fixed foreboding, but a shifting vigilance of lips and eyes that gave her the sense of his feeling himself invisibly surrounded.

Her hand shook so that she could hardly give him the clipping.

'This article – from the *Waukesha Sentinel* – that a man named Elwell has brought suit against you – that there was something wrong about the Blue Star Mine. I can't understand more than half.'

They continued to face each other as she spoke, and to her astonishment she saw that her words had the almost immediate effect of dissipating the strained watchfulness of his look.

'Oh, *that*!' He glanced down the printed slip, and then folded it with the gesture of one who handles something harmless and familiar. 'What's the matter with you this afternoon, Mary? I thought you'd got bad news.'

She stood before him with her undefinable terror subsiding slowly under the reassurance of his tone.

'You knew about this, then – it's all right?'

'Certainly I knew about it; and it's all right.'

'But what *is* it? I don't understand. What does this man accuse you of?'

'Pretty nearly every crime in the calendar.' Boyne had tossed the clipping down, and thrown himself into an armchair near the fire. 'Do you want to hear the story? It's not particularly interesting – just a squabble over interests in the Blue Star.'

'But who is this Elwell? I don't know the name.'

'Oh, he's a fellow I put into it – gave him a hand up. I told you all about him at the time.'

'I dare say. I must have forgotten.' Vainly she strained back among her memories. 'But if you helped him, why does he make this return?'

'Probably some shyster lawyer got hold of him and talked him over. It's all rather technical and complicated. I thought that kind of thing bored you.'

His wife felt a sting of compunction. Theoretically, she deprecated the American wife's detachment from her husband's professional interests, but in practice she had always found it difficult to fix her attention on Boyne's report of the transactions in which his varied interests involved him. Besides, she had felt during their years of exile, that, in a community where the amenities of living could be obtained only at the cost of efforts as arduous as her husband's professional labors, such brief leisure as he and she could command should be used as an escape from immediate preoccupations, a flight to the life they always dreamed of living. Once or twice, now that this new life had actually drawn its magic circle about them, she had asked herself if she had done right; but hitherto such conjectures had been no more than the retrospective excursions of an active fancy. Now, for the first time, it startled her a little to find how little she knew of the material foundation on which her happiness was built.

She glanced at her husband, and was again reassured by the composure of his face; yet she felt the need of more definite grounds for her reassurance.

'But doesn't this suit worry you? Why have you never spoken to me about it?'

He answered both questions at once. 'I didn't speak of it at first because it *did* worry me – annoyed me, rather. But it's all ancient history now. Your correspondent must have got hold of a back number of the *Sentinel.*'

She felt a quick thrill of relief. 'You mean it's over? He's lost his case?'

There was a just perceptible delay in Boyne's reply. 'This suit's been withdrawn – that's all.'

But she persisted, as if to exonerate herself from the inward charge of being too easily put off. 'Withdrawn it because he saw he had no chance?'

'Oh, he had no chance,' Boyne answered.

She was still struggling with a dimly felt perplexity at the back of her thoughts.

'How long ago was it withdrawn?'

He paused, as if with a slight return to his former uncertainty. 'I've just had the news now; but I've been expecting it.'

'Just now – in one of your letters?'

'Yes; in one of my letters.'

She made no answer, and was aware only, after a short interval of waiting, that he had risen, and, strolling across the room, had placed himself on the sofa at her side. She felt him, as he did so, pass an arm about her, she felt his hand seek hers and clasp it, and turning slowly, drawn by the warmth of his cheek, she met his smiling eyes.

'It's all right – it's all right?' she questioned, through the flood of her dissolving doubts; and 'I give you my word it was never righter!' he laughed back at her, holding her close.

• III •

ONE of the strangest things she was afterward to recall out of all the next day's strangeness was the sudden and complete recovery of her sense of security.

It was in the air when she woke in her low-ceiled, dusky room; it went with her downstairs to the breakfast table, flashed out at her from the fire, and reduplicated itself from the flanks of the urn and the sturdy flutings of the Georgian teapot. It was as if in some roundabout way, all her diffused fears of the previous day, with their moment of sharp concentration about the newspaper article – as if this dim questioning of the future, and startled return upon the past, had between them liquidated the arrears of some haunting moral obligation. If she had indeed been careless of her husband's affairs, it was, her new state seemed to prove, because her faith in him instinctively justified such carelessness; and his right to her faith had now affirmed itself in the very face of menace and suspicion. She had never seen him more untroubled, more naturally and unconsciously himself, than after the cross-examination to which she had subjected him: it was almost as if he had been aware of her doubts, and had wanted the air cleared as much as she did.

It was as clear, thank heaven, as the bright outer light that surprised her almost with a touch of summer when she issued from the house for her daily round of the gardens. She had left Boyne at his desk, indulging herself, as she passed the library door, by a last peep at his quiet face, where he bent, pipe in mouth, above his papers; and now she had her own morning's task to perform. The task involved, on such charmed winter days, almost as much happy loitering about the different quarters of her domain as if spring were already at work there. There were such endless possibilities still before her, such opportunities to bring out the latent graces of the old place, without a single irreverent touch of alteration, that the winter was all too short to plan what spring and autumn executed. And her recovered sense of safety gave, on this particular morning, a peculiar zest to her progress through the sweet still place. She went first to the kitchen garden, where the espaliered pear trees drew complicated patterns on the walls, and pigeons were fluttering and preening about the silvery-slated roof of their cot. There was something wrong about the piping of the hothouse, and she was expecting an authority from Dorchester, who was to drive out between trains and make a diagnosis of the boiler. But when she dipped into the damp heat of the greenhouses, among the spiced scents and waxy pinks and reds of old-fashioned exotics – even the flora of Lyng was in the note! – she learned that the great man had not arrived, and, the day being too rare to waste in an artificial atmosphere, she came out again and paced along the springy turf of the bowling green to the gardens behind the house. At their farther end rose a grass terrace, looking across the fish pond and yew hedges to the long house front with its twisted chimney stacks and blue roof angles all drenched in the pale gold moisture of the air.

Seen thus, across the level tracery of the gardens, it sent her, from open windows and hospitably smoking chimneys, the look of some warm human presence, of a mind slowly ripened on a sunny wall of experience. She had never before had such a sense of her intimacy with it, such a conviction that its secrets were all beneficent, kept, as they said to children, 'for one's good,' such a trust in its power to gather up her life and Ned's into the harmonious pattern of the long long story it sat there weaving in the sun.

She heard steps behind her, and turned, expecting to see the gardener accompanied by the engineer, from Dorchester. But only one figure was in sight, that of a youngish slightly built man, who, for reasons she could not on the spot have given, did not remotely resemble her notion of an authority on hothouse boilers. The newcomer, on seeing her, lifted his hat, and paused with the air of a gentleman – perhaps a traveler – who wishes to make it known that his intrusion is involuntary. Lyng occasionally attracted the more cultivated traveler, and Mary half expected to see the stranger dissemble a camera, or justify his presence by producing it. But he made no gesture of any sort, and after a moment she asked, in a tone responding to the courteous hesitation of his attitude: 'Is there anyone you wish to see?'

'I came to see Mr. Boyne,' he answered. His intonation, rather than his accent, was faintly American, and Mary, at the note, looked at him more closely. The brim of his soft felt hat cast a shade on his face, which, thus obscured, wore to her shortsighted gaze a look of seriousness, as of a person arriving on business, and civilly but firmly aware of his rights.

Past experience had made her equally sensible to such claims; but she was jealous of her husband's morning hours, and doubtful of his having given anyone the right to intrude on them.

'Have you an appointment with my husband?' she asked.

The visitor hesitated, as if unprepared for the question.

'I think he expects me,' he replied.

It was Mary's turn to hesitate. 'You see this is his time for work: he never sees anyone in the morning.'

He looked at her a moment without answering; then, as if accepting her decision, he began to move away. As he turned, Mary saw him pause and glance up at the peaceful house front. Something in his air suggested weariness and disappointment, the dejection of the traveler who has come from far off and whose hours are limited by the timetable. It occurred to her that if this were the case her refusal might have made his errand vain, and a sense of compunction caused her to hasten after him.

'May I ask if you have come a long way?'

He gave her the same grave look. 'Yes – I have come a long way.'

'Then, if you'll go to the house, no doubt my husband will see you now. You'll find him in the library.'

She did not know why she had added the last phrase, except from a vague impulse to atone for her previous inhospitality. The visitor seemed about to express his thanks, but her attention was distracted by the approach of the gardener with a companion who bore all the marks of being the expert from Dorchester.

'This way,' she said, waving the stranger to the house; and an instant later she had forgotten him in the absorption of her meeting with the boiler maker.

The encounter led to such far-reaching results that the engineer ended by finding it expedient to ignore his train, and Mary was beguiled into spending the remainder of the morning in absorbed confabulation among the flower pots. When the colloquy ended, she was surprised to find that it was nearly luncheon time, and she half expected, as she hurried back to the house, to see her husband coming out to meet her. But she found no one in the court but an undergardener raking the gravel, and the hall, when she entered it, was so silent that she guessed Boyne to be still at work.

Not wishing to disturb him, she turned into the drawing room, and there, at her writing table, lost herself in renewed calculations of the outlay to which the morning's conference had pledged her. The fact that she could permit herself such follies had not yet lost its novelty; and somehow, in contrast to the vague fears of the previous days, it now seemed an element of her recovered security, of the sense that, as Ned had said, things in general had never been 'righter.'

She was still luxuriating in a lavish play of figures when the parlormaid, from the threshold, roused her with an inquiry as to the expediency of serving luncheon. It was one of their jokes that Trimmle announced luncheon as if she were divulging a state secret, and Mary, intent upon her papers, merely murmured an absent-minded assent.

She felt Trimmle wavering doubtfully on the threshold, as if in rebuke of such unconsidered assent; then her retreating steps sounded down the passage, and Mary, pushing away her papers, crossed the hall and went to the library door. It was still closed, and she wavered in her turn, disliking to disturb her husband, yet anxious that he should not exceed his usual measure of work. As she stood there, balancing her impulses, Trimmle returned with the announcement of luncheon, and Mary, thus impelled, opened the library door.

Boyne was not at his desk, and she peered about her, expecting to discover him before the bookshelves, somewhere down the length of the room; but her call brought no response, and gradually it became clear to her that he was not there.

She turned back to the parlormaid.

'Mr. Boyne must be upstairs. Please tell him that luncheon is ready.'

Trimmle appeared to hesitate between the obvious duty of obedience and an equally obvious conviction of the foolishness of the injunction laid on her. The struggle resulted in her saying: 'If you please, Madam, Mr. Boyne's not upstairs.'

'Not in his room? Are you sure?'

'I'm sure, Madam.'

Mary consulted the clock. 'Where is he, then?'

'He's gone out,' Trimmle announced, with the superior air of one who has respectfully waited for the question that a well-ordered mind would have put first.

Mary's conjecture had been right, then. Boyne must have gone to the gardens to meet her, and since she had missed him, it was clear that he had taken the shorter way by the south door, instead of going round to the court. She crossed the hall to the French window opening directly on the yew garden, but the parlormaid, after another moment of inner conflict, decided to bring out: 'Please, Madam, Mr. Boyne didn't go that way.'

Mary turned back. 'Where *did* he go? And when?'

'He went out of the front door, up the drive, Madam.' It was a matter of principle with Trimmle never to answer more than one question at a time.

'Up the drive? At this hour?' Mary went to the door herself, and glanced across the court through the tunnel of bare limes. But its perspective was as empty as when she had scanned it on entering.

'Did Mr. Boyne leave no message?'

Trimmle seemed to surrender herself to a last struggle with the forces of chaos.

'No, Madam. He just went out with the gentleman.'

'The gentleman? What gentleman?' Mary wheeled about, as if to front this new factor.

'The gentleman who called, Madam,' said Trimmle resignedly.

'When did a gentleman call? Do explain yourself, Trimmle!'

Only the fact that Mary was very hungry, and that she wanted to consult her husband about the greenhouses, would have caused her to lay so unusual an injunction on her attendant; and even now she was detached enough to note in Trimmle's eye the dawning defiance of the respectful subordinate who has been pressed too hard.

'I couldn't exactly say the hour, Madam, because I didn't let the gentleman in,' she replied, with an air of discreetly ignoring the irregularity of her mistress's course.

'You didn't let him in?'

'No, Madam. When the bell rang I was dressing, and Agnes – '

'Go and ask Agnes, then,' said Mary.

Trimmle still wore her look of patient magnanimity. 'Agnes would not know, Madam, for she had unfortunately burnt her hand in trimming the wick of the new lamp from town' – Trimmle, as Mary was aware, had always been opposed to the new lamp – 'and so Mrs. Dockett sent the kitchenmaid instead.'

Mary looked again at the clock. 'It's after two! Go and ask the kitchenmaid if Mr. Boyne left any word.'

She went into luncheon without waiting, and Trimmle presently brought her there the kitchenmaid's statement that the gentleman had called about eleven o'clock, and that Mr. Boyne had gone out with him without leaving any message. The kitchenmaid did not even know the caller's name, for he had written it on a slip of paper, which he had folded and handed to her, with the injunction to deliver it at once to Mr. Boyne.

Mary finished her luncheon, still wondering, and when it was over, and Trimmle had brought the coffee to the drawing room, her wonder had deepened to a first faint tinge of disquietude. It was unlike Boyne to absent himself without explanation at so unwonted an hour, and the difficulty of identifying the visitor whose summons he had apparently obeyed made his disappearance the more unaccountable. Mary Boyne's experience as the wife of a busy engineer, subject to sudden calls and compelled to keep irregular hours, had trained her to the philosophic acceptance of surprises; but since Boyne's withdrawal from business he had adopted a Benedictine regularity of life. As if to make up for the dispersed and agitated years, with their 'stand-up' lunches, and dinners rattled down to the joltings of the dining cars, he cultivated the last refinements of punctuality and monotony, discouraging his wife's fancy for the unexpected, and declaring that to a delicate taste there were infinite gradations of pleasure in the recurrences of habit.

Still, since no life can completely defend itself from the unforeseen, it was evident that all Boyne's precautions would sooner or later prove unavailable, and Mary concluded that he had cut short a tiresome visit by walking with his caller to the station, or at least accompanying him for part of the way.

This conclusion relieved her from further preoccupation, and she went out herself to take up her conference with the gardener. Thence she walked to the village post office, a mile or so away; and when she turned toward home the early twilight was setting in.

She had taken a footpath across the downs, and as Boyne, meanwhile, had probably returned from the station by the highroad, there was little likelihood of their meeting. She felt sure, however, of his having reached the house before her; so sure that, when she entered it herself, without even pausing to inquire of Trimmle, she made directly for the library. But the library was still empty, and with an unwonted exactness of visual memory she observed that the papers on her husband's desk lay precisely as they had lain when she had gone in to call him to luncheon.

Then of a sudden she was seized by a vague dread of the unknown. She had closed the door behind her on entering, and as she stood alone in the long silent room, her dread seemed to take shape and sound, to be there breathing, and lurking among the shadows. Her shortsighted eyes strained through them, half-discerning an actual presence, something aloof, that watched and knew; and in the recoil from that intangible presence she threw herself on the bell rope and gave it a sharp pull.

The sharp summons brought Trimmle in precipitately with a lamp, and Mary breathed again at this sobering reappearance of the usual.

'You may bring tea if Mr. Boyne is in,' she said, to justify her ring.

'Very well, Madam. But Mr. Boyne is not in,' said Trimmle, putting down the lamp.

'Not in? You mean he's come back and gone out again?'

'No, Madam. He's never been back.'

The dread stirred again, and Mary knew that now it had her fast.

'Not since he went out with – the gentleman?'

'Not since he went out with the gentleman.'

'But who *was* the gentleman?' Mary insisted, with the shrill note of someone trying to be heard through a confusion of noises.

'That I couldn't say, Madam.' Trimmle, standing there by the lamp, seemed suddenly to grow less round and rosy, as though eclipsed by the same creeping shade of apprehension.

'But the kitchenmaid knows – wasn't it the kitchenmaid who let him in?'

'She doesn't know either, Madam, for he wrote his name on a folded paper.'

Mary, through her agitation, was aware that they were both designating the unknown visitor by a vague pronoun, instead of the conventional formula which, till then, had kept their allusions within the bounds of conformity. And at the same moment her mind caught at the suggestion of the folded paper.

'But he must have a name! Where's the paper?'

She moved to the desk, and began to turn over the documents that littered it. The first that caught her eye was an unfinished letter in her husband's hand, with his pen lying across it, as though dropped there at a sudden summons.

'My dear Parvis' – who was Parvis? – 'I have just received your letter announcing Elwell's death, and while I suppose there is now no further risk of trouble, it might be safer – '

She tossed the sheet aside, and continued her search; but no folded paper was discoverable among the letters and pages of manuscript which had been swept together in a heap, as if by a hurried or a startled gesture.

'But the kitchenmaid *saw* him. Send her here,' she commanded, wondering at her dullness in not thinking sooner of so simple a solution.

Trimmle vanished in a flash, as if thankful to be out of the room, and when she reappeared, conducting the agitated underling, Mary had regained her self-possession, and had her questions ready.

The gentleman was a stranger, yes – that she understood. But what had he said? And, above all, what had he looked like? The first question was easily enough answered, for the disconcerting reason that he had said so little – had merely asked for Mr. Boyne, and, scribbling something on a bit of paper, had requested that it should at once be carried in to him.

'Then you don't know what he wrote? You're not sure it *was* his name?'

The kitchenmaid was not sure, but supposed it was, since he had written it in answer to her inquiry as to whom she should announce.

'And when you carried the paper in to Mr. Boyne, what did he say?'

'The kitchenmaid did not think that Mr. Boyne had said anything, but she could not be sure, for just as she had handed him the paper and he was opening it, she had become aware that the visitor had followed her into the library, and she had slipped out, leaving the two gentlemen together.

'But then, if you left them in the library, how do you know that they went out of the house?'

This question plunged the witness into a momentary inarticulateness, from which she was rescued by Trimmle, who, by means of ingenious circumlocutions, elicited the statement that before she could cross the hall to the back passage she had heard the two gentlemen behind her, and had seen them go out of the front door together.

'Then, if you saw the strange gentleman twice, you must be able to tell me what he looked like.'

But with this final challenge to her powers of expression it became clear that the limit of the kitchenmaid's endurance had been reached. The obligation of going to the front door to 'show in' a visitor was in itself so subversive of the fundamental order of things that it had thrown her faculties into hopeless disarray, and she could only stammer out, after various panting efforts: 'His hat, mum, was different-like, as you might say – '

'Different? How different?' Mary flashed out, her own mind, in the same instant, leaping back to an image left on it that morning, and then lost under layers of subsequent impressions.

'His hat had a wide brim, you mean, and his face was pale – a youngish face?' Mary pressed her, with a white-lipped intensity of interrogation. But if the kitchenmaid found any adequate answer to this challenge, it was swept away for her listener down the rushing current of her own convictions. The stranger – the stranger in the garden! Why had Mary not thought of him before? She needed no one now to tell her that it was he who had called for her husband and gone away with him. But who was he, and why had Boyne obeyed him?

• IV •

It leaped out at her suddenly, like a grin out of the dark, that they had often called England so little – 'such a confoundedly hard place to get lost in.'

A confoundedly hard place to get lost in! That had been her husband's phrase. And now, with the whole machinery of official investigation sweeping its flashlights from shore to shore, and across the dividing straits; now, with Boyne's name blazing from the walls of every town and village, his portrait (how that wrung her!) hawked up and down the country like the image of a hunted criminal; now the little compact populous island, so policed, surveyed and administered, revealed itself as a Sphinxlike guardian of abysmal mysteries, staring back into his wife's anguished eyes as if with the wicked joy of knowing something they would never know!

In the fortnight since Boyne's disappearance there had been no word of him, no trace of his movements. Even the usual misleading reports that raise expectancy in tortured bosoms had been few and fleeting. No one but the kitchenmaid had seen Boyne leave the house, and no one else had seen 'the gentleman' who accompanied him. All inquiries in the neighborhood failed to elicit the memory of a stranger's presence that day in the neighborhood of Lyng. And no one had met Edward Boyne, either alone or in company, in any of the neighboring villages, or on the road across the downs, or at either of the local railway stations. The sunny English noon had swallowed him as completely as if he had gone out into Cimmerian night.

Mary, while every official means of investigation was working as its highest pressure, had ransacked her husband's papers for any trace of antecedent complications, of entanglements or obligations unknown to her, that might throw a ray into the darkness. But if any such had existed in the background of Boyne's life, they had vanished like the slip of paper on which the visitor had written his name. There remained no possible thread of guidance except – if it were indeed an exception – the letter which Boyne had apparently been in the art of writing when he received his mysterious summons. That letter, read and reread by his wife, and submitted by her to the police, yielded little enough to feed conjecture.

'I have just heard of Elwell's death, and while I suppose there is now no further risk of trouble, it might be safer – ' That was all. The 'risk of trouble' was easily explained by the newspaper clipping which had apprised Mary of the suit brought against her husband by one of his associates in the Blue Star enterprise. The only new information conveyed by the letter was the fact of its showing Boyne, when he wrote it, to be still apprehensive of the results of the suit, though he had told his wife that it had been withdrawn, and though the letter itself proved that the plaintiff was dead. It took several days of cabling to fix the identity of the 'Parvis' to whom the fragment was addressed, but even after these inquiries had shown him to be a Waukesha lawyer, no new facts concerning the Elwell suit were elicited. He appeared to have had no direct concern in it, but to have been conversant with the facts merely as an acquaintance, and possible intermediary; and he declared himself unable to guess with what object Boyne intended to seek his assistance.

This negative information, sole fruit of the first fortnight's search, was not increased by a jot during the slow weeks that followed. Mary knew that the investigations were still being carried on, but she had a vague sense of their gradually slackening, as the actual march of time seemed to slacken. It was as though the days, flying horror-struck from the shrouded image of the one inscrutable day, gained assurance as the distance lengthened, till at last they fell back into their normal gait. And so with the human imaginations at work on the dark event. No doubt it occupied them still, but week by week and hour by hour it grew less absorbing, took up less space, was slowly but inevitably crowded out of the foreground of consciousness by the new problems perpetually bubbling up from the cloudy caldron of human experience.

Even Mary Boyne's consciousness gradually felt the same lowering of velocity. It still swayed with the incessant oscillations of conjecture; but they were slower, more rhythmical in their beat. There were even moments of weariness when, like the victim of some poison which leaves the brain clear, but holds the body motionless, she saw herself domesticated with the Horror, accepting its perpetual presence as one of the fixed conditions of life.

These moments lengthened into hours and days, till she passed into a phase of stolid acquiescence. She watched the routine of daily life with the incurious eye of a savage on whom the meaningless processes of civilization make but the faintest impression. She had come to regard herself as part of the routine, a spoke of the wheel, revolving with its motion; she felt almost like the furniture of the room in which she sat, an insensate object to be dusted and pushed about with the chairs and tables. And this deepening apathy held her fast at Lyng, in spite of the entreaties of friends and the usual medical recommendation of 'change.' Her friends supposed that her refusal to move was inspired by the belief that her husband would one day return to the spot from which he had vanished, and a beautiful legend grew up about this imaginary state of waiting. But in reality she had no such belief: the depths of anguish enclosing her were no longer lighted by flashes of hope.

She was sure that Boyne would never come back, that he had gone out of her sight as completely as if Death itself had waited that day on the threshold. She had even renounced, one by one, the various theories as to his disappearance which had been advanced by the press, the police, and her own agonized imagination. In sheer lassitude her mind turned from these alternatives of horror, and sank back into the blank fact that he was gone.

No, she would never know what had become of him – no one would ever know. But the house *knew*; the library in which she spent her long lonely evenings knew. For it was here that the last scene had been enacted, here that the stranger had come, and spoken the word which had caused Boyne to rise and follow him. The floor she trod had felt his tread; the books on the shelves had seen his face; and there were moments when the intense consciousness of the old dusky walls seemed about to break out into some audible revelation of their secret. But the revelation never came, and she knew it would never come. Lyng was not one of the garrulous old houses that betray the secrets entrusted to them. Its very legend proved that it had always been the mute accomplice, the incorruptible custodian, of the mysteries it had surprised. And Mary Boyne, sitting face to face with its silence, felt the futility of seeking to break it by any human means.

• V •

'I DON'T say it *wasn't* straight, and yet I don't say it *was* straight. It was business.'

Mary, at the words, lifted her head with a start, and looked intently at the speaker.

When, half an hour before, a card with 'Mr. Parvis' on it had been brought up to her, she had been immediately aware that the name had been a part of her consciousness ever since she had read it and at the head of Boyne's unfinished letter. In the library she had found awaiting her a small sallow man with a bald head and gold eyeglasses, and it sent a tremor through her to know that this was the person to whom her husband's last known thought had been directed.

Parvis, civilly, but without vain preamble – in the manner of a man who has his watch in his hand – had set forth the object of his visit. He had 'run over' to England on business, and finding himself in the neighborhood of Dorchester, had not wished to leave it without paying his respects to Mrs. Boyne; and without asking her, if the occasion offered, what she meant to do about Bob Elwell's family.

The words touched the spring of some obscure dread in Mary's bosom. Did her visitor, after all, know what Boyne had meant by his unfinished phrase? She asked for an elucidation of his question, and noticed at once that he seemed surprised at her continued ignorance of the subject. Was it possible that she really knew as little as she said?

'I know nothing – you must tell me,' she faltered out; and her visitor thereupon proceeded to unfold his story. It threw, even to her confused perceptions, and imperfectly initiated vision, a lurid glare on the whole hazy episode of the Blue Star Mine. Her husband had made his money in that brilliant speculation at the cost of 'getting ahead' of someone less alert to seize the chance; and the victim of his ingenuity was young Robert Elwell, who had 'put him on' to the Blue Star scheme.

Parvis, at Mary's first cry, had thrown her a sobering glance through his impartial glasses.

'Bob Elwell wasn't smart enough, that's all; if he had been, he might have turned round and served Boyne the same way. It's the kind of thing that happens everyday in business. I guess it's what the scientists call the survival of the fittest – see?' said Mr. Parvis, evidently pleased with the aptness of his analogy.

Mary felt a physical shrinking from the next question she tried to frame: it was as though the words on her lips had a taste that nauseated her.

'But then – you accuse my husband of doing something dishonorable?'

Mr. Parvis surveyed the question dispassionately. 'Oh, no, I don't. I don't even say it wasn't straight.' He glanced up and down the long lines of books, as if one of them might have supplied him with the definition he sought. 'I don't say it *wasn't* straight, and yet I don't say it *was* straight. It was business.' After all, no definition in his category could be more comprehensive than that.

Mary sat staring at him with a look of terror. He seemed to her like the indifferent emissary of some evil power.

'But Mr. Elwell's lawyers apparently did not take your view, since I suppose the suit was withdrawn by their advice.'

'Oh, yes; they knew he hadn't a leg to stand on, technically. It was when they advised him to withdraw the suit that he got desperate. You see, he'd borrowed most of the money he lost in the Blue Star, and he was up a tree. That's why he shot himself when they told him he had no show.'

The horror was sweeping over Mary in great deafening waves.

'He shot himself? He killed himself because of *that*?'

'Well, he didn't kill himself, exactly. He dragged on two months before he died.' Parvis emitted the statement as unemotionally as a gramophone grinding out its record.

'You mean that he tried to kill himself, and failed? And tried again?'

'Oh, he didn't have to *try* again,' said Parvis grimly.

They sat opposite each other in silence, he swinging his eyeglasses thoughtfully about his finger, she, motionless, her arms stretched along her knees in an attitude of rigid tension.

'But if you knew all this,' she began at length, hardly able to force her voice above a whisper, 'how is it that when I wrote you at the time of my husband's disappearance you said you didn't understand his letter?'

Parvis received this without perceptible embarrassment: 'Why, I didn't understand it – strictly speaking. And it wasn't the time to talk about it, if I had. The Elwell business was settled when the suit was withdrawn. Nothing I could have told you would have helped you to find your husband.'

Mary continued to scrutinize him. 'Then why are you telling me now?'

Still Parvis did not hesitate. 'Well, to begin with, I supposed you knew more than you appear to – I mean about the circumstances of Elwell's death. And then people are talking of it now; the whole matter's been raked up again. And I thought if you didn't know you ought to.'

She remained silent, and he continued: 'You see, it's only come out lately what a bad state Elwell's affairs were in. His wife's a proud woman, and she fought on as long as she could, going out to work, and taking sewing at home when she got too sick – something with the heart, I believe. But she had his mother to look after, and the children, and she broke down under it, and finally had to ask for help. That called attention to the case, and the papers took it up, and a subscription was started. Everybody out there liked Bob Elwell, and most of the prominent names in the place are down on the list, and people began to wonder why – '

Parvis broke off to fumble in an inner pocket. 'Here,' he continued, 'here's an account of the whole thing from the *Sentinel* – a little sensational, of course. But I guess you'd better look it over.'

He held out a newspaper to Mary, who unfolded it slowly, remembering, as she did so, the evening when, in that same room, the perusal of a clipping from the *Sentinel* had first shaken the depths of her security.

As she opened the paper, her eyes, shrinking from the glaring headlines, 'Widow of Boyne's Victim Forced to Appeal for Aid,' ran down the column of text to two portraits inserted in it. The first was her husband's, taken from a photograph made the year they had come to England. It was the picture of him that she liked best, the one that stood on the writing table upstairs in her bedroom. As the eyes in the photograph met hers, she felt it would be impossible to read what was said of him, and closed her lids with the sharpness of the pain.

'I thought if you felt disposed to put your name down – ' she heard Parvis continue.

She opened her eyes with an effort, and they fell on the other portrait. It was that of a youngish man, slightly built, with features somewhat blurred by the shadow of a projecting hat brim. Where had she seen that outline before? She stared at it confusedly, her heart hammering in her ears. Then she gave a cry.

'This is the man – the man who came for my husband!'

She heard Parvis start to his feet, and was dimly aware that she had slipped backward into the corner of the sofa, and that he was bending above her in alarm. She straightened herself, and reached out for the paper, which she had dropped.

'It's the man! I should know him anywhere!' she persisted in a voice that sounded to her own ears like a scream.

Parvis's answer seemed to come to her from far off, down endless fog-muffled windings.

'Mrs. Boyne, you're not very well. Shall I call somebody? Shall I get a glass of water?'

'No, no, no!' She threw herself toward him, her hand frantically clutching the newspaper. 'I tell you, it's the man! I *know* him! He spoke to me in the garden!'

Parvis took the journal from her, directing his glasses to the portrait. 'It can't be, Mrs. Boyne. It's Robert Elwell.'

'Robert Elwell?' Her white stare seemed to travel into space. 'Then it was Robert Elwell who came for him.'

'Came for Boyne? The day he went away from here?' Parvis's voice dropped as hers rose. He bent over, laying a fraternal hand on her, as if to coax her gently back into her seat. 'Why, Elwell was dead! Don't you remember?'

Mary sat with her eyes fixed on the picture, unconscious of what he was saying.

'Don't you remember Boyne's unfinished letter to me – the one you found on his desk that day? It was written just after he'd heard of Elwell's death.' She noticed an odd shake in Parvis's unemotional voice. 'Surely you remember!' he urged her.

Yes, she remembered: that was the profoundest horror of it. Elwell had died the day before her husband's disappearance; and this was Elwell's portrait; and it was the portrait of the man who had spoken to her in the garden. She lifted her head and looked slowly about the library. The library could have borne witness that it was also the portrait of the man who had come in that day to call Boyne from his unfinished letter. Through the misty surgings of her brain she heard the faint boom of half-forgotten words – words spoken by Alida Stair on the lawn at Pangbourne before Boyne and his wife had ever seen the house at Lyng, or had imagined that they might one day live there.

'This was the man who spoke to me,' she repeated.

She looked again at Parvis. He was trying to conceal his disturbance under what he probably imagined to be an expression of indulgent commiseration; but the edges of his lips were blue. 'He thinks me mad; but I'm not mad,' she reflected; and suddenly there flashed upon her a way of justifying her strange affirmation.

She sat quiet, controlling the quiver of her lips, and waiting till she could trust her voice; then she said, looking straight at Parvis: 'Will you answer me one question, please? When was it that Robert Elwell tried to kill himself?'

'When – when?' Parvis stammered.

'Yes; the date. Please try to remember.'

She saw that he was growing still more afraid of her. 'I have a reason,' she insisted.

'Yes, yes. Only I can't remember. About two months before, I should say.'

'I want the date,' she repeated.

Parvis picked up the newspaper. 'We might see here,' he said, still humoring her. He ran his eyes down the page. 'Here it is. Last October – the – '

She caught the words from him. 'The 20th, wasn't it?' With a sharp look at her, he verified. 'Yes, the 20th. Then you *did* know?'

'I know now.' Her gaze continued to travel past him. 'Sunday, the 20th – that was the day he came first.'

Parvis's voice was almost inaudible. 'Came *here* first?'

'Yes.'

'You saw him twice, then?'

'Yes, twice.' She just breathed it at him. 'He came first on the 20th of October. I remember the date because it was the day we went up Meldon Steep for the first time.' She felt a faint gasp of inward laughter at the thought that but for that she might have forgotten.

Parvis continued to scrutinize her, as if trying to intercept her gaze.

'We saw him from the roof,' she went on. 'He came down the lime avenue toward the house. He was dressed just as he is in that picture. My husband saw him first. He was frightened, and ran down ahead of me; but there was no one there. He had vanished.'

'Elwell had vanished?' Parvis faltered.

'Yes.' Their two whispers seemed to grope for each other. 'I couldn't think what had happened. I see now. He *tried* to come then; but he wasn't dead enough – he couldn't reach us. He had to wait for two months to die; and then he came back again – and Ned went with him.'

She nodded at Parvis with the look of triumph of a child who has worked out a difficult puzzle. But suddenly she lifted her hands with a desperate gesture, pressing them to her temples.

'Oh, my God! I sent him to Ned – I told him where to go! I sent him to this room!' she screamed.

She felt the walls of books rush toward her, like inward falling ruins; and she heard Parvis, a long way off, through the ruins, crying to her, and struggling to get at her. But she was numb to his touch, she did not know what he was saying. Through the tumult she heard but one clear note, the voice of Alida Stair, speaking on the lawn at Pangbourne.

'You won't know till afterward,' it said. 'You won't know till long, long afterward.'

The Bolted Door

HUBERT GRANICE, pacing the length of his pleasant lamplit library, paused to compare his watch with the clock on the chimney piece.

Three minutes to eight.

In exactly three minutes Mr. Peter Ascham, of the eminent legal firm of Ascham and Pettilow, would have his punctual hand on the doorbell of the flat. It was a comfort to reflect that Ascham was so punctual – the suspense was beginning to make his host nervous. And the sound of the doorbell would be the beginning of the end – after that there'd be no going back, by God – no going back!

Granice resumed his pacing. Each time he reached the end of the room opposite the door he caught his reflection in the Florentine mirror above the fine old *crédence* he had picked up at Dijon – saw himself spare, quick moving, carefully brushed and dressed, but furrowed, gray about the temples, with a stoop which he corrected by a spasmodic straightening of the shoulders whenever a glass confronted him: a tired middle-aged man, baffled, beaten, worn out.

As he summed himself up thus for the third or fourth time the door opened and he turned with a thrill of relief to greet his guest. But it was only the manservant who entered, advancing silently over the mossy surface of the old Turkey rug.

'Mr. Ascham telephones, sir, to say he's unexpectedly detained and can't be here till eight-thirty.'

Granice made a curt gesture of annoyance. It was becoming harder and harder for him to control these reflexes. He turned on his heel, tossing to the servant over his shoulder: 'Very good. Put off dinner.'

Down his spine he felt the man's injured stare. Mr. Granice had always been so mild-spoken to his people – no doubt the odd change in his manner had already been noticed and discussed belowstairs. And very likely they suspected the cause. He stood drumming on the writing table till he heard the servant go out; then he threw himself into a chair, propping his elbows on the table and resting his chin on his locked hands.

Another half hour alone with it!

He wondered irritably what could have detained his guest. Some professional matter, no doubt – the punctilious lawyer would have allowed nothing less to interfere with a dinner engagement, more especially since Granice, in his note, had said: 'I shall want a little business chat afterward.'

But what professional matter could have come up at that unprofessional hour? Perhaps some other soul in misery had called on the lawyer; and, after all, Granice's note had given no hint of his own need! No doubt Ascham thought he merely wanted to make another change in his will. Since he had come into his little property, ten years earlier, Granice had been perpetually tinkering with his will.

Suddenly another thought pulled him up, sending a flush to his temples. He remembered a word he had tossed to the lawyer some six weeks earlier, at the Century Club. 'Yes – my play's as good as taken. I shall be calling on you soon to go over the contract. Those theatrical chaps are so slippery – I won't trust anybody but you to tie the knot for me!' That, of course, was what Ascham would think he was wanted for. Granice, at the idea, broke into an audible laugh – a queer stage laugh, like the cackle of a baffled villain in a melodrama. The absurdity, the unnaturalness of the sound abashed him, and he compressed his lips angrily. Would he take to soliloquy next?

He lowered his arms and pulled open the upper drawer of the writing table. In the right-hand corner lay a manuscript, bound in paper folders, and tied with a string beneath which a letter had been slipped. Next to the manuscript was a revolver. Granice stared a moment at these oddly associated objects; then he took the letter from under the string and slowly began to open it. He had known he should do so from the moment his hand touched the drawer. Whenever his eye fell on that letter some relentless force compelled him to reread it.

It was dated about four weeks back, under the letterhead of 'The Diversity Theater.'

My Dear Mr. Granice:

I have given the matter my best consideration for the last month, and it's no use – the play won't do. I have talked it over with Miss Melrose – and you know there isn't a gamer artist on our stage – and I regret to tell you she feels just as I do about it. It isn't the poetry that scares her – or me either. We both want to do all we can to help along the poetic drama – we believe the public's ready for it, and we're willing to take a big financial risk in order to be the first to give them what they want. *But we don't believe they could be made to want this.* The fact is, there isn't enough drama in your play to the allowance of poetry – the thing drags all through. You've got a big idea, but it's not out of swaddling clothes.

If this was your first play I'd say: *Try again.* But it has been just the same with all the others you've shown me. And you remember the result of *The Lee Shore* where you carried all the expenses of production yourself, and we couldn't fill the theater for a week. Yet *The Lee Shore* was a modern problem play – much easier to swing than blank verse. It isn't as if you hadn't tried all kinds – '

Granice folded the letter and put it carefully back into the envelope. Why on earth was he rereading it, when he knew every phrase in it by heart, when for a month past he had seen it, night after night, stand out in letters of flame against the darkness of his sleepless lids?

'It has been just the same with all the others you've shown me.'

That was the way they dismissed ten years of passionate unremitting work!

'You remember the result of "The Lee Shore."'

Good God – as if he were likely to forget it! He relived it all now in a drowning flash: the persistant rejection of the play, his resolve to put it on at his own cost, to spend ten thousand dollars of his inheritance on testing his chance of success – the fever of preparation, the dry-mouthed agony of the 'first night,' the flat fall, the stupid press, his secret rush to Europe to escape the condolence of his friends!

'It isn't as if you hadn't tried all kinds.'

No – he had tried all kinds: comedy, tragedy, prose and verse, the light curtain-raiser, the short sharp drama, the bourgeois-realistic and the lyrical-romantic – finally deciding that he would no longer 'prostitute his talent' to win popularity, but would impose on the public his own theory of art in the form of five acts of blank verse. Yes, he had offered them everything – and always with the same result.

Ten years of it – ten years of dogged work and unrelieved failure. The ten years from forty to fifty – the best ten years of his life! And if one counted the years before, the years of dreams, assimilation, preparation – then call it half a man's lifetime: half a man's lifetime thrown away!

And what was he to do with the remaining half? Well, he had settled that, thank God! He turned and glanced anxiously at the clock. Ten minutes past eight – only ten minutes had been consumed in that stormy rush through his past! And he must wait another twenty minutes for Ascham. It was one of the worst symptoms of his case that, in proportion as he had grown to shrink from human company, he dreaded more and more to be alone. . . . But why the devil was he waiting for Ascham? Why didn't he cut the knot himself? Since he was so unutterably sick of the whole business, why did he have to call in an outsider to rid him of this nightmare of living?

He opened the drawer again and laid his hand on the revolver. It was a slim ivory toy – just the instrument for a tired sufferer to give himself a 'hypodermic' with. Granice raised it in one hand, while with the other he felt under the thin hair at the back of his head, between the ear and the nape. He knew just where to place the muzzle: he had once got a surgeon to show him. And as he found the spot, and lifted the revolver to it, the inevitable phenomenon occurred. The hand that held the weapon began to shake, the tremor passed into his arm, his heart gave a leap which sent up a wave of deadly nausea to his throat, he smelt the powder, he sickened at the crash of the bullet through his skull, and a sweat broke out over his forehead and ran down his quivering face. . . .

He laid away the revolver and, pulling out his handkerchief, passed it tremulously over his brow and temples. It was of no use – he knew he could never do it in that way. His attempts at self-destruction were as futile as his snatches at fame! He couldn't make himself a real life, and he couldn't get rid of the life he had. And that was why he had sent for Ascham to help him. . . .

The lawyer, over the cheese and Burgundy, began to excuse himself for his delay.

'I didn't like to say anything while your man was about; but the fact is, I was sent for on a rather unusual matter – '

'Oh, it's all right,' said Granice cheerfully. He was beginning to feel the reaction that food and company always produced in him. It was not any recovered pleasure in life that he felt, but only a deeper withdrawal into himself. It was easier to go on automatically with the social gestures than to uncover to any human eye the abyss within him.

'My dear fellow, it's sacrilege to keep a dinner waiting – especially the production of an artist like yours.' Mr. Ascham sipped his Burgundy luxuriously. 'But the fact is, Mrs. Ashgrove sent for me.'

Granice raised his head with a movement of surprise. For a moment he was shaken out of his self-absorption.

'Mrs. Ashgrove?'

Ascham smiled. 'I thought you'd be interested; I know your passion for *causes célèbres*. And this promises to be one. Of course it's out of our line entirely – we never touch criminal cases. But she wanted to consult me as a friend. Ashgrove was a distant connection of my wife's. And, by Jove, it *is* a queer case!' The servant re-entered, and Ascham snapped his lips shut.

Would the gentlemen have their coffee in the dining room?

'No – serve it in the library,' said Granice, rising. He led the way back to the curtained confidential room. He was really curious to hear what Ascham had to tell him.

While the coffee and cigars were being served he fidgeted about, glancing at his letters – the usual meaningless notes and bills – and picking up the evening paper. As he unfolded it a headline caught his eye.

ROSE MELROSE WANTS TO PLAY POETRY.
THINKS SHE HAS FOUND HER POET.

He read on with a thumping heart – found the name of a young author he had barely heard of, saw the title of a play, a 'poetic drama,' dance before his eyes, and dropped the paper, sick, disgusted. It was true, then – she *was* 'game' – it was not the manner but the matter she mistrusted!

Granice turned to the servant, who seemed to be purposely lingering. 'I shan't need you this evening, Flint. I'll lock up myself.'

He fancied that the man's acquiescence implied surprise. What was going on, Flint seemed to wonder, that Mr. Granice should want him out of the way? Probably he would find a pretext for coming back to see. Granice suddenly felt himself enveloped in a network of espionage.

As the door closed he threw himself into an armchair and leaned forward to take a light from Ascham's cigar.

'Tell me about Mrs. Ashgrove,' he said, seeming to himself to speak stiffly, as if his lips were cracked.

'Mrs. Ashgrove? Well, there's not much to *tell.*'

'And you couldn't if there were?' Granice smiled.

'Probably not. As a matter of fact, she wanted my advice about her choice of counsel. There was nothing especially confidential in our talk.'

'And what's your impression, now you've seen her?'

'My impression is, very distinctly, *that nothing will ever be known.*'

'Ah – ?' Granice murmured, puffing at his cigar.

'I'm more and more convinced that whoever poisoned Ashgrove knew his business, and will consequently never be found out. That's a capital cigar you've given me.'

'You like it? I get them over from Cuba.' Granice examined his own reflectively. 'Then you believe in the theory that the clever criminals never *are* caught?'

'Of course I do. Look about you – look back for the last dozen years – none of the big murder problems are ever solved.' The lawyer ruminated behind his blue cloud. 'Why, take the instance in your own family: I'd forgotten I had an illustration at hand! Take old Joseph Lenman's murder – do you suppose that will ever be explained?'

As the words dropped from Ascham's lips his host looked about the library, and every object in it stared back at him with a stale unescapable familiarity. How sick he was of looking at that room! It was as dull as the face of a wife one has tired of. He cleared his throat slowly; then he turned his head to the lawyer and said: 'I could explain the Lenman murder myself.'

Ascham's eye kindled: he shared Granice's interest in criminal cases.

'By Jove! You've had a theory all this time? It's odd you never mentioned it. Go ahead and tell me. There are certain features in the Lenman case not unlike this Ashgrove affair, and your idea may be a help.'

Granice paused and his eye reverted instinctively to the table drawer in which the revolver and the manuscript lay side by side. What if he were to try another appeal to Rose Melrose? Then he looked at the notes and bills on the table, and the horror of taking up again the lifeless routine of life – of performing the same automatic gestures another day – dispelled his fleeting impulse.

'It's not an idea. I *know* who murdered Joseph Lenman.'

Ascham settled himself comfortable in his chair, prepared for enjoyment.

'You *know*? Well, who did?' he laughed.

'I did,' said Granice, rising to his feet.

He stood before Ascham, and the lawyer lay back, staring up at him. Then he broke into another laugh.

'Why, this is glorious! You murdered him, did you? To inherit his money, I suppose? Better and better! Go on, my boy! Unbosom yourself! Tell me all about it! confession is good for the soul.'

Granice waited till the lawyer had shaken the last peal of laughter from his throat; then he repeated doggedly: 'I murdered him.'

The two men looked at each other for a long moment, and this time Ascham did not laugh.

'Granice!'

'I murdered him – to get his money, as you say.'

There was another pause, and Granice, with a vague sense of amusement, saw his guest's look gradually change from pleasantry to apprehension.

'What's the joke, my dear fellow? I fail to see.'

'It's not a joke. It's the truth. I murdered him.' He had spoken painfully at first, as if there were a knot in his throat;

but each time he repeated the words he found they were easier to say.

Ascham laid down his cigar. 'What's the matter? Aren't you well? What on earth are you driving at?'

'I'm perfectly well. But I murdered my cousin, Joseph Lenman, and I want it known that I murdered him.'

'*You want it known*?'

'Yes. That's why I sent for you. I'm sick of living, and when I try to kill myself I funk it.' He spoke quite naturally now, as if the knot in his throat had been untied.

'Good Lord – good Lord,' the lawyer gasped.

'But I suppose,' Granice continued, 'there's no doubt this would be murder in the first degree? I'm sure of the chair if I own up?'

Ascham drew a long breath; then he said slowly: 'Sit down, Granice. Let's talk.'

• II •

GRANICE told his story simply, connectedly.

He began by a quick survey of his early years – the years of drudgery and privation. His father, a charming man who could never say 'no,' had so signally failed to say it on certain essential occasions that when he died he left an illegitimate family and a mortgaged estate. His lawful kin found themselves hanging over a gulf of debt, and young Granice, to support his mother and sister, had to leave Harvard and bury himself at eighteen in a broker's office. He loathed his work, and he was always poor, always worried and often ill. A few years later his mother died, but his sister, a helpless creature, remained on his hands. His own health gave out, and he had to go away for six months, and work harder than ever when he came back. He had no knack for business, no head for figures, not the dimmest insight into the mysteries of commerce. He wanted to travel and write – those were his inmost longings. And as the years dragged on, and he neared middle-age without making any more money, or acquiring any firmer health, a sick despair possessed him. He tried writing, but he always came home from the office so tired that his brain could not work. For half the year he did not reach his dim uptown flat till after dark, and could only 'brush up' for dinner, and afterward lie on the lounge with his pipe, while his sister droned through the evening paper. Sometimes he spent an evening at the theater; or he dined out or, more rarely, strayed off with an acquaintance or two in quest of what is known as 'pleasure.' And in summer, when he and Kate went to the sea side for a month, he dozed through the days in utter weariness. Once he fell in love with a charming girl – but what had he to offer her, in God's name? She seemed to like him, and in common decency he had to drop out of the running. Apparently no one replaced him, for she never married, but grew stoutish, grayish, philanthropic – yet how sweet she had been when he first kissed her! One more wasted life, he reflected. . . .

But the stage had always been his master passion. He would have sold his soul for the time and freedom to write plays! It was *in him* – he could not remember when it had not been his deepest-seated instinct. As the years passed it became a morbid, a relentless obsession – yet with every year the material conditions were more and more against it. He felt himself growing middle-aged, and he watched the reflection of the process in his sister's wasted face. At eighteen she had been pretty, and as full of enthusiasm as he. Now she was sour, trivial, insignificant – she had missed her chance of life. And she had no resources, poor creature, was fashioned simply for the primitive functions she had been denied the chance to fulfill! It exasperated him to think of it – and to reflect that even now a little travel, a little health, a little money, might transform her, make her young and desirable. . . . The chief fruit of his experience was that there is no such fixed state as age or youth – there is only health as against sickness, wealth as against poverty; and age or youth as the outcome of the lot one draws.

At this point in his narrative Granice stood up, and went to lean against the mantelpiece, looking down at Ascham, who had not moved from his seat, or changed his attitude of spellbound attention.

'Then came the summer when we went to Wrenfield to be near old Lenman – my mother's cousin, as you know. Some of the family always mounted guard over him – generally a niece or so. But that year they were all scattered, and one of the nieces offered to lend us her cottage if we'd relieve her of duty for two months. It was a nuisance for me, of course, for Wrenfield is two hours from town; but my mother, who was a slave to family observances, had always been good to the old man, so it was natural that we should be called on – and there was the saving of rent and the good air for Kate. So we went.

'You never knew Joseph Lenman? Well, picture to yourself an amoeba, or some primitive organism of that sort, under a Titan's microscope. He was large, undifferentiated, inert – since I could remember him he had done nothing but take his temperature and read the *Churchman*. Oh, and cultivate melons – that was his hobby. Not vulgar out-of-door melons – his were grown under glass. He had acres of it at Wrenfield – his big kitchen garden was surrounded by blinking battalions of greenhouses. And in nearly all of them melons were grown: early melons and late, French, English, Domestic – dwarf melons and monsters: every shape, color and variety. They were petted and nursed like children – a staff of trained attendants waited on them. I'm not sure they didn't have a doctor to take their temperature; at any rate the place was full of thermometers. And they didn't sprawl on the ground like ordinary melons; they were trained against the glass like nectarines, and each melon hung in a net which sustained its weight and left it free on all sides to the sun and air.

'It used to strike me sometimes that old Lenman was just like one of his own melons – the pale-fleshed English kind. His life, apathetic and motionless, hung in a net of gold, in an equable warm ventilated atmosphere, high above earthly worries. The cardinal rule of his existence was not to let himself be "worried." . . . I remember his advising me to try it myself, one day when I spoke to him about Kate's bad health, and her need of a change. "I always make it a rule not to let myself worry," he said complacently. "It's the worst thing for the liver – and you look to me as if you had a liver. Take my advice and be cheerful. You'll make yourself happier and others too." And all he had to do was to write a check, and send the poor girl off for a holiday!

'The hardest part of it was that the money half belonged to us already. The old skinflint only had it for life, in trust for us and the others. But his life was a good deal sounder than mine or Kate's – and one could picture him taking extra care of it for the joke of keeping us waiting. I always felt that the sight of our hungry eyes was a tonic to him.

'Well, I tried to see if I couldn't reach him through his vanity. I flattered him, feigned a passionate interest in his melons. And he was taken in, and used to discourse on them by the hour. On fine days he was driven to the greenhouses in his pony chair, and waddled through them, prodding and leering at the fruit, like a fat Turk in his seraglio. When he bragged to me of the expense of growing them I was reminded of a hideous old Lothario bragging of what his pleasures cost. And the resemblance was completed by the fact that he couldn't eat as much as a mouthful of his melons – had lived for years on butter milk and toast.

'But, after all, it's my only hobby – why shouldn't I indulge it?' he said sentimentally. As if I'd ever been able to indulge any of mine! On the keep of those melons Kate and I could have lived like gods. . . .

'One day toward the end of the summer, when Kate was too unwell to drag herself up to the big house, she asked me to go and spend the afternoon with cousin Joseph. It was a lovely soft September afternoon – a day to lie under a Roman stone pine, with one's eyes on the sky, and let the cosmic harmonies rush through one. Perhaps the vision was suggested by the fact that, as I entered cousin Joseph's hideous black walnut library, I passed one of the undergardeners, a handsome Italian, who dashed out in such a hurry that he nearly knocked me down. I remember thinking it queer that the fellow, whom I had often seen about the melon houses, did not bow to me or even seem to see me.

'Cousin Joseph sat in his usual seat, behind the darkened windows, his fat hands folded on his protuberant waistcoat, the last number of the *Churchman* at his elbow, and near it, on a huge dish, a melon – the fattest melon I'd ever seen. As I looked at it I pictured the ecstasy of contemplation from which I must have roused him, and congratulated myself on finding him in such a mood, since I had made up my mind to ask him a favor. Then I noticed that his face, instead of looking as calm as an eggshell, was distorted and whimpering – and without stopping to greet me he pointed passionately to the melon.

' "Look at it, look at it – did you ever see such a beauty? Such firmness – roundness – such delicious smoothness to the touch?" It was as if he had said "she" instead of "it," and when he put out his senile hand and touched the melon I positively had to look the other way.

'Then he told me what had happened. The Italian under-gardener, who had been specially recommended for the melon houses – though it was against my cousin's principles to employ a Papist – had been assigned to the care of the monster: for it had revealed itself, early in its existence, as destined to become a monster, to surpass its plumpest pulpiest sisters, carry off prizes at agricultural shows, and be photographed and celebrated in every gardening paper in the land. The Italian had done well – seemed to have a sense of responsibility. And that very morning he had been ordered to pick the melon, which was to be shown next day at the county fair, and to bring it in for Mr. Lenman to gaze on its blond virginity. But in picking it, what had the damned scoundrelly Jesuit done but drop it – drop it crash on the spout of a watering pot, so that it received a deep gash in its firm pale rotundity, and was henceforth but a bruised, ruined, fallen melon?

'The old man's rage was fearful in its impotence – he shook, spluttered and strangled with it. He had just had the Italian up and had sacked him on the spot, without wages or character – had threatened to have him arrested if he was ever caught prowling about Wrenfield. "By God, and I'll do it – I'll write to Washington – I'll have the pauper scoundrel deported! I'll show him what money can do!" As likely as not there was some murderous blackhand business under it – it would be found that the fellow was a member of a "gang". Those Italians would murder you for a quarter. He meant to have the police look into it. . . . And then he grew frightened at his own excitement. "But I must calm myself," he said. He took his temperature, rang for his drops, and turned to the *Churchman*. He had been reading an article on Nestorianism when the melon was brought in. He asked me to go on with it, and I read to him for an hour, in the dim close room, with a fat fly buzzing stealthily about the fallen melon.

'All the while one phrase of the old man's buzzed in my brain like the fly about the melon. "*I'll show him what money can do*!" Good heaven! If *I* could but show the old man! If I could make him see his power of giving happiness as a new outlet for his monstrous egotism! I tried to tell him something about my situation and Kate's – spoke of my ill-health, my unsuccessful drudgery, my longing to write, to make myself a name – I stammered out an entreaty for a loan. "I can guarantee to repay you, sir – I've a half-written play as security. . . ."

'I shall never forget his glassy stare. His face had grown as smooth as an eggshell again – his eyes peered over his fat cheeks like sentinels over a slippery rampart.

' "A half-written play – a play of *yours* as security?" He looked at me almost fearfully, as if detecting the first symptoms of insanity. "Do you understand anything of business?" he inquired. I laughed and answered: "No, not much."

'He leaned back with closed lids. "All this excitement has been too much for me," he said. "If you'll excuse me, I'll prepare for my nap." And I stumbled out of the room, blindly, like the Italian.'

Granice moved away from the mantelpiece, and walked across to the tray set out with decanters and soda water. He poured himself a tall glass of soda water, emptied it, and glanced at Ascham's dead cigar.

'Better light another,' he suggested.

The lawyer shook his head, and Granice went on with his tale. He told of his mounting obsession – how the murderous impulse had waked in him on the instant of his cousin's refusal, and he had muttered to himself: 'By God, if you won't, I'll make you.' He spoke more tranquilly as the narrative proceeded, as though his rage had died down once the resolve to act on it was taken. He applied his whole mind to the question of how the old man was to be 'disposed of.' Suddenly he remembered the outcry: 'Those Italians would murder you for a quarter!' But no definite project presented itself: he simply waited for an inspiration.

Granice and his sister moved to town a day or two afterward. But the cousins, who had returned, kept them informed of the old man's condition. One day, about three weeks later, Granice, on getting home, found Kate excited over a report from Wrenfield. The Italian had been there again – had somehow slipped into the house, made his way up to the library, and 'used threatening language.' The housekeeper found cousin Joseph gasping, the whites of his eyes showing 'something awful.' The doctor was sent for, and the attack warded off; and the police had ordered the Italian from the neighborhood.

But cousin Joseph, thereafter, languished, had 'nerves,' and lost his taste for toast and buttermilk. The doctor called in a colleague, and the consultation amused and excited the old man – he became once more an important figure. The medical men reassured the family – too completely! – and to the patient they recommended a more varied diet: advised him to take whatever 'tempted him.' And so one day, tremulously, prayer-fully, he decided on a tiny bit of melon. It was brought up with ceremony, and consumed in the presence of the housekeeper and a hovering cousin; and twenty minutes later he was dead. . . .

'But you remember the circumstances,' Granice went on; 'how suspicion turned at once on the Italian? In spite of the hint the police had given him he had been seen hanging about the house since "the scene." It was said that he had tender relations with the kitchenmaid, and the rest seemed easy to explain. But when they looked round to ask him for the explanation he was gone – gone clean out of sight. He had been "warned" to leave Wrenfield, and he had taken the warning so to heart that no one ever laid eyes on him again.'

Granice paused. He had dropped into a chair opposite the lawyer's and he sat for a moment, his head thrown back, looking about the familiar room. Everything in it had grown grimacing and alien, and each strange insistent object seemed craning forward from its place to hear him.

'It was I who put the stuff in the melon,' he said. 'And I don't want you to think I'm sorry for it. This isn't "remorse," understand. I'm glad the old skinflint is dead – I'm glad the others have their money. But mine's no use to me any more. My sister married miserably, and died. And I've never had what I wanted.'

Ascham continued to stare; then he said: 'What on earth was your object, then?'

'Why, to *get* what I wanted – what I fancied was in reach! I wanted change, rest, *life*, for both of us – wanted, above all, for myself, the chance to write! I traveled, got back my health, and came home to tie myself up to my work. And I've slaved at it steadily for ten years without reward – without the most distant hope of success! Nobody will look at my stuff. And now I'm fifty, and I'm beaten, and I know it.' His chin dropped forward on his breast. 'I want to chuck the whole business,' he ended.

• III •

It was after midnight when Ascham left.

His hand on Granice's shoulder, as he turned to go – 'District Attorney be hanged; see a doctor, see a doctor!' he had cried; and so, with an exaggerated laugh, had pulled on his coat and departed.

Granice turned back into the library. It had never occurred to him that Ascham would not believe his story. For three hours he had explained, elucidated, patiently and painfully gone over every detail – but without once breaking down the iron incredulity of the lawyer's eye.

At first Ascham had feigned to be convinced – but that, as Granice now perceived, was simply to get him to expose himself, to entrap him into contradictions. And when the attempt failed, when Granice triumphantly met and refuted each disconcerting question, the lawyer dropped the mask, and broke out with a good-humored laugh: 'By Jove, Granice, you'll write a successful play yet. The way you've worked this all out is a marvel.'

'Granice swung about furiously – that last sneer about the play inflamed him. Was all the world in a conspiracy to deride his failure?

'I did it, I did it,' he muttered, his rage spending itself against the impenetrable surface of the other's mockery; and Ascham answered with a quieting smile: 'Ever read any of those books on hallucinations? I've got a fairly good medico-legal library. I could send you one or two if you like. . . .'

Left alone, Granice cowered down in the chair before his writing table. He understood that Ascham thought him off his head.

'Good God – what if they all think me crazy?'

The horror of it broke out over him in a cold sweat – he sat there and shook, his eyes hidden in his hands. But gradually, as he began to rehearse his story for the thousandth time, he saw again how incontrovertible it was, and felt sure that any criminal lawyer would believe him.

'That's the trouble – Ascham's not a criminal lawyer. And then he's a friend. What a fool I was to talk to a friend! Even if he did believe me, he'd never let me see it – his instinct would be to cover the whole thing up . . . But in that case – if he *did* believe me – he might think it a kindness to get me shut up in an asylum. . . .' Granice began to tremble again. 'Good heaven! If he should bring in an expert – one of those damned alienists! Ascham and Pettilow can do anything – their word always goes. If Ascham drops a hint that I'd better be shut up, I'll be in a strait-jacket by tomorrow! And he'd do it from the kindest motives – be quite right to do it if he thinks I'm a murderer!'

The vision froze him to his chair. He pressed his fists to his bursting temples and tried to think. For the first time he hoped that Ascham had not believed his story.

'But he did – he did! I can see it now – I noticed what a queer eye he cocked at me. Good God, what shall I do – what shall I do?'

He started up and looked at the clock. Half-past one. What if Ascham should think the case urgent, rout out an alienist, and come back with him? Granice jumped to his feet, and his gesture brushed the morning paper from the table. As he stooped to pick it up the movement started a new train of association.

He sat down again, and reached for the telephone book in the rack by his chair.

'Give me three-o-ten . . . yes.'

The new idea in his mind had revived his energy. He would act – act at once. It was only by thus planning ahead, committing himself to some unavoidable line of conduct, that he could pull himself through the meaningless days. Each time he reached a fresh decision it was like coming out of a foggy weltering sea into a calm harbor with lights. One of the queerest phases of his long agony was the relief produced by these momentary lulls.

'That the office of the *Investigator*? Yes? Give me Mr. Denver, please . . . Hallo, Denver . . . Yes, Hubert Granice . . . Just caught you? Going straight home? Can I come and see you . . . yes, now . . . have a talk? It's rather urgent . . . Yes, might give you some first-rate "copy". . . . All right!' He hung up the receiver with a laugh. It had been a happy thought to call up the editor of the *Investigator* – Robert Denver was the very man he needed. . . .

Granice put out the lights in the library – it was odd how the automatic gestures persisted! – went into the hall, put on his hat and overcoat, and let himself out of the flat. In the hall, a sleepy elevator boy blinked at him and then dropped his head on his arms. Granice passed out into the street. At the corner of Fifth Avenue he hailed a cab, and called out an uptown address. The long thoroughfare stretched before him, dim and deserted, like an ancient avenue of tombs. But from Denver's house a friendly beam fell on the pavement; and as Granice sprang from his cab the editor's electric turned the corner.

The two men grasped hands, and Denver, feeling for his latchkey, ushered Granice into the hall.

'Disturb me? Not a bit. You might have, at ten tomorrow morning . . . but this is my liveliest hour . . . you know my habits of old.'

Granice had known Robert Denver for fifteen years – watched his rise through all the stages of journalism to the Olympian pinnacle of the *Investigator's* editorial office. In the thick-set man with grizzling hair there were few traces left of the hungry-eyed young reporter who, on his way home in the small hours, used to 'bob in' on Granice, while the latter sat grinding at his plays. Denver had to pass Granice's flat on the way to his own, and it became a habit, if he saw a light in the window, and Granice's shadow against the blind, to go in, smoke a pipe, and discuss the universe.

'Well – this is like old times – a good old habit reversed.' The editor smote his visitor genially on the shoulder. 'Reminds me of the nights when I used to rout you out. How's the play, by the way? There *is* a play, I suppose? It's as safe to ask you that as to say to some men: 'How's the baby?'

Denver laughed good-naturedly, and Granice thought how thick and heavy he had grown. It was evident, even to Granice's tortured nerves, that the words had not been uttered in malice – and the fact gave him a new measure of his insignificance. Denver did not even know that he had been a failure! The fact hurt more than Ascham's irony.

'Come in – come in.' The editor led the way into a small cheerful room, where there were cigars and decanters. He pushed an armchair toward his visitor, and dropped into another with a comfortable groan.

'Now, then – help yourself. And let's hear all about it.'

He beamed at Granice over his pipe bowl, and the latter, lighting his cigar, said to himself: 'Success makes men comfortable, but it makes them stupid.'

Then he turned, and began: 'Denver, I want to tell you – '

*

The clock ticked rhythmically on the mantelpiece. The room was gradually filled with drifting blue layers of smoke, and through them the editor's face came and went like the moon through a moving sky. Once the hour struck – then the rhythmical ticking began again. The atmosphere grew denser and heavier, and beads of perspiration began to roll from Granice's forehead.

'Do you mind if I open the window?'

'No. It *is* stuffy in here. Wait – I'll do it myself.' Denver pushed down the upper sash, and returned to his chair. 'Well – go on,' he said, filling another pipe. His composure exasperated Granice.

'There's no use in my going on if you don't believe me.'

The editor remained unmoved. 'Who says I don't believe you? And how can I tell till you've finished?'

Granice went on, ashamed of his outburst. 'It was simple enough, as you'll see. From the day the old man said to me "Those Italians would murder you for a quarter" I dropped everything and just worked at my scheme. It struck me at once that I must find a way of getting to Wrenfield and back in a night – and that led to the idea of a motor. A motor – that never occurred to you? You wonder where I got the money, I suppose. Well, I had a thousand or so put by, and I nosed around till I found what I wanted – a secondhand racer. I knew how to drive a car, and I tried the thing and found it was all right. Times were bad, and I bought it for my price, and stored it away. Where? Why, in one of those no-questions-asked garages where they keep motors that are not for family use. I had a lively cousin who had put me up to that dodge, and I looked about till I found a queer hole where they took in my car like a baby in a foundling asylum. . . . Then I practiced running to Wrenfield and back in a night. I knew the way pretty well, for I'd done it often with the same lively cousin – and in the small hours, too. The distance is over ninety miles, and on the third trial I did it under two hours. But my arms were so lame that I could hardly get dressed the next morning.

'Well, then came the report about the Italian's threats, and I saw I must act. . . . I meant to break into the old man's room, shoot him, and get away again. It was a big risk, but I thought I could manage it. Then we heard that he was ill – that there'd been a consultation. Perhaps the fates were going to do it for me! Good Lord, if that could only be! . . .'

Granice stopped and wiped his forehead: the open window did not seem to have cooled the room.

'Then came word that he was better; and the day after, when I came up from my office, I found Kate laughing over the news that he was to try a bit of melon. The housekeeper had just telephoned her – all Wrenfield was in a flutter. The doctor himself had picked out the melon, one of the little French ones that are hardly bigger than a large tomato – and the patient was to eat it at his breakfast the next morning.

'In a flash I saw my chance. It was a bare chance, no more. But I knew the ways of the house – I was sure the melon would be brought in overnight and put in the pantry icebox. If there were only one melon in the icebox I could be fairly sure it was the one I wanted. Melons didn't lie around loose in that house – every one was known, numbered, catalogued. The old man was beset by the dread that the servants would eat them, and he took all sorts of mean precautions to prevent it. Yes, I felt pretty sure of my melon . . . and poisoning was much safer than shooting. It would have been the devil and all to get into his bedroom without his rousing the house; but I ought to be able to break into the pantry without much trouble.

'It was a cloudy night, too – everything served me. I dined quietly, and sat down at my desk. Kate had one of her usual headaches, and went to bed early. As soon as she was gone I slipped out. I had got together a sort of disguise – red beard and queer-looking ulster. I shoved them into a bag, and went round to the garage. There was no one there but a half-drunken machinist whom I'd never seen before. That served me, too. They were always changing machinists, and this new fellow didn't even bother to ask if the car belonged to me. It was a very easy-going place. . . .

'Well, I jumped in, ran up Broadway, and let the car go as soon as I was out of Harlem. Dark as it was, I could trust myself to strike a sharp pace. In the shadow of a wood I stopped a second and got into the beard and ulster. Then away again – it was just eleven-thirty when I got to Wrenfield.

'I left the car in a lane behind the Lenman place, and slipped through the kitchen garden. The melon houses winked at me through the dark – I remember thinking that they knew what I wanted to know. . . . By the stable a dog came out growling –

but he nosed me out, jumped on me, and went back. . . . The house was as dark as the grave. I knew everybody went to bed by ten. But there might be a prowling servant – the kitchenmaid might have come down to let in her Italian. I had to risk that, of course. I crept around by the back door and hid in the shrubbery. Then I listened. It was all as silent as death. I crossed over to the house, pried open the pantry window, and climbed in. I had a little electric lamp in my pocket, and shielding it with my cap I groped my way to the icebox, opened it – and there was the little French melon . . . only one.

'I stopped to listen – I was quite cool. Then I pulled out my bottle of stuff and my syringe, and gave each section of the melon a hypodermic. It was all done inside of three minutes – at ten minutes to twelve I was back in the car. I got out of the lane as quietly as I could, struck a back road, and let the car out as soon as I was beyond the last houses. I only stopped once on the way in, to drop the beard and ulster into a pond. I had a big stone ready to weight them with and they went down plump, like a dead body – and at two I was back at my desk.'

Granice stopped speaking and looked across the smoke fumes at his listener; but Denver's face remained inscrutable.

At length he said: 'Why did you want to tell me this?'

The question startled Granice. He was about to explain, as he had explained to Ascham; but suddenly it occurred to him that if his motive had not seemed convincing to the lawyer it would carry much less weight with Denver. Both were successful men, and success does not understand the subtle agony of failure. Granice cast about for another reason.

'Why, I – the thing haunts me . . . remorse, I suppose you'd call it. . . .'

Denver struck the ashes from his empty pipe.

'Remorse? Bosh!' he said energetically.

Granice's heart sank. 'You don't believe in – *remorse*?'

'Not an atom: in the man of action. The mere fact of your talking of remorse proves to me that you're not the man to have planned and put through such a job.'

Granice groaned. 'Well – I lied to you about remorse. I've never felt any.'

Denver's lips tightened sceptically about his freshly-filled pipe. 'What *was* your motive, then? You must have had one.'

'I'll tell you' – And Granice began once more to rehearse the story of his failure, of his loathing for life. 'Don't say you don't believe me this time . . . that this isn't a real reason!' he stammered out as he ended.

Denver meditated. 'No, I won't say that. I've seen too many queer things. There's always a reason for wanting to get out of life – the wonder is that we find so many for staying in!'

Granice's heart grew light. 'Then you *do* believe me?'

'Believe that you're sick of the job? Yes. And that you haven't the nerve to pull the trigger? Oh, yes – that's easy enough, too. But all that doesn't make you a murderer – though I don't say it proves you could never have been one.'

'I *have* been one, Denver – I swear to you.'

'Perhaps.' Again the journalist mused. 'Just tell me one or two things.'

'Oh, go ahead. You won't stump me!' Granice heard himself say with a laugh.

'Well – how did you make all those trial trips without exciting your sister's curiosity? I knew your night habits pretty well at that time, remember. You were seldom out late. Didn't the change in your ways surprise her?'

'No; because she was away at the time. She went to pay several visits in the country after we came back from Wrenfield, and had only been in town a night or two before – before I did the job.'

'And that night she went to bed with a headache?

'Yes – blinding. She didn't know anything when she had that kind. And her room was at the back of the flat.'

There was another pause in Denver's interrogatory. 'And when you got back – she didn't hear you? You got in without her knowing it?'

'Yes. I went straight to my work – took it up at the word where I'd left off – *why, Denver, don't you remember*?' Granice passionately interjected.

'Remember – ?'

'Yes; how you found me – when you looked in that morning, between two and three . . . your usual hour . . . ?'

'Yes,' the editor nodded.

Granice gave a short laugh. 'In my old coat – with my pipe: looked as if I'd been working all night, didn't I? Well, I hadn't been in my chair ten minutes!'

Denver uncrossed his legs and then crossed them again. 'I didn't know whether *you* remembered that.'

'What?'

'My coming in that particular night – or morning.'

Granice swung round in his chair. 'Why, man alive! that's why I'm here now. Because it was you who spoke for me at the inquest, when they looked round to see what all the old man's heirs had been doing that night – you who testified to having dropped in and found me at my desk as usual. . . . I thought *that* would appeal to your journalistic sense if nothing else would!'

Denver smiled. 'Oh, my journalistic sense is still susceptible enough – and the idea's picturesque, I grant you: asking the man who proved your alibi to establish your guilt.'

'That's it – that's it!' Granice's laugh had a ring of triumph.

'Well, but how about the other chap's testimony – I mean that young doctor: what was his name? Ned Ranney. Don't you remember my testifying that I'd met him at the elevated station, and told him I was on my way to smoke a pipe with you, and his saying: 'All right; you'll find him in. I passed the house two hours ago, and saw his shadow against the blind, as usual.' And the lady with the toothache in the flat across the way: she corroborated his statement, you remember.'

'Yes; I remember.'

'Well, then?'

'Simple enough. Before starting I rigged up a kind of mannequin with old coats and a cushion – something to cast a shadow on the blind. All you fellows were used to seeing my shadow there in the small hours – I counted on that, and knew you'd take any vague outline as mine.'

'Simple enough, as you say. But the woman with the toothache saw the shadow move – you remember she said she saw you sink forward, as if you'd fallen asleep.'

'Yes; and she was right. It *did* move. I suppose some extra-heavy dray must have jolted by the flimsy building – at any rate, something gave my mannequin a jar, and when I came back he had sunk forward, half over the table.'

There was a long silence between the two men. Granice, with a throbbing heart, watched Denver refill his pipe. The editor, at any rate, did not sneer and flout him. After all, journalism gave a deeper insight than the law into the fantastic possibilities of life, prepared one better to allow for the incalculableness of human impulses.

'Well?' Granice faltered out.

Denver stood up with a shrug. 'Look here, man – what's wrong with you? Make a clean breast of it! Nerves gone to smash? I'd like to take you to see a chap I know – an ex-prizefighter – who's a wonder at pulling fellows in your state out of their hole – '

'Oh, oh – ' Granice broke in. He stood up also, and the two men eyed each other. 'You don't believe me, then?'

'This yarn – how can I? There wasn't a flaw in your alibi.'

'But haven't I filled it full of them now?'

Denver shook his head. 'I might think so if I hadn't happened to know that you *wanted* to. There's the hitch, don't you see?'

Granice groaned. 'No, I didn't. You mean my wanting to be found guilty – ?'

'Of course! If somebody else had accused you, the story might have been worth looking into. As it is, a child could have invented it. It doesn't do much credit to your ingenuity.'

Granice turned sullenly toward the door. What was the use of arguing? But on the threshold a sudden impulse drew him back. 'Look here, Denver – I dare say you're right. But will you do just one thing to prove it? Put my statement in the *Investigator*, just as I've made it. Ridicule it as much you like. Only give the other fellows a chance at it – men who don't know anything about me. Set them talking and looking about. I don't care a damn whether *you* believe me – what I want is to convince the Grand Jury! I ought'nt to have come to a man who knows me – your cursed incredulity is infectious. I don't put my case well, because I know in advance it's discredited, and I almost end by not believing it myself. That's why I can't convince *you*. It's a vicious circle.' He laid a hand on Denver's arm. Send a stenographer, and put my statement in the paper.'

But Denver did not warm to the idea. 'My dear fellow, you seem to forget that all the evidence was pretty thoroughly sifted at the time, every possible clue followed up. The public would have been ready enough then to believe that you murdered old Lenman – you or anybody else. All they wanted was a murderer – the most improbable would have served. But your alibi was too confoundedly complete. And nothing you've told me has shaken it.' Denver laid his cool hand over the other's burning fingers.

'Look here, old fellow, go home and work up a better case – then come in and submit it to the *Investigator*.'

• IV •

THE perspiration was rolling off Granice's forehead. Every few minutes he had to draw out his handkerchief and wipe the moisture from his face.

For an hour and a half he had been talking steadily, putting his case to the District Attorney. Luckily he had a speaking acquaintance with Allonby, and had obtained, without much difficulty, a private audience on the very day after his talk with Robert Denver. In the interval between he had hurried home, got out of his evening clothes, and gone forth again at once into the dreary dawn. His fear of Ascham and the alienist made it impossible for him to remain in his rooms. And it seemed to him that the only way of averting that hideous peril was to establish, in some sane impartial mind, the proof of his guilt. Even if he had not been so incurably sick of life, the electric chair seemed now the only alternative to the strait-jacket.

As he paused to wipe his forehead he saw the District Attorney glance at his watch. The gesture was significant, and Granice lifted an appealing hand. 'I don't expect you to believe me now – but can't you put me under arrest, and have the thing looked into?'

Allonby smiled faintly under his heavy grayish mustache. He had a ruddy face, full and jovial, in which his keen professional eyes seemed to keep watch over impulses not strictly professional.

'Well, I don't know that we need lock you up just yet. But of course I'm bound to look into your statement – '

Granice rose with an exquisite sense of relief. Surely Allonby wouldn't have said that if he hadn't believed him!

'That's all right. Then I needn't detain you. I can be found at any time at my apartment.' He gave the address.

The District Attorney smiled again, more openly. 'What do you say to leaving it for an hour or two this evening? I'm giving a little supper at Rector's – quiet little affair: just Miss Melrose – I think you know her – and a friend or two; and if you'll join us. . . .'

Granice stumbled out of the office without knowing what reply he had made.

He waited for four days – four days of concentrated horror. During the first twenty-four hours the fear of Ascham's alienist dogged him; and as that subsided, it was replaced by the growing conviction that his avowal had made no impression on the District Attorney. Evidently, if he had been going to look into the case, Allonby would have been heard from before now. . . . And that mocking invitation to supper showed clearly enough how little the story had impressed him!

Granice was overcome by the futility of any further attempt to inculpate himself. He was chained to life – a 'prisoner of consciousness.' Where was it he had read the phrase? Well, he was learning what it meant. In the long night hours, when his brain seemed ablaze, he was visited by a sense of his fixed identity, of his irreducible, inexpugnable *selfness,* keener, more insidious, more unescapable, than any sensation he had ever known. He had not guessed that the mind was capable of such intricacies of self-realization, of penetrating so deep into its own dark windings. Often he woke from his brief snatches of sleep with the feeling that something material was clinging to him, was on his hands and face, and in his throat – and as his brain cleared he understood that it was the sense of his own personality that stuck to him like some thick viscous substance.

Then, in the first morning hours, he would rise and look out of his window at the awakening activities of the street – at the street cleaners, the ash cart drivers, and the other dingy workers flitting by through the sallow winter light. Oh, to be one of them – any of them – to take his chance in any of their skins! they were the toilers – the men whose lot was pitied – the victims wept over and ranted about by altruists and economists; and how thankfully he would have taken up the load of any one of them, if only he might have shaken off his own! But, no – the iron circle of consciousness held them too: each one was handcuffed to his own detested ego. Why wish to be any one man rather than another? The only absolute good was not to be. . . . And Flint, coming in to draw his bath, would ask if he preferred his eggs scrambled or poached that morning?

On the fifth day he wrote a long letter to Allonby; and for the succeeding two days he had the occupation of waiting for an answer. He hardly stirred from his rooms in his fear of missing the letter by a moment; but would the District Attorney write, or send a representative: a policeman, a 'secret agent,' or some other mysterious emissary of the law?

On the third morning Flint, stepping softly – as if, confound it! his master were ill – entered the library where Granice sat behind an unread newspaper, and proffered a card on a tray.

Granice read the name – J. B. Hewson – and underneath, in pencil, 'From the District Attorney's office.' He started up with a thumping heart, and signed an assent to the servant.

Mr. Hewson was a sallow nondescript man of about fifty – the kind of man of whom one is sure to see a specimen in any crowd. 'Just the type of the successful detective,' Granice reflected as he shook hands with his visitor.

It was in that character that Mr. Hewson briefly introduced himself. He had been sent by the District Attorney to have 'a quiet talk' with Mr. Granice – to ask him to repeat the statement he had made about the Lenman murder.

His manner was so quiet, so reasonable and receptive, that Granice's self-confidence returned. Here was a sensible man – a man who knew his business – it would be easy enough to make *him* see through that ridiculous alibi! Granice offered Mr. Hewson a cigar, and lighting one himself – to prove his coolness – began again to tell his story.

He was conscious, as he proceeded, of telling it better than ever before. Practice helped, no doubt; and his listener's detached, impartial attitude helped still more. He could see that Hewson, at least, had not decided in advance to disbelieve him, and the sense of being trusted made him more lucid and more consecutive. Yes, this time his words would certainly convince. . . .

• V •

DESPAIRINGLY, Granice gazed up and down the street. Beside him stood a young man with bright prominent eyes, a smooth but not too smoothly-shaven face, and an Irish smile. The young man's nimble glance followed Granice's.

'Sure of the number, are you?' he asked briskly.

'Oh, yes – it was 104.'

'Well, then, the new building has swallowed it up – that's certain.'

He tilted his head back and surveyed the half-finished front of a brick and limestone flat house that reared its flimsy elegance above the adjacent row of tottering tenements and stables.

'Dead sure?' he repeated.

'Yes,' said Granice, discouraged. 'And even if I hadn't been, I know the garage was just opposite Leffler's over there.' He pointed across the street to a tumble-down building with a blotched sign on which the words 'Livery and Boarding' were still faintly discernible.

The young man glanced at the stable. 'Well, that's something – may get a clue there. Leffler's – same name there, anyhow. You remember that name?'

'Yes – distinctly.'

Granice had felt a return of confidence since he had enlisted the interest of the *Explorer's* 'smartest' reporter. If there were moments when he hardly believed his own story, there were others when it seemed impossible that everyone should not believe it; and young Peter McCarren, peering, listening, questioning, jotting down notes, inspired him with new hope. McCarren had fastened on the case at once, 'like a leech,' as he phrased it – jumped at it, thrilled to it, and settled down to 'draw the last drop of fact from it, and not let go till he had.' No one else had treated Granice in that way – even Allonby's detective had not taken a single note. And though a week had elapsed since the visit of that authorized official, nothing had been heard from the District Attorney's office: Allonby had apparently dropped the matter again. But McCarren wasn't going to drop it – not he! He hung on Granice's footsteps. They had spent the greater part of the previous day together, and now they were off again, running down fresh clues.

But at Leffler's they got none, after all. Leffler's was no longer a stable. It was condemned to demolition, and in the respite between sentence and execution it had become a vague place of storage, a hospital for broken-down carriages and carts, presided over by a bleary-eyed old woman who knew nothing of Flood's garage across the way – did not even remember what had stood there before the new flat house began to rise.

'Well – we may run Leffler down somewhere; I've seen harder jobs done,' said McCarren, cheerfully noting down the name.

As they walked back toward Sixth Avenue he added, in a less sanguine tone: 'I'd undertake now to put the thing through if you could only put me on the track of that cyanide.'

Granice's heart sank. Yes – there was the weak spot; he had felt it from the first! But he still hoped to convince McCarren that his case was strong enough without it; and he urged the reporter to come back to his rooms and sum up the facts with him again.

'Sorry, Mr. Granice, but I'm due at the office now. Besides, it'd be no use till I get some fresh stuff to work on. Suppose I call you up tomorrow or next day?'

He plunged into a trolley and left Granice gazing desolately after him.

Two days later he reappeared at the apartment, a shade less jaunty in demeanor.

'Well, Mr. Granice, the stars in their courses are against you, as the bard says. Can't get a trace of Flood, or of Leffler either. And you say you bought the motor through Flood, and sold it through him, too?'

'Yes,' said Granice wearily.

'Who bought it, do you know?'

Granice wrinkled his brows. 'Why, Flood – yes, Flood himself. I sold it back to him three months later.'

'Flood? The devil! And I've ransacked the town for Flood. That kind of business disappears as if the earth had swallowed it.'

Granice, discouraged, kept silence.

'That brings us back to the poison,' McCarren continued, his notebook out. 'Just go over that again, will you?'

And Granice went over it again. It had all been so simple at the time – and he had been so clever in covering up his traces! As soon as he decided on poison he looked about for an acquaintance who manufactured chemicals; and there was Jim Dawes, a Harvard classmate, in the dyeing business – just the man. But at the last moment it occurred to him that suspicion might turn toward so obvious an opportunity, and he decided on a more tortuous course. Another friend, Carrick Venn, a student of medicine whose own ill-health had kept him from the practice of his profession, amused his leisure with experiments in physics, for the execution of which he had set up a simple laboratory. Granice had the habit of dropping in to smoke a cigar with him on Sunday afternoons, and the friends generally sat in Venn's workshop, at the back of the old family house in Stuyvesant Square. Off this workshop was the cupboard of supplies, with its row of deadly bottles. Carrick Venn was an original, a man of restless curious tastes, and his place, on a Sunday, was often full of visitors: a cheerful crowd of journalists, scribblers, painters, experimenters in diverse forms of expression. Coming and going among so many, it was easy enough to pass unperceived; and one afternoon Granice, arriving before Venn had returned home, found himself alone in the workshop, and quickly slipping into the cupboard, transferred the drug to this pocket.

But that had happened ten years ago; and Venn, poor fellow, was long since dead of his dragging ailment. His old father was dead, too, the house in Stuyvesant Square had been turned into a boardinghouse, and the shifting life of New York had passed its sponge over every trace of their history. Even the optimistic McCarren seemed to acknowledge the hopelessness of seeking for proof in that direction.

'And there's the third door slammed in our faces.' He shut his notebook, and throwing back his head, rested his bright inquisitive eyes on Granice's anxious face.

'Look here, Mr. Granice – you see the weak spot, don't you?'

The other made a despairing motion. 'I see so many!'

'Yes: but the one that weakens all the others. Why the deuce do you want this thing known? Why do you want to put your head into the noose?'

Granice looked at him hopelessly, trying to take the measure of his quick light irreverent mind. No one so full of cheerful animal life would believe in the craving for death as a sufficient motive; and Granice racked his brain for one more convincing. But suddenly he saw the reporter's face soften, and melt to an artless sentimentalism.

Mr. Granice – has the memory of this thing always haunted you?'

Granice stared a moment, and then leapt at the opening. 'That's it – the memory of it . . . always. . . .'

McCarren nodded vehemently. 'Dogged your steps, eh? Wouldn't let you sleep? The time came when you *had* to make a clean breast of it?'

'I had to. Can't you understand?'

The reporter struck his fist on the table. 'God, sir! I don't suppose there's a human being with a drop of warm blood in him that can't picture the deadly horrors of remorse – '

The Celtic imagination was aflame, and Granice mutely thanked him for the word. What neither Ascham nor Denver would accept as a conceivable motive the Irish reporter seized on as the most adequate; and, as he said, once one could find a convincing motive, the difficulties of the case became so many incentives to effort.

'Remorse – *remorse*,' he repeated, rolling the word under his tongue with an accent that was a clue to the psychology of the popular drama; and Granice, perversely, said to himself: 'If I could only have struck that note I should have been running in six theaters at once.'

He saw that from that moment McCarren's professional zeal would be fanned by emotional curiosity; and he profited by the fact to propose that they should dine together, and go on afterward to some music hall or theater. It was becoming necessary to Granice to feel himself an object of preoccupation, to find himself in another mind. He took a kind of gray penumbral pleasure in riveting McCarren's attention on his case; and to feign the grimaces of moral anguish became an engrossing game. He had not entered a theater for months; but he sat out the meaningless performances, sustained by the sense of the reporter's observation.

Between the acts McCarren amused him with anecdotes about the audience: he knew everyone by sight, and could lift the curtain from each physiognomy. Granice listened indulgently. He had lost all interest in his kind, but he knew that he was himself the real center of McCarren's attention, and that every word the latter spoke had an indirect bearing on his own problem.

See that fellow over there – the little dried-up man in the third row, pulling his mustache? *His* memoirs would be worth publishing,' McCarren said suddenly in the last *entr'acte*.

Granice, following his glance, recognized the detective from Allonby's office. For a moment he had the thrilling sense that he was being shadowed.

'Caesar, if *he* could talk – !' McCarren continued. 'Know who he is, of course? Dr. John B. Stell, the biggest alienist in the country – '

Granice, with a start, bent again between the heads in front of him. '*That* man – the fourth from the aisle? You're mistaken. That's not Dr. Stell.'

McCarren laughed. 'Well, I guess I've been in court often enough to know Stell when I see him. He testifies in nearly all the big cases where they plead insanity.'

A shiver ran down Granice's spine, but he repeated obstinately: 'that's not Dr. Stell.'

'Not Stell? Why, man, I *know* him. Look – here he comes. If it isn't Stell, he won't speak to me.'

The little dried-up man was moving slowly up the aisle. As he neared McCarren he made a gesture of recognition.

'How'do, Doctor Stell? Pretty slim show, ain't it?' the reporter cheerfully flung out at him. And Mr. J. B. Hewson, with a nod of assent, passed on.

Granice sat benumbed. He knew that he had not been mistaken – the man who had just passed was the same man whom Allonby had sent to see him: a physician disguised as a detective. Allonby, then, had thought him insane, like the other, had regarded his confession as the maundering of a maniac. The discovery froze Granice with horror – he saw the madhouse gaping for him.

'Isn't there a man a good deal like him – a detective named J. B. Hewson?'

But he knew in advance what McCarren's answer would be. 'Hewson? J. B. Hewson? Never heard of him. But that was J. B. Stell fast enough – I guess he can be trusted to know himself, and you saw he answered to his name.'

• VI •

SOME days passed before Granice could obtain a word with the District Attorney: he began to think that Allonby avoided him.

But when they were face to face Allonby's jovial countenance showed no sign of embarrassment. He waved his visitor to a chair, and leaned across his desk with the encouraging smile of a consulting physician.

Granice broke out at once: 'That detective you sent me the other day – '

Allonby raised a deprecating hand.

'– I know: it was Stell the alienist. Why did you do that, Allonby?'

The other's face did not lose its composure. 'Because I looked up your story first – and there's nothing in it.'

'Nothing in it?' Granice furiously interposed.

'Absolutely nothing. If there is, why the deuce don't you bring me proof? I know you've been talking to Peter Ascham, and to Denver, and to that little ferret McCarren of the *Explorer*. Have any of them been able to make out a case for you? No. Well, what am I to do?'

Granice's lips began to tremble. 'Why did you play me that trick?'

'About Stell? I had to, my dear fellow: it's part of my business, Stell *is* a detective, if you come to that – every doctor is.'

The trembling of Granice's lips increased, communicating itself in a long quiver to his facial muscles. He forced a laugh through his dry throat. 'Well – and what did he detect?'

'In you? Oh, he thinks it's overwork – overwork and too much smoking. If you look in on him someday at his office he'll show you the record of hundreds of cases like yours, and tell you what treatment he recommends. It's one of the commonest forms of hallucination. Have a cigar, all the same.'

'But, Allonby I killed that man!'

The District Attorney's large hand, outstretched on his desk, had an almost imperceptible gesture, and a moment later, as if in answer to the call of an electric bell, a clerk looked in from the outer office.

'Sorry, my dear fellow – lot of people waiting. Drop in on Stell some morning,' Allonby said, shaking hands.

McCarren had to own himself beaten: there was absolutely no flaw in the alibi. And since his duty to his journal obviously forbade his wasting time on insoluble mysteries, he ceased to frequent Granice, who dropped back into a deeper isolation. For a day or two after his visit to Allonby he continued to live in dread of Dr. Stell. Why might not Allonby have deceived him as to the alienist's diagnosis? What if he were really being shadowed, not by a police agent but by a mad doctor? To have the truth out, he determined to call on Dr. Stell.

The physician received him kindly, and reverted without embarrassment to their previous meeting. 'We have to do that occasionally, Mr. Granice; it's one of our methods. And you had given Allonby a fright.'

Granice was silent. He would have liked to reaffirm his guilt, to produce the fresh arguments which had occurred to him since his last talk with the physician; but he feared his eagerness might be taken for a symptom of derangement, and he affected to smile away Dr. Stell's allusion.

'You think, then, it's a case of brain fag – nothing more?'

'Nothing more. I should advise you to knock off tobacco you smoke a good deal, don't you?'

He developed his treatment, recommending massage, gymnastics, travel, or any form of diversion that did not – that in short –

Granice interrupted him impatiently. 'Oh, I loathe all that – and I'm sick of traveling.'

'H'm. Then some larger interest – politics, reform, philanthropy? Something to take you out of yourself.'

'Yes. I understand,' said Granice wearily.

'Above all, don't lose heart. I see hundreds of cases like yours,' the doctor added cheerfully from the threshold.

On the doorstep Granice stood still and laughed. Hundreds of cases like his – the case of a man who had committed a murder, who confessed his guilt, and whom no one would believe! Why, there had never been a case like it in the world. What a good figure Stell would have made in a play: the great alienist who couldn't read a man's mind any better than that!

Granice saw huge comic opportunities in the type.

But as he walked away, his fears dispelled, the sense of listlessness returned on him. For the first time since his avowal to Peter Ascham he found himself without an occupation, and understood that he had been carried through the past weeks only by the necessity of constant action. Now his life had once more become a stagnant backwater, and as he stood on the street corner watching the tides of traffic sweep by, he asked himself desparingly how much longer he could endure to float about in the sluggish circle of his consciousness.

The thought of self-destruction came back to him; but again his flesh recoiled. He yearned for death from other hands, but he could never take it from his own. And, aside from his insuperable physical fear, another motive restrained him. He was possessed by the dogged desire to establish the truth of his story. He refused to be swept aside as an irresponsible dreamer – even if he had to kill himself in the end, he would not do so before proving to society that he had deserved death from it.

He began to write long letters to the papers; but after the first had been published and commented on, public curiosity was quelled by a brief statement from the District Attorney's office, and the rest of his communications remained unprinted. Ascham came to see him, and begged him to travel. Robert Denver dropped in, and tried to joke him, out of his delusion; till Granice, mistrustful of their motives, began to dread the reappearance of Dr. Stell, and set a guard on his lips. But the words he kept back engendered others and still others in his brain. His inner self became a humming factory of arguments, and he spent long hours reciting and writing down elaborate statements, which he constantly retouched and developed. Then his activity began to languish under the lack of an audience, the sense of being buried beneath deepening drifts of indifference. In a passion of resentment he swore that he would prove himself a murderer, even if he had to commit another crime to do it; and for a night or two the thought flamed red on his sleeplessness. But daylight dispelled it. The determining impulse was lacking and he hated to choose his victim promiscuously. . . . So he was thrown back on the struggle to impose the truth of his story. As fast as one channel closed on him he tried to pierce another through the sliding sands of incredulity. But every issue seemed blocked, and the whole human race leagued together to cheat one man of the right to die.

Thus viewed, the situation became so monstrous that he lost his last shred of self-restraint in contemplating it. What if he were really the victim of some mocking experiment, the center of a ring of holiday-makers jeering at a poor creature in its blind dashes against the solid walls of consiousness? But, no – men were not so uniformly cruel: there were flaws in the close surface of their indifference, cracks of weakness and pity here and there. . . .

Granice began to think that his mistake lay in having appealed to persons more or less familiar with his past, and to whom the visible conformities of his life seemed a complete disproof of its one fierce secret deviation. The general tendency was to take for the whole of life the slit seen between the blinders of habit: and in his walk down that narrow vista Granice cut a correct enough figure. To a vision free to follow his whole orbit his story would be more intelligible: it would be easier to convince a chance idler in the street than the trained intelligence hampered by a sense of his antecedents. This idea shot up in him with the tropic luxuriance of each new seed of thought, and he began to walk the streets, and to frequent out-of-the-way chophouses and bars in his search for the impartial stranger to whom he should disclose himself.

At first every face looked encouragement; but at the crucial moment he always held back. So much was at stake, and it was so essential that his first choice be decisive. He dreaded stupidity, timidity, intolerance. The imaginative eye, the furrowed brow, were what he sought. He must reveal himself only to a heart versed in the tortuous motions of the human will; and he began to hate the dull benevolence of the average face. Once or twice, obscurely, allusively, he made a beginning – once sitting down by a man in a basement chophouse, another day approaching a lounger on an east side wharf. But in both cases the premonition of failure checked him on the brink of avowal. His dread of being taken for a man in the clutch of a fixed idea gave him an abnormal keenness in reading the expression of his listeners, and he had provided himself in advance with a series of verbal alternatives, trap doors of evasion from the first dart of ridicule or suspicion.

He passed the greater part of the day in the streets, coming home at irregular hours, dreading the silence and orderliness of his apartment, and the mute scrutiny of Flint. His real life was spent in a world so remote from this familiar setting that he sometimes had the sense of a living metempsychosis, a furtive passage from one identity to another – yet the other as unescapably himself!

One humiliation he was spared: the desire to live never revived in him. Not for a moment was he tempted to a shabby pact with existing conditions. He wanted to die, wanted it with the fixed unwavering desire which alone attains its end. And still the end eluded him! It would not always, of course – he had full faith in the dark star of his destiny. And he could prove it best by repeating his story, persistently and indefatigably, pouring it into indifferent ears, hammering it into dull brains, till at last it kindled a spark, and some one of the careless millions paused, listened, believed. . . .

It was a mild March day, and he had been loitering on the west side docks, looking at faces. He was becoming an expert in physiognomies: his eagerness no longer made rash darts and awkward recoils. He knew now the face he needed, as clearly as if it had come to him in a vision; and not till he found it would he speak. As he walked eastward through the shabby streets he had a premonition that he should find it that morning. Perhaps it was the promise of spring in the air – certainly he felt calmer than for days. . . .

He turned into Washington Square, struck across it obliquely, and walked up University Place. Its heterogeneous passers always attracted him – they were less hurried than in Broadway, less enclosed and classified than in Fifth Avenue. He walked slowly, watching for his face.

At Union Square he had a relapse into discouragement, like a votary who has watched too long for a sign from the altar. Perhaps, after all, he should never find his face. . . . The air was languid, and he felt tired. He walked between the bald grass plots and the twisted trees, making for a seat. Presently he passed a bench on which a girl sat alone, and something as definite as the twitch of a cord caused him to stop before her. He had never dreamed of telling his story to a girl, had hardly looked at the women's faces as they passed. His case was man's work: how could a woman help him? But this girl's face was extraordinary – quiet and wide as an evening sky. It suggested a hundred images of space, distance, mystery, like ships he had seen, as a boy, berthed by a familiar wharf, but with the breath of far seas and strange harbors in their shrouds. . . . Certainly this girl would understand. He went up to her, lifting his hat, observing the forms – wishing her to see at once that he was 'a gentleman.'

'I am a stranger to you,' he began sitting down beside her, 'but your face is so extremely intelligent that I feel . . . I feel it is the face I've waited for . . . looked for everywhere; and I want to tell you – '

The girl's eyes widened: she rose to her feet. She was escaping him!

In his dismay he ran a few steps after her, and caught her by the arm.

'Here – wait – listen! Oh, don't scream, you fool!' he shouted out.

He felt a hand on his own arm; turned and confronted a policeman. Instantly he understood that he was being arrested, and something hard within him was loosened and ran to tears.

'Ah, you know – you *know* I'm guilty?'

He was conscious that a crowd was forming, and that the girl had disappeared. But what did he care about the girl? It was the policeman who had understood him. He turned and followed, the crowd at his heels. . . .

• VII •

In the charming place in which he found himself there were so many sympathetic faces that he felt more than ever convinced of the certainty of making himself heard.

It was a bad blow, at first, to find that he had not been arrested for murder; but Ascham, who had come at once, convinced him that he needed rest, and the time to 'review' his statements; it appeared that reiteration had made them a little confused and contradictory. To this end he had readily acquiesced in his removal to a large quiet establishment, with an open space and trees about it, where he had found a number of intelligent companions, some, like himself, engaged in preparing or reviewing statements of their cases, and others ready to lend an attentive ear to his own recital.

For a time he was content to let himself go on the current of this new existence; but although his auditors gave him for the most part an encouraging attention, which, in some, went the length of really brilliant and helpful suggestion, he gradually felt a recurrence of his doubts. Either his hearers were not sincere, or else they had less power to help him than they boasted. His endless conferences resulted in nothing, and the long rest produced an increased mental lucidity which made inaction more and more unbearable. At length he discovered that on certain days visitors from the outer world were admitted to his retreat; and he wrote out long and logically constructed relations of his crime, and furtively slipped them into the hands of these messengers of hope.

This gave him a fresh lease of patience, and he now lived only to watch for the visitors' days, and scan the faces that swept by him like stars seen and lost in the rifts of a hurrying sky.

Mostly, these faces were strange and less intelligent than those of his companions. But they represented his last means of access to the world, a kind of subterranean channel on which he could set his 'statements' afloat, like paper boats which a mysterious current might sweep out into the open seas of life.

One day, however, his attention was arrested by a familiar contour, a pair of bright prominent eyes, and a chin insufficiently shaved. He sprang up and stood in the path of Peter McCarren.

The journalist looked at him doubtfully, then held out his hand with a startled '*Why* – ?'

'You didn't know me? I'm so changed?' Granice faltered, feeling the rebound of the other's wonder.

'Why, no; but you're looking quieter – smoothed out,' McCarren smiled.

'Yes: that's what I'm here for – to rest. And I've taken the opportunity to write out a clearer statement – '

Granice's hand shook so that he could hardly draw the paper from his pocket. As he did so he noticed that the reporter was accompanied by a tall man with compassionate eyes. It came to Granice in a wild thrill of conviction that this was the face he had waited for. . . .

'Perhaps your friend – he *is* your friend? – would glance over it – or I could put the case in a few words if you have time?' Granice's voice shook like his hand. If this chance escaped him he felt that his last hope was gone. McCarren and the stranger looked at each other, and the reporter glanced at his watch.

'I'm sorry we can't stay and talk it over now, Mr. Granice; but my friend has an engagement, and we're rather pressed – '

Granice continued to proffer the paper. 'I'm sorry – I think I could have explained. But you'll take this, at any rate?'

The stranger looked at him gently. 'Certainly – I'll take it.' He had his hand out. 'Good-bye.'

'Good-bye,' Granice echoed.

He stood watching the two men move away from him through the long hall; and as he watched them a tear ran down his face. But as soon as they were out of sight he turned and walked toward his room, beginning to hope again, already planning a new statement. . . .

Outside the building the two men stood still, and the journalist's companion looked up curiously at the long rows of barred windows.

'So that was Granice?'

'Yes – that was Granice, poor devil,' said McCarren.

'Strange case! I suppose there's never been one just like it? He's still absolutely convinced that he committed that murder?'

'Absolutely. Yes.'

The stranger reflected. 'And there was no conceivable ground for the idea? No one could make out how it started? A quiet conventional sort of fellow like that – where do you suppose he got such a delusion? Did you ever get the least clue to it?'

McCarren stood still, his hands in his pockets, his head cocked up in contemplation of the windows. Then he turned his bright hard gaze on his companion.

'That was the queer part of it. I've never spoken of it – but I *did* get a clue.'

'By Jove! That's interesting. What was it?'

McCarren formed his red lips into a whistle. 'Why – that it wasn't a delusion.'

'He produced his effect – the other turned a startled glance on him.

'He murdered the man all right. I tumbled on the truth by the merest accident, when I'd pretty nearly chucked the whole job.'

'He murdered him – murdered his cousin?'

'Sure as you live. Only don't split on me. It's about the queerest business I ever ran into. . . . *Do about it*? Why, what was I to do? I couldn't hang the poor devil, could I? Lord, but I was glad when they collared him, and had him stowed away safe in there!'

The tall man listened with a grave face, grasping Granice's statement in his hand.

'Here – take this; it makes me sick,' he said abruptly, thrusting the paper at the reporter; and the two men turned and walked in silence to the gates.

The Temperate Zone

'TRAVELING, SIR,' a curt parlormaid announced from Mrs. Donald Paul's threshold in Kensington; adding, as young Willis French's glance slipped over her shoulder down a narrow and somewhat conventional perspective of white paneling and black prints: 'If there's any message you'd like to write – '

He did not know if there were or not; but he instantly saw that his hesitation would hold the house door open a minute longer, and thus give him more time to stamp on his memory the details of the cramped London hall, beyond which there seemed no present hope of penetrating.

'Could you tell me where?' he asked, in a tone implying that the question of his having something to write might be determined by the nature of the answer.

The parlormaid scrutinized him more carefully. 'Not exactly, sir: Mr. and Mrs. Paul are away motoring, and I believe they're to cross over to the continent in a day or two.' She seemed to have gathered confidence from another look at him, and he was glad he had waited to unpack his town clothes, instead of rushing, as he had first thought of doing, straight from the steamer train to the house. 'If it's for something important, I could give you the address,' she finally condescended, apparently reassured by her inspection.

'It *is* important,' said the young man almost solemnly; and she handed him a sheet of gold-monogrammed note paper across which was tumbled, in large loose characters: 'Hotel Nouveau Luxe, Paris.'

The unexpectedness of the address left Willis French staring. There was nothing to excite surprise in the fact of the Donald

Pauls having gone to Paris; or even in their having gone there in their motor; but that they should be lodged at the Nouveau Luxe seemed to sap the very base of probability.

'Are you *sure* they're staying there?'

To the parlormaid, at this point, it evidently began to look as if, in spite of his reassuring clothes, the caller might have designs on the umbrellas.

'I couldn't say, sir. It's the address, sir,' she returned, adroitly taking her precautions about the door.

These were not lost on the visitor, who, both to tranquilize her and to gain time, turned back toward the quiet Kensington street and stood gazing doubtfully up and down its uneventful length.

All things considered, he had no cause to regret the turn the affair had taken; the only regret he allowed himself was that of not being able instantly to cross the threshold hallowed by his young enthusiasm. But even that privilege might soon be his; and meanwhile he was to have the unforeseen good luck of following Mrs. Donald Paul to Paris. His business in coming to Europe had been simply and solely to see the Donald Pauls; and had they been in London he would have been obliged, their conference over, to return at once to New York, whence he had been sent, at his publisher's expense, to obtain from Mrs. Paul certain details necessary for the completion of his book: 'The Art of Horace Fingall.' And now, by a turn of what he fondly called his luck – as if no one else's had ever been quite as rare – he found his vacation prolonged, and his prospect of enjoyment increased, by the failure to meet the lady in London.

Willis French had more than once had occasion to remark that he owed some of his luckiest moments to his failures. He had tried his hand at several of the arts, only to find, in each case, the same impassable gulf between vision and execution; but his ill success, which he always promptly recognized, had left him leisure to note and enjoy all the incidental compensations of the attempt. And how great some of these compensations were, he had never more keenly felt than on the day when two of the greatest came back to him merged in one glorious opportunity.

It was probable, for example, that if he had drawn a directer profit from his months of study in a certain famous Parisian *atelier*, his labors would have left him less time in which to observe and study Horace Fingall, on the days when the great painter made his round among the students; just as, if he had written better poetry, Mrs. Morland, with whom his old friend Lady Brankhurst had once contrived to have him spend a Sunday in the country, might have given him, during their long confidential talk, less of her sweet compassion and her bracing wisdom. Both Horace Fingall and Emily Morland had, professionally speaking, discouraged their young disciple, the one had said 'don't write' as decidedly as the other had said 'don't paint'; but both had let him feel that interesting failures may be worth more in the end than dull successes, and that there is range enough for the artistic sensibilities outside the region of production. The fact of the young man's taking their criticism without flinching (as he himself had been thankfully aware of doing) no doubt increased their liking, and thus let him farther into their intimacy. The insight into two such natures seemed, even at the moment, to outweigh any personal success within his reach; and as time removed him from the experience he had less and less occasion to question the completeness of the compensation.

Since then, as it happened, his two great initiators had died within a few months of each other, Emily Morland prematurely, and at the moment when her exquisite art was gaining new warmth from the personal happiness at last opening to her, and Horace Fingall in his late golden prime, when his genius also seemed to be winged for new flights. Except for the nearness of the two death dates, there was nothing to bring together in the public mind the figures of the painter and the poet, and Willis French's two experiences remained associated in his thoughts only because they had been the greatest revelations of temperament he had ever known. No one but Emily Morland had ever renewed in him that sense of being in the presence of greatness that he had first felt on meeting Horace Fingall. He had often wondered if the only two beings to whom he owed this emotion had ever known each other, and he had concluded that, even in this day of universal meetings, it was unlikely. Fingall, after leaving the United States for Paris toward his fortieth year, had never absented himself from France except on short occasional visits to his native country; and Mrs. Morland, when she at last broke away from her depressing isolation in a Staffordhire parsonage, and set up her own house in London, had been drawn from there only by one or two holiday journeys in Italy. Nothing, moreover, could have been more unlike than the mental quality and the general attitude of the two artists. The only point of resemblance between them lay in the effect they produced of the divine emanation of genius. Willis French's speculations as to the result of a meeting between them had always resulted in the belief that they would not have got on. The two emanations would have neutralized each other, and he suspected that both natures lacked the complementary qualities which might have bridged the gulf between them. And now chance had after all linked their names before posterity, through the fact that the widow of the one had married the man who had been betrothed to the other! . . .

French's brief glimpses of Fingall and Mrs. Morland had left in him an intense curiosity to know something more of their personal history, and when his publisher had suggested his writing a book on the painter his first thought had been that here was an occasion to obtain the desired light, and to obtain it, at one stroke, through the woman who had been the preponderating influence in Fingall's art, and the man for whom Emily Morland had written her greatest poems.

That Donald Paul should have met and married the widow of Horace Fingall was one of the facts on which young French's imagination had always most appreciatively dwelt. It was strange indeed that these two custodians of great memories, for both of whom any other marriage would have been a derogation, should have found the one way of remaining on the heights; and it was almost equally strange that their inspiration should turn out to be Willis French's opportunity!

At the very outset, the wonder of it was brought home to him by his having to ask for Mrs. Paul at what had once been Mrs. Morland's house. Mrs. Morland had of course bequeathed the house to Donald Paul; and equally of course it was there that, on his marriage to Mrs. Fingall, Donald Paul had taken his wife. If that wife had been any other, the thought would have been one to shrink from; but to French's mind no threshold was too sacred for the feet of Horace Fingall's widow.

Musing on these things as he glanced up and down the quiet street, the young man, with his sharp professional instinct for missing no chance that delay might cancel, wondered how, before turning from the door, he might get a glimpse of the house which was still – which, in spite of everything, would always be – Emily Morland's.

'You were not thinking of looking at the house, sir?'

French turned back with a start of joy. 'Why, yes – I was!' he said instantly.

The parlormaid opened the door a little wider. 'Of course, properly speaking, you should have a card from the agent; but Mrs. Paul *did* say, if anyone was *very* anxious – May I ask, sir, if you know Mrs. Paul?'

The young man lowered his voice reverentially to answer: 'No; but I knew Mrs. Morland.'

The parlormaid looked as if he had misunderstood her question. After a moment's thought she replied: 'I don't think I recall the name.'

They gazed at each other across incalculable distances, and Willis French found no reply. 'What on earth can she suppose I want to see the house for?' he could only wonder.

Her next question told him. 'If it's very urgent, sir – ' another glance at the cut of his coat seemed to strengthen her, and she moved back far enough to let him get a foot across the threshold. 'Would it be to hire or to buy?'

Again they stared at each other till French saw his own wonder reflected in the servant's doubtful face; then the truth came to him in a rush. The house was not being shown to him because it had once been Emily Morland's and he had been recognized as a pilgrim to the shrine of genius, but because it was Mrs. Donald Paul's and he had been taken for a possible purchaser!

All his disenchantment rose to his lips; but it was checked there by the leap of prudence. He saw that if he showed his wonder he might lose his chance.

'Oh, it would be to buy!' he said; for, though the mere thought of hiring was desecration, few things would have seemed more possible to him, had his fortune been on the scale of his enthusiasm, than to become the permanent custodian of the house.

The feeling threw such conviction into his words that the parlormaid yielded another step.

'The drawing room in this way,' she said as he bared his head.

• II •

It was odd how, as he paced up and down the Embankment late that evening, musing over the vision vouchsafed him, one detail continued to detach itself with discordant sharpness from the harmonious blur.

The parlormaid who had never heard of Mrs. Morland, and who consequently could not know that the house had ever been hers, had naturally enough explained it to him in terms of its new owners' habits. French's imagination had so promptly anticipated this that he had, almost without a shock, heard Mrs. Morland's library described as 'the gentlemans' study,' and marked how an upstairs sitting room with faded Venetian furniture and rows of old books in golden-brown calf had been turned, by the intrusion of a large pink toilet table, into 'the lady's dressing room, sir.' It did not offend him that the dwelling should be used as suited the convenience of the persons who lived in it; he was never for expecting life to stop, and the Historic House which has been turned into a show had always seemed to him as dead as a blown egg. He had small patience with the kind of reverence which treats fine things as if their fineness made them useless. Nothing, he thought, was too fine for natural uses, nothing in life too good for life, he liked the absent and unknown Donald Pauls the better for living naturally in this house which had come to them naturally, and not shrinking into the mere keepers of a shrine. But he had winced at just one thing: at seeing there, on the writing table which had once been Emily Morland's, and must still, he quickly noted, be much as she had left it – at seeing there, among pens and pencils and ink-stained paper cutters, halfway between a lacquer cup full of elastic bands and a blotting book with her initials on it, one solitary object of irrelevant newness: an immense expensively framed photograph of Fingall's picture of his wife.

The portrait – the famous first one, now in the Luxembourg – was so beautiful, and so expressive of what lovers of Fingall's art most loved in it, that Willis French was grieved to see it so indelicately and almost insolently out of place. If ever a thing of beauty can give offence, Mrs. Fingall's portrait on Emily Morland's writing table gave offence. Its presence there shook down all manner of French's faiths. There was something shockingly crude in the way it made the woman in possession triumph over the woman who was gone.

It would have been different, he felt at once, if Mrs. Morland had lived long enough to marry the man she loved; then the dead and the living woman would have faced each other on an equality. But Mrs. Morland, to secure her two brief years of happiness, had had to defy conventions and endure affronts. When, breaking away from the unhappy conditions of her married life, she had at last won London and freedom, it was only to learn that the Reverend Ambrose Morland, informed of her desire to remarry, and of his indisputable right to divorce her, found himself, on religious grounds, unable to set her free. From this situation she sought no sensational escape. Perhaps because the man she loved was younger than herself, she chose to make no open claim on him, to place no lien on his future; she simply let it be known to their few nearest friends that he and she belonged to each other as completely as a man and woman of active minds and complex interests can ever belong to each other when such life as they live together must be lived in secret. To a woman like Mrs. Morland the situation could not be other than difficult and unsatisfying. If her personal distinction saved her from social slights it could not save her from social subserviences. Never once, in the short course of her love history, had she been able to declare her happiness openly, or to let it reveal itself in her conduct; and it seemed, as one considered her case, small solace to remember that some of her most moving verse was the expression of that very privation.

At last her husband's death had freed her, and her coming marriage to Donald Paul been announced; but her own health had already failed, and a few weeks later she too was dead, and Donald Paul lost in the crowd about her grave, behind the Morland relations who, rather generously as people thought, came up from Staffordshire for the funeral of the woman who had brought scandal and glory to their name.

So, tragically and inarticulately, Emily Morland's life had gone out; and now, in the house where she and her lover had spent their short secret hours, on the very table at which she had sat and imperishably written down her love, he had put the portrait of the other woman, her successor; the woman to whom had been given the one great thing she had lacked. . . .

Well, that was life too, French supposed: the ceaseless ruthless turning of the wheel! If only – yes, here was where the real pang lay – if only the supplanting face had not been so different from the face supplanted! Standing there before Mrs. Fingall's image, how could he not recall his first sight of Emily Morland, how not feel again the sudden drop of all his expectations when the one woman he had not noticed on entering Lady Brankhurst's drawing room, the sallow woman with dull hair and a dowdy dress, had turned out to be his immortal? Afterward, of course, when she began to talk, and he was let into the deep world of her eyes, her face became as satisfying as some grave early sculpture which, the imagination once touched by it, makes more finished graces trivial. But there remained the fact that she was what it called plain, and that her successor was beautiful; and it hurt him to see that perfect face, so all-expressive and all-satisfying, in the very spot where Emily Morland, to make her beauty visible, had had to clothe it in poetry. What would she not have given, French wondered, just once to let her face speak for her instead?

The sense of injustice was so strong in him that when he returned to his hotel he went at once to his portmanteau and, pulling out Mrs. Morland's last volume, sat down to reread the famous love sonnets. It was as if he wanted to make up to her for the slight of which he had been the unwilling witness. . . .

The next day, when he set out for France, his mood had changed. After all, Mrs. Morland had had her compensations. She had been inspired, which, on the whole, is more worth-while than to inspire. And then his own adventure was almost in his grasp; and he was at the age when each moment seems to stretch out to the horizon.

The day was fine, and as he sat on the deck of the steamer watching the white cliffs fade, the thought of Mrs. Morland was displaced by the vision of her successor. He recalled the day when Mrs. Fingall had first looked out at him from her husband's famous portrait of her, so frail, so pale under the gloom and glory of her hair, and he had been told how the sight of her had suddenly drawn the painter's genius from its long eclipse. Fingall had found her among the art students of one of the Parisian studios which he fitfully inspected, had rescued her from financial difficulties and married her within a few weeks of their meeting: French had

had the tale from Lady Brankhurst, who was an encyclopedia of illustrious biographies.

'Poor little Bessy Reck – a little American waif sent out from some prairie burrow to "learn art" – that was literally how she expressed it! She hadn't a relation of her own, I believe: the people of the place she came from had taken pity on her and scraped together enough money for her passage and for two years of the Latin Quarter. After that she was to live on the sale of her pictures! And suddenly she met Fingall, and found out what she was really made for.'

So far Lady Brankhurst had been satisfying, as she always was when she trod on solid fact. But she never knew anything about her friends except what had happened to them, and when questioned as to what Mrs. Fingall was really like she became vague and slightly irritable.

'Oh, well, he transformed her, of course: for one thing he made her do her hair differently. Imagine; she used to puff it out over her forehead! And when we went to the studio she was always dressed in the most marvellous Eastern things. Fingall drank cups and cups of Turkish coffee, and she learned to make it herself – it *is* better, of course, but so messy to make! The studio was full of Siamese cats. It was somewhere over near the Luxembourg – very picturesque, but one *did* smell the drains. I used always to take my salts with me; and the stairs were pitch black.' That was all.

But from her very omissions French had constructed the vision of something too fine and imponderable not to escape Lady Brankhurst, and had rejoiced in the thought that, of what must have been the most complete of blisses, hardly anything was exposed to crude comment but the stairs which led to it.

Of Donald Paul he had been able to learn even less, though Lady Brankhurst had so many more facts to give. Donald Paul's life lay open for everybody in London to read. He had been first a 'dear boy,' with a large and eminently respectable family connection, and then a not especially rising young barrister, who occupied his briefless leisure by occasionally writing things for the reviews. He had written an article about Mrs. Morland, and when, soon afterward, he happened to meet her, he had suddenly realized that he hadn't understood her poetry in the least, and had told her so and written another article – under her guidance, the malicious whispered, and boundlessly enthusiastic, of course;

people said it was that which had made her fall in love with him. But Lady Brankhurst thought it was more likely to have been his looks – with which French, on general principles, was inclined to agree. 'What sort of looks?' he asked. 'Oh, like an old picture, you know'; and at that shadowy stage of development the image of Donald Paul had hung. French, in spite of an extensive search, had not even been able to find out where the fateful articles on Mrs. Morland's verse had been published; and light on that point was one of the many lesser results he now hoped for.

Meanwhile, settled in his chair on deck, he was so busy elaborating his own picture of the couple he was hastening to that he hardly noticed the slim figure of traveler with a sallow keen face and small dark beard who hovered near, as if for recognition.

'André Jolyesse – you don't remember me?' the gentleman at length reminded him in beautifully correct English; and French woke to the fact that it was of course Jolyesse, the eminent international portrait painter, whose expensively gloved hand he was shaking.

'We crossed together on the "Gothic" the last time I went to the States,' Monsieur Jolyesse reminded him, 'and you were so amiable as to introduce me to several charming persons, who added greatly to the enjoyment of my visit.'

'Of course, of course,' French assented; and seeing that the painter was in need of a listener, the young man reluctantly lifted his rugs from the next chair.

It was because Jolyesse, on the steamer, had been so shamelessly in quest of an article that French, to escape his importunities, had passed him on to the charming persons referred to; and if he again hung about in this way, and recalled himself, it was doubtless for a similarly shameless purpose. But French was more than ever steeled against the celebrating of such art as that of Jolyesse; and, to cut off a possible renewal of the request, he managed – in answer to a question as to what he was doing with himself – to mention casually that he had abandoned art criticism for the writing of books.

The portrait painter was far too polite to let his attention visibly drop at this announcement; too polite, even, not to ask with a show of interest if he might know the subject of the work. Mr. French was at the moment engaged on.

'Horace Fingall – *bigre*!' he murmured, as if the aridity of the task impressed him while it provoked his pity. 'Fingall – Fingall – '

he repeated, his incredulous face smilingly turned to French, while he drew a cigarette from a gold case as flat as an envelope.

French gave back the smile. It delighted him, it gave him a new sense of the importance of his task, to know that Jolyesse, in spite of Fingall's posthumous leap to fame, still took that view of him. And then, with a start of wonder, the young man remembered that the two men must have known each other, that they must have had at least casual encounters in the crowded promiscuous life of the painters' Paris. The possibility was so rich in humor that he was moved to question his companion.

'You must have come across Fingall now and then, I suppose?'

Monsieur Jolyesse shrugged his shoulders. 'Not for years. He was a savage – he had no sense of solidarity. And envious – !' The artist waved the ringed hand that held his cigarette. 'Could one help it if one sold more pictures than he did? But it was gall and wormwood to him, poor devil. Of course he sells *now* – tremendously high, I believe. But that's what happens: when an unsuccessful man dies, the dealers seize on him and make him a factitious reputation. Only it doesn't last. You'd better make haste to finish your book; that sort of celebrity collapses like a soap bubble. Forgive me,' he added, with a touch of studied compunction, 'for speaking in this way of your compatriot. Fingall had aptitudes – immense, no doubt – but no technique, and no sense of beauty; none whatever.'

French, rejoicing, let the commentary flow on; he even felt the need to stimulate its flow.

'But how about his portrait of his wife – you must know it?'

Jolyesse flung away his cigarette to lift his hands in protest. 'That consumptive witch in the Luxembourg? *Ah, mais non*! She looks like a vegetarian vampire. *Voyez vous, si l'on a beaucoup aimé les femmes* – ' the painter's smile was evidently intended to justify his championship of female loveliness. He puffed away the subject with his cigarette smoke, and turned to glance down the deck. 'There – by Jove, that's what I call a handsome woman! Over there, with the sable cloak and the brand new traveling bags. A honeymoon outfit, *hein*? If your poor Fingall had had the luck to do *that* kind – ! I'd like the chance myself.'

French, following his glance, saw that it rested on a tall and extremely elegant young woman who was just settling herself in a deck chair with the assistance of an attentive maid and a hovering steward. A young man, of equal height and almost superior elegance, strolled up to tuck a rug over her shining boot tips before seating himself at her side; and French had to own that, at least as a moment's ornament, the lady was worth all the trouble spent on her. She seemed, in truth, framed by nature to bloom from one of Monsieur Jolyesse's canvases, so completely did she embody the kind of beauty it was his mission to immortalize. It was annoying that eyes like forest pools and a mouth like a tropical flower should so fit into that particular type; but then the object of Monsieur Jolyesse's admiration had the air of wearing her features, like her clothes, simply because they were the latest fashion, and not because they were a part of her being. Her inner state was probably a much less complicated affair than her lovely exterior: it was a state, French guessed, of easy apathetic good humor, galvanised by the occasional need of a cigarette, and by a gentle enjoyment of her companion's conversation. French had wondered, since his childhood, what the Olympian lovers in fashion plates found to say to each other. Now he knew. They said (he strolled nearer to the couple to catch it): 'Did you wire about reserving a compartment?' and 'I haven't seen my golf clubs since we came on board' and 'I do hope Marshall's brought enough of that new stuff for my face' – and lastly, after a dreamy pause: 'I *know* Gwen gave me a book to read when we started, but I can't think where on earth I've put it.'

It was odd too that, handsome and young as they still were (both well on the warm side of forty), this striking couple were curiously undefinably old-fashioned – in just the same way as Jolyesse's art. They belonged, for all their up-to-date attire, to a period before the triumph of the slack and the slouching: it was as if their elegance had pined too long in the bud, and its related flowering had a tinge of staleness.

French mused on these things while he listened to Jolyesse's guesses as to the class and nationality of the couple, and finally, in answer to the insistent question: 'But where do you think they come from?' replied a little impatiently: 'Oh, from the rue de la Paix, of course!' He was tired of the subject, and of his companion, and wanted to get back to his thoughts of Horace Fingall.

'Ah, I hope so – then I may run across them yet!' Jolyesse, as he gathered up his bags, shot a last glance at the beauty. 'I'll haunt the dressmakers till I find her – she looks as if she spent most of her time with them. And the young man evidently refuses her nothing. You'll see, I'll have her in the next Salon!' He turned back to add: 'She might be a compatriot of yours. Women who look as if they came out of the depths of history usually turn out to be from your newest Territory. If you run across her, do say a good word for me. My full-lengths are fifty thousand francs now – to Americans.'

• III •

ALL that first evening in Paris the vision of his book grew and grew in French's mind. Much as he loved the great city, nothing it could give him was comparable, at that particular hour, to the rapture of his complete withdrawal from it into the sanctuary of his own thoughts. The very next day he was to see Horace Fingall's widow, and perhaps to put his finger on the clue to the labyrinth: that mysterious tormenting question of the relation between the creative artist's personal experience and its ideal expression. He was to try to guess how much of Mrs. Fingall, beside her features, had passed into her husband's painting; and merely to ponder on that opportunity was to plunge himself into the heart of his subject. Fingall's art had at last received recognition, genuine from the few, but mainly, no doubt, inspired by the motives to which Jolyesse had sneeringly alluded; and, intolerable as it was to French to think that snobbishness and cupidity were the chief elements in the general acclamation of his idol, he could not forget that he owed to these baser ingredients the chance to utter his own panegyric. It was because the vulgar herd at last wanted to know what to say, when it heard Fingall mentioned, that Willis French was to be allowed to tell them; such was the base rubble the Temple of Fame was built of! Yes, but future generations would enrich its face with lasting marbles; and it was to be French's privilege to put the first slab in place.

The young man, thus brooding, lost himself in the alluring and perplexing alternatives of his plan. The particular way of dealing with a man's art depended, of course, so much on its relation to his private life, and on the chance of a real insight into that. Fingall's life had been obdurately closed and aloof; would it be his widow's wish that it should remain so? Or would she understand that any serious attempt to analyze so complex and individual an art must be preceded by a reverent scrutiny of the artist's personality? Would she, above all, understand how reverent French's scrutiny would be, and consent, for the sake of her husband's glory, to guide and enlighten it? Her attitude, of course, as he was nervously aware, would greatly depend on his: on his finding the right words and the convincing tone. He could almost have prayed for guidance, for some supernatural light on what to say to her! It was late that night when, turning from his open window above the throbbing city, he murmured to himself: 'I wonder what on earth we shall begin by saying to each other?'

Her sitting room at the Nouveau Luxe was empty when he was shown into it the next day, though a friendly note had assured him that she would be in by five. But he was not sorry she was late, for the room had its secrets to reveal. The most conspicuous of these was a large photograph of a handsome young man, in a frame which French instantly recognized as the mate of the one he had noticed on Mrs. Morland's writing table. Well – it was natural, and rather charming, that the happy couple should choose the same frame for each other's portraits, and there was nothing offensive to Fingall's memory in the fact of Donald Paul's picture being the most prominent object in his wife's drawing room.

Only – if this were indeed Donald Paul, where had French seen him already? He was still questioning the lines of the pleasant oft-repeated face when his answer entered the room in the shape of a splendidly draped and feathered lady.

'I'm sorry! The dressmakers are *such* beasts – they've been sticking pins in me ever since two o'clock.' She held out her hand with a click of bracelets slipping down to the slim wrist. 'Donald! Do come – it's Mr. French,' she called back over her shoulder; and the gentleman of the photograph came in after her.

The three stood looking at each other for an interval deeply momentous to French, obviously less stirring to his hosts; then Donald Paul said, in a fresh voice a good deal younger than his ingenuous middle-aged face: 'We've met somewhere before, surely. Wasn't it the other day at Brighton – at the Metropole?'

His wife looked at him and smiled, wrinkling her perfect brows a little in the effort to help his memory. 'We go to so many hotels! *I* think it was at the Regina at Harrogate.' She appealed to their visitor for corroboration.

'Wasn't it simply yesterday, on the Channel?' French suggested, the words buzzing a little in his own ears; and Mrs. Paul instantly remembered.

'Of course! How stupid of me!' Her random sweetness grew more concentrated. 'You were talking to a dark man with a beard – André Jolyesse, wasn't it? I *told* my husband it was Jolyesse. How awfully interesting that you should know him! Do sit down and let me give you some tea while you tell us all about him.'

French, as he took the cup from her hand, remembered that, a few hours earlier, he had been wondering what he and she would first say to each other.

It was dark when he walked away from the blazing front of the Nouveau Luxe. Mrs. Donald Paul had given him two generous hours, and had filled them with talk of her first husband; yet as French turned from the hotel he had the feeling that what he brought away with him had hardly added a grain to his previous knowledge of Horace Fingall. It was perhaps because he was still too blankly bewildered – or because he had not yet found the link between what had been and what was – that he had been able to sift only so infinitesimal a residue out of Mrs. Paul's abundance. And his first duty, plainly, if he were ever to thread a way through the tangle, was to readjust himself and try to see things from a different point of view.

His one definite impression was that Mrs. Paul was very much pleased that he should have come to Paris to see her, and acutely, though artlessly, aware of the importance of his mission. Artlessness, in fact, seemed her salient quality: there looked out of her great Sphinx eyes a consciousness as cloudless as a child's. But one thing he speedily discovered: she was keenly alive to her first husband's greatness. On that point French saw that she needed no enlightenment. He was even surprised, sitting opposite to her in all the blatancy of hotel mirrors and gilding, to catch on her lips the echoes of so different a setting. But he gradually perceived that the words she used had no meaning for her save, as it were, a symbolic one: they were like the mysterious price marks with which dealers label their treasures. She knew that her husband had been proud and isolated, that he had 'painted only for himself' and had 'simply despised popularity'; but she rejoiced that he was now at last receiving 'the kind of recognition even *he* would have cared for'; and when French, at this point, interposed, with an impulse of self-vindication: 'I didn't know that, as yet, much had been written about him that he would have liked,' she opened her fathomless eyes a little wider, and answered: 'Oh, but the dealers are simply fighting for his things.'

The shock was severe; but presently French rallied enough to understand that she was not moved by a spirit of cupidity, but was simply applying the only measure of greatness she knew. In Fingall's lifetime she had learned her lesson, and no doubt repeated it correctly – her conscientious desire for correctness was disarming – but now that he was gone his teaching had got mixed with other formulas, and she was serenely persuaded that, in any art, the proof and corollary of greatness was to become a best seller. 'Of course he was his own worst enemy,' she sighed. 'Even when people *came* to buy he managed to send them away discouraged. Whereas now – !'

In the first chill of his disillusionment French thought for a moment of flight. Mrs. Paul had promised him all the documentation he required: she had met him more than halfway in her lavish fixing of hours and offering of material. But everything in him shrank from repeating the experience he had just been subjected to. What was the use of seeing her again, even though her plans included a visit to Fingall's former studio? She had told him nothing whatever about Fingall, and she had told him only too much about herself. To do that, she had not even had to open her beautiful lips. On his way to her hotel he had stopped in at the Luxembourg, and filled his eyes again with her famous image. Everything she was said to have done for Fingall's genius seemed to burn in the depths of that quiet face. It was like an inexhaustible reservoir of beauty, a still pool into which the imagination could perpetually dip and draw up new treasure. And now, side by side with the painter's vision of her, hung French's own: the vision of the too-smiling beauty set in glasses and glitter, preoccupied with dressmakers and theater stalls, and affirming her husband's genius in terms of the auction room and the stock exchange!

'Oh, hang it – what can she give me? I'll go straight back to New York,' the young man suddenly resolved. The resolve even carried him precipitately back to his hotel; but on its threshold another thought arrested him. Horace Fingall had not been the only object of his pilgrimage: he had come to Paris to learn what he could of Emily Morland too. That purpose he had naturally not avowed at the Nouveau Luxe: it was hardly the moment to confess his double quest. But the manifest friendliness of Donald Paul convinced him that there would be no difficulty in obtaining whatever enlightenment it was in the young man's power to give. Donald Paul, at first sight, seemed hardly more expressive than his wife; but though his last avatar was one so remote from literature, at least he had once touched its borders and even worn its livery. His great romance had originated in the accident of his having written an article about its heroine; and transient and unproductive as that phase of his experience had probably been, it must have given him a sense of values more applicable than Mrs. Paul's to French's purpose.

Luck continued to favor him; for the next morning, as he went down the stairs of his hotel, he met Donald Paul coming up.

His visitor, fresh and handsome as his photograph, and dressed in exactly the right clothes for the hour and the occasion, held out an eager hand.

'I'm so glad – I hoped I'd catch you,' he smiled at the descending French; and then, as if to tone down what might seem an excess of warmth, or at least make it appear the mere overflow of his natural spirits, he added: 'My wife rushed me off to say how sorry she is that she can't take you to the studio this morning. She'd quite forgotten an appointment with her dressmaker – *one* of her dressmakers!' Donald Paul stressed it with a frank laugh; his desire, evidently, was to forestall French's surprise. 'You see,' he explained, perhaps guessing that a sense of values was expected of him, 'it's rather more of a business for her than for – well, the average woman. These people – the big ones – are really artists themselves nowadays, aren't they? And they all regard her as a sort of Inspiration; she really tries out the coming fashions for them – lots of things succeed or fail as they happen to look on *her*.' Here he seemed to think another laugh necessary. 'She's always been an inspiration; it's come to be a sort of obligation to her. You see, I'm sure?'

French protested that he saw – and that any other day was as convenient –

'Ah, but that's the deuce of it! The fact is, we're off for Biarritz the day after tomorrow; and St. Moritz later. We shan't be back here, I suppose, till the early spring. And of course *you* have your plans; ah, going back to America next week? Jove, that is bad.' He frowned over it with an artless boyish anxiety. 'And tomorrow – well, you know what a woman's last day in Paris is likely to be, when she's had only three of them! Should you mind most awfully – think it hopelessly inadequate, I mean – if I offered to take you to the studio instead?' He reddened a little, evidently not so much at the intrusion of his own person into the setting of his predecessor's life, as at his conscious inability to talk about Horace Fingall in any way that could possibly interest Willis French.

'Of course,' he went on, 'I shall be a wretched substitute . . . I know so little . . . so little in any sense . . . I never met him,' he avowed, as if excusing an unaccountable negligence. 'You know how savagely he kept to himself. . . . Poor Bessy – *she* could tell you something about that!' But he pulled up sharp at this involuntary lapse into the personal, and let his smile of interrogation and readiness say the rest for him.

'Go with you? But of course – I shall be delighted,' French responded; and a light of relief shone in Mr. Paul's transparent eyes.

'That's very kind of you; and of course she can tell you all about it later – add the details. She told me to say that if you didn't mind turning up again this afternoon late, she'll be ready to answer any questions. Naturally, she's used to that too!'

This sent a slight shiver through French, with its hint of glib replies insensibly shaped by repeated questionings. He knew, of course, that after Fingall's death there had been an outpouring of articles on him in the journals and the art reviews of every country: to correct their mistakes and fill up their omissions was the particular purpose of his book. But it took the bloom – another layer of bloom – from his enthusiasm to feel that Mrs. Paul's information, meagre as it was, had already been robbed of its spontaneity, that she had only been reciting to him what previous interrogators had been capable of suggesting, and had themselves expected to hear.

Perhaps Mr. Paul read the disappointment in his looks, and misinterpreted it, for he added: 'You can't think how I feel the absurdity of trying to talk to *you* about Fingall!'

His modesty was disarming. French answered with sincerity: 'I assure you I shall like nothing better than going there with you,' and Donald Paul, who was evidently used to assuming that the sentiments of others were as genuine as his own, at once brightened into recovered boyishness.

'That's jolly. Taxi!' he cried, and they were off.

• IV •

ALMOST as soon as they entered the flat, French had again to hail the reappearance of his 'luck.' Better, a thousand times better, to stand in this place with Donald Paul than with Horace Fingall's widow!

Donald Paul, slipping the key into the rusty lock, had opened the door and drawn back to let the visitor pass. The studio was cold and empty – how empty and how cold! No one had lived in the flat since Fingall's death: during the first months following it the widow had used the studio to store his pictures, and only now that the last were sold, or distributed for sale among the dealers, had the place been put in the hands of the agents – like Mrs. Morland's house in Kensington.

In the wintry overhead light the dust showed thick on the rough paint-stained floor, on the few canvases leaning against the walls, and the painter's inconceivably meager 'properties.' French had known that Fingall's studio would not be the upholstered setting for afternoon teas of Lady Brankhurst's vision, but he had not dared to expect such a scornful bareness. He looked about him reverently.

Donald Paul remained silent; then he gave one of his shy laughs. 'Not much in the way of cozy corners, eh? Looks rather as if it had been cleared for a prize fight.'

French turned to him. 'Well, it *was*. When he wrestled with the Angel until dawn.

Mr. Paul's open gaze was shadowed by a faint perplexity, and for half a second French wondered if his metaphor had been taken as referring to the former Mrs. Fingall. But in another moment his companion's eyes cleared. 'Of course – I see! Like What's-in-his name: in the Bible, wasn't he?' He stopped, and began again impulsively: 'I like that idea, you know; he *did* wrestle with his work! Bessy says he used to paint a thing over twenty times – or thirty, if necessary. It drove his sitters nearly mad. That's why he had to wait so long for success, I suppose.' His glance seemed to appeal to French to corroborate this rather adventurous view.

'One of the reasons,' French assented.

His eyes were traveling slowly and greedily about the vast cold room. He had instantly noted that, in Lady Brankhurst's description of the place, nothing was exact but the blackness of the stairs that led there. The rest she must have got up from muddled memories of other studios – that of Jolyesse, no doubt, among the number. French could see Jolyesse, in a setting of bibelots, dispensing Turkish coffee to fashionable sitters. But the nakedness of Fingall's studio had assuredly never been draped: as they beheld it now, so it must have been when the great man painted there – save, indeed, for the pictures once so closely covering the walls (as French saw from the number of empty nails) that to enter it must have been like walking into the heart of a sunset.

None were left. Paul had moved away and stood looking out of the window, and timidly, tentatively, French turned around, one after another, the canvases against the wall. All were as bare as the room, though already prepared for future splendors by the hand from which the brush had dropped so abruptly. On one only a few charcoal strokes hinted at a head – unless indeed it were a landscape? The more French looked the less intelligible it became – the mere first stammer of an unuttered message. The young man put it back with a sigh. He would have liked, beyond almost everything, here under Fingall's roof to discover just one of his pictures.

'If you'd care to see the other rooms? You know he and Bessy lived here,' he heard his companion suggest.

'Oh, immensely!'

Donald Paul opened a door, struck a match in a dark passage, and preceded him.

'Nothing's changed.'

The rooms, which were few and small, were still furnished; and this gave French the measure of their humbleness – for they were almost as devoid of comfort as the studio. Fingall must have lived so intensely and constantly in his own inner vision that nothing external mattered. He must have been almost as detached from the visible world as a great musician or a great ascetic; at least till one sat him down before a face or a landscape – and then what he looked at became the whole of the visible world to him.

'Rather doleful diggings for a young woman,' Donald Paul commented with a half-apologetic smile, as if to say: 'Can you wonder that she likes the Nouveau Luxe?'

French acquiesced. 'I suppose, like all the very greatest of them, he was indifferent to lots of things we think important.'

'Yes – and then . . .' Paul hesitated, 'then they were so frightfully poor. He didn't know how to manage – how to get on with people, either sitters or dealers. For years he sold nothing, literally nothing. It *was* hard on her. She saw so well what he ought to have done; but he wouldn't listen to her!'

'Oh – ' French stammered; and saw the other faintly redden.

'I don't mean, of course, that an artist, a great creative artist, isn't always different . . . on the contrary . . .' Paul hesitated again. 'I understand all that . . . I've experienced it. . . .' His handsome face softened, and French, mollified, murmured to himself: 'He was awfully kind to Emily Morland – I'm sure he was.'

'Only,' Mrs. Paul's husband continued with a deepening earnestness, as if he were trying to explain to French something not quite clear to himself, 'only, if you're not a great creative artist yourself, it is hard sometimes, sitting by and looking on and feeling that if your were just allowed to say a word – Of course,' he added abruptly, 'he was very good to her in other ways; very grateful. She was his inspiration.'

'It's something to have been that,' French said; and at the words his companion's color deepened to a flush which took in his neck and ears, and spread up to his white forehead.

'It's everything,' he agreed, almost solemnly.

French had wandered up to a bookshelf in what had apparently been Fingall's dressing room. He had seen no other books about, and was curious to learn what these had to tell him. They were chiefly old Tauchnitz novels – mild mid-Victorian fiction rubbing elbows with a few odd volumes of Dumas, Maupassant and Zola. But under a loose pile the critic, with beating heart, had detected a shabby sketchbook. His hand shook as he opened it; but its pages were blank, and he reflected ironically that had they not been the dealers would never have left it there.

'They've been over the place with a fine toothcomb,' he muttered to himself.

'What have you got hold of?' Donald Paul asked, coming up.

French continued mechanically to flutter the blank pages; then his hand paused at one which was scribbled over with dots and diagrams, and marginal notes in Fingall's small cramped writing.

'Tea party,' it was cryptically entitled, with a date beneath; and on the next page, under the heading 'For tea party,' a single figure stood out – the figure of a dowdily-dressed woman seated in a low chair, a cup in her hand, and looking up as if to speak to someone who was not yet sketched in. The drawing, in three chalks on a gray ground, was rapidly but carefully executed: one of those light and perfect things which used to fall from Fingall like stray petals from a great tree in bloom. The woman's attitude was full of an ardent interest; from the forward thrust of her clumsily-shod foot to the tilt of her head and the highlight on her eyeglasses, everything about her seemed electrified by some eager shock of ideas. 'Who was talking to her – and what could he have been saying?' was the first thought the little drawing suggested. But it merely flashed through French's mind, for he had almost instantly recognized the portrait – just touched with caricature, yet living, human, even tender – of the woman he least expected to see there.

'Then she *did* know him!' he triumphed out aloud, forgetting who was at his elbow. He flushed up at his blunder and put the book in his companion's hand.

Donald Paul stared at the page.

'She – who?'

French stood confounded. There she sat – Emily Morland – acquiver in every line with life and sound and color: French could hear her very voice running up and down its happy scales! And beside him stood her lover, and did not recognize her. . . .

'Oh – ' Paul stammered at length. 'It's – you mean?' He looked again. 'You think he meant it for Mrs. Morland?' Without waiting for an answer he fixed French with his large boyish gaze, and exclaimed abruptly: 'Then you knew her?'

'Oh, I saw her only once – just once.' French couldn't resist laying a little stress on the *once*.

But Donald Paul took the answer unresentfully. 'And yet you recognized her. I suppose you're more used than I am to Fingall's way of drawing. Do you think he was ever very good at likenesses? I *do* see now, of course . . . but, come, I call it a caricature, don't you?'

'Oh, what does that matter?'

'You mean, you think it's so clever?'

'I think it's magnificent!' said French with emotion.

The other still looked at him ingeniously, but with a dawning light of eagerness. It recalled to French the suppressed, the exaggerated warmth of his greeting on the hotel stairs. 'What is it he wants of me? For he wants something.'

'I never knew, either,' Paul continued, 'that she and Fingall had met. Some one must have brought her here, I suppose. It's curious.' He pondered, still holding the book. 'And I didn't know *you* knew her,' he concluded.

'Oh, how should you? She was probably unconscious of the fact herself. I spent a day with her once in the country, years ago. Naturally, I've never forgotten it.'

Donald Paul's eyes continued obscurely to entreat him. 'That's wonderful!'

'What – that one should never forget having once met Emily Morland?' French rejoined, with a smile he could not repress.

'No,' said Emily Morland's lover with simplicity. 'But the coincidence. You see, I'd made up my mind to ask you – ' He broke off, and looked down at the sketch, as if seeking guidance where doubtless he had so often found it. 'The fact is,' he began again, 'I'm going to write her 'Life.' She left me all her papers – I dare say you know about all that. It's a trust – a sacred trust; but it's also a most tremendous undertaking! And yesterday, after hearing something of what you're planning about Fingall, I realized how little I'd really thought the book out, how unprepared I was – what a lot more there was in that sort of thing than I'd at first imagined. I used to write – a little; just short reviews, and that kind of thing. But my hand's out nowadays; and besides, this is so different. And then, my time's not quite my own any longer. . . . So I made up my mind that I'd consult you, ask you if you'd help me . . . oh, as much as ever you're willing. . . .' His smile was irresistible. 'I asked Bessy. And she thought you'd understand.'

'Understand?' gasped French. 'Understand?'

'You see,' Paul hurried on, 'there are heaps and heaps of letters – her beautiful letters! I don't mean' – his voice trembled slightly – 'only the ones to me; though some of those . . . well,

I'll leave it to you to judge. . . . But lots of others too, that all sorts of people have sent me. Apparently everybody kept her letters. And I'm simply swamped in them,' he ended helplessly, 'unless you will. . . .'

French's voice was as unsteady as his. 'Unless I will? There's nothing on earth I'd have asked . . . if I could have imagined it. . . .'

'Oh, really?' Paul's voice dropped back with relief to its everyday tone. He was clearly unprepared for exaltation. 'It's amazingly kind of you – so kind that I don't in the least know how to thank you.'

He paused, his hand still between the pages of the sketchbook. Suddenly he opened it and glanced down again at the drawing, and then at French.

'Meanwhile – if you really like this thing; you *do*?' He smiled a little incredulously and bent his handsome head to give the leaf a closer look. 'Yes, there are his initials; well, that makes it all the more. . . .' He tore out the page and handed it to French. 'Do take it,' he said. 'I wish I had something better of her to give you – but there's literally nothing else; nothing except the beautiful enlarged photograph she had done for me the year we met; and that, of course – '

• V •

MRS. PAUL, as French had foreseen she would be, was late at their second appointment; later even than at the first. But what did French care? He could have waited contentedly for a week in that blatant drawing room, with such hopes in his bosom and such a treasure already locked up in his portmanteau. And when at last she came she was just as cordial, as voluble and as unhelpful as ever.

The great difficulty, of course, was that she and her husband were leaving Paris so soon, and that French, for his part, was under orders to return at once to America. 'The things I could tell you if we only had the time!' she sighed regretfully. But this left French unmoved, for he knew by now how little she really had to tell. Still, he had a good many more questions to ask, a good many more dates and facts to get at, than could be crowded into their confused hour over a laden tea table, with belated parcels perpetually arriving, the telephone ringing, and the maid putting in her head to ask if the orange-and-silver brocade was to go to Biarritz, or to be sent straight on with the furs and the sports clothes to St. Moritz.

Finally, in the hurried parenthesis between these weightier matters, he extracted from her the promise to meet him in Paris in March – March at the latest – and give him a week, a whole week. 'It will be so much easier, then, of course,' she agreed. 'It's the deadest season of the year in Paris. There'll be nobody to bother us, and we can really settle down to work' – her lovely eyes kindled at the thought – 'and I can give you all the papers you need, and tell you everything you want to know.'

With that he had to be content, and he could afford to be – now. He rose to take leave; but suddenly she rose also, a new eagerness in her eyes. She moved toward the door with him, and there her look detained him.

'And Donald's book too; you can get to work with Donald at the same time, can't you?' She smiled on him confidentially. 'He's told me that you've promised to help him out – it's so angelically good of you! I do assure you he appreciates it immensely. Perhaps he's a little too modest about his own ability; but it *is* a terrible burden to have had imposed on him, isn't it, just as he and I were having our first real holiday! It's been a nightmare to him all these months. Reading all those letters and manuscripts, and deciding – Why don't authors do those things for themselves?' She appealed to French, half indignantly. 'But after all,' she concluded, her smile deepening, 'I understand that you should be willing to take the trouble, in return for the precious thing he's given you.'

French's heart gave a frightened thump: her smile had suddenly become too significant.

'The precious thing?'

She laughed. 'Do you mean to say you've forgotten it already? Well, if you have, I don't think you deserve it. The portrait of Mrs. Morland – the *only* one, apparently! A signed drawing of Horace's; it's something of a prize, you'll admit. Donald tells me that you and he made the discovery of the sketchbook together. I can't for the life of me imagine how it ever escaped those harpies of dealers. You can fancy how they went through everything . . . like detectives after fingerprints, I used to say! Poor me – they used to have me out of bed everyday at daylight! How furious they'd be if they knew what they've missed!' She paused and laughed again, leaning in the doorway in one of her long Artemis attitudes.

French felt his head spinning. He dared not meet her eyes, for fear of discovering in them the unmasked cupidity he fancied he had once before detected there. He felt too sick for any thought but flight; but every nerve in him cried out: 'Whatever she says or does, she shall never have that drawing back!'

She said and did nothing; which made it even more difficult for him. It gave him the feeling that if he moved she would move too – with a spring, as if she herself were a detective, and suspected him of having the treasure in his pocket ('Thank God I haven't!' he thought). And she had him so entirely at her mercy, with all the Fingall dates and documents still in her hold; there was nothing he could do but go – pick up the portmanteau with the drawing in it, and fly by the next train, if need be!

The idea traversed him in a flash, and then gave way again to the desolating sense of who she was, and what it was that they were maneuvering and watching each other about. That was the worst of all – worse even than giving up the drawing, or renouncing the book on Fingall. He felt that he must get away at any cost, rather than prolong their silent duel; and, sick at heart, he reached out for the doorknob.

'Oh, no!' she exclaimed, her hand coming down on his wrist.

He forced an answering smile. 'No?'

She shook her head, her eyes still on his. 'You're not going like that.' Though she held him playfully her long fine fingers seemed as strong as steel. 'After all, business is business, isn't it? We ordinary mortals, who don't live in the clouds among the gods, can't afford to give nothing for nothing. . . . *You* don't – so why should I?'

He had never seen her so close before, and as her face hovered over him, so warm, persuasive, confident, he noted in it, with a kind of savage satisfaction, the first faint lines of age.

'So why should I?' she repeated gaily. He stood silent, imprisoned; and she went on, throwing her head back a little, and letting her gaze filter down on him through her rich lowered lashes: 'But I know you'll agree with me that it's only fair. After all, Donald has set you the example. He's given you something awfully valuable in return for the favor you're going to do him – the immense favor. Poor darling – there never was anybody as generous as Donald! Don't be alarmed; I'm not going to ask you to give me a present on *that* scale.' She drew herself up and threw back her lids, as if challenging him. 'You'd have difficulty in finding one – anybody would!'

French was still speechless, bewildered, not daring to think ahead, and all the while confusedly aware that his misery was feeding some obscure springs of amusement in her.

'In return for the equally immense favor I'm going to do you – coming back to Paris in March, and giving you a whole week – what are you going to give *me*? Have you ever thought about *that*?' she flung out at him; and then, before he could answer: 'Oh, don't look so miserable – don't rack your brains over it! I told you I wasn't grasping – I'm not going to ask for anything unattainable. Only, you see' – she paused, her face grown suddenly tender and young again – 'you see, Donald wants so dreadfully to have a portrait of me, one for his very own, by a painter he really admires; a *likeness*, simply, you see, not one of those wild things poor Horace used to do of me – and what I want is to beg and implore you to ask Jolyesse if he'll do me. I can't ask him myself: Horace despised his things, and was always ridiculing him, and Jolyesse knew it. It's all very well – but, as I used to tell Horace, success does mean something after all, doesn't it? And no one has been more of a success than Jolyesse – I hear his prices have doubled again. Well, that's a proof, in a way . . . what's the use of denying it? Only it makes it more difficult for poor me, who can't afford him, even if I dared to ask!' She wrinkled her perfect brows in mock distress. 'But if *you* would – an old friend like you – if you'd ask it as a personal favor, and make him see that for the widow of a colleague he ought to make a reduction in his price – really a *big* reduction! – I'm sure he'd do it. After all, it's not my fault if my husband didn't like his pictures. And I should be so grateful to you, and so would Donald.'

She dropped French's arm and held out both her shining hands to him. 'You *will* – you really will? Oh, you dear good man, you!' He had slipped his hands out of hers, but she caught him again, this time not menacingly but exuberantly.

'If you could arrange it for when I'm here in March, that would be simply perfect, wouldn't it? You can, you think? Oh, bless you! And mind, he's got to make it a full-length!' she called after him joyfully across the threshold.

Diagnosis

NOTHING TO WORRY ABOUT – absolutely nothing. Of course not . . . just what they all say!' Paul Dorrance walked away from his writing table to the window of his high-perched flat. The window looked south, over the crowded towering New York below Wall Street which was the visible center and symbol of his life's work. He drew a great breath of relief – for under his surface incredulity a secret reassurance was slowly beginning to unfold. The two eminent physicians he had just seen had told him he would be all right again in a few months; that his dark fears were delusions; that all he needed was to get away from work till he had recovered his balance of body and brain. Dorrance had smiled acquiescence and muttered inwardly: 'Infernal humbugs; as if I didn't know how I felt!'; yet hardly a quarter of an hour later their words had woven magic passes about him, and with a timid avidity he had surrendered to the sense of returning life. 'By George, I *do* feel better,' he muttered, and swung about to his desk, remembering he had not breakfasted. The first time in months that he had remembered that! He touched the bell at his elbow, and with a half-apologetic smile told his servant that . . . well, yes . . . the doctors said he ought to eat more. . . . Perhaps he'd have an egg or two with his coffee . . . yes, with bacon. . . . He chafed with impatience till the tray was brought.

Breakfast over, he glanced through the papers with the leisurely eye of a man before whom the human comedy is likely to go on unrolling itself for many years. 'Nothing to be in a hurry about, after all,' was his half-conscious thought. That line which had so haunted him lately, about 'Time's wingèd chariot,' relapsed into the region of pure aesthetics, now that in his case the wings were apparently to be refurled. 'No reason whatever why you shouldn't live to be an old man.' That was pleasant hearing, at forty-nine. What did they call an old man, nowadays? He had always imagined that he shouldn't care to live to be an old man; now he began by asking himself what he understood by the term 'old.' Nothing that applied to himself, certainly; even if he were to be mysteriously metamorphosed into an old man at some far distant day – what then? It was too far off to visualize, it did not affect his imagination. Why, old age no longer began short of seventy; almost every day the papers told of hearty old folk celebrating their hundredth birthdays – sometimes by re-marriage. Dorrance lost himself in pleasant musings over the increased longevity of the race, evoking visions of contemporaries of his grandparents, infirm and toothless at an age which found their descendants still carnivorous and alert.

The papers read, his mind drifted agreeably among the rich possibilities of travel. A busy man ordered to interrupt his work could not possibly stay in New York. Names suggestive of idleness and summer clothes floated before him: the West Indies, the Canaries, Morocco – why not Morocco, where he had never been? And from there he could work his way up through Spain. He rose to reach for a volume from the shelves where his travel books were ranged – but as he stood fluttering its pages, in a state of almost thoughtless beatitude, something twitched him out of his dream. 'I suppose I ought to tell her – ' he said aloud.

Certainly he ought to tell her; but the mere thought let loose a landslide of complications, obligations, explanations . . . their suffocating descent made him gasp for breadth. He leaned against the desk, closing his eyes.

But of course she would understand. The doctors said he was going to be all right – that would be enough for her. She would see the necessity of his going away for some months; a year perhaps. She couldn't go with him; that was certain! So what was there to make a fuss about? Gradually, insidiously, there stole into his mind the thought – at first a mere thread of a suggestion – that this might be the moment to let her see, oh, ever so gently, that things couldn't go on forever – nothing did – and that, at his age, and with this new prospect of restored health, a man might reasonably be supposed to have his own views, his own plans; might think of marriage; marriage with a young girl; children; a place in the country . . . his mind wandered into that dream as it had into the dream of travel. . . .

Well, meanwhile he must let her know what the diagnosis was. She had been awfully worried about him, he knew, though all along she had kept up so bravely. (Should he, in the independence of his recovered health, confess under his breath that he celebrated 'braveness' sometimes got a little on his nerves?) Yes, it had been hard for her; harder than for anyone; he owed it to her to tell her at once that everything was all right; all right as far as *he* was concerned. And in her beautiful unselfishness nothing else would matter to her – at first. Poor child! He could hear her happy voice! 'Really – really and truly? They both said so? You're *sure*? Oh, of course, I've always known . . . haven't I always told you?' Bless her, yes; but he'd known all along what she was thinking. . . . He turned to the desk, and took up the telephone.

As he did so, his glance lit on a sheet of paper on the rug at his feet. He had keen eyes: he saw at once that the letterhead bore the name of the eminent consultant whom his own physician had brought in that morning. Perhaps the paper was one of the three or four prescriptions they had left with him; a chance gust from door or window might have snatched it from the table where the others lay. He stooped and picked it up –

That was the truth, then. That paper on the floor held his fate. The two doctors had written out their diagnosis, and forgotten to pocket it when they left. There were their two signatures; and the date. There was no mistake. . . . Paul Dorrance sat for a long time with the paper on the desk before him. He propped his chin on his locked hands, shut his eyes, and tried to grope his way through the illimitable darkness. . . .

Anything, anything but the sights and sounds of the world outside! If he had had the energy to move he would have jumped up, drawn the curtains shut, and cowered in his armchair in absolute blackness till he could come to some sort of terms with this new reality – for him henceforth the sole reality. For what did anything matter now except that he was doomed – was dying? That these two scoundrels had known it, and had lied to him? And that, having lied to him, in their callous professional haste, they had tossed his death sentence down before him, forgotten to carry it away, left it there staring up at him from the floor?

Yes; it would be easier to bear in a pitch-black room, a room from which all sights and sounds, all suggestions of life, were excluded. But the effort of getting up to draw the curtains was too great. It was easier to go on sitting there, in the darkness created by pressing his fists against his lids. 'Now, then, my good fellow – this is what it'll be like in the grave. . . .'

Yes; but if he had known the grave was *there*, so close, so all-including, so infinitely more important and real than any of the trash one had tossed the years away for; if somebody had told him . . . he might have done a good many things differently, put matters in a truer perspective, discriminated, selected, weighed. . . . Or, no! A thousand times no! Be beaten like that? Go slinking off to his grave before it was dug for him? His folly had been that he had not packed enough into life; that he had always been sorting, discriminating, trying for a perspective, choosing, weighing – God! When there was barely time to seize life before the cup that held it was cracked, and gulp it down while you had a throat that could swallow!

Ah, well – no use in retrospection. What was done was done: what undone must remain so to all eternity. Eternity – what did the word mean? How could the least fringe of its meaning be grasped by ephemeral creatures groping blindly through a few short years to the grave? Ah, the pity of it – pity, pity! That was the feeling that rose to the surface of his thoughts. Pity for all the millions of blind gropers like himself, the millions and millions who thought themselves alive, as he had, and suddenly found themselves dead; as he had! Poor mortals all, with that seed of annihilation that made them brothers – how he longed to help them, how he winced at the thought that he must so often have hurt them, brushing by in his fatuous vitality! How many other lives had he used up in his short span of living? Not consciously, of course – that was the worst of it! The old nurse who had slaved for him when he was a child, and then vanished from his life, to be found again, years after, poor, neglected, dying – well, for her he had done what he could. And that thin young man in his office, with the irritating cough, who might perhaps have been saved if he had been got away sooner? Stuck on to the end because there was a family to support – of course! And the old bookkeeper whom Dorrance had inherited from his father, who was deaf and half blind, and wouldn't go either till he had to be gently told – ?

All that had been been, as it were, the stuff out of which he, Paul Dorrance, had built up his easy, affluent, successful life. But, no, what nonsense! He had been fair enough, kind enough, whenever he found out what was wrong; only he hadn't really pitied them, had considered his debt discharged when he had drawn a cheque or rung up a Home for Incurables. Whereas pity, he now saw – oh, curse it, he was talking like a Russian novel! Nonsense . . . nonsense . . . everybody's turn came sooner or later. The only way to reform the world was to reform Death out of it. And instead of that, Death was always there, was there now, at the door, in the room, at his elbow . . . *his* Death, his own private and particular end-of-everything. *Now*! He snatched his hands away from his face. They were wet.

A bell rang hesitatingly and the door opened behind him. He heard the servant say: 'Mrs. Welwood.' He stood up, blinking at the harsh impact of light and life. 'Mrs. Welwood.' Everything was going on again, going on again . . . people were behaving exactly as if he were not doomed . . . the door shut.

'Eleanor!'

She came up to him quickly. How close, alive, oppressive everyone seemed! She seldom came to his flat – he wondered dully why she had come today.

She stammered: 'What has happened? You promised to telephone at ten. I've been ringing and ringing. They said nobody answered. . . .'

Ah, yes: he remembered now. He looked at the receiver. It lay on the desk, where he had dropped it when his eye had lit on that paper. All that had happened in his other life – before. . . . Well, here she was. How pale she looked, her eyelids a little swollen. And yet how strong, how healthy – how obviously undiseased. Queer! She'd been crying too! Instinctively he turned, and put himself between her and the light.

'What's all the fuss about, dear?' he began jauntily.

She colored a little, hesitating as if he had caught her at fault. 'Why, it's nearly one o'clock; and you told me the consultation was to be at nine. And you promised. . . .'

Oh, yes; of course. He had promised. . . . With the hard morning light on her pale face and thin lips, she looked twenty years older. Older than what? After all, she was well over forty, and had never been beautiful. Had he ever thought her beautiful? Poor Eleanor – oh, poor Eleanor!

'Well, yes; it's my fault,' he conceded. 'I suppose I telephoned to somebody' (this fib to gain time) 'and forgot to hang up the receiver. There it lies; I'm convicted!' He took both her hands – how they trembled! – and drew her to him.

This was Eleanor Welwood, for fifteen years past the heaviest burden on his conscience. As he stood there, holding her hands, he tried to recover a glimpse of the beginnings, and of his own state of mind at the time. He had been captivated; but never to the point of wishing she were free to marry him. Her husband was a pleasant enough fellow; they all belonged to the same little social group; it was a delightful relation, just as it was. And Dorrance had the pretext of his old mother, alone and infirm, who lived with him and whom he could not leave. It was tacitly understood that old Mrs. Dorrance's habits must not be disturbed by any change in the household. So love, on his part, imperceptibly cooled (or should he say ripened?) into friendship; and when his mother's death left him free, there still remained the convenient obstacle of Horace Welwood. Horace Welwood did not die; but one day, as the phrase is, he 'allowed' his wife to divorce him. The news had cost Dorrance a sleepless night or two. The divorce was obtained by Mrs. Welwood, discreetly, in a distant and accommodating state; but it was really Welwood who had repudiated his wife, and because of Paul Dorrance. Dorrance knew this, and was aware that Mrs. Welwood knew he knew it. But he had kept his head, she had silenced her heart; and life went on as before, except that since the divorce it was easier to see her, and he could telephone to her house whenever he chose. And they continued to be the dearest of friends.

He had often gone over all this in his mind, with an increasing satisfaction in his own shrewdness. He had kept his freedom, kept his old love's devotion – or as much of it as he wanted – and proved to himself that life was not half bad if you knew how to manage it. That was what he used to think – and then, suddenly, two or three hours ago, he had begun to think differently about everything, and what had seemed shrewdness now unmasked itself as a pitiless egotism.

He continued to look at Mrs. Welwood, as if searching her face for something it was essential he should find there. He saw her lips begin to tremble, the tears still on her lashes, her features gradually dissolving in a blur of apprehension and incredulity. 'Ah – this is beyond her! She won't be "brave" now,' he thought with an uncontrollable satisfaction. It seemed necessary, at the moment, that someone should feel the shock of his doom as he was feeling it – should *die with him*, at least morally, since he had to die. And the strange insight which had come to him – this queer 'behind-the-veil' penetration he was suddenly conscious of – had already told him that most of the people he knew, however sorry they might think they were, would really not be in the least affected by his fate, would remain as inwardly unmoved as he had been when, in the plenitude of his vigour, someone had said before him: 'Ah, poor so-and-so – didn't you know? The doctors say it's all up to him.'

With Eleanor it was different. As he held her there under his eyes he could almost trace the course of his own agony in her paling dissolving face, could almost see her as she might one day look if she were his widow – *his widow*! Poor thing. At least if she were that she could proclaim her love and her anguish, could abandon herself to open mourning on his grave. Perhaps that was the only comfort it was still in his power to give her . . . or in hers to give him. For the grave might be less cold if watered by her warm tears. The thought made his own well up, and he pressed her closer. At that moment his first wish was to see how she would look if she were really happy. His friend – his only friend! How he would make up to her now for his past callousness!

'Eleanor – '

'Oh, won't you tell me?' she entreated.

'Yes. Of course. Only I want you to promise me something first – '

'Yes. . . .'

'To do what I want you – whatever I want you to.'

She could not still the trembling of her hands, though he pressed them so close. She could scarcely articulate: 'Haven't I, always – ?'

Slowly he pronounced: 'I want you to marry me.'

Her trembling grew more violent, and then subsided. The shadow of her terrible fear seemed to fall from her, as the shadow of living falls from the face of the newly dead. Her face looked young and transparent; he watched the blood rise to her lips and cheeks.

'Oh, Paul, Paul – then the news is *good*?'

He felt a slight shrinking at her obtuseness. After all, she was alive (it wasn't her fault), she was merely alive, like all the rest. . . . Magnanimously he rejoined: 'Never mind about the news now.' But to himself he muttered: *'Sancta Simplicitas!'*

She had thought he had asked her to marry him because the news was good!

• II •

THEY were married almost immediately, and with as little circumstance as possible. Dorrance's ill-health, already vaguely known of in his immediate group of friends, was a sufficient pretext for hastening and simplifying the ceremony; and the next day the couple sailed for France.

Dorrance had not seen again the two doctors who had pronounced his doom. He had forbidden Mrs. Welwood to speak of the diagnosis, to him or to anyone else. 'For God's sake, don't let's dramatize the thing,' he commanded her; and she acquiesced.

He had shown her the paper as soon as she had promised to marry him; and had hastened, as she read it, to inform her that of course he had no intention of holding her to her promise. 'I only wanted to hear you say "yes,"' he explained, on a note of emotion so genuine that it deceived himself as completely as it did her. He was sure he would not accept his offer to release her; if he had not been sure he might not have dared to make it. For he understood now that he must marry her; he simply could not live out these last months alone. For a moment his thoughts had played sentimentally with the idea that he was marrying her to acquit an old debt, to make her happy before it was to late; but that delusion had been swept away like a straw on the torrent of his secret fears. A new form of egotism, fiercer and more impatient than the other, was dictating his words and gestures – and he knew it. He was marrying simply to put a sentinel between himself and the presence lurking on his threshold – with the same blind instinct of self-preservation which had made men, in old days, propitiate death by the lavish sacrifice of life. And, confident as he was, he had felt an obscure dread of her failing him till his ring was actually on her finger; and a great ecstasy of reassurance and gratitude as he walked out into the street with that captive hand on his arm. Could it be that together they would be able to cheat death after all?

They landed at Genoa, and traveled by slow stages toward the Austrian Alps. The journey seemed to do Dorrance good; he was bearing the fatigue better than he had expected; and he was conscious that his attentive companion noted the improvement, though she forbore to emphasize it. 'Above all, don't be too cheerful,' he had warned her, half smilingly, on the day when he had told her of his doom. 'Marry me if you think you can stand it; but don't try to make me think I'm going to get well.'

She had obeyed him to the letter, watching over his comfort, sparing him all needless fatigue and agitation, carefully serving up to him, on the bright surface of her vigilance, the flowers of travel stripped of their thorns. The very qualities which had made her a perfect mistress – self-effacement, opportuneness, the art of being present and visible only when he required her to be – made her (he had to own it) a perfect wife for a man cut off from everything but the contemplation of his own end.

They were bound for Vienna, where a celebrated specialist was said to have found new ways of relieving the suffering caused by such cases as Dorrance's – sometimes even (though Dorrance and his wife took care not to mention this to each other) of checking the disease, even holding it for years in abeyance. 'I owe it to the poor child to give the thing a trial,' the invalid speciously argued, disguising his own passionate impatience to put himself in the great man's hands. 'If she *wants* to drag out her life with a half-dead man, why should I prevent her?' he thought, trying to sum up all the hopeful possibilities on which the new diagnostician might base his verdict. . . . 'Certainly,' Dorrance thought, 'I have had less pain lately. . . .'

It had been agreed that he should go to the specialist's alone; his wife was to wait for him at their hotel. 'But you'll come straight back afterward? You'll take a taxi – you won't walk?' she had pleaded, for the first time betraying her impatience. 'She knows the hours are numbered, and she can't bear to lose one,' he thought, a choking in his throat; and as he bent to kiss her he had a vision of what it would have been, after the interview that lay ahead of him, the verdict he had already discounted, to walk back to an hotel in which no one awaited him, climb to an empty room and sit down alone with his doom. 'Bless you, child, of course I'll take a taxi. . . .'

Now the consultation was over, and he had descended from the specialist's door, and stood alone in the summer twilight, watching the trees darken against the illumination of the street lamps. What a divine thing a summer evening was, even in a crowded city street! He wondered that he had never before felt its peculiar loveliness. Through the trees the sky was deepening from pearl gray to blue as the stars came out. He stood there, unconscious of the hour, gazing at the people hurrying to and fro on the pavement, the traffic flowing by in an unbroken stream, all the ceaseless tides of the city's life which had seemed to him, half an hour ago, forever suspended. . . .

'No, it's too lovely; I'll walk,' he said, rousing himself, and took a direction opposite to that in which his hotel lay. 'After all,' he thought 'there's no hurry. . . . What a charming town Vienna is – I think I should like to live here,' he mused as he wandered on under the trees. . . .

When at last he reached his hotel he stopped short on the threshold and asked himself: 'How am I going to tell her?' He realized that during his two hours' perambulations since he had left the doctor's office he had thought out nothing, planned nothing, not even let his imagination glance at the future, but simply allowed himself to be absorbed into the softly palpitating life about him, like a tired traveller sinking, at his journey's end, into a warm bath. Only now, at the foot of the stairs, did he see the future facing him, and understand that he knew no more how to prepare for the return to life than he had for the leaving it. . . . 'If only she takes it quietly – without too much fuss,' he thought, shrinking in advance from any disturbance of those still waters into which it was so beatific to subside.

'That New York diagnosis was a mistake – an utter mistake,' he began vehemently, and then paused, arrested, silenced, by something in his wife's face which seemed to oppose an invisible resistance to what he was in the act of saying. He had hoped she would not be too emotional – and now: what was it? Did he really resent the mask of composure she had no doubt struggled to adjust during her long hours of waiting? He stood and stared at her. 'I suppose you don't believe it? he broke off, with an aimless irritated laugh.

She came to him eagerly. 'But of course I do, of course!' She seemed to hesitate for a second. 'What I never did believe,' she said abruptly, 'was the other – the New York diagnosis.'

He continued to stare, vaguely resentful of this new attitude, and of the hint of secret criticism it conveyed. He felt himself suddenly diminished in her eyes, as though she were retrospectively stripping him of some prerogative. If she had not believed in the New York diagnosis, what must her secret view of him have been all the while? 'Oh, you never believed in it? And may I ask why?' He heard the edge of sarcasm in his voice.

She gave a little laugh that sounded almost as aimless as his. 'I – I don't know. I suppose I couldn't *bear* to, simply; I couldn't believe fate could be so cruel.'

Still with a tinge of sarcasm he rejoined: 'I'm glad you had your incredulity to sustain you.' Inwardly he was saying: 'Not a tear . . . not an outbreak of emotion . . .' and his heart, dilated by the immense inrush of returning life, now contracted as if an invisible plug had been removed from it, and its fullness were slowly ebbing. 'It's a queer business, anyhow,' he mumbled.

'What is, dear?'

'This being alive again. I'm not sure I know yet what it consists in.'

She came up and put her arms about him, almost shyly. 'We'll try to find out, love – together.'

• III •

THIS magnificent gift of life, which the Viennese doctor had restored to him as lightly as his New York colleagues had withdrawn it, lay before Paul Dorrance like something external, outside of himself, an honour, an official rank, unexpectedly thrust on him: he did not discover till then how completely he had dissociated himself from the whole business of living. It was as if life were a growth which the surgeon's knife had already extirpated, leaving him, disembodied, on the pale verge of nonentity. All the while that he had kept saying to himself: 'In a few weeks more I shall be dead,' had he not really known that he was dead already?

'But what are we to do, then, dearest?' he heard his wife asking. 'What do you want? Would you like to go home at once? Do you want me to cable to have the flat got ready?'

He looked at her in astonishment, wounded by such unperceivingness. Go home – to New York? To his old life there? Did she really think of it as something possible, even simple and natural? Why, the small space he had occupied there had closed up already; he felt himself as completely excluded from that other life as if his absence had lasted for years. And what did she mean by 'going home'? The old Paul Dorrance who had made his will, wound up his affairs, resigned from his clubs and directorships, pensioned off his old servants and married his old mistress – that Dorrance was as dead as if he had taken that final step for which all those others were but the hasty preparation. He *was* dead; this new man, to whom the doctor had said: 'Cancer? Nothing of the sort – not a trace of it. Go home and tell your wife that in a few months you'll be as sound as any man of fifty I ever met – ' this new Dorrance, with his new health, his new leisure and his new wife, was an intruder for whom a whole new existence would have to be planned out. And how could anything be decided until one got to know the new Paul Dorrance a little better?

Conscious that his wife was waiting for his answer, he said: 'Oh, this fellow here may be all wrong. Anyhow, he wants me to take a cure somewhere first – I've got the name written down. After that we'll see. . . . But wouldn't you rather travel for a year or so? How about South Africa or India next winter?' he ventured at random, after trying to think of some point of the globe even more remote from New York.

• IV •

THE cure was successful, the Viennese specialist's diagnosis proved to be correct; and the Paul Dorrances celebrated the event by two years of foreign travel. But Dorrance never felt again the unconditioned ecstasy he had tasted as he walked out from the doctor's door into the lamplit summer streets. After that, at the very moment of re-entering his hotel, the effort of readjustment had begun; and ever since it had gone on.

For a few months the wanderers, weary of change, had settled in Florence, captivated by an arcaded villa on a cypress-walled hill, and the new Paul Dorrance, whom it was now the other's incessant task to study and placate, had toyed with the idea of a middle life of cultivated leisure. But he soon grew tired of his opportunities, and found it necessary to move on, and forget in strenuous travel his incapacity for assimilation and reflection. And before the two years were over the old Paul Dorrance, who had constituted himself the other's courier and prime minister, discovered that the old and the new were one, and that the original Paul Dorrance was there, unchanged, unchangeable, and impatient to get back to his old niche because it was too late to adapt himself to any other. So the flat was reopened and the Dorrances returned to New York.

The completeness of his identity with the old Paul Dorrance was indelibly impressed on the new one on the first evening of his return home. There he was, the same man in the same setting as when, two years earlier, he had glanced down from the same armchair and seen the diagnosis of the consulting physicians at his feet. The hour was late, the room profoundly still; no touch of outward reality intervened between him and that hallucinating vision. He almost saw the paper on the floor, and with the same gesture as before he covered his eyes to shut it out. Two years ago – and nothing was changed, after so many changes, except that he should not hear the hesitating ring at the door, should not again see Eleanor Welwood, pale and questioning, on the threshold. Eleanor Welwood did not ring his doorbell now; she had her own latchkey; she was no longer Eleanor Welwood but Eleanor Dorrance, and asleep at this moment in the bedroom which had been Dorrance's, and was now encumbered with feminine properties, while his own were uncomfortably wedged into the cramped guest room of the flat.

Yes – that was the only change in his life; and how aptly the change in the rooms symbolized it! During their travels, even after Dorrance's return to health, his wife's presence had been like a soft accompaniment of music, a painted background to the idle episodes of convalescence; now that he was about to fit himself into the familiar furrow of old habits and relations he felt as if she were already expanding and crowding him into a corner. He did not mind about the room – so he assured himself, though with a twinge of regret for the slant of winter sun which never reached the guest room; what he minded was that he now recognized as the huge practical joke that fate had played on him. He had never meant, he the healthy, vigorous, middle-aged Paul Dorrance, to marry this faded woman for whom he had so long ceased to feel anything but a friendly tenderness. It was the bogey of death, starting out from the warm folds of his closely-curtained life, that had tricked him into the marriage, and then left him to expiate his folly.

Poor Eleanor! It was not her fault if he had imagined, in a moment of morbid retrospection, that happiness would transform and enlarge her. Under the surface changes she was still the same: a perfect companion while he was ill and lonely, an unwitting encumbrance now that (unchanged also) he was restored to the life from which his instinct of self-preservation had so long excluded her. Why had he not trusted to that instinct, which had warned him she was the woman for a sentimental parenthesis, not for the pitiless continuity of marriage? Why, even her face declared it. A lovely profile, yes; but somehow the full face was inadequate. . .

Dorrance suddenly remembered another face; that of a girl they had met in Cairo the previous winter. He felt the shock of her young fairness, saw the fruity bloom of her cheeks, the light animal vigor of every movement, he heard her rich beckoning laugh, and met the eyes questioning his under the queer slant of her lids. Someone had said: 'She's had an offer from a man who can give her everything a woman wants; but she's refused, and no one can make out why. . . .' Dorrance knew. . . . She had written to him since, and he had not answered her letters. And now here he was, installed once more in the old routine he could not live without, yet from which all the old savor was gone. 'I wonder why I was so scared of dying,' he thought; then the truth flashed on him. 'Why, you fool, you've been dead all the time. That first diagnosis was the true one. Only they put it on the physical plane by mistake. . . .' The next day he began to insert himself painfully into his furrow.

• V •

ONE evening some two years later, as Paul Dorrance put his latchkey into his door, he said to himself reluctantly: 'Perhaps I really ought to take her away for a change.'

There was nothing nowadays that he dreaded as much as change. He had had his fill of the unexpected, and it had not agreed with him. Now that he had fitted himself once more into his furrow all he asked was to stay there. It had even become an effort, when summer came, to put off his New York habits and go with his wife to their little place in the country. And the idea that he might have to go away with her in mid-February was positively disturbing.

For the past ten years she had been fighting a bad bronchitis, following on influenza. But 'fighting' was hardly the right word. She, usually so elastic, so indomitable, had not shown her usual resiliency, and Dorrance, from the vantage ground of his recovered health, wondered a little at her lack of spirit. She mustn't not let herself go, he warned her gently. 'I was in a good deal tighter place myself not so many years ago – and look at me now. Don't you let the doctors scare you.' She had promised him again that morning that she wouldn't, and he had gone off to his office without waiting for the physician's visit. But during the day he began in an odd way to feel his wife's nearness. It was as though she needed him, as though there were something she wanted to say; and he concluded that she probably knew she ought to go south, and had been afraid to tell him so. 'Poor child – of course I'll take her if the doctor says it's really necessary.' Hadn't he always done everything he could for her? It seemed to him that they had been married for years and years, and that as a husband he had behind him a long and irreproachable record. Why, he hadn't even answered that girl's letters. . . .

As he opened the door of the flat a strange woman in a nurse's dress crossed the hall. Instantly Dorrance felt the alien atmosphere of the place, the sense of something absorbing and exclusive which ignores and averts itself from the common doings of men. He had felt that same atmosphere, in all its somber implications, the day he had picked up the cancer diagnosis from the floor.

The nurse stopped to say 'Pneumonia,' and hurried down the passage to his wife's room. The doctor was coming back at nine o'clock; he had left a note in the library, the butler said. Dorrance knew what was in the note before he opened it. Precipitately, with the vertical drop of a bird of prey, death was descending on his house again. And this time there was no mistake in the diagnosis.

The nurse said he could come in for a minute; but he wasn't to stay long, for she didn't like the way the temperature was rising . . . and there, between the chalk-white pillows, in the green-shaded light, he saw his wife's face. What struck him first was the way it had shrunk and narrowed after a few hours of fever; then, that though it wore a just-perceptible smile of welcome, there was no sign of the tremor of illumination which usually greeted his appearance. He remembered how once, encountering that light, he had grumbled inwardly: 'I wish to God she wouldn't always unroll a red carpet when I come in – ' and then been ashamed of his thought. She never embarrassed him by any public show of feeling; that subtle play of light remained invisible to others, and his irritation was caused simply by knowing it was there. 'I don't want to be anybody's sun and moon,' he concluded. But now she was looking at him with a new, an almost critical equality of expression. His first thought was: 'Is it possible she doesn't know me?' But her eyes met his with a glance of recognition, and he understood that the change was simply due to her being enclosed in a world of her own, complete, and independent of his.

'Please, now – ' the nurse reminded him; and obediently he stole out of the room.

The next day there was a slight improvement; the doctors were encouraged; the day nurse said: 'If only it goes on like this – '; and as Dorrance opened the door of his wife's room he thought: 'If only she looks more like her own self – !'

But she did not. She was still in that new and self-contained world which he had immediately identified as the one he had lived in during the months when he had thought he was to die. 'After all, I didn't die,' he reminded himself; but the reminder brought no solace, for he knew exactly what his wife was feeling, he had tested the impenetrability of the barrier which shut her off from the living. 'The truth is, one doesn't only die once,' he mused, aware that he had died already; and the memory of the process, now being re-enacted before him, laid a chill on his heart. If only he could have helped her, made her understand! But the barrier was there, the transparent barrier through which everything on the hither side looked so different. And today it was he who was on the hither side.

Then he remembered how, in his loneliness, he had yearned for the beings already so remote, and the beings on the living side; and he felt for his wife the same rush of pity as when he had thought himself dying, and known what agony his death would cost her.

That day he was allowed to stay for five minutes; the next day ten; she continued to improve, and the doctors would have been perfectly satisfied if her heart had not shown signs of weakness. Hearts, however, medically speaking, are relatively easy to deal with; and to Dorrance she seemed much stronger.

Soon the improvement became so marked that the doctor made no objection to his sitting with her for an hour or two; the nurse was sent for a walk, and Dorrance was allowed to read the morning paper to the invalid. But when he took it up his wife stretched out her hand. 'No – I want to talk to you.'

He smiled, and met her smile. It was as if she had found a slit in the barrier and were reaching out to him. 'Dear – but won't talking tire you?'

'I don't know. Perhaps.' She waited. 'You see, I'm talking to you all the time, while I lie here. . . .'

He knew – he knew! How her pangs went through him! 'But you see, dear, raising your voice. . . .'

She smiled incredulously, that remote behind-the-barrier smile he had felt so often on his own lips. Though she could reach through to him the dividing line was still there, and her eyes met his with a look of weary omniscience.

'But there's no hurry,' he argued. 'Why not wait a day or two? Try to lie there and not even think.'

'Not think!' She raised herself on a weak elbow. 'I want to think every minute – every second. I want to relive everything, day by day, to the last atom of time. . . .'

'Time? But there'll be plenty of time!'

She continued to lean on her elbow, fixing her illumined eyes on him. She did not seem to hear what he said; her attention was concentrated on some secret vision of which he felt himself the mere transparent mask.

'Well,' she exclaimed, with a sudden passionate energy, 'it was worth it! I always knew – '

Dorrance bent toward her. 'What was worth – ?' But she had sunk back with closed eyes, and lay there reabsorbed into the cleft of the pillows, merged in the inanimate, a mere part of the furniture of the sick-room. Dorrance waited for a moment, hardly understanding the change; then he started up, rang, called, and in a few minutes the professionals were in possession, the air was full of ether and camphor, the telephone ringing, the disarray of death in the room. Dorrance knew that he would never know what she had found worth it. . . .

• VI •

HE sat in his library, waiting. Waiting for what? Life was over for him now that she was dead. Until after the funeral a sort of factitious excitement had kept him on his feet. Now there was nothing left but to go over and over those last days. Every detail of them stood out before him in unbearable relief; and one of the most salient had been the unexpected appearance in the sick room of Dorrance's former doctor – the very doctor who, with the cancer specialist, had signed the diagnosis of Dorrance's case. Dorrance, since that day, had naturally never consulted him professionally; and it chanced that they had never met. But Eleanor's physician, summoned at the moment of her last heart attack, without even stopping to notify Dorrance, had called in his colleague. The latter had a high standing as a consultant (the idea made Dorrance smile); and besides, what did it matter? By that time they all knew – nurses, doctors and most of all Dorrance himself – that nothing was possible but to ease the pangs of Eleanor's last hours. And Dorrance had met his former doctor without resentment; hardly even with surprise.

But the doctor had not forgotten that he and his former patient had been old friends; and the day after the funeral, late in the evening, had thought it proper to ring the widower's doorbell and present his condolences. Dorrance, at his entrance, looked up in surprise, at first resenting the intrusion, then secretly relieved at the momentary release from the fiery wheel of his own thoughts. 'The man is a fool – but perhaps,' Dorrance reflected, 'he'll give me something that will make me sleep. . . .'

The two men sat down, and the doctor began to talk gently of Eleanor. He had known her for many years, though not professionally. He spoke of her goodness, her charity, the many instances he had come across his poor patients of her discreet and untiring ministrations. Dorrance, who had dreaded hearing her spoken of, and by this man above all others, found himself listening with a curious avidity to these reminiscences. He needed no one to tell him of Eleanor's kindness, her devotion – yet at the moment such praise was sweet to him. And he took up the theme; but not without a secret stir of vindictiveness, a vague desire to make the doctor suffer for the results of his now-distant blunder. 'She always gave too much of herself – that was the trouble. No one knows that better than I do. She was never really the same after those months of incessant anxiety about me that you doctors made her undergo.' He had not intended to say anything of the sort; but as he spoke the resentment he had thought extinct was fanned into flame by his words. He had forgiven the two doctors for himself, but he suddenly found he could not forgive them for Eleanor, and he had an angry wish to let them know it. 'That diagnosis of yours nearly killed her, though it didn't kill *me,*' he concluded sardonically.

The doctor had followed this outburst with a look of visible perplexity. In the crowded life of a fashionable physician, what room was there to remember a mistaken diagnosis? The sight of his forgetfulness made Dorrance continue with rising irritation: 'The shock of it *did* kill her – I see that now.'

'Diagnosis – what diagnosis?' echoed the doctor blankly.

'I see you don't remember,' said Dorrance.

'Well, no; I don't, for the moment.'

'I'll remind you, then. When you came to see me with that cancer specialist four or five years ago, one of you dropped your diagnosis by mistake in going out. . . .'

'Oh, *that*?' The doctor's face lit up with sudden recollection. 'Of course! The diagnosis of the other poor fellow we'd been to see before coming to you. I remember it all now. Your wife – Mrs. Welwood then, wasn't she? – brought the paper back to me a few hours later – before I'd even missed it. I think she said you'd picked it up after we left, and thought it was meant for *you*.' The doctor gave an easy retrospective laugh. 'Luckily I was able to reassure her at once.' He leaned back comfortably in his armchair and shifted his voice to the pitch of condolence. 'A beautiful life, your wife's was. I only wish it had been in our power to prolong it. But these cases of heart failure . . . you must tell yourself that at least you had a few happy years; and so many of us haven't even that.' The doctor stood up and held out his hand.

'Wait a moment, please,' Dorrance said hurriedly. 'There's something I want to ask you.' His brain was whirling so that he could not remember what he had started to say. 'I can't sleep. . . .' he began.

'Yes?' said the doctor, assuming a professional look, but with a furtive glance at his wrist watch.

Dorrance's throat felt dry and his head empty. He struggled with the difficulty of ordering his thoughts, and fitting rational words of them.

'Yes – but no matter about my sleeping. What I meant was: do I understand you to say that the diagnosis you dropped in leaving was not intended for me?'

The doctor stared. 'Good Lord, no – of course it wasn't. You never had a symptom. Didn't we both tell you so at the time?'

'Yes,' Dorrance slowly acquiesced.

'Well, if you didn't believe us, your scare was a short one, anyhow,' the doctor continued with a mild jocularity; and he put his hand out again.

'Oh, wait,' Dorrance repeated. 'What I really wanted to ask was what day you said my wife returned the diagnosis to you? But I suppose you don't remember.'

The doctor reflected. 'Yes, I do; it all comes back to me now. It was the very same day. We called on you in the morning, didn't we?'

'Yes; at nine o'clock,' said Dorrance, the dryness returning to his throat.

'Well, Mrs. Welwood brought the diagnosis back to me directly afterward.'

'You think it was the very same day?' (Dorrance wondered to himself why he continued to insist on this particular point.)

The doctor took another stolen glance at his watch. 'I'm sure it was. I remember now that it was my consultation day, and that she caught me at two o'clock, before I saw my first patient. We had a good laugh over the scare you'd had.'

'I see,' said Dorrance.

'Your wife had one of the sweetest laughs I ever heard,' continued the doctor, with an expression of melancholy reminiscence.

There was a silence, and Dorrance was conscious that his visitor was looking at him with growing perplexity. He too gave a slight laugh. 'I thought perhaps it was the day after,' he mumbled vaguely. 'Anyhow, you did give me a good scare.'

'Yes,' said the doctor. 'But it didn't last long, did it? I asked your wife to make my peace with you. You know such things will happen to hurried doctors. I hope she persuaded you to forgive me?'

'Oh, yes,' said Dorrance, as he followed the doctor to the door to let him out.

'Well, now about that sleeping – ' the doctor checked himself on the threshold to ask.

'Sleeping?' Dorrance stared. 'Oh, I shall sleep all right tonight,' he said with sudden decision, as he closed the door on his visitor.

The Day of the Funeral

HIS WIFE had said: 'If you don't give her up I'll throw myself from the roof.' He had not given her up, and his wife had thrown herself from the roof.

Nothing of this had of course come out in the inquest. Luckily Mrs. Trenham had left no letters or diary – no papers of any sort, in fact; not even a little mound of ashes on the hearth. She was the kind of woman who never seemed to have many material appurtenances or encumbrances. And Dr. Lanscomb, who had attended her ever since her husband had been called to his professorship at Kingsborough, testified that she had always been excessively emotional and high-strung, and never 'quite right' since her only child had died. The doctor's evidence closed the inquiry; the whole business had not lasted more than ten minutes.

Then, after another endless interval of forty-eight hours, came the funeral. Ambrose Trenham could never afterward recall what he did during those forty-eight hours. His wife's relations lived at the other end of the continent, in California; he himself had no immediate family; and the house – suddenly became strange and unfamiliar, a house that seemed never to have been his – had been given over to benevolent neighbors, soft-stepping motherly women, and to glib, subservient men who looked like a cross between book agents and revivalists. These men took measures, discussed technical questions in undertones with the motherly women, and presently came back with a coffin with plated handles. Someone asked Trenham what was to be engraved on the plate on the lid, and he said: 'Nothing.' He understood afterward that the answer had not been what was expected; but at the time everyone evidently ascribed it to his being incapacitated by grief.

Before the funeral one horrible moment stood out from the others, though all were horrible. It was when Mrs. Cossett, the wife of the professor of English Literature, came to him and said: 'Do you want to see her?'

'See her – ?' Trenham gasped, not understanding.

Mrs. Cossett looked surprised, and a little shocked. 'The time has come – they must close the coffin. . . .'

'Oh, let them close it,' was on the tip of the widower's tongue; but he saw from Mrs. Cossett's expression that something very different was expected of him. He got up and followed her out of the room and up the stairs. . . . He looked at his wife. Her face had been spared. . . .

That too was over now, and the funeral as well. Somehow, after all, the time had worn on. At the funeral, Trenham had discovered in himself – he, the absent-minded, the unobservant – an uncanny faculty for singling out every one whom he knew in the crowded church. It was incredible; sitting in the front pew, his head bowed forward on his hands, he seemed suddenly gifted with the power of knowing who was behind him and on either side. And when the service was over, and to the sound of 'O Paradise' he turned to walk down the nave behind the coffin, though his head was still bowed, and he was not conscious of looking to the right or the left, face after face thrust itself forward into his field of vision – and among them, yes: of a sudden, Barbara Wake's!

The shock was terrible; Trenham had been so sure she would not come. Afterward he understood that she had had to – for the sake of appearances. 'Appearances' still ruled at Kingsborough – where didn't they, in the university world, and more especially in New England? But at the moment, and for a long time, Trenham had felt horrified, and outraged in what now seemed his holiest feelings. What right had she? How dare she? It was indecent. . . . In the reaction produced by the shock of seeing her, his remorse for what had happened hardened into icy hate of the woman who had been the cause of the tragedy. The sole cause – for in a flash Trenham had thrown off his own share in the disaster. 'The woman tempted me – ' Yes, she had! It was what his poor wronged Milly had always said: 'You're so weak: and she's always tempting you – '

He used to laugh at the idea of Barbara Wake as a temptress; one of poor Milly's delusions! It seemed to him, then, that he was always pursuing, the girl evading; but now he saw her as his wife had seen her, and despised her accordingly. The indecency of her coming to the funeral! To have another look at him, he supposed . . . she was insatiable . . . it was as if she could never fill her eyes with him. But, if he could help it, they should never be laid on him again. . . .

• II •

His indignation grew; it filled the remaining hours of the endless day, the empty hours after the funeral was over; it occupied and sustained him. The President of the University, an old friend, had driven him back to his lonely house, had wanted to get out and come in with him. But Trenham had refused, had shaken hands at the gate, and walked alone up the path to his front door. A cold lunch was waiting on the dining-room table. He left it untouched, poured out some whiskey and water, carried the glass into his study, lit his pipe and sat down in his armchair to think, not of his wife, with whom the inquest seemed somehow to have settled his account, but of Barbara Wake. With her he must settle his account himself. And he had known at once how he would do it; simply by tying up all her letters, and the little photograph he always carried in his notecase (the only likeness he had of her), and sending them back without a word.

A word! What word indeed could equal the emphasis of that silence? Barbara Wake had all the feminine passion for going over and over things; talking them inside out; in that respect she was as bad as poor Milly had been, and nothing would humiliate and exasperate her as much as an uncommented gesture of dismissal. It was so fortifying to visualize that scene – the scene of her opening the packet alone in her room – that Trenham's sense of weariness disappeared, his pulses begun to drum excitedly, and he was torn by a pang of hunger, the first he had felt in days. Was the cold meat still on the table, he wondered? Shamefacedly he stole back to the dining room. But the table had been cleared, of course – just today! On ordinary days the maid would leave the empty dishes for hours unremoved; it was one of poor Milly's household grievances. How often he had said to her, impatiently: 'Good Lord, what does it matter?' and she had answered: 'But,

Ambrose, the flies!' . . . And now, of all days, the fool of a maid had cleared away everything. He went back to his study, sat down again, and suddenly felt too hungry to think of anything but his hunger. Even his vengeance no longer nourished him; he felt as if nothing would replace that slice of pressed beef, with potato salad and pickles, of which his eyes had rejected the disgusted glimpse an hour or two earlier.

He fought his hunger for a while longer; then he got up and rang. Promptly, attentively, Jane, the middle-aged disapproving maid, appeared – usually one had to rip out the bell before she disturbed herself. Trenham felt sheepish at having to confess his hunger to her, as if it made him appear unfeeling, unheroic; but he could not help himself. He stammered out that he supposed he ought to eat something . . . and Jane, at once, was all tearful sympathy. 'That's right, sir; you must *try* . . . you must force yourself. . . .' Yes, he said; he realized that. He would force himself. 'We were saying in the kitchen, Katy and me, that you couldn't go on any longer this way. . . .' He could hardly wait till she had used up her phrases and got back to the pantry. . . . Through the half-open dining-room door he listened avidly to her steps coming and going, to the clatter of china, the rattle of the knife basket. He met her at the door when she returned to tell him that his lunch was ready . . . and that Katy had scrambled some eggs for him the way he liked them.

At the dining-room table, when the door had closed on her, he squared his elbows, bent his head over his plate, and emptied every dish. Had he ever before known the complex exquisiteness of a slice of pressed beef? He filled his glass again, leaned luxuriously, waited without hurry for the cheese and biscuits, the black coffee, and a slice of apple pie apologetically added from the maids' dinner – and then – oh, resurrection! – felt for his cigar case, and calmly, carelessly almost, under Jane's moist and thankful eyes, cut his Corona and lit it.

'Now he's saved,' her devout look seemed to say.

• III •

THE letters must be returned at once. But to whom could he entrust them? Certainly not to either one of the maidservants. And there was no one else but the slow-witted man who looked after the garden and the furnace, and who would have been too much dazed by such a commission to execute it without first receiving the most elaborate and reiterated explanations, and then would probably have delivered the packet to Professor Wake, or posted it – the latter a possibility to be at all costs avoided, since Trenham's writing might have been recognized by someone at the post office, one of the chief centers of gossip at Kingsborough. How it complicated everything to live in a small, prying community! He had no reason to suppose that any one divined the cause of his wife's death, yet he was aware that people had seen him more than once in out-of-the-way places, and at queer hours, with Barbara Wake; and if his wife knew, why should not others suspect? For a while, at any rate, it behooved him to avoid all appearance of wishing to communicate with the girl. Returning a packet to her on the very day of the funeral would seem particularly suspicious. . . .

Thus, after coffee and cigar, and a nip of old Cognac, argued the normal sensible man that Trenham had become again. But if his nerves had been steadied by food his will had been strengthened by it, and instead of a weak, vacillating wish to let Barbara Wake feel the weight of his scorn he was now animated by the furious resolution to crush her with it, and at once. That packet should be returned to her before night.

He shut the study door, drew out his keys, and unlocked the cabinet in which he kept the letters. He had no need now to listen for his wife's step, or to place himself between the cabinet and the door of the study, as he used to when he thought he heard her coming. Now, had he chosen, he could have spread the letters out all over the table. Jane and Katy were busy in the kitchen, and the rest of the house was his to do what he liked in. He could have sat down and read the serried pages one by one, lingeringly, gloatingly, as he had so often longed to do when the risk was too great – and now they were but so much noisome rubbish to him, to be crammed into a big envelope, and sealed up out of sight. He began to hunt for an envelope. . . .

God! What dozens and dozens of letters there were! And all written within eighteen months. No wonder poor Milly . . . but what a blind reckless fool he had been! The reason of their abundance was, of course, the difficulty of meeting. . . .

So often he and Barbara had had to write because they couldn't contrive to see each other . . . but still, this bombardment of letters was monstrous, inexcusable. . . . He hunted for a long time for an envelope big enough to contain them; finally found one, a huge linen-lined envelope meant for college documents, and jammed the letters into it with averted head. But what, he thought suddenly, if she mistook his silence, imagined he had sent her the letters simply as a measure of prudence? No – that was hardly likely, now that all need of prudence was over; but she might affect to think so, use the idea as a pretext to write and ask what he meant, what she was to understand by his returning her letters without a word. It might give her an opening, which was probably what she was hoping for, and certainly what he was most determined she should not have.

He found a sheet of note paper, shook his fountain pen, wrote a few words (hardly looking at the page as he did so), and thrust the note in among the letters. His hands turned clammy as he touched them; he felt cold and sick . . . and the cursed flap of the envelope wouldn't stick – those linen envelopes were always so stiff. And where the devil was the sealing wax? He rummaged frantically among the odds and ends on his desk. A provision of sealing wax used always to be kept in the lower left-hand drawer. He groped about in it and found only some yellowing newspaper clippings. Milly used to be so careful about seeing that his writing table was properly supplied; but lately – ah, his poor poor Milly! If she could only know how he was suffering and atoning already. . . . Some string, then. . . . He fished some string out of another drawer. He would have to make it do instead of sealing wax; he would have to try to tie a double knot. But his fingers, always clumsy, were twitching like a drug fiend's; the letters seemed to burn them through the envelope. With a shaking hand he addressed the packet, and sat there, his eyes turned from it, while he tried again to think out some safe means of having it delivered. . . .

• IV •

HE dined hungrily, as he had lunched; and after dinner he took his hat from its peg in the hall, and said to Jane: 'I think I'll smoke my cigar in the campus.'

That was a good idea; he saw at once that she thought it a hopeful sign, his wanting to take the air after being mewed up in the house for so long. The night was cold and moonless, and the college grounds, at that hour, would be a desert . . . after all, delivering the letters himself was the safest way: openly, at the girl's own door, without any mystery. . . . If Malvina, the Wakes' old maid, should chance to open the door, he'd pull the packet out and say at once: 'Oh, Malvina, I've found some books that Miss Barbara lent me last year, and as I'm going away – ' He had gradually learned that there was nothing as safe as simplicity.

He was reassured by the fact that the night was so dark. It felt queer, unnatural somehow, to be walking abroad again like the Ambrose Trenham he used to be; he was glad there were so few people about, and that the Kingsborough suburbs were so scantily lit. He walked on, his elbow hitting now and then against the bundle, which bulged out of his pocket. Every time he felt it a sort of nausea rose in him. Professor Wake's house stood halfway down one of the quietest of Kingsborough's outlying streets. It was withdrawn from the road under the hanging boughs of old elms; he could just catch a glint of light from one or two windows. And suddenly, as he was almost abreast of the gate, Barbara Wake came out of it.

For a moment she stood glancing about her; then she turned in the direction of the narrow lane bounding the farther side of the property. What took her there, Trenham wondered? His first impulse had been to draw back, and let her go her way; then he saw how providential the encounter was. The lane was dark, deserted – a mere passage between widely scattered houses, all asleep in their gardens. The chilly night had sent people home early; there was not a soul in sight. In another moment the packet would be in her hands, and he would have left her, just silently raising his hat.

He remembered now where she was going. The garage, built in the far corner of the garden, opened into the lane. The Wakes had no chauffeur, and Barbara, who drove the car, was sole mistress of the garage and of its keys. Trenham and she had met there sometimes; a desolate trysting place! But what could they do, in a town like Kingsborough? At one time she had talked of setting up a studio – she dabbled in painting; but the suggestion had alarmed him (he knew the talk it would create), and he had discouraged her. Most often they took the train and went to Ditson, a manufacturing town an hour away, where no one knew them . . . but what could she be going to the garage for at this hour?

The thought of his wife rushed into Trenham's mind. The discovery that she had lived there beside him, knowing all, and that suddenly, when she found she could not regain his affection, life had seemed worthless, and without a moment's hesitation she had left it. . . . Why, if he had known the quiet woman at his side had such springs of passion in her, how differently he would have regarded her, how little this girl's insipid endearments would have mattered to him! He was a man who could not live without tenderness, without demonstrative tenderness; his own shyness and reticence had to be perpetually broken down, laughingly scattered to the winds. His wife, he now saw, had been too much like him, had secretly suffered from the same inhibitions. She had always seemed ashamed, and frightened by her feeling for him, and half repelled, half fascinated by his response. At times he imagined that she found him physically distasteful, and wondered how, that being the case, she could be so fiercely jealous of him. Now he understood that her cold reluctant surrender concealed a passion so violent that it humiliated her, and so incomprehensible that she had never mastered its language. She reminded him of a clumsy little girl he had once known at a dancing class he had been sent to as a boy – a little girl who had a feverish passion for dancing, but could never learn the steps. And because he too had felt the irresistible need to join in the immemorial love dance he had ended by choosing a partner more skilled in its intricacies. . . .

These thoughts wandered through his mind as he stood watching Barbara Wake. Slowly he took a few steps down the lane; then he halted again. He had not yet made up his mind what to do. If she were going to the garage to get something she had forgotten (as was most probable, at that hour) she would no doubt be coming back in a few moments, and he could meet her and hand her the letters. Above all, he wanted to avoid going into the garage. To do so at that moment would have been a profanation of Milly's memory. He would have liked to efface from his own all recollection of the furtive hours spent there; but the vision returned with intolerable acuity as the girl's slim figure, receding from him, reached the door. How often he had stood at that corner, under those heavy trees, watching for her to appear and slip in ahead of him – so that they should not be seen entering together. The elaborate precautions with which their meetings had been surrounded – how pitiably futile they now seemed! They had not even achieved their purpose, but had only belittled his love and robbed it of its spontaniety. Real passion ought to be free, reckless, audacious, unhampered by the fear of a wife's feelings, of the university's regulations, the president's friendship, the deadly risk of losing one's job and wrecking one's career. It seemed to him now that the love he had given to Barbara Wake was almost as niggardly as that which he had doled out to his wife. . . .

He walked down the lane and saw that Barbara was going into the garage. It was so dark that he could hardly make out her movements; but as he reached the door she drew out her electric lamp (that recalled memories too), and by its flash he saw her slim gloveless hand put the key into the lock. The key turned, the door creaked, and all was darkness. . . .

The glimpse of her hand reminded him of the first time he had dared to hold it in his and press a kiss on the palm. They had met accidentally in the train, both of them on their way home from Boston, and he had proposed that they should get off at the last station before Kingsborough, and walk back by a short cut he knew, through the woods and along the King river. It was a shining summer day, and the girl had been amused at the idea and had accepted. . . . He could see now every line, every curve of her hand, a quick strong young hand, with long fingers, slightly blunt at the tips, and a sensuous elastic palm. It would be queer to have to carry on life without ever again knowing the feel of that hand. . . .

Of course he would go away; he would have to. If possible he would leave the following week. Perhaps the faculty would let him advance his sabbatical year. If not, they would probably let him off for the winter term, and perhaps after that he might make up his mind to resign, and look for a professorship elsewhere – in the South, or in California – as far away from that girl as possible. Meanwhile what he wanted was to get away to some hot climate, steamy, tropical, where one could lie out all night on a white beach and hear the palms chatter to the waves, and the trade winds blow from God knew where . . . one of those fiery flowery islands where marriage and love were not regarded so solemnly, and a man could follow his instinct without calling down a catastrophe, or feeling himself morally degraded. . . . Above all, he never wanted to see again a woman who argued and worried and reproached, and dramatized things that ought to be as simple as eating and drinking. . . .

Barbara, he had to admit, had never been frightened or worried, had never reproached him. The girl had the true sporting instinct; he never remembered her being afraid of risks, or nervous about 'appearances.' Once or twice, at moments when detection seemed imminent, she had half frightened him by her cool resourcefulness. He sneered at the remembrance. 'An old hand, no doubt!' But the sneer did not help him. Whose fault was it if the girl had had to master the arts of dissimulation? Whose but his? He alone (he saw in sudden terror) was responsible for what he supposed would be called her downfall. Poor child – poor Barbara! Was it possible that he, the seducer, the corrupter, had presumed to judge her? The thought was monstrous. . . . His resentment had already vanished like a puff of mist. The feeling of his responsibility, which had seemed so abhorrent, was now almost sweet to him. He was responsible – he owed her something! Thank heaven for that! For now he could raise his passion into a duty, and thus disguised and moralized, could once more – oh, could he, dared he? – admit it openly into his life. The mere possibility made him suddenly feel less cold and desolate. That the something – not – himself that made for righteousness should take on the tender lineaments, the human warmth of love, should come to sit by his hearth in the shape of Barbara – how warm, how happy and reassured it made him! He had a swift vision of her, actually sitting there in the shabby old leather chair (he would have it re-covered), her slim feet on the faded Turkey rug (he would have it replaced). It was almost a pity – he thought madly – that they would probably not be able to stay on at Kingsborough, there, in that very house where for so long he had not even dared to look at her letters. . . . Of course, if they did decide to, he would have it all done over for her.

• V •

THE garage door creaked and again he saw the flash of the electric lamp on her bare hand as she turned the key; then she moved toward him in the darkness.

'Barbara!'

She stopped short at his whisper. They drew closer to each other. 'You wanted to see me?' she whispered back. Her voice flowed over him like summer air.

'Can we go in there – ?' he gestured.

'Into the garage? Yes – I suppose so.'

They turned and walked in silence through the obscurity. The comfort of her nearness was indescribable.

She unlocked the door again, and he followed her in. 'Take care; I left the wheel jack somewhere,' she warned him. Automatically he produced a match, and she lit the candle in an old broken-paned lantern that hung on a nail against the wall. How familiar it all was – how often he had brought out his matchbox and she had lit that candle! In the little pool of yellowish light they stood and looked at each other.

'You didn't expect me?' he stammered.

'I'm not sure I didn't,' she returned softly, and he just caught her smile in the half-light. The divineness of it!

'I didn't suppose I should see you. I just wandered out. . . .' He suddenly felt the difficulty of accounting for himself.

'My poor Ambrose!' She laid her hand on his arm. 'How I've ached for you – '

Yes; that was right; the tender sympathizing friend . . . anything else, at that moment, would have been unthinkable. He drew a breath of relief and self-satisfaction. Her pity made him feel almost heroic – had he not lost sight of his own sufferings in the thought of hers? 'It's been awful – ' he muttered.

'Yes; I know.'

She sat down on the step of the old Packard, and he found a wooden stool and dragged it into the candle ray.

'I'm glad you came,' she began, still in the same soft healing voice, 'because I'm going away tomorrow early, and – '

He started to his feet, upsetting the stool with a crash. 'Going away? Early tomorrow?' Why hadn't he known of this? He felt weak and injured. Where could she be going in this sudden way?

If they hadn't happened to meet, would he have known nothing of it till she was gone? His heart grew small and cold.

She was saying quietly: 'You must see – it's better. I'm going out to the Jim Southwicks, in California. They're always asking me. Mother and father think it's on account of my colds . . . the winter climate here . . . they think I'm right.' She paused, but he could find nothing to say. The future had become a featureless desert. 'I wanted to see you before going,' she continued, 'and I didn't exactly know . . . I hoped you'd come – '

'When are you coming back?' he interrupted desperately.

'Oh, I don't know; they want me for the winter, of course. There's a crazy plan about Hawaii and Samoa . . . sounds lovely, doesn't it? And from there on. . . . But I don't know. . . .'

He felt a suffocation in his throat. If he didn't cry out, do something at once to stop her, he would choke. 'You can't go – you can't leave me like this!' It seemed to him that his voice had risen to a shout.

'Ambrose – ' she murmured, subdued, half warning.

'You can't. How can you? It's madness. You don't understand. You say you ought to go – it's better you should go. What do you mean – why better? Are you afraid of what people might say? Is that it? How can they say anything when they know we're going to be married? Don't you know we're going to be married?' he burst out weakly, his words stumbling over each other in the effort to make her understand.

She hesitated a moment, and he stood waiting in an agony of suspense. How women loved to make men suffer! At last she said in a constrained voice: 'I don't think we ought to talk of all this yet – '

Rebuking him – she was actually rebuking him for his magnanimity! But couldn't she see – couldn't she understand? Or was it that she really enjoyed torturing him? 'How can I help talking of it, when you tell me you're going away tomorrow morning? Did you really mean to go without even telling me?'

'If I hadn't seen you I should have written,' she faltered.

'Well, now I'm here you needn't write. All you've got to do is to answer me,' he retorted almost angrily. The calm way in which she dealt with the situation was enough to madden a man – actually as if she hadn't made up her mind, good God! 'What are you afraid of?' he burst out harshly.

'I'm not afraid – only I didn't expect . . . I thought we'd talk of all this later . . . if you feel the same when I come back – if we both do.'

'If we both do!' Ah, there was the sting – the devil's claw! What was it? Was she being superhumanly magnanimous – or proud, over-sensitive, afraid that he might be making the proposal out of pity? Poor girl – poor child! That must be it. He loved her all the more for it, bless her! Or was it (ah, now again the claw tightened), was it that she really didn't want to commit herself, wanted to reserve her freedom for this crazy expedition, to see whether she couldn't do better by looking about out there – she, so young, so fresh and radiant – than by binding herself in advance to an elderly professor at Kingsborough? Hawaii – Samoa – swarming with rich idle yachtsmen and young naval officers (he had an excruciating vision of a throng of *Madame Butterfly* tenors in immaculate white duck and gold braid) – cocktails, fox-trot, moonlight in the tropics . . . he felt suddenly middle-aged, round shouldered, shabby, with thinning graying hair. . . . Of course what she wanted was to look round and see what her chances were! He retrieved the fallen stool, set it up again, and sat down on it.

'I suppose you're not sure you'll feel the same when you get back? Is that it?' he suggested bitterly.

Again she hesitated. 'I don't think we ought to decide now – tonight. . . .'

His anger blazed. 'Why oughtn't we? Tell me that! I've decided. Why shouldn't you?'

'You haven't really decided either,' she returned gently.

'I haven't – haven't I? Now what do you mean by that?' He forced a laugh that was meant to be playful but sounded defiant. He was aware that his voice and words were getting out of hand – but what business had she to keep him on the stretch like this?

'I mean, after what you've been through. . . .'

'After what I've been through? But don't you see that's the very reason? I'm at the breaking point – I can't bear any more.'

'I know; I know.' She got up and came close, laying a quiet hand on his shoulder. 'I've suffered for you too. The shock it must have been. That's the reason why I don't want to say anything now that you might – '

He shook off her hand, and sprang up. 'What hypocrisy!' He heard himself beginning to shout again. 'I suppose what you mean is that you want to be free to marry out there if you see anybody you like better. Then why not admit it at once?'

'Because it's not what I mean. I don't want to marry anyone else, Ambrose.'

Oh, the melting music of it! He lifted his hands and hid his burning eyes in them. The sound of her voice wove magic passes above his forehead. Was it possible that such bliss could come out of such anguish? He forgot the place – forgot the day – and abruptly, blindly, caught her by the arm, and flung his own about her.

'Oh, Ambrose – ' he heard her, reproachful, panting. He struggled with her, feverish for her lips.

In the semiobscurity there was the sound of something crashing to the floor between them. They drew apart, and she looked at him, bewildered. 'What was that?'

What was it? He knew well enough; a shiver of cold ran over him. The letters, of course – her letters! The bulging clumsily-tied envelope had dropped out of his pocket onto the floor of the garage; in the fall the string had come undone, and the mass of papers had tumbled out, scattering themselves like a pack of cards at Barbara's feet. She picked up her electric lamp, and bending over shot its sharp ray on them.

'Why, they're letters! Ambrose – are they my letters?' She waited; but silence lay on him like lead. 'Was that what you came for?' she exclaimed.

If there was an answer to that he couldn't find it, and stupidly, without knowing what he was doing, he bent down and began to gather up the letters.

For a while he was aware of her standing there motionless, watching him; then she too bent over, and took up the gaping linen envelope. 'Miss Barbara Wake,' she read out; and suddenly she began to laugh. 'Why,' she said, 'there's something left in it! A letter for *me*? Is that it?'

He put his hand out. 'Barbara – don't! Barbara – I implore you!'

She turned the electric ray on the sheet of paper, which detached itself from the shadows with the solidity of a graven tablet. Slowly she read out, in a cool measured voice, almost as though she were parodying his poor phrases: ' "November tenth. . . . You will probably feel as I do" (no – don't snatch! Ambrose, I forbid you!) "You will probably feel, as I do, that after what has happened you and I can never" – ' She broke off and raised her eyes to Trenham's. ' "After what has happened"? I don't understand. What do you mean? What *has* happened, Ambrose – between you and me?'

He had retreated a few steps, and stood leaning against the side of the motor. 'I didn't say "between you and me."'

'What did you say?' She turned the light once more on the fatal page. ' "You and I can never wish to meet again."' Her hand sank, and she stood facing him in silence.

Feeling her gaze fixed on him, he muttered miserably: 'I asked you not to read the thing.'

'But if it was meant for me why do you want me not to read it?'

'Can't you see? It doesn't mean anything. I was raving mad when I wrote it. . . .'

'But you wrote it only a few hours ago. It's dated today. How can you have changed so in a few hours? And you say: "After what has happened." That must mean something. What does it mean? What *has* happened?'

He thought he would go mad indeed if she repeated the word again. 'Oh, don't – !' he exclaimed.

'Don't what?'

'Say it over and over – "what has happened?" Can't you understand that just at first – '

He broke off, and she prompted him: 'Just at first – ?'

'I couldn't bear the horror alone. Like a miserable coward I let myself think you were partly responsible – I wanted to think so, you understand. . . .'

Her face seemed to grow white and wavering in the shadows. 'What do you mean? Responsible for what?'

He straightened his shoulders and said slowly: 'Responsible for her death. I was too weak to carry it alone.'

'Her death?' There was a silence that seemed to make the shadowy place darker. He could hardly see her face now, she was so far off. 'How could I be responsible?' she broke off, and then began again: 'Are you – trying to tell me – that it wasn't an accident?'

'No – it wasn't an accident.'

'She – '

'Well, can't you guess?' he stammered, panting.

'You mean – she killed herself?'

'Yes.'

'Because of us?'

He could not speak, and after a moment she hurried on: 'But what makes you think so? What proof have you? Did she tell anyone? Did she leave a message – a letter?'

He summoned his voice to his dry throat. 'No; nothing.'

'Well, then – ?'

'She'd told me beforehand; she'd warned me – '

'Warned you?'

'That if I went on seeing you . . . and I did go on seeing you . . . she warned me again and again. Do you understand now?' he exclaimed, twisting round on her fiercely, like an animal turning on its torturer.

There was an interval of silence – endless it seemed to him. She did not speak or move; but suddenly he heard a low sobbing sound. She was weeping, weeping like a frightened child. . . . well, of all the unexpected turns of fate! A moment ago he had seemed to feel her strength flowing into his cold veins, had thought to himself: 'I shall never again be alone with my horror – ' and now the horror had spread from him to her, and he felt her inwardly recoiling as though she shuddered away from the contagion.

'Oh, how dreadful, how dreadful – ' She began to cry again, like a child swept by a fresh gust of misery as the last subsides.

'Why dreadful?' he burst out, unnerved by the continuance of her soft unremitting sobs. 'You must have known she didn't like it – didn't you?'

Through her lament a whisper issued: 'I never dreamed she knew.'

'You mean to say you thought we'd deceived her? All those months? In a one-horse place where everybody is on the watch to see what everybody else is doing? Likely, isn't it? My God – '

'I never dreamed . . . I never dreamed. . . .' she reiterated.

'His exasperation broke out again. 'Well, now you begin to see what I've suffered – '

'Suffered? *You* suffered?' She uttered a low sound of derision. 'I see what she must have suffered – what we both of us must have made her suffer.'

'Ah, at least you say "both of us"!'

She made no answer, and through her silence he felt again that she was inwardly shrinking, averting herself from him. What! His accomplice deserting him? She acknowledged that she was his accomplice – she said 'both of us' – and yet she was drawing back from him, flying from him, leaving him alone! Ah, no – she shouldn't escape as easily as that, she shouldn't leave him; he couldn't face that sense of being alone again. 'Barbara!' he cried out, as if the actual distance between them had already doubled.

She still remained silent, and he hurried on, almost cringingly: 'Don't think I blame you, child – don't think. . . .'

'Oh, what does it matter, when I blame myself?' she wailed out, her face in her hands.

'Blame yourself? What folly! When you say you didn't know – '

'Of course I didn't know! How can you imagine – ? But this dreadful thing has happened; and *you* knew it might happen . . . you knew it all along . . . all the while it was in the back of your mind . . . the days when we used to meet here . . . and the days when we went to Ditson . . . oh, that horrible room at Ditson! All that time she was sitting at home alone, knowing everything, and hating me as if I'd been her murderess. . . .'

'Good God, Barbara! Don't you suppose I blame myself?'

'But if you blamed yourself how could you go on, how could you let me think she didn't care?'

'I didn't suppose she did,' he muttered sullenly.

'But you say she told you – she warned you! Over and over again she warned you.'

'Well, I didn't want to believe her – and so I didn't. When a man's infatuated. . . . Don't you see it's hard enough to bear without all this? Haven't you any pity for me, Barbara?'

'Pity?' she repeated slowly. 'The only pity I feel is for *her* – for what she must have gone through, day after day, week after week, sitting there all alone and knowing . . . imagining exactly what you were saying to me . . . the way you kissed me . . . and watching the clock, and counting the hours . . . and then having you come back, and explained, and pretend – I suppose you *did* pretend? . . . and all the while secretly knowing you were lying, and yet longing to believe you . . . and having warned you, and seeing that her warnings made no difference . . . that you didn't care if she died or not . . . that you were doing all you could to kill her . . . that you were probably counting the days till she was dead!' Her passionate apostrophe broke down in a sob, and again she stood weeping like an inconsolable child.

Trenham was struck silent. It was true. He had never been really able to enter into poor Milly's imaginings, the matter of her lonely musings; and here was this girl to whom, in a flash, that solitary mind lay bare. Yes; that must have been the way Milly felt – he knew it now – and the way poor Barbara herself would feel if he ever betrayed her. Ah, but he was never going to betray her – the thought was monstrous! Never for a moment would he cease to love her. This catastrophe had bound them together as a happy wooing could never have done. It was her love for him, her fear for their future, that was shaking her to the soul, giving her this unnatural power to enter into Milly's mind. If only he could find words to reassure her, now, at once. But he could not think of any.

'Barbara – Barbara,' he kept on repeating, as if her name were a sort of incantation.

'Oh, think of it – those lonely endless hours! I wonder if you ever did think of them before? When you used to go home after one of our meetings, did you remember each time what she'd told you, and begin to wonder, as you got near the house, if she'd done it *that day*?'

'Barbara – '

'Perhaps you did – perhaps you were even vexed with her for being so slow about it. Were you?'

'Oh, Barbara – Barbara. . . .'

'And when the day came at last, were you surprised? Had you got so impatient waiting that you'd begun to believe she'd never do it? Were these days when you went almost mad at having to wait so long for your freedom? It was the way I used to feel when I was rushing for the train to Ditson, and father would call me at the last minute to write letters for him, or mother to replace her on some charity committee; there were days when I could have *killed* them, almost, for interfering with me, making me miss one of our precious hours together. *Killed them*, I say! Don't you suppose I know how murderers feel? How *you* feel – for you're a murderer, you know! And now you come here, when the earth's hardly covered her, and try to kiss me, and ask me to marry you – and think, I suppose, that by doing so you're covering up her memory more securely, you're pounding down the earth on her a little harder. . . .'

She broke off, as if her own words terrified her, and hid her eyes from the vision they called up.

Trenham stood without moving. He had gathered up the letters, and they lay in a neat pile on the floor between himself and her, because there seemed no other place to put them. He said to himself (reflecting how many million men must have said the same thing at such moments): 'After this she'll calm down, and by tomorrow she'll be telling me how sorry she is. . . .' But the reflection did not seem to help him. She might forget – but he would not. He had forgotten too easily before; he had an idea that his future would be burdened with long arrears of remembrance. Just as the girl described Milly, so he would see her in the years to come. He would have to pay the interest on his oblivion; and it would not help much to have Barbara pay it with him. The job was probably one that would have to be accomplished alone. At last words shaped themselves without his knowing it. 'I'd better go,' he said.

Unconsciously he had expected an answer, an appeal; a protest, perhaps. But none came. He moved away a few steps in the direction of the door. As he did so he heard Barbara break into a laugh, and the sound, so unnatural in that place, and at that moment, brought him abruptly to a halt.

'Yes – ?' he said, half turning, as though she had called him.

'And I sent a wreath – I sent her a wreath! It's on her grave now – it hasn't even had time to fade!'

'Oh – ' he gasped, as if she had struck him across the face. They stood forlornly confronting each other. Her last words seemed to have created an icy void between them. Within himself a voice whispered: 'She can't find anything worse than that.' But he saw by the faint twitch of her lips that she was groping, groping –

'And the worst of it is,' she broke out, 'that if I didn't go away, and we were to drag on here together, after a time I might even drift into forgiving you.'

Yes; she was right; that was certainly the worst of it. Human imagination could not go beyond that, he thought. He moved away again stiffly.

'Well, you *are* going away, aren't you?' he said.

'Yes; I'm going.'

He walked back slowly through the dark deserted streets. His brain, reeling with the shock of the encounter, gradually cleared, and looked about on the new world within itself. At first the inside of his head was like a deserted house out of which all the furniture had been moved, down to the last familiar encumbrances. It was empty, absolutely empty. But gradually a small speck of consciousness appeared in the dreary void, like a mouse scurrying across bare floors. He stopped on a street corner to say to himself: 'But after all nothing is changed – absolutely nothing. I went there to tell her that we should probably never want to see each other again; and she agreed with me. She agreed with me – that's all.'

It was a relief, almost, to have even that little thought stirring about in the resonant of his brain. He walked on more quickly, reflecting, as he reached his own corner: 'In a minute it's going to rain.' He smiled a little at his unconscious precaution in hurrying home to escape the rain. 'Jane will begin to fret – she'll be sure to notice that I didn't take my umbrella.' And his cold heart felt a faint warmth at the thought that someone in the huge hostile world would really care whether he had taken his umbrella or not. 'But probably she's in bed and asleep,' he mused, despondently.

On his doorstep he paused and began to grope for his latchkey. He felt impatiently in one pocket after another – but the key was not to be found. He had an idea that he had left it lying on his study table when he came in after – after what? Why, that very morning, after the funeral! He had flung the key down among his papers – and Jane would never notice that it was there. She would never think of looking; she had been bidden often enough on no account to meddle with the things on his desk. And besides she would take for granted that he had the key in his pocket. And here he stood, in the middle of the night, locked out of his own house –

A sudden exasperation possessed him. He was aware that he must have lost all sense of proportion, all perspective, for he felt as baffled and as angry as when Barbara's furious words had beaten down on him. Yes; it made him just as unhappy to find himself locked out of his house – he could have sat down on the doorstep and cried. And here was the rain beginning. . . .

He put his hand to the bell; but did the front doorbell ring in the far-off attic where the maids were lodged? And was there the least chance of the faint tinkle from the pantry mounting two flights, and penetrating to their sleep-muffled ears? Utterly improbable, he knew. And if he couldn't make them hear he would have to spend the night at a hotel – the night of his wife's funeral! And the next morning all Kingsborough would know of it, from the President of the University to the boy who delivered the milk. . . .

But his hand had hardly touched the bell when he felt a vibration of life in the house. First there was a faint flash of light through the transom above the front door; then, scarcely distinguishable from the noises of the night, a step sounded far off; it grew louder on the hall floor, and after an interval that seemed endless the door was flung open by a Jane still irreproachably capped and aproned.

'Why, Jane – I didn't think you'd be awake! I forgot my key. . . .'

'I know, sir. I found it. I was waiting.' She took his wet coat from him. Dear, dear! And you hadn't your umbrella.'

He stepped into his own hall, and heard her close and bar the door behind him. He liked to listen to that familiar slipping of the bolts and clink of the chain. He liked to think that she minded about his not having his umbrella. It was his own house, after all – and this friendly hand was shutting him safely into it. The dreadful sense of loneliness melted a little at the old reassuring touch of habit.

'Thank you, Jane; sorry I kept you up,' he muttered, nodding to her as he went upstairs.

Confession

THIS IS THE WAY it began; stupidly, trivally, out of nothing as fatal things do.

I was sitting at the corner table in the hotel restaurant; I mean the left-hand corner as you enter from the hall . . . as if that mattered! A table in that angle, with a view over the mountains, was too good for an unaccompanied traveler, and I had it only because the headwaiter was a good-natured fellow who . . . as if that mattered, either! Why can't I come to the point?

The point is that, entering the restaurant that day with the doubtful step of the newly-arrived, she was given the table next to me. Colossal Event – eh? But if you've ever known what it is, after a winter of semi-invalidism on the Nile, to be told that, before you're fit to go back and take up your job in New York – before that little leak in your lung is patched up tight – you've got to undergo another three or four months of convalescence on top of an Alp; if you've dragged through all those stages of recovery, first among one pack of hotel idlers, then among another, you'll know what small incidents can become Colossal Events against the empty horizon of your idleness.

Not that a New York banker's office (even before the depression) commanded a very wide horizon, as I understand horizons; but before arguing that point with me, wait and see what it's like to look out day after day on a dead-level of inoccupation, and you'll know what a towering affair it may become to have your temperature go up a point, or a woman you haven't seen before stroll into the dining room, and sit down at the table next to yours.

But what magnified this very ordinary incident for me was the immediate sense of something out of the ordinary in the woman herself. Beauty? No; not even. (I say 'even' because there are far deadlier weapons, as we all know.) No, she was not beautiful; she was not particularly young; and though she carried herself well, and was well-dressed (though overexpensively, I thought), there was nothing in that to single her out in a fashionable crowd.

What then? Well, what struck me first in her was a shy but intense curiosity about everything in that assemblage of commonplace and shopworn people. Here was a woman, evidently well-bred and well-off, to whom a fashionable hotel restaurant in the Engadine during the summer was apparently a sight so unusual, and composed of elements so novel and inexplicable, that she could hardly remember to eat in the subdued excitement of watching all that was going on about her.

As to her own appearance, it obviously did not preoccupy her – or figured only as an element of her general and rather graceful timidity. She was so busy observing all the dull commonplace people about her that it had presumably never occurred to her that she, who was neither dull nor commonplace, might be herself the subject of observation. (Already I found myself resenting any too protracted stare from the other tables.)

Well, to come down to particulars: she was middling tall, slight, almost thin; pale, with a long somewhat narrow face and dark hair; and her wide blue-gray eyes were so light and clear that her hair and complexion seemed dusky in contrast. A melancholy mouth, which lit up suddenly when she smiled – but her smiles were rare. Dress, sober, costly, severely 'ladylike'; her whole appearance, shall I say a trifle old-fashioned – or perhaps merely provincial? But certainly it was not only her dress which singled her out from the standardized beauties at the other tables. Perhaps it was the fact that her air of social inexperience was combined with a look, about the mouth and eyes, of having had more experience, of some other sort, than any woman in the room.

But of what sort? That was what baffled me. I could only sum it up by saying to myself that she was different; which, of course, is what every man feels about the woman he is about to fall in love with, no matter how painfully usual she may appear to others. But I had no idea that I was going to fall in love with the lady at the next table, and when I defined her as 'different' I did not mean it subjectively, did not mean different to *me*, but in herself, mysteriously, and independently of the particular impression she made on me. In short, she appeared, in spite of her dress and bearing, to be a little uncertain and ill at ease in the ordinary social scene, but at home and sure of herself elsewhere. Where?

I was still asking myself this when she was joined by a companion. One of the things one learns in traveling is to find out about people by studying their associates; and I wished that the lady who interested me had not furnished me with this particular kind of clue. The woman who joined her was probably of about her own age; but that seemed to be the only point of resemblance between them. The newcomer was stout, with mahogany-dyed hair, and small eyes set too close to a coarse nose. Her complexion, through a careless powdering, was flushed, and netted with little red veins, and her chin sloped back under a vulgar mouth to a heavy white throat. I had hoped she was only a chance acquaintance of the dark lady's; but she took her seat without speaking, and began to study the menu without as much as a glance at her companion. They were fellow travelers, then; and though the newcomer was as richly dressed as the other, and I judged more fashionably, I detected at once that she was a subordinate, probably a paid one, and that she sought to conceal it by an exaggerated assumption of equality. But how could the one woman have chosen the other as a companion? It disturbed my mental picture of the dark lady to have to fit into it what was evidently no chance association.

'Have you ordered my beer?' the last comer asked, drawing off her long gloves from thick red fingers crammed with rings (the dark lady wore none, I had noticed.)

'No, I haven't,' said the other.

Her tone somehow suggested: 'Why should I? Can't you ask for what you want yourself?' But a moment later she had signed to the headwaiter, and said, in a low tone: 'Miss Wilpert's Pilsener, please – as usual.'

'Yes; *as usual*. Only nobody ever remembers it! I used to be a lot better served when I had to wait on myself.'

The dark lady gave a faint laugh of protest.

Miss Wilpert, after a critical glance at the dish presented to her, transferred a copious portion to her plate, and squared herself before it. I could almost imagine a napkin tucked into the neck of her dress, below the crease in her heavy white throat.

'There were three women ahead of me at the hairdresser's,' she grumbled.

The dark lady glanced at her absently. 'It doesn't matter.'

'What doesn't matter?' snapped her companion. 'That I should be kept there two hours, and have to wait till two o'clock for my lunch?'

'I meant that your being late didn't matter to me.'

'I dare say not,' retorted Miss Wilpert. She poured down a draft of Pilsener, and set the empty glass beside her plate. 'So you're in the "nothing matters" mood again, are you?' she said, looking critically at her companion.

The latter smiled faintly. 'Yes.'

'Well, then – what are we staying here for? You needn't sacrifice yourself for me, you know.'

A lady, finishing her lunch, crossed the room, and in passing out stopped to speak to my neighbor. 'Oh, Mrs. Ingram' (so her name was Ingram), 'can't we persuade you to join us at bridge when you've had your coffee?'

Mrs. Ingram smiled, but shook her head. 'Thank you so much. But you know I don't play cards.'

'Principles!' jerked out Miss Wilpert, wiping her rouged lips after a second glass of Pilsener. She waved her fat hand toward the retreating lady. 'I'll join up with you in half an hour,' she cried in a penetrating tone.

'Oh, do,' said the lady with an indifferent nod.

I had finished my lunch, drunk my coffee, and smoked more than my strict ration of cigarettes. There was no other excuse for lingering, and I got up and walked out of the restaurant. My friend Antoine, the headwaiter, was standing near the door, and in passing I let my lips shape the inaudible question: 'The lady at the next table?'

Antoine knew everyone, and also everyone's history. I wondered why he hesitated for a moment before replying: 'Ah – Mrs. Ingram? Yes. From California.'

'Er – regular visitor?'

'No. I think on her first trip to Europe.'

'Ah. Then the other lady's showing her about?'

Antoine gave a shrug. 'I think not. She seems also new.'

'I like the table you've given me, Antoine,' I remarked; and he nodded compliantly.

I was surprised, therefore, that when I came down to dinner that evening I had been assigned to another seat, on the farther side of the restaurant. I asked for Antoine, but it was his evening off, and the understudy who replaced him could only say that I had been moved by Antoine's express orders. 'Perhaps it was on account of the draft, sir.'

'Draft be blowed! Can't I be given back my table?'

He was very sorry, but, as I could see, the table had been allotted to an infirm old lady, whom it would be difficult, and indeed impossible, to disturb.

'Very well, then. At lunch tomorrow I shall expect to have it back,' I said severely.

In looking back over the convalescent life, it is hard to recall the exaggerated importance every trifle assumes when there are only trifles to occupy one. I was furious at having had my place changed; and still more so when, the next day at lunch, Antoine, as a matter of course, conducted me to the table I had indignantly rejected the night before.

'What does this mean? I told you I wanted to go back to that corner table – '

Not a muscle moved in his noncommittal yet all-communicating face. 'So sorry, sir.'

'Sorry? Why, you promised me – '

'What can I do? Those ladies have our most expensive suite; and they're here for the season.'

'Well, what's the matter with the ladies? I've no objection to them. They're my compatriots.'

Antoine gave me a spectral smile. 'That appears to be the reason, sir.'

'The reason? They've given you a reason for asking to have me moved?'

'The big red one did. The other, Mrs. Ingram, as you can see, is quite different – though both are a little odd,' he added thoughtfully.

'Well – the big red one?'

'The *dame de compagnie*. You must excuse me, sir; but she says she doesn't like Americans. And as the management is anxious to oblige Mrs. Ingram – '

I gave a haughty laugh. 'I see. Whereas a humble lodger like myself – But there are other hotels at Mont Soleil, you may remind the management from me.'

'Oh, Monsieur, Monsieur – you can't be so severe on a lady's whim,' Antoine murmured reprovingly.

Of course I couldn't. Antoine's advice was always educational. I shrugged, and accepting my banishment, looked about for another interesting neighbor to watch instead of Mrs. Ingram. But I found that no one else interested me. . . .

• II •

'DON'T you think you might tell me now,' I said to Mrs. Ingram a few days later, 'why your friend insisted on banishing me to the farther end of the restaurant?'

I need hardly say that, in spite of Miss Wilpert's prejudice against her compatriots, she had not been able to prevent my making the acquaintance of Mrs. Ingram. I forgot how it came about – the pretext of a dropped letter, a deck chair to be moved out of the sun, or one of the hundred devices which bring two people together when they are living idle lives under the same roof. I had not gained my end without difficulty, however, for the ill-assorted pair were almost always together. But luckily Miss Wilpert played bridge, and Mrs. Ingram did not, and before long I had learned to profit by this opportunity, and in the course of time to make the fullest use of it.

Yet after a fortnight I had to own that I did not know much more about Mrs. Ingram than when I had first seen her. She was younger than I had thought, probably not over thirty-two or three; she was wealthy; she was shy; she came from California, or at any rate had lived there. For the last two years or more she appeared to have traveled, encircling the globe, and making long stays in places as far apart as Ceylon, Tenerife, Rio and Cairo. She seemed, on the whole, to have enjoyed these wanderings. She asked me many questions about the countries she had visited, and I saw that she belonged to the class of intelligent but untaught travelers who can learn more by verbal explanations than from books. Unprepared as she was for the sights awaiting her, she had necessarily observed little, and understood less; but she had been struck by the more conspicuous features of the journey, and the Taj, the Parthenon and the Pyramids had not escaped her. On the subject of her travels she was at least superficially communicative; and as she never alluded to husband or child, or to any other friend or relative, I was driven to conclude that Miss Wilpert had been her only companion. This deepened the mystery, and made me feel that I knew no more of her real self than on the day when I had first seen her; but, perhaps partly for that reason, I found her increasingly interesting. It was clear that she shrank from strangers, but I could not help seeing that with me she was happy and at ease, and as ready as I was to profit by our opportunities of being together. It was only when Miss Wilpert appeared that her old shyness returned, and I suspected that she was reluctant to let her companion see what good friends we had become.

I had put my indiscreet question about Miss Wilpert somewhat abruptly, in the hope of startling Mrs. Ingram out of her usual reserve; and I saw by the quick rise of color under her pale skin that I had nearly succeeded. But after a moment she replied, with a smile: 'I can't believe Cassie ever said anything so silly.'

'You can't? Then I wish you'd ask her; and if it was just an invention of that headwaiter's I'll make him give me back my table before he's a day older.'

Mrs. Ingram still smiled. 'I hope you won't make a fuss about such a trifle. Perhaps Cassie did say something foolish. She's not used to traveling, and sometimes takes odd notions.'

The ambiguity of the answer was obviously meant to warn me off; but having risked one question I was determined to risk another. 'Miss Wilpert's a very old friend, I suppose?'

'Yes; very,' said Mrs. Ingram noncommittally.

'And was she always with you when you were at home?'

My question seemed to find her unprepared. 'At home – ?'

'I mean, where you lived. California, wasn't it?'

She looked relieved. 'Oh, yes; Cassie Wilpert was with me in California.'

'But there she must have had to associate with her compatriots?'

'Yes; that's one reason why she was so glad when I decided to travel,' said Mrs. Ingram with a faint touch of irony, and then added: 'Poor Cassie was very unhappy at one time; there were people who were unkind to her. That accounts for her prejudices, I suppose.'

'I'm sorry I'm one of them. What can I do to make up to her?'

I fancied I saw a slight look of alarm in Mrs. Ingram's eyes. 'Oh, you'd much better leave her alone.'

'But she's always with you; and I don't want to leave you alone.'

Mrs. Ingram smiled, and then sighed. 'We shall be going soon now.'

'And then Miss Wilpert will be rid of me?'

Mrs. Ingram looked at me quickly; her eyes were plaintive, almost entreating. 'I shall never leave her; she's been like a – a sister to me,' she murmured, answering a question I had not put.

The word startled me; and I noticed that Mrs. Ingram had hesitated a moment before pronouncing it. A sister to her – that coarse red-handed woman? The words sounded as if they had been spoken by rote. I saw at once that they did not express the speaker's real feeling, and that, whatever that was, she did not mean to let me find it out.

Some of the bridge players with whom Miss Wilpert consorted were coming toward us, and I stood up to leave. 'Don't let Miss Wilpert carry you off on my account. I promise you I'll keep out of her way,' I said laughing.

Mrs. Ingram straightened herself almost imperiously. 'I'm not at Miss Wilpert's orders; she can't take me away from any place I choose to stay in,' she said; but a moment later, lowering her voice, she breathed to me quickly: 'Go now; I see her coming.'

• III •

I DON'T mind telling you that I was not altogether happy about my attitude toward Mrs. Ingram. I'm not given to prying into other people's secrets; yet I had not scrupled to try to trap her into revealing hers. For that there was a secret I was now convinced; and I excused myself for trying to get to the bottom of it by the fact that I was sure I should find

Miss Wilpert there, and that the idea was abhorrent to me. The relation between the two women, I had by now discovered, was one of mutual animosity; not the kind of animosity which may be the disguise of more complicated sentiments, but the simple incompatibility that was bound to exist between two women so different in class and character. Miss Wilpert was a coarse, uneducated woman, with, as far as I could see, no redeeming qualities, moral or mental, to bridge the distance between herself and her companion; and the mystery was that any past tie or obligation, however strong, should have made Mrs. Ingram tolerate her.

I knew how easily rich and idle women may become dependent on some vulgar tyrannical housekeeper or companion who renders them services and saves them trouble; but I saw at once that this theory did not explain the situation. On the contrary, it was Miss Wilpert who was dependent on Mrs. Ingram, who looked to her as guide, interpreter, and manager of their strange association. Miss Wilpert possessed no language but her own, and of that only a local vernacular which made it difficult to explain her wants (and they were many) even to the polyglot servants of a Swiss hotel. Mrs. Ingram spoke a carefully acquired if laborious French, and was conscientiously preparing for a winter in Naples by taking a daily lesson in Italian; and I noticed that whenever an order was to be given, an excursion planned, or any slight change effected in the day's arrangement, Miss Wilpert, suddenly embarrassed and helpless, always waited for Mrs. Ingram to interpret for her. It was obvious, therefore, that she was a burden and not a help to her employer, and that I must look deeper to discover the nature of their bond.

Mrs. Ingram, guidebook in hand, appealed to me one day about their autumn plans. 'I think we shall be leaving next week; and they say here we ought not to miss the Italian lakes.'

'Leaving next week? But why? The lakes are not at their best till after the middle of September. You'll find them very stuffy after this high air.'

Mrs. Ingram sighed. 'Cassie's tired of it here. She says she doesn't like the people.'

I looked at her, and then ventured with a smile: 'Don't you mean that she doesn't like me?'

'I don't see why you think that – '

'Well, I dare say it sounds rather fatuous. But you *do* know why I think it; and you think it yourself.' I hesitated a moment, and then went on, lowering my voice: 'Since you attach such importance to Miss Wilpert's opinions, it's natural I should want to know why she dislikes seeing me with you.'

Mrs. Ingram looked at me helplessly. 'Well, if she doesn't like you – '

'Yes; but in reality I don't think it's me she dislikes, but the fact of my being with you.'

She looked disturbed at this. 'But if she dislikes you, it's natural she shouldn't want you to be with me.'

'And do her likes and dislikes regulate all your friendships?'

'Friendships? I've so few; I know hardly anyone,' said Mrs. Ingram, looking away.

'You'd have as many as you chose if she'd let you,' I broke out angrily.

She drew herself up with the air of dignity she could assume on occasion. 'I don't know why you find so much pleasure in saying disagreeable things to me about my – my friend.'

The answer rushed to my lips: 'Why did she begin by saying disagreeable things about me?' – but just in time I saw that I was on the brink of a futile wrangle with the woman whom, at that moment, I was the most anxious not to displease. How anxious, indeed, I now saw for the first time, in the light of my own anger. For what on earth did I care for the disapproval of a creature like Miss Wilpert, except as it interfered with my growing wish to stand well with Kate Ingram? The answer I did make sprang to my lips before I could repress it. 'Because – you must know by this time. Because I can't bear that anything or any one should come between us.'

'Between us – ?'

I pressed on, hardly knowing what I was saying. 'Because nothing matters to me as much as what you feel about me. In fact, nothing else matters at all.'

The words had rushed out, lighting up the depths of my feeling as much to myself as to Mrs. Ingram. Only then did I remember how little I knew of the woman to whom they were addressed – not even her maiden name, nor as much as one fact of her past history. I did not even know if she were married, widowed or divorced. All I did know was that I had fallen in love with her – and had told her so.

She sat motionless, without a word. But suddenly her eyes filled, and I saw that her lips were trembling too much for her to speak.

'Kate – ' I entreated; but she drew back, shaking her head.

'No – '

'Why "no"? Because I've made you angry – ?'

She shook her head again. 'I feel that you're a true friend – '

'I want you to feel much more than that.'

'It's all I can ever feel – for anyone. I shall never – never . . .' She broke down, and sat struggling with her tears.

'Do you say that because you're not free?'

'Oh, no – oh, no – '

'Then is it because you don't like me? Tell me that, and I won't trouble you again.'

We were sitting alone in a deserted corner of the lounge. The diners had scattered to the wide verandahs, the card room or the bar. Miss Wilpert was safely engaged with a party of bridge players in the farthest room of the suite, and I had imagined that at last I should be able to have my talk out with Mrs. Ingram. I had hardly meant it to take so grave a turn; but now that I had spoken I knew my choice was made.

'If you tell me you don't like me, I won't trouble you any more,' I repeated, trying to keep her eyes on mine. Her lids quivered, and she looked down at her uneasy hands. I had often noticed that her hands were the only unquiet things about her, and now she sat clasping and unclasping them without ceasing.

'I can't tell you that I don't like you,' she said, very low. I leaned over to capture those restless fingers, and quiet them in mine; but at the same moment she gave a start, and I saw that she was not looking at me, but over my shoulder at someone who must have crossed the lounge behind me. I turned and saw a man I had not noticed before in the hotel, but whose short square-shouldered figure struck me as vaguely familiar.

'Is that someone you know?' I asked, surprised by the look in her face.

'N-no. I thought it was . . . I must have been mistaken. . . .' I saw that she was struggling to recover her self-control, and I looked again at the newcomer, who had stopped on his way to the bar to speak to one of the hall porters.

'Why, I believe it's Jimmy Shreve – Shreve of the New York *Evening Star*,' I said. 'It looks like him. Do you know him?'

'No.'

'Then, please – won't you answer the question I was just asking you?'

She had grown very pale, and was twisting her long fingers distressfully. 'Oh, not now; not now. . . .'

'Why not now? After what you've told me, do you suppose I'm going to be put off without a reason?'

'There's my reason!' she exclaimed with a nervous laugh. I looked around, and saw Miss Wilpert approaching. She looked unusually large and flushed, and her elaborate evening dress showed a displeasing expanse of too-white skin.

'Ah, that's your reason? I thought so!' I broke out bitterly.

One of Mrs. Ingram's quick blushes overswept her. 'I didn't mean that – you've no right to say so. I only meant that I'd promised to go with her. . . .'

Miss Wilpert was already towering over us, loud-breathing and crimson. I suspected that in the intervals of bridge she had more than once sought refreshment at the bar. 'Well, so this is where you've hidden yourself away, is it? I've hunted for you all over the place; but I didn't suppose you'd choose a dark corner under the stairs. I presume you've forgotten that you asked them to reserve seats for us for those Javanese dances. They won't keep our places much longer; the ballroom's packed already.'

I sat still, almost holding my breath, and watched the two women. I guessed that a crucial point in the struggle between them had been reached, and that a word from me might wreck my chances. Mrs. Ingram's color faded quickly, as it always did, but she forced a nervous smile. 'I'd no idea it was so late.'

'Well, if your watch has stopped, there's the hall clock right in front of you,' said Miss Wilpert, with quick panting breaths between the words. She waited a moment. 'Are you coming?'

Mrs. Ingram leaned back in her deep armchair. 'Well, no – I don't believe I am.'

'You're *not*?'

'No. I think I like it better here.'

'But you must be crazy! You asked that Italian Countess to keep us two seats next to hers – '

'Well, you can go and ask her to excuse me – say I'm tired. The ballroom's always so hot.'

'Land's sake! How'm I going to tell her all that in Italian? You know she don't speak a word of English. She'll think it's pretty funny if you don't come; and so will the others. You always say you hate to have people talk about you; and yet here you sit, stowed away in this dark corner, like a schoolgirl with her boy friend at a Commencement dance – '

Mrs. Ingram stood up quickly. 'Cassie, I'm afraid you must have been losing at bridge. I never heard you talk so foolishly. But of course I'll come if you think the Countess expects us.' She turned to me with a little smile, and suddenly, shyly, held out her hand. 'You'll tell me the rest tomorrow morning,' she said, looking straight at me for an instant; then she turned and followed Cassie Wilpert.

I stood watching them with a thumping heart. I didn't know what held these women together, but I felt that in the last few minutes a link of the chain between them had been loosened, and I could hardly wait to see it snap.

I was still standing there when the man who had attracted Mrs. Ingram's notice came out of the bar, and walked toward me; and I saw that it was in fact my old acquaintance Jimmy Shreve, the bright particular ornament of the *Evening Star*. We had not met for a year or more, and his surprise at the encounter was as great as mine. 'Funny, coming across you in this jazz crowd. I'm here to get away from my newspaper; but what has brought you?'

I explained that I had been ill the previous year, and, by the doctor's orders, was working out in the Alps the last months of my convalescence; and he listened with the absent-minded sympathy which one's friends give to one's ailments, particularly when they are on the mend.

'Well – well – too bad you've had such a mean time. Glad you're out of it now, anyway,' he muttered, snapping a reluctant cigarette lighter, and finally having recourse to mine. As he bent over it he said suddenly: 'Well, what about Kate Spain?'

I looked at him in bewilderment. For a moment the question was so unintelligible that I wondered if he too were a sufferer, and had been sent to the heights for medical reasons; but his sharp little professional eyes, burned with a steady spark of curiosity as he took a close-up of me across the lighter. And then I understood; at least I understood the allusion, though its relevance escaped me.

'Kate Spain? Oh, you mean that murder trial at Cayuga? You got me a card for it, didn't you? But I wasn't able to go.'

'I remember. But you've made up for it since, I see.' He continued to twinkle at me meaningly; but I was still groping. 'What do you think of her?' he repeated.

'Think of her? Why on earth should I think of her at all?'

He drew back and squared his sturdy shoulders in evident enjoyment. 'Why, because you've been talking to her as hard as you could for the last two hours,' he chuckled.

I stood looking at him blankly. Again it occurred to me that under his tight journalistic mask something had loosened and gone adrift. But I looked at the steadiness of the stumpy fingers which held his cigarette. The man had himself under perfect control.

'Kate Spain?' I said, collecting myself. 'Does that lady I was talking to really look to you like a murderess?'

Shreve made a dubious gesture. 'I'm not so sure what murderesses look like. But, as it happens, Kate Spain was acquitted.'

'So she was. Still, I don't think I'll tell Mrs. Ingram that she looks like her.'

Shreve smiled incredulously. 'Mrs. Ingram? Is that what you call her?'

'It's her name. I was with Mrs. Ingram, of California.'

'No, you weren't. You were with Kate Spain. She knows me well enough – ask her. I met her face to face just now, going into the ballroom. She was with a red-headed Jezebel that I don't know.'

'Ah, you don't know the red-headed lady? Well, that shows you're mistaken. For Miss Cassie Wilpert has lived with Mrs. Ingram as her companion for several years. They're inseparable.'

Shreve tossed away his cigarette and stood staring at me. 'Cassie Wilpert? Is that what that great dressed-up prize fighter with all the jewelry calls herself? Why, see here, Severance, Cassie was the servant girl's name, sure enough: Cassie – don't you remember? It was her evidence that got Kate Spain off. But at the trial she was a thin haggard Irish girl in dirty calico. To be sure, I suppose old Ezra Spain starved his servant as thoroughly as he starved his daughter. You remember Cassie's description of the daily fare: Sunday, boiled mutton; Monday, cold mutton; Tuesday, mutton hash; Wednesday, mutton stew – and I forget what day the dog got the mutton bone. Why, it was Cassie who knocked the prosecution all to pieces. At first it was doubtful how the case would go; but she testified that she and Kate Spain were out shopping together when the old man was murdered; and the prosecution was never able to shake her evidence.'

Remember it? Of course I remembered every detail of it, with a precision which startled me, considering I had never, to my knowledge, given the Kate Spain trial a thought since the talk about it had died out with the woman's acquittal. Now it all came back to me, every scrap of evidence, all the sordid and sinister gossip let loose by the trial: the tale of Ezra Spain, the wealthy miser and tyrant, of whom no one in his native town had a good word to say, who was reported to have let his wife die of neglect because he would not sent for a doctor till it was too late, and who had been too mean to supply her with food and medicines, or to provide a trained nurse for her. After his wife's death his daughter had continued to live with him, browbeaten and starved in her turn, and apparently lacking the courage to cast herself penniless and inexperienced upon the world. It had been almost with a sense of relief that Cayuga had learned of the old man's murder by a wandering tramp who had found him alone in the house, and had killed him in his sleep, and got away with what little money there was. Now at last, people said, that poor persecuted daughter with the wistful eyes and the frightened smile would be free, would be rich, would be able to come out of her prison, and marry and enjoy her life, instead of wasting and dying as her mother had died. And then came the incredible rumor that, instead of coming out of prison – the prison of her father's house – she was to go into another, the kind one entered in handcuffs, between two jailers: was to go there accused of her father's murder.

'I've got it now! Cassie Donovan – that was the servant's name,' Shreve suddenly exclaimed. 'Don't you remember?'

'No, I don't. But this woman's name, as I've told you, isn't Donovan – it's Wilpert, Miss Wilpert.'

'Her new name, you mean? Yes. And Kate Spain's new name, you say, is Mrs. Ingram. Can't you see that the first thing they'd do, when they left Cayuga, would be to change their names?'

'Why should they, when nothing was proved against them? And you say yourself you didn't recognize Miss Wilpert,' I insisted, struggling to maintain my incredulity.

'No; I didn't remember that she might have got fat and dyed her hair. I guess they do themselves like fighting cocks now, to make up for past privations. They say the old man cut up even fatter than people expected. But prosperity hasn't changed Kate Spain. I knew her at once; I'd have known her anywhere. And she knew me.'

'She didn't know you,' I broke out; 'she said she was mistaken.'

Shreve pounced on this in a flash. 'Ah – so at first she thought she did?' He laughed. 'I don't wonder she said afterward she was mistaken. I don't dye my hair yet, but I'm afraid I've put on nearly as much weight as Cassie Donovan.' He paused again, and then added: 'All the same, Severance, she did know me.'

I looked at the little journalist and laughed back at him.

'What are you laughing at?'

'At you. At such a perfect case of professional deformation. Wherever you go you're bound to spot a criminal; but I should have thought even Mont Soleil could have produced a likelier specimen than my friend Mrs. Ingram.'

He looked a little startled at my tone. 'Oh, see here, if she's such a friend I'm sorry I said anything.'

I rose to heights of tolerance. 'Nothing you can say can harm her, my dear fellow.'

'Harm her? Why on earth should it? I don't want to harm her.'

'Then don't go about spreading such ridiculous gossip. I don't suppose anyone cares to be mistaken for a woman who's been tried for her life; and if I were a relation of Mrs. Ingram's I'm bound to tell you I should feel obliged to put a stop to your talk.'

He stared in surprise, and I thought he was going to retort in the same tone; but he was a fair-minded little fellow, and after a moment I could see he'd understood. 'All right, Severance; of course I don't want to do anything that'll bother her. . . .'

'Then don't go on talking as if you still thought she was Kate Spain.'

He gave a hopeless shrug. 'All right. I won't. Only she *is*, you know; what'll you bet on it, old man?'

'Good night,' I said with a nod, and turned away. It was obviously a fixed idea with him; and what harm could such a crank do to me, much less to a woman like Mrs. Ingram?

As I left him he called after me: 'If she ain't, who is she? Tell me that, and I'll believe you.'

I walked away without answering.

• IV •

I WENT up to bed laughing inwardly at poor Jimmy Shreve. His craving for the sensational had certainly deformed his critical faculty. How it would amuse Mrs. Ingram to hear that he had identified her with the wretched Kate Spain! Well, she should hear it; we'd laugh over it together the next day. For she had said, in bidding me good night: 'You'll tell me the rest in the morning.' And that meant – could only mean – that she was going to listen to me, and if she were going to listen, she must be going to answer as I wished her to. . . .

Those were my thoughts as I went up to my room. They were scarcely less confident while I was undressing. I had the hope, the promise almost, of what, at the moment, I most wished for – the only thing I wished for, in fact. I was amazed at the intensity with which I wished it. From the first I had tried to explain away my passion by regarding it as the idle man's tendency to fall into sentimental traps; but I had always known that what I felt was not of that nature. This quiet woman with the wide pale eyes and melancholy mouth had taken possession of me; she seemed always to have inhabited my mind and heart; and as I lay down to sleep I tried to analyze what it was in her that made her seem already a part of me.

But as soon as my light was out I knew I was going to lie awake all night; and all sorts of unsought problems instantly crowded out my sentimental musings. I had laughed at Shreve's inept question: 'If she ain't Kate Spain, who is she?' But now an insistent voice within me echoed: Who is she? What, in short, did I know of her? Not one single fact which would have permitted me to disprove his preposterous assertion. Who was she? Was she married, unmarried, divorced, a widow? Had she children, parents, relations distant or near? Where had she lived before going to California, and when had she gone there? I knew neither her birthplace, nor her maiden name, or indeed any fact about her except the all-dominating fact of herself.

In rehearsing our many talks with the pitiless lucidity of sleeplessness I saw that she had the rare gift of being a perfect listener; the kind whose silence supplies the inaudible questions and answers most qualified to draw one on. And I had been drawn on; ridiculously, fatuously, drawn on. She was in possession of all the chief facts of my modest history. She knew who I was, where I came from, who were my friends, my family, my antecedents; she was fully informed as to my plans, my hopes, my preferences, my tastes and hobbies. I had even confided to her my passion for Brahms and for book collecting, and my dislike for the wireless, and for one of my brothers-in-law. And in return for these confidences she had given me – what? An understanding smile, and the occasional murmur: 'Oh, do you feel that too? I've always felt it.'

Such was the actual extent of my acquaintance with Mrs. Ingram; and I perceived that, though I had laughed at Jimmy Shreve's inept assertion, I should have been utterly unable to disprove it. I did not know who Mrs. Ingram was, or even one single fact about her.

From that point to supposing that she could be Kate Spain was obviously a long way. She might be – well, let's say almost anything; but not a woman accused of murder, and acquitted only because the circumstantial evidence was insufficient to hang her. I dismissed the grotesque supposition at once; there were problems enough to keep me awake without that.

When I said that I knew nothing of Mrs. Ingram I was mistaken. I knew one fact about her; that she could put up with Cassie Wilpert. It was only a clue, but I had felt from the first that it was a vital one. What conceivable interest or obligation could make a woman like Mrs. Ingram endure such an intimacy? If I knew that, I should know all I cared to know about her; not only about her outward circumstances but her inmost self.

Hitherto, in indulging my feeling for her, I had been disposed to slip past the awkward obstacle of Cassie Wilpert; but now I was resolved to face it. I meant to ask Kate Ingram to marry me. If she refused, her private affairs were obviously no business of mine; but if she accepted I meant to have the Wilpert question out with her at once.

It seemed a long time before daylight came; and then there were more hours to be passed before I could reasonably present myself to Mrs. Ingram. But at nine I sent a line to ask when she would see me; and a few minutes later my note was returned to me by the floor waiter.

'But this isn't an answer; it's my own note,' I exclaimed.

Yes; it was my own note. He had brought it back because the lady had already left the hotel.

'Left? Gone out, you mean?'

'No; left with all her luggage. The two ladies went an hour ago.'

In a few minutes I was dressed and had hurried down to the concierge. It was a mistake, I was sure; of course Mrs. Ingram had not left. The floor waiter, whom I had long since classed as an idiot, had simply gone to the wrong door. But no; the concierge shook his head. It was not a mistake. Mrs. Ingram and Miss Wilpert had gone away suddenly that morning by motor. The chauffeur's orders were to take them to Italy; to Baveno or Stresa, he thought; but he wasn't sure, and the ladies had left no address. The hotel servants said they had been up all night packing. The heavy luggage was to be sent to Milan; the concierge had orders to direct it to the station. That was all the information he could give – and I thought he looked at me queerly as he gave it.

• V •

I DID not see Jimmy Shreve again before leaving Mont Soleil that day; indeed I exercised all my ingenuity in keeping out of his way. If I were to ask any further explanations, it was of Mrs. Ingram that I meant to ask them. Either she was Kate Spain, or she was not; and either way, she was the woman to whom I had declared my love. I should have thought nothing of Shreve's insinuations if I had not recalled Mrs. Ingram's start when she first saw him. She herself had owned that she had taken him for someone she knew; but even this would not have meant much if she and her companion had not disappeared from the hotel a few hours later, without leaving a message for me, or an address with the hall porter.

I did not for a moment suppose that this disappearance was connected with my talk of the previous evening with Mrs. Ingram. She herself had expressed the wish to prolong that talk when Miss Wilpert interrupted it; and failing that, she had spontaneously suggested that we should meet again the next morning. It would have been less painful to think that she had fled before the ardor of my wooing than before the dread of what Shreve might reveal about her; but I knew the latter reason was the more likely.

The discovery stunned me. It took me some hours to get beyond the incredible idea that this woman, whose ways were so gentle, with whose whole nature I felt myself in such delightful harmony, had stood her trial as a murderess – and the murderess of her own father. But the more I revolved this possibility the less I believed in it. There might have been other – and perhaps not very creditable – reasons for her abrupt flight; but that she should be flying because she knew that Shreve had recognized her seemed, on further thought, impossible.

Then I began to look at the question from another angle. Supposing she *were* Kate Spain? Well, her father had been assassinated by a passing tramp; so the jury had decided. Probably suspicion would never have rested on her if it had not been notorious in Cayuga that the old man was a selfish miser, who for years had made his daughter's life intolerable. To those who knew the circumstances it had seemed conceivable, seemed almost natural, that the poor creature should finally turn against him. Yet she had had no difficulty in proving her innocence; it was clearly established that she was out of the house when the crime was committed. Her having been suspected, and tried, was simply one of those horrible blunders of which innocent persons have so often been the victims. Do what she would to live it down, her name would always remain associated with that sordid tragedy; and wasn't it natural that she should flee from any reminder of it, any suspicion that she had been recognized, and her identity proclaimed by a scandal-mongering journalist? If she were Kate Spain, the dread of having the fact made known to everyone in that crowded hotel was enough to drive her out of it. But if her departure had another cause, in no way connected with Shreve's arrival, might it not have been inspired by a sudden whim of Cassie Wilpert's? Mrs. Ingram had told me that Cassie was bored and wanted to get away; and it was all too clear that, however loudly she proclaimed her independence, she always ended by obeying Miss Wilpert.

It was a melancholy alternative. Poor woman – poor woman either way, I thought. And by the time I had reached this conclusion, I was in the train which was hurrying me to Milan. Whatever happened I must see her, and hear from her own lips what she was flying from.

I hadn't much hope of running down the fugitives at Stresa or Baveno. It was not likely that they would go to either of the places they had mentioned to the concierge; but I went to both the next morning, and carried out a minute inspection of all the hotel lists. As I had foreseen, the travelers were not to be found, and I was at a loss to know where to turn next. I knew, however, that the luggage the ladies had sent to Milan was not likely to arrive till the next day, and concluded that they would probably wait for it in the neighborhood; and suddenly I remembered that I had once advised Mrs. Ingram – who was complaining that she was growing tired of fashionable hotels – to try a little *pension* on the lake of Orta, where she would be miles away from 'palaces', and from the kind of people who frequent them. It was not likely that she would have remembered this place; but I had put a pencil stroke beside the name in her guidebook, and that might recall it to her. Orta, at any rate, was not far off; and I decided to hire a car at Stresa, and go there before carrying on my journey.

• VI •

I DON'T suppose I shall ever get out of my eyes the memory of the public sitting room in the *pension* at Orta. It was there that I waited for Mrs. Ingram to come down, wondering if she would, and what we should say to each other when she did.

There were three windows in a row, with clean heavily starched Nottingham lace curtains carefully draped to exclude the best part of the matchless view over lake and mountains. To make up for this privation the opposite wall was adorned with a huge oil painting of a Swiss waterfall. In the middle of the room was a table of sham ebony, with ivory inlays, most of which had long since worked out of their grooves, and on the table the usual dusty collection of tourist magazines, fashion papers, and tattered copies of *Zion's Weekly* and the *Christian Science Monitor*.

What is the human mind made of, that mine, at such a moment, should have minutely and indelibly registered these depressing details? I even remember smiling at the thought of the impression my favorite *pension* must have made on travelers who had just moved out of the most expensive suite in the Mont Soleil Palace.

And then Mrs. Ingram came in.

My first impression was that something about her dress or the arrangement of her hair had changed her. Then I saw that two dabs of rouge had been unskilfully applied to her pale cheeks, and a cloud of powder dashed over the dark semicircles under her eyes. She must have undergone some terrible moral strain since our parting to feel the need of such a disguise.

'I thought I should find you here,' I said.

She let me take her two hands, but at first she could not speak. Then she said, in an altered voice: 'You must have wondered – '

'Yes; I wondered.'

'It was Cassie who suddenly decided – '

'I supposed so.'

She looked at me beseechingly. 'But she was right, you know.'

'Right – about what?'

Her rouged lips began to tremble, and she drew her hands out of mine.

'Before you say anything else,' I interrupted, 'there's one thing you must let me say. I want you to marry me.'

I had not meant to bring it out so abruptly; but something in her pitiful attempt to conceal her distress had drawn me closer to her, drawn me past all doubts and distrusts, all thought of evasion or delay.

She looked at me, still without speaking, and two tears ran over her lids, and streaked the untidy powder on her cheeks.

'No - no - no!' she exclaimed, lifting her thin hand and pressing it against my lips. I drew it down and held it fast.

'Why not? You knew I was going to ask you, the day before yesterday, and when we were interrupted you promised to hear me the next morning. You yourself said: "tomorrow morning."'

'Yes; but I didn't know then – '

'You didn't know – ?'

I was still holding her, and my eyes were fixed on hers. She gave me back my look, deeply and desperately. Then she freed herself.

'Let me go. I'm Kate Spain,' she said.

We stood facing each other without speaking. Then I gave a laugh, and answered, in a voice that sounded to me as though I were shouting: 'Well, I want to marry you, Kate Spain.'

She shrank back, her hands clasped across her breast. 'You knew already? That man told you?'

'Who – Jimmy Shreve? What does it matter if he did? Was that the reason you ran away from me?' She nodded.

'And you thought I wouldn't find you?'

'I thought you wouldn't try.'

'You thought that, having told you one day that I loved you, I'd let you go out of my life the next?'

She gave me another long look. 'You – you're generous. I'm grateful. But you can't marry Kate Spain,' she said, with a little smile like the grimace on a dying face.

I had no doubt in my own mind that I could; the first sight of her had carried that conviction home, and I answered: 'Can't I, though? That's what we'll see.'

'You don't know what my life is. How would you like, wherever you went, to have some one suddenly whisper behind you: "Look. That's Kate Spain"?'

I looked at her, and for a moment found no answer. My first impulse of passionate pity had swept me past the shock of her confession; as long as she was herself, I seemed to feel, it mattered nothing to me that she was also Kate Spain. But her last words called up a sudden vision of the life she must have led since her acquittal; the life I was asking to share with her. I recalled my helpless wrath when Shreve had told me who she was; and now I seemed to hear the ugly whisper – 'Kate Spain, Kate Spain' – following us from place to place, from house to house; following my wife and me.

She took my hesitation for an answer. 'You hadn't thought of that, had you? But I think of nothing else, day and night. For three years now I've been running away from the sound of my name. I tried California first; it was at the other end of the country, and some of my mother's relations lived there. They were kind to me, everybody was kind; but wherever I went I heard my name: Kate

Spain – Kate Spain! I couldn't go to church, or to the theater, or into a shop to buy a spool of thread, without hearing it. What was the use of calling myself Mrs. Ingram, when, wherever I went, I heard Kate Spain? The very school children knew who I was, and rushed out to see me when I passed. I used to get letters from people who collected autographs, and wanted my signature: "Kate Spain, you know." And when I tried shutting myself up, people said: "What's she afraid of? Has she got something to hide, after all?" and I saw that it made my cousins uncomfortable, and shy with me, because I couldn't lead a normal life like theirs. . . . After a year I couldn't stand it, and so we came away, and went round the world. . . . But wherever we go it begins again: and I know now I can never get away from it.' She broke down, and hid her face for a moment. Then she looked up at me and said: 'And so you must go away, you see.'

I continued to look at her without speaking: I wanted the full strength of my will to go out to her in my answer. 'I see, on the contrary, that I must stay.'

She gave me a startled glance. 'No – no.'

'Yes, yes. Because all you say is a nervous dream; natural enough, after what you've been through, but quite unrelated to reality. You say you've thought of nothing else, day and night; but why think of it at all – in that way? Your real name is Kate Spain. Well – what of it? Why try to disguise it? You've never done anything to disgrace it. You've suffered through it, but never been abased. If you want to get rid of it there's a much simpler way; and that is to take mine instead. But meanwhile, if people ask you if you're Kate Spain, try saying yes, you are, instead of running away from them.'

She listened with bent head and interlocked hands, and I saw a softness creep about her lips. But after I had ceased she looked up at me sadly. 'You've never been tried for your life,' she said.

The words struck to the roots of my optimism. I remembered in a flash that when I had first seen her I had thought there was a look about her mouth and eyes unlike that of any other woman I had known; as if she had had a different experience from theirs. Now I knew what that experience was: the black shadow of the criminal court, and the long lonely fight to save her neck. And I'd been trying to talk reason to a woman who'd been through that!

'My poor girl – my poor child!' I held out my arms, and she fell into them and wept out her agony. There were no more words to be said; no words could help her. Only the sense of human nearness, human pity, of a man's arms about her, and his heart against hers, could draw her out of her icy hell into the common warmth of day.

Perhaps it was the thought of that healing warmth which made me suddenly want to take her away from the Nottingham lace curtains and the Swiss waterfall. For a while we sat silent, and I held her close; then I said: 'Come out for a walk with me. There are beautiful walks close by, up through the beechwoods.'

She looked at me with a timid smile. I knew now that she would do all I told her to; but before we started out I must rid my mind of another load. 'I want to have you all to myself for the rest of the day. Where's Miss Wilpert?' I asked.

Miss Wilpert was away in Milan, she said, and would not be back till late. She had gone to see about passport visas and passages on a cruising liner which was sailing from Genoa to the Aegean in a few days. The ladies thought of taking the cruise. I made no answer, and we walked out through the *pension* garden, and mounted the path to the beechwoods.

We wandered on for a long time, saying hardly anything to each other; then we sat down on the mossy steps of one of the little pilgrimage chapels among the trees. It is a place full of sweet solitude, and gradually it laid its quieting touch on the tormented creature at my side.

As we sat there the day slipped down the sky, and we watched, through the great branches, the lake turning golden and then fading, and the moon rising above the mountains. I put my hand on hers. 'And now let's make some plans,' I said.

I saw the apprehensive look come back to her eyes. 'Plans – oh, why, today?'

'Isn't it natural that two people who've decided to live together should want to talk over their future? When are we going to be married – to begin with?'

She hesitated for a long time, clasping and unclasping her unhappy hands. She had passed the stage of resistance, and I was almost sure she would not turn to it again. I waited, and at length she said, looking away from me: 'But you don't like Cassie.'

The words were a shock, though I suppose I must have expected them. On the whole, I was glad they had been spoken; I had not known how to bring the subject up, and it was better she should do it for me.

'Let's say, dear, that Cassie and I don't like each other. Isn't that nearer the truth?'

'Well, perhaps; but – '

'Well, that being so, Cassie will certainly be quite as anxious to strike out for herself as I shall be to – '

She interrupted me with a sudden exclamation. 'No, no! She'll never leave me – never.'

'Never leave you? Not when you're my wife?'

She hung her head, and began her miserable finger-weaving again. 'No; not even if she lets me – '

'Lets you – ?'

'Marry you,' she said in a whisper.

I mastered her hands, and forced her to turn around to me. 'Kate – look at me; straight at me. Shall I tell you something? Your worst enemy's not Kate Spain; it's Cassie Wilpert.'

She freed herself from my hold and drew back. 'My worst enemy? Cassie – she's been my only friend!'

'At the time of the trial, yes. I understand that; I understand your boundless gratitude for the help she gave you. I think I feel about that as you'd want me to. But there are other ways of showing your gratitude than by sharing the rest of your life with her.'

She listened, drooping again. 'I've tried every other way,' she said at length, below her breath.

'What other ways?'

'Oh, everything. I'm rich you know, now,' she interrupted herself, her color rising. 'I offered her the house at Cayuga – it's a good house; they say it's very valuable. She could have sold it if she didn't want to live there. And of course I would have continued the allowance I'm giving her – I would have doubled it. But what she wanted was to stay with me; the new life she was leading amused her. She was a poor servant girl, you know; and she had a dreadful time when – when my father was alive. She was our only help. . . . I suppose you read about it all . . . and even then she was good to me. . . . She dared to speak to him as I didn't. . . . And then, at the trial . . . the trial lasted a whole month; and it was a month with thirty-one days. . . . Oh, don't make me go back to it – for God's sake don't!' she burst out, sobbing.

It was impossible to carry on the discussion. All I thought of was to comfort her. I helped her to her feet, whispering to her as if she had been a frightened child, and putting my arm about her to guide her down the path. She leaned on me, pressing her arm against mine. At length she said: 'You see it can't be; I always told you it could never be.'

'I see more and more that it must be; but we won't talk about that now,' I answered.

We dined quietly in a corner of the *pension* dining room, which was filled by a colony of British old maids and retired army officers and civil servants – all so remote from the world of the 'Ezra Spain case' that, if Shreve had been there to proclaim Mrs. Ingram's identity, the hated syllables would have waked no echo. I pointed this out to Mrs. Ingram, and reminded her that in a few years all memory of the trial would have died out, even in her own country, and she would be able to come and go unobserved and undisturbed. She shook her head and murmured: 'Cassie doesn't think so', but when I suggested that Miss Wilpert might have her own reasons for cultivating this illusion, she did not take up the remark, and let me turn to pleasanter topics.

After dinner it was warm enough to wander down to the shore in the moonlight, and there, sitting in the little square along the lakeside, she seemed at last to cast off her haunting torment, and abandon herself to the strange new sense of happiness and safety. But presently the church bell rang the hour, and she started up, insisting that we must get back to the *pension* before Miss Wilpert's arrival. She would be there soon now, and Mrs. Ingram did not wish her to know of my presence till the next day.

I agreed to this, but stipulated that the next morning the news of our approaching marriage should be broken to Miss Wilpert, and that as soon as possible afterward I should be told of the result. I wanted to make sure of seeing Kate the moment her talk with Miss Wilpert was over, so that I could explain away – and above all, laugh away – the inevitable threats and menaces before they grew to giants in her tormented imagination. She promised to meet me between eleven and twelve in the deserted writing room, which we were fairly sure of having to ourselves at that hour; and from there I could take her up the hillside to have our talk out undisturbed.

• VII •

I DID not get much sleep that night, and the next morning before the *pension* was up I went out for a short row on the lake. The exercise braced my nerves, and when I got back I was prepared to face with composure whatever further disturbances were in store. I did not think they would be as bad as they appeared to my poor friend's distracted mind, and was convinced that if I could keep a firm hold on her will the worst would soon be over. It was not much past nine, and I was just finishing the *café au lait* I had ordered on returning from my row, when there was a knock at my door. It was not the casual knock of a tired servant coming to remove a tray, but a sharp nervous rap immediately followed by a second; and, before I could answer, the door opened and Miss Wilpert appeared. She came directly in, shut the door behind her, and stood looking at me with a flushed and lowering stare. But it was a look I was fairly used to seeing when her face was turned to mine, and my first thought was one of relief. If there was a scene ahead, it was best that I should bear the brunt of it; I was not half so much afraid of Miss Wilpert as of the Miss Wilpert of Kate's imagination.

I stood up and pushed forward my only armchair. 'Do you want to see me, Miss Wilpert? Do sit down.'

My visitor ignored the suggestion. 'Want to see you? God knows I don't . . . I wish we'd never laid eyes on you either of us,' she retorted in a thick passionate voice. If the hour had not been so early I should have suspected her of having already fortified herself for the encounter.

'Then, if you won't sit down, and don't want to see me – ' I began affably; but she interrupted me.

'I don't *want* to see you; but I've got to. You don't suppose I'd be here if I didn't have something to say to you?'

'Then you'd better sit down, after all.'

She shook her head, and remained leaning in the window jamb, one elbow propped on the sill. 'What I want to know is: what business has a dandified gentleman like you to go round worming women's secrets out of them?'

Now we were coming to the point. 'If I've laid myself open to the charge,' I said quietly, 'at least it's not because I've tried to worm out yours.'

The retort took her by surprise. Her flush darkened, and she fixed her small suspicious eyes on mine.

'*My* secrets?' she flamed out. 'What do you know about my secrets?' she pulled herself together with a nervous laugh. 'What an old fool I am! You're only trying to get out of answering my question. What I want to know is what call you have to pry into my friend's private affairs?'

I hesitated, struggling again with my anger. 'If I've pried into them, as you call it, I did so, as you probably know, only after I'd asked Mrs. Ingram to be my wife.'

Miss Wilpert's laugh became an angry whinny. 'Exactly! If indeed you didn't ask her to be your wife to get her secret out of her. She's so unsuspicious that the idea never crossed her mind till I told her what I thought of the trick you'd played on her.'

'Ah, you suggested it was a trick? And how did she take the suggestion?'

Miss Wilpert stood for a moment without speaking; then she came up to the table and brought her red fist down on it with a bang. 'I tell you she'll never marry you!' she shouted.

I was on the verge of shouting back at her; but I controlled myself, conscious that we had reached the danger point in our struggle. I said nothing, and waited.

'Don't you hear what I say?' she challenged me.

'Yes; but I refuse to take what you say from anyone but Mrs. Ingram.' My composure seemed to steady Miss Wilpert. She looked at me dubiously, and then dropped into the chair I had pushed forward. 'You mean you want her to tell you herself?'

'Yes.' I sat down also, and again waited.

Miss Wilpert drew a crumpled handkerchief across her lips. 'Well, I can get her to tell you – easy enough. She'll do anything I tell her. Only I thought you'd want to act like a gentleman, and spare her another painful scene – '

'Not if she's unwilling to spare me one.'

Miss Wilpert considered this with a puzzled stare. 'She'll tell you just what I'm telling you – you can take my word for that.'

'I don't want anybody's word but hers.'

'If you think such a lot of her I'd have thought you'd rather have gone away quietly, instead of tormenting her any more.' Still I was silent, and she pulled her chair up to the table, and stretched her thick arms across it. 'See here, Mr. Severance – now you listen to me.'

'I'm listening.'

'You know I love Kate so that I wouldn't harm a hair of her head,' she whimpered. I made no comment, and she went on, in a voice grown oddly and unsteady: 'But I don't want to quarrel with you. What's the use?'

'None whatever. I'm glad you realize it.'

'Well, then let's you and me talk it over like old friends. Kate can't marry you, Mr. Severance. Is that plain? She can't marry you, and she can't marry anybody else. All I want is to spare her more scenes. Won't you take my word for it, and just slip off quietly if I promise you I'll make it all right, so she'll bear you no ill will?'

I listened to this extraordinary proposal as composedly as I could; but it was impossible to repress a slight laugh. Miss Wilpert took my laugh for an answer, and her discolored face crimsoned furiously. 'Well?'

'Nonsense, Miss Wilpert. Of course I won't take your orders to go away.'

She rested her elbows on the table, and her chin on her crossed hands. I saw she was making an immense effort to control herself. 'See here, young man, now you listen. . . .'

Still I sat silent, and she sat looking at me, her thick lower lip groping queerly, as if it were feeling for words she could not find.

'I tell you – ' she stammered.

I stood up. 'If vague threats are all you have to tell me, perhaps we'd better bring our talk to an end.'

She rose also. 'To an end? Any minute, if you'll agree to go away.'

'Can't you see that such arguments are wasted on me?'

'You mean to see her?'

'Of course I do – at once, if you'll excuse me.'

She drew back unsteadily, and put herself between me and the door. 'You're going to her now? But I tell you you can't! You'll half kill her. Is that what you're after?'

'What I'm after, first of all, is to put an end to this useless talk,' I said, moving toward the door. She flung herself heavily backward, and stood against it, stretching out her two arms to block my way. 'She can't marry – she can't marry you!' she screamed.

I stood silent, my hands in my pockets. 'You – you don't believe me?' she repeated.

'I've nothing more to say to you, Miss Wilpert.'

'Ah, you've nothing more to say to me? Is that the tune? Then I'll tell you that I've something more to say to you; and you're not going out of this room till you've heard it. And you'll wish you were dead when you have.'

'If it's anything about Mrs. Ingram, I refuse to hear it; and if you force me to, it will be exactly as if you were speaking to a man who's stone deaf. So you'd better ask yourself if it's worth-while.'

She leaned against the door, her heavy head dropped queerly forward. 'Worth-while – worth-while? It'll be worth your while not to hear it – I'll give you a last chance,' she said.

'I should be much obliged if you'd leave my room, Miss Wilpert.'

' "Much obliged?"' she simpered, mimicking me. 'You'd be much obliged, would you? Hear him, girls – ain't he stylish? Well, I'm going to leave your room in a minute, young gentleman; but not till you've heard your death sentence.'

I smiled. 'I shan't hear it, you know. I shall be stone deaf.'

She gave a little screaming laugh, and her arms dropped to her sides. 'Stone deaf, he says. And to the day of his death he'll never get out of his ears what I'm going to tell him. . . .' She moved forward again, lurching a little; she seemed to be trying to take the few steps back to the table, and I noticed that she had left her handbag on it. I took it up. 'You want your bag?'

'My bag?' Her jaw fell slightly, and began to tremble again. 'Yes, yes . . . my bag . . . give it to me. Then you'll know all about Kate Spain. . . .' She got as far as the armchair, dropped into it sideways and sat with hanging head, and arms lolling at her sides. She seemed to have forgotten about the bag, though I had put it beside her.

I stared at her, horrified. Was she as drunk as all that – or was she ill, and desperately ill? I felt cold about the heart, and went up, and took hold of her. 'Miss Wilpert – won't you get up? Aren't you well?'

Her swollen lips formed a thin laugh, and I saw a thread of foam in their corners. 'Kate Spain . . . I'll tell you. . . .' Her head sank down onto her creased white throat. Her arms hung lifeless; she neither spoke nor moved.

• VIII •

AFTER the first moment of distress and bewilderment, and the two or three agitated hours spent in consultations, telephonings, engaging of nurses, and inquiring about nursing homes, I was at last able to have a few words with Mrs. Ingram.

Miss Wilpert's case was clear enough; a stroke induced by sudden excitement, which would certainly – as the doctors summoned from Milan advised us – result in softening of the brain, probably followed by death in a few weeks. The direct cause had been the poor woman's fit of rage against me; but the doctors told me privately that in her deteriorated condition any shock might have brought about the same result. Continual overindulgence in food and drink – in drink especially – had made her, physiologically, an old woman before her time; all her organs were worn out, and the best that could be hoped was the bodily resistance which sometimes develops when the mind fails would not keep her too long from dying.

I had to break this as gently as I could do Mrs. Ingram, and the same time to defend myself against the painful inferences she might draw from the way in which the attack had happened. She knew – as the whole horrified *pension* knew – that Miss Wilpert had been taken suddenly ill in my room; and anyone living on the same floor must have been aware that an angry discussion had preceded the attack. But Kate Ingram knew more; she, and she alone, knew Cassie Wilpert had gone to my room, and when I found myself alone with her instantly read that knowledge in her face. This being so, I thought it better to make no pretense.

'You saw Miss Wilpert, I suppose, before she came to me?' I asked.

She made a faint assenting motion; I saw that she was too shaken to speak.

'And she told you, probably, that she was going to tell me I must not marry you.'

'Yes – she told me.'

I sat down beside her and took her hand. 'I don't know what she meant,' I went on, 'or how she intended to prevent it; for before she could say anything more – '

Kate Ingram turned to me quickly. I could see the life rushing back to her striken face. 'You mean – she didn't say anything more?'

'She had no time to.'

'Not a word more?'

'Nothing – '

Mrs. Ingram gave me one long look; then her head sank between her hands. I sat beside her in silence, and at last she dropped her hands and looked up again. 'You've been very good to me,' she said.

'Then, my dear, you must be good too. I want you to go to your room at once and take a long rest. Everything is arranged; the nurse has come. Early tomorrow morning the ambulance will be here. You can trust me to see that things are looked after.'

Her eyes rested on me, as if she were trying to grope for the thoughts beyond this screen of words. 'You're sure she said nothing more?' she repeated.

'On my honor, nothing.'

She got up and went obediently to her room.

It was perfectly clear to me that Mrs. Ingram's docility during those first grim days was due chiefly to the fact of her own helplessness. Little of the practical experience of everyday life had come into her melancholy existence, and I was not surprised that, in a strange country and among unfamiliar faces, she should turn to me for support. The shock of what had occurred, and God knows what secret dread behind it, had prostrated the poor creature, and the painful details still to be dealt with made my nearness a necessity. But, as far as our personal relations were concerned, I knew that sooner or later an emotional reaction would come.

For the moment it was kept off by other cares. Mrs. Ingram turned to me as to an old friend, and I was careful to make no other claim on her. She was installed at the nursing home in Milan to which her companion had been transported; and I saw her there two or three times daily. Happily for the sick woman, the end was near; she never regained consciousness, and before the month was out she was dead. Her life ended without a struggle, and Mrs. Ingram was spared the sight of protracted suffering; but the shock of the separation was inevitable. I knew she did not love Cassie Wilpert, and I measured her profound isolation when I saw that the death of this woman left her virtually alone.

When we returned from the funeral I drove her back to the hotel where she had engaged rooms, and she asked me to come to see her there the next afternoon.

At Orta, after Cassie Wilpert's sudden seizure, and before the arrival of the doctors, I had handed her bag over to Mrs. Ingram, and had said: 'You'd better lock it up. If she gets worse the police might ask for it.'

She turned ashy pale. 'The police – ?'

'Oh, you know there are endless formalities of that kind in all Latin countries. I should advise you to look through the bag yourself, and see if there's anything in it she might prefer not to have you keep. If there is, you'd better destroy it.'

I knew at the time that she had guessed I was referring to some particular paper; but she took the bag from me without speaking. And now, when I came to the hotel at her summons, I wondered whether she would allude to the matter, whether in the interval it has passed out of her mind, or whether she had decided to say nothing. There was no doubt that the bag had contained something which Miss Wilpert was determined that I should see; but, after all, it might have been only a newspaper report of the Spain trial. The unhappy creature's brain was already so confused that she might have attached importance to some document that had no real significance. I hoped it was so, for my one desire was to put out of my mind the memory of Cassie Wilpert, and of what her association with Mrs. Ingram had meant.

At the hotel I was asked to come up to Mrs. Ingram's private sitting room. She kept me waiting for a little while, and when she appeared she looked so frail and ill in her black dress that I feared she might be on the verge of a nervous breakdown.

'You look too tired to see anyone today. You ought to go straight to bed and let me send for the doctor,' I said.

'No – no.' She shook her head, and signed to me to sit down. 'It's only . . . the strangeness of everything. I'm not used to being alone. I think I'd better go away from here tomorrow,' she began excitedly.

'I think you had, dear. I'll make any arrangements you like, if you'll tell me where you want to go. And I'll come and join you, and arrange as soon as possible about our marriage. Such matters can be managed fairly quickly in France.'

'In France?' she echoed absently, with a little smile.

'Or wherever else you like. We might go to Rome.'

She continued to smile; a strained mournful smile, which began to frighten me. Then she spoke. 'I shall never forget what you've been to me. But we must say good-bye now. I can't marry you. Cassie did what was right – she only wanted to spare me the pain of telling you.'

I looked at her steadily. 'When you say you can't marry me,' I asked, 'do you mean that you're already married, and can't free yourself?'

She seemed surprised. 'Oh, no. I'm not married – I was never married.'

'Then, my dear – '

She raised one hand to silence me; with the other she opened her little black handbag and drew out a sealed envelope. 'This is the reason. It's what she meant to show you – '

I broke in at once: 'I don't want to see anything she meant to show me. I told her so then, and I tell you so now. Whatever is in that envelope, I refuse to look at it.'

Mrs. Ingram gave me a startled glance. 'No, no. You must read it. Don't force me to tell you – that would be worse. . . .'

I jumped up and stood looking down into her anguished face. Even if I hadn't loved her, I should have pitied her then beyond all mortal pity.

'Kate,' I said, bending over her, and putting my hand on her icy-cold one, 'when I asked you to marry me I buried all such questions, and I'm not going to dig them up again today – or any other day. The past's the past. It's at an end for us both, and tomorrow I mean to marry you, and begin our future.'

She smiled again, strangely, I thought, and then suddenly began to cry. Then she flung her arms about my neck, and pressed herself against me. 'Say good-bye to me now – say good-bye to Kate Spain,' she whispered.

'Good-bye to Kate Spain, yes; but not to Kate Severance.'

'There'll never be a Kate Severance. There never can be. Oh, won't you understand – won't you spare me? Cassie was right; she tried to do her duty when she saw I couldn't do it. . . .'

She broke into terrible sobs, and I pressed my lips against hers to silence her. She let me hold her for a while, and when she drew back from me I saw that the battle was half-won. But she stretched out her hand toward the envelope. 'You must read it – '

I shook my head. 'I won't read it. But I'll take it and keep it. Will that satisfy you, Kate Severance?' I asked. For it had suddenly occurred to me that, if I tore the paper up before her, I should only force her, in her present mood, to the more cruel alternative of telling me what it contained.

I saw at once that my suggestion quieted her. 'You will take it, then? You'll read it tonight? You'll promise me?'

'No, my dear. All I promise you is to take it with me, and not to destroy it.'

She took a long sobbing breath, and drew me to her again. 'It's as if you'd read it already, isn't it?' she said below her breath.

'It's as if it had never existed – because it never will exist for me.' I held her fast, and kissed her again. And when I left her I carried the sealed envelope away with me.

• IX •

ALL that happened seven years ago; and the envelope lies before me now, still sealed. Why should I have opened it?

As I carried it home that night at Milan, as I drew it out of my pocket and locked it away among my papers, it was as transparent as glass to me. I had no need to open it. Already it had given me the measure of the woman who, deliberately, determinedly, had thrust it into my hands. Even as she was in the act of doing so, I had understood that with Cassie Wilpert's death the one danger she had to fear had been removed; and that, knowing herself at last free, at last safe, she had voluntarily placed her fate in my keeping.'

'Greater love hath no man – certainly no woman,' I thought. Cassie Wilpert, and Cassie Wilpert alone, held Kate Spain's secret – the secret which would doubtless have destroyed her in the eyes of the world, as it was meant to destroy her in mine. And that secret, when it had been safely buried with Cassie Wilpert, Kate Spain had deliberately dug up again, and put into my hands.

It took her some time to understand the use I meant to make of it. She did not dream, at first, that it had given me a complete insight into her character, and that that was all I wanted of it. Weeks of patient waiting, of quiet reasoning, of obstinate insistence, were required to persuade her that I was determined to judge her, not by her past, whatever it might have been, but by what she had unconsciously revealed of herself since I had known her and loved her.

'You can't marry me – you know why you can't marry me,' she had gone on endlessly repeating; till one day I had turned on her, and declared abruptly: 'Whatever happens, this is to be our last talk on the subject. I will never return to it again, or let you return to it. But I swear one thing to you now; if you know how your father died, and have kept silence to shield someone – to shield I don't care who' – I looked straight into her eyes as I said this – 'if this is your reason for thinking you ought not to marry me, then I tell you now that it weighs nothing with me, and never will.'

She gave me back my look, long and deeply; then she bent and kissed my hands. That was all.

I had hazarded a great deal in saying what I did; and I knew the risk I was taking. It was easy to answer for the present; but how could I tell what the future, our strange incalculable future together, might bring? It was that which she dreaded, I knew; not for myself, but for me. But I was ready to risk it, and a few weeks after that final talk – for final I insisted on its being – I gained my point, and we were married.

We were married; and for five years we lived our strange perilous dream of happiness. That fresh unfading happiness which now and then mocks the lot of poor mortals; but not often – and never for long.

At the end of five years my wife died; and since then I have lived alone among memories so made of light and darkness that sometimes I am blind with remembered joy, and sometimes numb under present sorrow. I don't know yet which will end by winning the day with me; but in my uncertainty I am putting old things in order – and there on my desk lies the paper I have never read, and beside it the candle with which I shall presently burn it.

List of Sources

'The Lamp of Psyche' was first collected in *Early Uncollected Stories*, 1895; 'A Journey' in *The Greater Inclination*, 1899; 'The Line of Least Resistance' in *Early Uncollected Stories*, 1900; 'The Moving Finger' in *Crucial Instances*, 1901; 'Expiation' in *The Descent of Man*, 1904; '*Les Metteurs en Scène*' (originally published in French) in *Uncollected Stories*, 1908; 'Full Circle', 'The Daunt Diana', 'Afterward', and 'The Bolted Door' in *Tales of Men and Ghosts*, 1909; 'The Temperate Zone' in *Here and Beyond*, 1924; 'Diagnosis' and 'The Day of the Funeral' in *Human Nature*, 1933; and 'Confession' in *The World Over*, 1936.